Mummy Said the F-word

FIONA GIBSON

HODDER

First published in Great Britain in 2008 by Hodder & Stoughton
An Hachette Livre UK company

1

Copyright © Fiona Gibson 2008

The right of Fiona Gibson to be identified as the Author
of the Work has been asserted by her in accordance
with the Copyright, Designs and Patents Act 1988.

A CIP catalogue record for this title is available from the British Library

ISBN 978 0 340 83835 8

Typeset in Plantin Light by Hewer Text UK Ltd, Edinburgh
Printed and bound by Clays Ltd, St Ives plc

Hodder & Stoughton policy is to use papers that are natural, renewable
and recyclable products and made from wood grown in sustainable
forests. The logging and manufacturing processes are expected to
conform to the environmental regulations of the country of origin.

Hodder & Stoughton Ltd
A division of Hodder Headline
338 Euston Road
London NW1 3BH

www.hodder.co.uk

For Margery and Keith, with all my love

ACKNOWLEDGEMENTS

Huge thanks to: Jenny Tucker for accidentally providing the title (thanks also to Pedro, the daddy who said the f-word). Cathy Gillian for being the best writing pal I could wish for. Tania Cheston for running with me and being so helpful with plots. The brain-boosting Dolphinton writers: Vicki Feaver, Elizabeth Dobie, Margaret Dunn and Amanda McLean. Kirsty Scott, Wendy Rigg, Anita Naik and Daniel Blythe for stacks of encouragement and perky-up emails. Jane Wright at the *Sunday Herald* for giving me the chance to be an agony aunt for a year. Wendy Varley and Ellie Stott for reading the early manuscript and offering lashings of encouragement. Chris, Sue and Jill at Atkinson Pryce bookshop. All at Hodder, especially my editors Sara Kinsella and Isobel Akenhead, and publicist Eleni Fostiropoulos. Jen and Tony at www.bluex2.com for my website. Finally, my gorgeous family Jimmy, Sam, Dex and Erin for always being there, making me laugh, keeping me sane and agreeing that we really are rubbish at keeping fish.

www.fionagibson.com

PROLOGUE

A copy of *Bambino* magazine lies on our kitchen table. I pick it up, idly flicking through, about to fling it bin-wards. 'Britain's weekly parenting bible,' reads the line beneath the shimmering pink logo, as if no parent could possibly consider raising a child without it.

The magazine falls open at the problem page. 'When Daddy Strays,' reads the headline above one of the problems. I glance through the open door of our basement kitchen. My husband, Martin, is in the garden, talking urgently on his mobile. He has taken the day off work with life-threatening man-flu, but must be in constant contact with his office, *naturellement*. Our son Travis is enjoying the June sunshine and trying to catch butterflies to stuff into his toy ambulance.

My skin prickles as I glance back at the magazine. The agony aunt is called Harriet Pike. She is wearing an expensive-looking white shirt – the kind magazines always refer to as 'crisp' – and a terse smile that veers towards a sneer. In fact, she bears an uncanny resemblance to the woman who pulled a disgusted face when a nugget of dung tumbled out of Travis's dungaree leg in the fruit shop. Cat's-arse face. You become immune to people like that.

'Sassy, smart – she shoots from the hip,' reads the text along the top of Harriet's page. I start reading the 'Daddy Strays' bit. Not that I expect this Pike woman to say anything useful. I'm just curious, that's all. My friend Millie edits this magazine and is forever sending me copies, which I bin, virtually unread, although I never tell her that. Millie means well, and sends the magazines in the hope that they'll bring some sparkle to my life, ha ha.

What Pike has done is break down the fall-out from Daddy's affair into several steps – as if the unravelling of an entire life is as simple as baking a cake. 'Step one', I read, 'is grief.'

> You're grieving for the good times, the life you had together. Yet, however much you're hurting, bear in mind that infidelity is rarely one person's fault. Examine your own role, the part you had to play in all of this. Perhaps he felt dreadfully neglected. Second fiddle to your new baby.

What planet is this woman on? He shagged someone else, end of story! 'Hopefully,' Pike witters on, 'you might find it in your heart to forgive.' With a snort, I drop the magazine on to the table.

A cool breeze sneaks through the open back door. Finishing his call, Martin wanders into the kitchen. I look up and he's gawping at *Bambino*, which still lies open at the problem page. Our eyes meet. And I see it – guilt and utter terror – smeared across his face.

Shit. Something's wrong. My heart judders, and everything around me turns vague and fuzzy as if it's dissolving. So I haven't been imagining it. I'm not a paranoid idiot. I've suspected for ages that something's been going on – something that Martin couldn't possibly share with me, because I am only his wife of twelve years and the mother of our three children. I'd even wondered if he'd been made redundant and couldn't bring himself to tell me. My head had filled with images of him sitting in parks sipping coffee, trying to fill up the days.

Now, I *hope* it's something like that. It really wouldn't be too bad. I could work full-time, find an office job, and we'd manage OK. I'd even forgive all the lies.

Clutching his ambulance, Travis scampers in behind Martin and dances around him. He glances up at Daddy, whose face has turned an alarming purply-red. I grip the back of the chair, terrified of what might happen if I let go.

'Caitlin, I'm so sorry.'

I watch Martin's mouth. He never calls me Caitlin. From the start, I have always been Cait to him.

So I know it's something very bad.

'What . . . what's going on?' It comes out as a whisper.

Martin's face has turned pale now, as if his internal temperature control has gone haywire. He slumps on to a chair at the table.

'Brrrmmm,' hums Travis, making his ambulance perform a jaunty three-point turn on the floor.

'We can't talk about this now,' Martin murmurs, firing Travis a pleading look.

'Nee-naw!' cries our son. 'Want butterflies. C'mon, Daddy, let's play!'

I can't speak. My head is filled with a dull thumping noise.

'Daddy funny,' Travis announces. 'Daddy cry.'

He's right, although Martin's tears aren't falling properly. They're kind of blotting and making shiny patches around his eyes.

'Please go upstairs, Travis,' I murmur. 'Go up to Lola's room. She's got all her vet things out.' She, like her father, is off sick today. The house feels stale and germy.

'No,' Travis retorts, excavating a nostril with his finger.

'Please. Up you go. You love playing vets. You could be chief vet! Go on, darling, I'll come up in a minute.' If I had it, I would stuff a million pounds into his dungaree pockets if he'd go up to Lola's room.

'No like Lola. No like vets.' Travis studies his father in awe. Watching Martin crying is proving to be far more entertaining than a Junior Vet surgery with light-up X-ray machine and plastic kittens that wee in their litter tray. I pray for him to tire of this startling display and leave the room.

All these years together and I've never seen Martin cry. Sometimes I've wondered if he actually possesses tear ducts, or if they were switched off at some point during late childhood. Everything feels heightened. My heart is pounding frantically.

'Wee-wee,' Travis announces.

'Whatever it is,' I say calmly, 'you can tell me.'

'Cait,' Martin mumbles, 'there's someone else. I'm leaving you.'

I turn away from him and stare down at Travis, whose navy corduroy dungarees are slowly darkening around the groin, indicating the steady progression of wee.

'Mummy crying!' he says, grinning, as if my next party trick might prove even more of a hoot. Who needs a Junior Vet surgery with all of this going on? It's fantastic fun in our house.

I swipe my arm across my face, march towards Travis and plop him on my hip. Then I carry him out of the room, yearning to shrink myself down, squeeze into his ambulance and be taken to a warm, safe place where this kind of thing never happens.

Later, with our children safely decanted into their beds, I learn that her name is Daisy. Daisy, a pretty, delicate flower, had waltzed into Bink and Smithson, the architects' practice in Holborn where Martin works, to offer after-sales service. 'What sort of after-sales service?' I bark at him.

I am torturing him, dragging out every sordid detail. It should feel satisfying, but it doesn't. We sit facing each other across the cluttered kitchen table.

'She . . . she works for the water-cooler company. They'd installed some coolers, and—'

'Get to the point!'

'She . . . well, she came back, just to make sure the water had reached the right temperature . . . asked if there'd been any problems at bottle-changeover time . . .'

Right. And lingered at Martin's desk, laughing at his jokes, complimenting his choice of shirt and tie, making him feel so *good* and *young* again, and finally lunging at him – taking the defenceless kitten by such surprise that he found one hand plunging into her lacy 34C bra, and the other into her matching knickers.

'And she, um . . . we um . . . It just happened,' is how he puts it.

Naturally, his colleagues had gone home by this point. And I made that bit up, about her underwear matching. Water-Cooler Slapper doesn't strike me as someone who'd permit her peachy arse to come into contact with tragic saggy pants.

So Martin's hands had fallen into these places, in the way that Travis's foot *fell* against Eddie Templeton's butt during a row over a ripped painting at nursery. I hadn't realised that crucial parts of Martin's anatomy – hand, penis – are capable of behaving completely independently of his brain. Perhaps he needs to see a doctor about his nerve connections.

'When did this happen?' I ask dully.

'Um, three months ago. About three months.'

'So you've lied and lied.'

Martin nods slowly.

'And when's the first time you actually . . .' My voice fractures and I grip the table edge.

His Adam's apple bobs. 'That day. In the, er, at the office . . . the after-sales day.'

'What?' I yell. 'You mean you did it in your office? Jesus, Martin—'

'No, no . . . it wasn't . . . It was, um . . .' He tails off. 'In the loo.'

I open my mouth and shut it again. Oh, that's all right then. They only did it in the office loo. Not on his desk or anything. Let's crack open the fucking champagne. A horrible gulping noise comes from my gut.

Martin stares at me. His lips are pale and shrunken. 'I can't tell you how much I wish this hadn't happened.'

'Do you . . . d'you love her?' I hate myself for asking that, but I can't help it.

His mouth tightens, and he shakes his head. 'It's not . . . I don't know, Cait. All I know is, I can't be here any more, with you.'

'Then do it,' I snarl. 'Just get out.'

It's as if he's secretly yearned to do this for months and has finally been given permission.

The tension around him disperses. He gets up, walks out of the kitchen and heads upstairs to the hall. I hear him stepping outside, closing the front door behind him and unlocking his car. The engine starts. The sound of him driving away merges with all the other East London noises.

He's gone. I rest my head in my hands and shut my eyes tightly, kidding myself that when I reopen them, everything will be normal again. Martin will be his usual distant self, but at least he'll be here, still mine.

Nothing's changed when I open my eyes. 'It's natural to feel angry!' chirps that blasted woman in *Bambino* magazine. My family, my life, destroyed for a quickie in an office loo.

In terms of after-sales service, surely this is taking things a tad too far.

PART ONE

Forget computers, gadgets and all the trappings of our modern age. The greatest gift you can give a child is the warmth and stability of a loving family.

Harriet Pike, Bambino problem page, 18 February

Smug fuck.

Caitlin Brown, newly single mother of three

I

Did you know that the tongue is more responsible for bad breath than the gums or teeth? That it forms the perfect breeding ground for odorous bacteria in the form of an invisible layer of soft plaque? Sweep it away instantly with our new Antibacterial Tongue-Scraper, a snip at—

'Mum!'

I type, '£4.99 (special introductory price).'

'MUM! Where are you?' Lola's voice ricochets around the stairwell as she thunders down to the kitchen.

'I'm working,' I call back. 'Watch your DVD, colour your picture. I'll be finished in a minute.'

We've struck a bargain, Lola and me. She will allow me to bash out my sparkling copy for vitalworld.com, a website that seems to thrive on customers' paranoia about emitting bad smells. In the meantime – and we're talking one measly hour – she can watch her *Simpsons* DVD or colour in her zebra poster. I know that mothers are supposed to drip with guilt if they so much as try to nudge a toe back into the world of paid employment. However, since Martin's departure over eight months ago, I don't have a choice. And Lola's playdate with Bart Simpson is, I feel, hardly tantamount to infant neglect.

It's Friday, and we're just home from school. We live on a quiet terraced road a short walk from Bethnal Green tube station. The area was pretty cheap when Martin and I moved here, soon after getting married, but it's been gentrified and is now awash with young families. There are numerous all-terrain buggies and pleasing, wholesome activities for kids. Jake, my ten-year-old, is at football practice in the new sports hall, which for some reason he doggedly keeps attending, even though the coach commented that he spends most of the session examining his fingernails. Travis, who's three, is at his psychopathic mate Rory's birthday party. Good mothers accompany their offspring to parties and stay for the duration. However, Travis didn't want me to stay. 'Bye-bye, Mummy!' he yelled, waving gleefully. My third-born seems to regard being away from me as a fantastic treat.

I continue: 'It takes mere seconds to scrape the layer of mushroom-like spores from the tongue's surface.'

Bloody genius! The Booker Prize beckons. I picture myself striding on to a stage in some glittering ballroom to receive my award. I have swathes of rich chestnut hair (rather than nondescript light brown) and the perky breasts of a nineteen-year-old. I am no longer a dumped thirty-five-year-old mother in ratty jeans and an ancient Gap sweater that's felted in the wash.

'Mummy! I've been shouting and shouting and shouting.' Lola stalks into the kitchen and plonks herself on my lap, causing my swivel chair to wobble dangerously.

'Yes, hon. I heard you. This'll only take me a minute.'

'You always say that. It's never a minute. It's hours and hours and *hours*.'

She sighs dramatically. At just turned seven, she has mastered the art of cranking up my guilt to the max.

'I'm sorry, hon. The sooner you let me get on, the sooner I'll be finished, and then we can do something nice.'

'It's not fair,' she growls.

I peer over her shoulder at the screen. What else can I dredge up about this wretched scraper thingy? Ross, who commissions my copy, expects lashings of descriptive detail, and once ticked me off for not making some wart-freezing gizmo sound 'tempting' enough. My instinct was to behave in an extremely grown-up manner and tell him to fuck off, but when you're reliant on one client for 90 per cent of your income, you tend to button your lip. 'You need to lure visitors,' Ross urged me. 'Have them believing that our products are –' he snorted into the phone '– Truly life-changing.'

What the hell can I say? 'Never scrape if you have a new boyfriend staying over as he might assume you have some obsessive tongue-cleaning disorder. Small children, too, might find the process alarming.'

Apparently, you're meant to pay special attention to the furry region at the back of the tongue, a factlet that's causing my mid-afternoon sandwich to shift uneasily in my stomach. I'd always assumed that tongues self-cleaned, requiring no interference from their owners. It's a small step from colonic irrigation. Maybe that particular delight is yet to come: the Acme High-Pressure Rectal Hose. 'With the flick of a switch, sluice out those hard-to-reach areas.' I could dispatch one to Daisy to try out on my beloved ex. That'd liven up their Friday night.

'What's that?' Lola leans towards the screen.

'What's what, sweetheart?' Please go. Please let me finish.

'A tongoo-scrappa.'

'*Tongue-scraper*,' I snigger, winding my arms round her middle. 'You scrape your tongue with it if you've got smelly breath.'

'Ugh. My breath's not smelly.'

'No, darling. It's quite orangey, in fact.'

'Let me read more,' she demands.

'Lols, you wouldn't be interested. It's just boring stuff about the things that can go wrong with grown-ups' bodies.'

'Please. Just a teeny bit. I want to be here, with you.'

With a sigh, I scroll down so she can learn about high-absorbency deodorising insoles for those whose feet literally *gush* sweat, flooding their shoes, although not so far down as to expose her to discreet pads for mild bladder weakness.

'I need to get on now, OK? Watch another episode if you like, or do some colouring.'

'I can't,' she mutters into her T-shirt.

'Why not?'

'It, um . . . broke.'

'You've got plenty more felt pens. There's that pack of two hundred that Dad gave you.' My gaze is still fixed on the monitor.

'It's not *pens*. It's the telly.'

I spin her round on my lap so I can scrutinise her face. 'What about the telly?'

'My drink went in it.'

'*In* it? What part did it go in?'

I lean over her to press 'save', not wishing to lose one word of my literary masterpiece, and lift her off my knee. Lola scuttles behind me as I stomp from our basement kitchen up to the living room.

I loom over the TV and try to peer into the slits at the back. It's awfully dark in there and smells faintly of synthetic orange.

'What happened?' I demand, running a hand along the slits and detecting stickiness.

'It just went in,' she murmurs.

'What d'you mean, it just went in? This is a new TV! TVs cost money – they cost hundreds of pounds. Don't you understand that, Lola? Doesn't money mean anything to you?'

She lowers her gaze. Her eyelashes are so dark and luscious they look permanently wet.

'It didn't cost money. Millie was gonna throw it away, but you made her give it to us.'

I sigh. Her lush, wavy hair – reddish-brown, like the outside of almonds – falls around her lightly freckled face. Her lips, which curve beautifully – like her father's, although it pains me to admit it – are pursed, as if ready to whistle. And she's right. Millie had donated her unwanted TV to us. Martin took ours when he moved out – can you believe it? It had sentimental value, apparently, and was definitely 'his'. (It had been presented to him by the senior partners at work when they'd scooped a major award.) I was surprised he hadn't taken the fucking fridge while he was at it.

'So,' I say, 'your drink went in, and then what happened? Was there a bang or a fizzing noise or what?'

I am trying to remain calm. Since Martin walked out, my formerly extrovert daughter has clung, limpet-like, to me, and I'm loath to upset her. Learning that Daddy wasn't merely living with Slapper – or Daisy – but also Poppy, her four-year-old daughter, seemed to tear out her insides.

'It just went off,' Lola says meekly. She regards me with interest while I switch it on and off several times and bang its top with my fist.

'The thing is,' I rant, 'getting liquid inside electrical things is really dangerous. You could get a shock and die. That's why you're not allowed appliances in the bathroom.'

'What's an appliance?' she enquires.

'Like a fan heater or a microwave. An electrical thing.'

'We don't have a fan-eater.'

'Yes, and now we don't have a—' The phone starts ringing.

'Is the phone an appliance?' Lola asks as I snatch it.

'Hello, Cait.'

It's Martin, aka Wandering Dick, or Shagpants, as Millie is fond of calling him. I hold the receiver away from my ear, as if his voice might infect it.

'Hi,' I say curtly.

'I rang twice yesterday, left a message with Jake. Didn't he tell you?'

'Um, I think he mentioned it,' I say vaguely.

'He said you were in the bath.'

'That's right. Is that OK with you? Or would you prefer me to be filthy and haggard and stop washing my hair?'

'Is a hairdryer an appliance?' Lola chirps.

Martin snorts. It sounds like someone trying to clear a nasal blockage, and causes bile to rise in my throat.

'It was about this weekend,' he says. 'It's quite important.'

'It *is* this weekend,' I point out. 'It's Friday. TGI Friday. The weekend starts here.'

'For God's sake, Cait! Can't we have a normal adult conversation? Why do you insist on acting like a child?'

I yearn to remind him that his own behaviour has hardly been impeccable of late, but manage to keep a grip on myself for Lola's sake. 'Is there a problem,' I say lightly, 'about this weekend?'

'Yes. Look, I'm sorry, and I know it's my turn for the kids, but—'

'Don't tell me,' I snap. 'Something's come up.'

'Don't say it like that.' Martin emits another priggish snort. I picture his nostrils quivering damply, and wonder what had ever possessed me to have sex with the man, to fall crazily in love with him, to have to stop myself from squealing with joy when we met up at Batters Corner, which is where people around here met in those days. Seeing him standing there, waiting for *me*, would make me feel that it wasn't only the night, but my entire life that was just beginning.

'Martin,' I say coldly, 'I'm not saying it like anything. This is my normal voice.'

He exhales. 'It's Poppy's fifth birthday on Sunday. I'm sorry – I'd completely forgotten . . .'

'And?'

'Dad's electric toothbrush is an appliance!' Lola announces. 'Why can't I have one? They clean your teeth better so you don't need that scraper thing.'

'Well, um,' Martin mutters, 'let's not make this difficult . . .'

'You said you'd take the kids to Thorpe Park on Sunday, remember?'

'Yay!' Lola beams excitedly. 'Are *you* coming, Mummy?'

I shake my head fervently. Martin favours showy days out: to zoos, theme parks and chocolate factories, thus proving to our children that although he now lives with Daisy and Poppy, in Stoke Newington, he is still Father Superior and cares about his children. He's the hunky, baby-cradling Athena-poster daddy. He's *so good* with our three that strangers' children flock around him, and grown women weep. No wonder their knickers fly off when he strolls by. He's the Pied fucking Piper of Stoke Newington. Unfortunately, he is less keen to involve himself in the foraging for nits, or the application of verruca lotion.

Martin clears his throat. 'Any other time, it'd be fine, but on a birthday . . . Poppy wants, you know . . . one-to-one.'

'Can't she have one-to-one with her mother?' I enquire.

'Yes, of course . . .'

'But you feel you should be there too. On Poppy's special day. Just the three of you. I know maths isn't my strong point, Martin, but I'd make that *two*-to-one.' My voice has turned into a croak, which I don't like at all.

'Cait,' Martin says gently, 'it's not the right time for a huge get-together.'

So *that*'s how you think of your kids, I seethe: as an unruly rabble, crowding precious Poppy's day. What's she getting for her birthday? I wonder. A pony? Fifteen antelopes? A life-sized gingerbread house with a conservatory fashioned from melted-down clear lollies? That wretched child has everything. First time they'd met her, the kids took great delight in relaying a full inventory of her every plaything.

'So,' I growl, 'where are you taking her?'

'Um, Thorpe Park.'

'Jesus.' So many bad words swirl around in my head I fear they'll burst out of my ears.

'That's what she wants,' he adds. 'She's been looking forward to it for ages.'

'So have ours,' I hiss.

'I'll take them another time. We'll sort—'

'I know!' I blurt wildly. 'Take ours on Saturday, when it's not Poppy's birthday, and take Poppy on Sunday, when it *is* her—'

'I can't go to Thorpe Park twice in one weekend!' Martin blusters.

Lola sucks a tendril of hair fretfully.

'Why not?' I ask.

'Bloody hell, Cait. I hate those places. They're full of scream-ing, hyperactive kids dosed up on cheap sweets. They do my head in.'

'Do they? I thought you enjoyed your jolly days out with our children.'

A pause. 'You have to twist everything, don't you?'

I picture Martin's neck, with the tufts of fluffy hair growing down the back – greying a little now, I'd been pleased to note – and how I'd like to give that a damn good twist. Right round, until his eyes bulged and his veins stuck out. That would make a pleasant change from being so bloody mature and let's-be-reasonable-for-the-kids. I'm so controlled at kiddie-handover time that sometimes I fear that my heart will judder to a halt from the effort. *That* would show him.

'Or,' I continue, skirting round his remark, 'you could take all of them together and split up – so Daisy takes Poppy to one part, and you take ours to another, and the two families go around separately . . .' I tail off, overcome by the awful realisation that Martin doesn't view himself as belonging to a separate family from Daisy and Poppy. Of course he doesn't.

'Space issues' – his term – mean that he is unable to accommodate his own offspring more frequently than every other weekend. Daisy and Poppy are with him virtually all the time. He'll have read billions of bedtime stories, the way he used to with ours. *They* are Martin's family now. A woman with a glossy black bob, pert young-person's breasts and a precocious daughter who won't let Lola lay a finger on My Little Pony's mane brush. Over eight months on, when I'm supposed to have recovered from the break-up and be moving on, making a new life for myself – all the overly positive crap that fills magazines like *Bambino* – and I still yearn to stab him between the eyes. We're not even going through a divorce. I haven't set anything in motion, for the pathetic reason that being no longer married to me might make life easier for him. Martin hasn't dared to suggest it.

I finish the call, mentally totting up our scores: Martin, 1; Cait, O.

Lola gazes up at me, her dark eyes gleaming like Christmas-tree baubles. 'Why won't Daddy take us to Thorpe Park?' she asks.

'He says he'll still take you,' I babble, 'and he's really looking forward to it, but he can't do it this weekend because something else is happening.'

'Oh. What's happening?'

She knows, of course she does. She just wants me to say it. I scrabble for the least hurtful answer, my tongue flapping dryly in my mouth. 'He didn't say,' is all I can dredge up.

'He's taking Poppy instead, isn't he?' A tear wobbles dangerously, and I bend down to pull her close.

'It's her birthday,' I say softly. 'She just wants a special time.'

She fixes me with a stoic look, her brave face. 'So do I,' she mutters.

'Listen, we'll do something special too. I've just got to finish my work, OK? Then we'll pop out and pick up the boys and come back for tea. We'll have pancakes for afters, all right?'

'With lemon and sugar?'

'We'll buy a lemon on the way home. You can make the batter all by yourself.'

Lola musters a weak smile and plonks herself on the rug. I don't have it in me to go on about the buggered TV, not after her disappointment over Thorpe Park. Summoning every ounce of concentration, she draws a perfect crown on the biggest zebra's head. No matter what Martin does, or how often he lets her down, he's still King Daddy as far as his daughter's concerned. Which strikes me as more than a little unfair.

Down in the bowels of the house – our shadowy basement kitchen – I try to switch back into work mode, but it's useless. I can't face the tongue thing again, let alone corn creams and blackhead exterminators. Martin's calls often have that effect. It's as if he's hatching a plot to make me lose my Vitalworld job on top of everything else.

It's not that I want us to get back together. The thought of Martin touching me – or, indeed, inhabiting the same page of the A–Z – makes me want to vomit. No, what concerns me these days is his effect on the kids. It churns my insides to see Lola struggling to be brave and good. Jake has taken to cleaning his bedroom with alarming vigour. The first time I caught him lugging the Hoover upstairs, I assumed he needed it for a game.

'I want my room to be nice,' he'd muttered.

'But I make it nice!' I'd protested.

'It's not nice. It's horrible and dirty.'

Shortly afterwards, he'd bought a can of Mr Sheen (Spring Fresh fragrance) with his own pocket money. Whenever he uses it, its smell seems to permeate the entire house. Sometimes I can even taste it.

And Travis? He's too young to grasp the ins and outs, but is patently aware that Daddy no longer lives with us, and that another adult female plus offspring now feature in his life.

He knows that Dad used to put out his breakfast cereal and pour the milk from a great height, making sploshy white waterfalls. And now he doesn't.

I check my inbox. There's an email from Ross at Vitalworld.

Hi, Cait,
Hope all's good with you and the brood.

He always says 'brood'; it makes me feel like a plump hen.

Sorry to be a pain, but could you try a slight change of tone with your new batch of copy and make it bouncier? I've had feedback from the big cheeses and they'd like it more upbeat, hard sell – you know the kind of thing. I'm sure you won't find it a problem. Hope you haven't done too much work on it already.

Cheers, Cait, and have a great weekend,
Ross

I glare down at my product list:

- Gloss 'n' Gleam Anti-Dandruff Conditioning Masque

I start to write, 'Is anything worse than spotting a snowstorm on your shoulders?' and think, Yes! Lots of things are far worse than that. Like your husband announcing that he and his girlfriend are moving to a fancy new flat in Canary Wharf, as they want somewhere that feels like 'theirs' instead of just 'hers'. (Despite the fact that his extortionate maintenance payments – which, being Athena Daddy, he is *quite happy to make* – have rendered them bankrupt. Allegedly.) A flat with not one but two – count'em! – roof terraces.

- pile ointment
- Fresh Zone halitosis pills with extract of liquorice and clove
- Blackhead-Removal System
- Redeem Hair-Recovery Programme for Men
- Corn Care with natural beeswax. Also effective for heels, elbows and other scaly areas.

Who the hell buys this stuff? Lizards?

- Wind-Away tablets, to ease the discomfort of flatulence and trapped wind.

God, the human body can be terribly embarrassing sometimes. Having lost momentum with the tongue thing, I move on to the fart pills, trying to muster every upbeat cell in my body.

Maybe it's time I found myself a proper job.

This is all Martin's fault. I'd have nearly finished by now if he hadn't cancelled and thrown me off track. All it would need is a little 'bouncing up'.

Thorpe Park. It's opening weekend, to coincide with February half-term. For all I care, he can spend the entire weekend with Daisy and Poppy on the spinny rides he so hates. The kids and I will have a fantastic time doing, er . . . I'm sure I'll conjure up something.

As for Martin choosing birthday girl over his own flesh and blood, I won't utter one more word about it. Let them have their damn one-to-one. I'll rise above them like a dignified cloud.

2

Thorpe Park is as gaudy as the contents of an upended toy box.

'Come on!' Travis yelps, tugging his mittened hand free and tearing away.

I grab him by his dungaree strap. 'We'll have to stick together or we'll lose you. Look how busy it is here.'

'Wanna go on that!' he rages, indicating a terrifying roller coaster looping the loop.

'That's for bigger children, Travis. There are lots of other things you can go on.'

'Don't want baby things. Want big-boy things.' He juts out his bottom lip like a ramp.

Sam catches my eye and grins. I am part of a 'we' again – albeit temporarily – as, to my surprise and delight, my single-dad friend offered to come with us. Sam's ex-wife, mother to their ten-year-old son, Harvey, apparently swished off some years ago to 'find herself' in Cornwall with an old flame. Like me, Sam has been dumped on with ten tons of horse shit. Unlike me, he doesn't – as far as I'm aware – harbour resentment and hatred. Things seem to be terribly grown-up and respectful between Sam and Amelia. I once spotted a hand-drawn birthday card on his mantelpiece, in which she'd written, 'Happy birthday, babe. Love, Melly xxx,' which hardly hinted at mutual hatred.

'Aren't you worried we'll bump into them?' he asks, as our group straggles through the throng.

My plan had been to do precisely that, as a kind of up-yours gesture. I know – neither big nor clever. And now I'm not so sure I want to be here at all.

'I don't think it's likely,' I tell him, 'but if we do, I can handle it.' *I've got you*, I want to add.

He drapes a reassuring arm round my shoulders. Sweet, kind Sam. He'd be immensely fanciable – dark, dark eyes, lithe, slender body – to any woman whose libido hadn't been utterly quashed, as mine has.

'I just don't want you getting upset,' he says.

'Sam –' I turn to face him '– I really don't give a stuff about them. Come on, let's find the water-ride thing.'

My spirits have risen – probably due to Jake looking happy for once, instead of wearing his usual droopy 'yeah, yeah' face. We spend the morning milling from ride to ride, braving the Rumba Rapids and the tamest of the roller coasters, where two women in the car in front steal lusty glances at Sam when they think I'm not watching. I first met him a year ago, but we've been hanging out with the kids for six months or so, since Sam and Harvey moved into the next street and our sons became firm friends at school. Sam has hauled me out of a pit of depression, stopping me from feeling like a crushed eggshell at the bottom of the pedal bin of life. I am now a baked-bean can, roughly halfway up. Naturally, Bev and Marcia and the rest of the PTA mob assume that we're enjoying a rampant affair, based on the evidence that we hang out together and our sons are friends – plus, single mothers are gagging to shag the pants off anyone, of course. I ran into Marcia in the supermarket last week. She gave the contents of my trolley a quick once-over, as if expecting to glimpse ready-meals and gallons of gin.

After our café lunch, Sam whisks Travis to the toddler rides, while I jam myself on to the big wheel with the others. Big wheels I can handle. And it's from there, at its highest point, that I spot him. Martin, wearing a yolk-coloured T-shirt, with a child perched on his shoulders.

My stomach tightens and I grip Lola's hand. I shouldn't have brought them here, at least not today. Now there's no escape. My kids are about to be faced with their father and Poppy on her special day, and it's all my stupid, blundering fault. I gawp at

Poppy. All I know about Daisy's little darling has been gleaned from the kids following Daddy Weekends. Poppy has a 'special' chair at the table on which no one else is allowed to sit. She shuns any foods that are deemed 'soft'. She has a dolly's cot, high chair, buggy and camper van – and probably a timeshare in dolly's holiday villa in Mauritius. Because Martin ferries our children to and from his new pad, I have yet to have the pleasure of meeting her. Lola has told me that she refuses to wear anything non-pink, hence my private nickname for her, Pink Princess.

Martin looks utterly at ease with her. Poppy keeps twisting round excitedly, her legs dangling against his chest. He is gripping her ankles, keeping her steady and safe. Anyone would think he was her dad. On top of the dolly's high chair and timeshare, this child now has our children's father – albeit in a sick-making yellow T-shirt. Is he trying to look like a children's TV presenter, or a tub of margarine? The T-shirt is a precise match for those butter-substitute tubs: Utterly Butterly, I Can't Believe It's Not Butter – of course it's not butter, you thick twit.

Frantically, I plot our escape route to avoid confronting the charming birthday tableau. What was I thinking, hauling the kids here today? I'd wanted to make a point. (*He* might feel fine about disappointing our children. I most certainly do not.) I'd wanted to scream out the message: '*You* might think you're the only one who's allowed here on Poppy's birthday . . . but here we are! We've paid our entrance fee and we're going to damn well enjoy ourselves!' And I hadn't considered how wretched they'd feel, seeing Martin with his shiny new family. I am despicable. Imagine using your own children to make a point. They should be removed from my care.

If only we could escape without being spotted. I know – once we get off the ride, I'll tell Sam we have to leave immediately. I'll feign illness, a fainting fit – even death. Anything to get the hell out of this damn place. Fuck, the margarine blob is edging closer. As our big-wheel chair descends, I can see the back of Poppy's head, her ash-blonde curls clumped up with numerous hairclips and ribbons – a fine example of accessory overload.

'Mummy,' Lola protests, 'you're hurting my hand.'

'Sorry, sweetheart. I didn't realise.' I let go and wipe sweat from my palms on to my jeans. I am sweating all over, even though it's chilly enough for our breath to form pale clouds. Mercifully, there's no sign of Slapper. I have met her only once, a couple of months ago, when I ran into her and Martin Christmas shopping in Covent Garden. They'd been clutching each other's hands and had sprung apart as soon as they saw me. At least she had the decency to look horrified. My teeth were so tightly gritted I'd feared that they'd crumble to dust. I'd been so shattered by the effort of being *reasonable* and *mature* that I'd dived into a pub and ordered a glass of white wine, which I'd downed virtually in one. If I wound up in the Priory, I would be forwarding the bill to Martin.

'That was brilliant!' Harvey enthuses. 'Can we go on again?'

'Maybe later,' I say quickly. 'We're meeting your dad by the teacup ride so we'll have to get off really fast, OK, and hurry round that way.' I jab a hand in the opposite direction to the margarine blob.

'*Why* are we in a hurry?' Jake narrows his eyes suspiciously.

'Because . . . we want to go on as many rides as we can, don't we? There's so much to see, isn't there? Isn't this fantastic?' I realise I am hyperventilating and try to steady my breath.

Jake tosses his growing-out fringe from his eyes. I do my damnedest to blot out Martin from my line of sight, but the T-shirt shines gaudily, like a buttercup floating in a river. The wheel judders to a halt and we all clamber out.

'Mum, look!' Jake yelps. 'There's Dad!' He charges towards him, with Lola tearing after, hair flying behind her.

I watch them, with Harvey lurking at my side, as they grind to a standstill before their father and stare up at Poppy.

'Hello, Daddy,' Lola says, less gleeful now.

The grin spreads unsteadily over Martin's face. 'Hi, you guys!' He flings me a stern look as I approach.

Harvey, suddenly awkward and shy, has thrust his hands into his pockets and is staring at the ground.

Lola glares up at the small blonde appendage perched upon her dad's shoulders. Poppy crunches a sweet. Her unwavering gaze has a touch of smugness about it. She has pale porcelain skin, widely set pale-blue eyes like a doll's and is done up to the neck in a quilted pink jacket, its hood thickly edged with silver fur.

'So,' Martin smirks, 'fancy meeting you here.'

'The kids wanted to come,' I murmur.

'Yeah,' Jake asserts. 'Mum said you couldn't bring us so she would. Why couldn't we all have come together?'

'I, er, it was tricky,' Martin says with a tight laugh.

I feel myself shrinking and withering inside.

'Well,' Lola announces, 'we're all together now.'

Martin frowns and hisses, as if Harvey might be hearing-impaired, 'Isn't that Sam Blackwell's boy?'

'Yes, he is. His name's Harvey. Sam's taken Travis to the little ones' rides, so we'd better go. We're meeting them at—'

'What I can't understand,' Martin snaps, 'is why you had to come here today. To make a point, was it?'

Clearly, he's forgetting that an impressionable young person sporting six billion hair clips is drinking in his every word.

'Of course it wasn't,' I snap back.

'You really know how to make things awkward, Cait.'

I start to protest, but he launches a second attack: 'We could have talked, if it was that important. I never imagined you'd do this.'

'Dad, we went on the big wheel,' Jake mumbles.

'That's nice.' Martin responds with a stretched smile.

'Can *we* do that, Martin?' Poppy whispers. 'Can we go on the big wheel?'

'Later, darling,' he mumbles.

Darling now, is it?

'Where's Mummy?' she asks.

'She's gone to get—' He starts, glimpsing a face in the crowd and waving frantically. 'Look – here's Mummy now!'

Poppy swings round, grinning delightedly as Slapper approaches.

Daisy is smiling and clutching two hot drinks cups, but her smile wilts when she sees me. *Oh, fuck*, I can see in her eyes. *Oh, bollocks*. Her jaw has set rigid. She is wearing slim navy trousers, flat lilac pumps with bows at the front and a sheer sleeveless top patterned with tiny pink flowers. I am staring like a pervy old man.

She wobbles a little as a child buffets her, causing liquid to splosh through the holes in the lids.

'Mummy!' Poppy cries, but all Daisy can manage is a grimace.

I gawp at her top. It is wet and has turned virtually transparent. No jacket or sweater, in February! How very silly of her.

'Hello, Caitlin,' she says, handing a steaming cup to Martin. 'Fancy seeing you here.' A tremor appears beneath her left eye.

'Yes, fancy,' I say, unable to tear away my gaze from her magnificent breasts. These breasts, I notice with a plummeting heart, are unhampered by bra. They jut out like Barbie's with no visible means of support. They are cartoon breasts, the pneumatic tits of a thirteen-year-old boy's lurid sketch.

They do not look real.

'Why are you wet, Daisy?' Lola asks.

That's my girl.

'I know, stupid isn't it?' She laughs a little too loudly, swinging her hair, shampoo-ad-style. 'We went on the Rumba Rapids and my coat got soaked. Thought I'd be better without it.'

'But your top's wet as well,' Lola observes, 'and it's really cold today. Mummy made us wear gloves.'

Have a fiver, fabulous daughter of mine.

'Funny, isn't it?' I cut in. 'We went on the Rumba Rapids too and we're all perfectly dry. Guess we were just lucky.'

'I think it depends where you sit in the boat thing,' she says coolly.

I realise that as well as the small blonde appendage on his shoulders, Martin also has a coat jammed under his arm. Must be Daisy's. I can't ever recall him carrying *my* coat.

Harvey is regarding Daisy with an open sneer. Jake twiddles

his jacket zip distractedly. Firing me a look of defiance, Daisy takes Martin's hand. She grips it so tightly her knuckles whiten.

'Well,' Martin blusters, 'we're heading off for lunch in the café. Enjoy the rest of your day. I'll see you next weekend, OK, kids? We'll have lots of fun then. Fancy seeing what's on at the Science Museum?'

There's half-hearted nodding. Jake crushes a Smarties tube with his foot.

'We'll do something really special,' Martin concludes, and I glance down to check whether his insincerity is dripping all over the ground, forming puddles of lies.

Then I see Sam approaching with Travis, scanning the throng for us. He spots Martin and holds back. Our eyes meet and he frowns with concern.

'I'm sure they'll look forward to that,' I say stiffly, shepherding the children away.

'Bye!' Poppy calls after us, her 'I am five' badge glinting in the wintry sun.

She's only a kid. None of this is her fault. She didn't choose her mother or insist that she seduced unsuspecting males in their offices. Poppy has nothing whatsoever to do with Slapper's deluxe after-sales service. I try to smile at her, as any decent adult would, but it won't come. She's pointing at the highest roller coaster now, resting her chin on the top of Martin's head.

Gripping Lola's hand tightly, I will my eyes to behave as the birthday threesome disappears into the crowd.

3

We're home, and although it's dark and bitterly cold outside, the kids insist on surging out to crack iced puddles in the back garden. They dive in and out of the kitchen, demanding further ice-breaking implements. I locate gnarled plastic spades, but draw the line at dishing out ladles and serrated bread knives.

'Hope you're not depressed about Miss Wet T-Shirt,' Sam ventures when the kids are out of earshot.

I am loading fish fingers on to the grill. Daisy's breasts still shimmer pertly in my brain.

'Of course not,' I insist. 'You were right, though. It was a dumb idea to go today.'

'I didn't say that . . .'

'No, but you thought it. You tried to warn me. I was trying to prove that I didn't care and ended up making the kids feel awful.' My voice trembles. 'I shouldn't have put them through that.'

'Maybe it wasn't your smartest move,' Sam says gently, which is marginally better than, 'I told you so.'

He smiles and it's infectious, as if our mouth-raising mechanisms are somehow connected.

'Anyway,' I add, 'what did you think of Slapper?'

The kids are bickering in the garden. Too many children, too few frozen puddles to go round.

'Um . . . hard,' Sam murmurs.

'It's not that hard,' I retort. 'I mean, d'you think she's attractive? I don't mind. I mean, I *know* she is . . .'

'No – hard-*faced*. One of those brittle faces that looks like it'd crack and fall off if she laughed . . . Can she laugh, out of interest?'

Sam cheers me up, despite everything. 'I'm not sure. Actually, I meant her wet top and no bra and all that.'

He crinkles his brow. 'They were, um, very . . .'

'Pert?'

'Wet. They were very wet. Something warmer, like a polo-neck jumper, would've been more suitable.'

I laugh and tip peas into a pan. It wouldn't bother me, honestly, if Sam had been mesmerised by Slapper's display. He's a man, after all, yet he seems totally uninterested in meeting anyone. Maybe it's the still-hankering-after-the-ex thing. Or perhaps, like me, he has no urge to do it with anybody. I haven't slept with anyone – apart from Travis and Lola in the throes of a nightmare or chickenpox – since Martin left, and doubt if I ever will again. It's been over eight months and the thought of any man pawing my body still makes me feel nauseous. I have *tried* to fancy Sam, if only to reassure myself that I'm still capable of having lewd thoughts. I have done my utmost to imagine him naked, the two of us kissing passionately and my hands roaming all over his perfectly roamable body, but nothing happens. Not a tingle – not one iota of smut in my head. I have repeated the process with every man I know between the ages of twenty and eighty-five (a pretty generous catchment area, I'd have thought). Still nothing. My libido has died, like a plant that no one has bothered to water.

Sam mooches out to check on the kids, letting in an icy gust. It feels so right, him hanging out here with us. From the moment we met, sheltering from driving rain beneath the slide in the park, our friendship seemed inevitable.

'Hey,' he says, jutting his face round the doorway, 'you really are upset about today, aren't you?'

I nod mutely. 'I used the kids to get at Martin.'

'Oh, Cait. They're over it, and they had a great time. Just forget about Martin and Slapper.'

How can I? I think, as Sam comes over and hugs me.

'Listen.' Sam pulls away, fixing me with a stare. 'You don't want him back, do you?'

'God, no.' I turn away and yank out the grill pan.

'So stop obsessing. She's an idiot and they deserve each other. She's probably caught pneumonia by now.'

'Hope so.' I hate myself for caring, for imagining Martin helping Daisy to peel off her wet things, running her a hot bath, bringing her a glass of wine and administering a post-soak massage . . .

More than any of that, I hate it that I've turned into a sexless android at the age of thirty-five.

Later, after reading Lola and Travis's bedtime stories, I step into Jake's room to say goodnight. He has taken the books off his shelf and is wiping it with a yellow duster.

'Why are you doing that?' I ask faintly.

''Cause I want to,' he murmurs.

Inhaling deeply, I sit on the edge of his bed. Instantly, I'm shrouded in guilt. I should be helping, not sitting watching him; I should have cleaned the shelf, so he doesn't have to. At ten years old, he shouldn't fret about dust.

'Jake,' I venture, 'I'm really pleased that you're helping around the house, but you needn't spend so much time, you know . . . polishing and stuff.'

''S'all right,' he mumbles.

'What was wrong with your bookshelf anyway? You keep your books so tidy these days. Sam couldn't believe it last time he came into your room and—'

'There was a spider,' Jake snaps, gripping the duster. 'It ran over the top of my books.'

A nervous laugh crackles out of me. 'Not scared of spiders, are you, hon? You're always collecting bugs in the garden . . .'

'It means it's dirty in here. There's probably webs and stuff.'

I open my mouth to speak, but he turns away and gives the shelf another squoosh of Mr Sheen. I feel so empty, watching him rubbing vigorously with the duster. All I want is my old Jake back, who not so very long ago would clamber on to my lap and demand kisses. Jake whose room featured pyjamas strewn on the floor, faintly whiffing of pee, and ancient juice cups left festering on his windowsill.

Right now, I could *kiss* a festering juice cup.

'Then he followed me to the bathroom,' Millie enthuses next day over lunch, 'and honestly, Cait, you wouldn't believe it, the size of—'

'Shhh!' I indicate Travis, who is merrily rapping the table with a teaspoon.

We're in Marco's, a cramped and bustling Italian restaurant close to Millie's office near Leicester Square.

'What?' She blinks at me. 'He's a baby. He doesn't understand.'

'Of course he does! He can hear, you know. And talk and repeat things . . .'

'I'm not a baby,' Travis retorts.

'How old *is* he again?' Millie asks, as if he is incapable of comprehension or speech.

'Three.'

I manage not to add, 'You're his godmother, remember? The chosen one. Surely his birthday is indelibly printed on your brain?'

She frowns, knitting her immaculate brows, as if I have come up with some startling theory regarding infant development. Despite editing *Bambino*, Britain's so-called 'weekly parenting bible', Millie seems to know stuff-all about children. She has none of her own – her relationships tend to fizzle out after a few heady weeks – and I suspect she resents the ones she's forced to encounter, as if anyone under eleven years old should only be allowed to eat at McDonald's. On spying a small child in a restaurant, she reels back, as if their nappy is likely to spontaneously combust in her face. In fact, none of Millie's editorial staff are parents, 'Although we all *know* people with children,' she once told me, rather hotly.

She continues to rave breathlessly about her new man, who's a motorcycle courier (at the moment) but really a sculptor who does amazing things with rusting window frames. 'Incredible legs,' she breathes. 'You know that lovely muscle men have on the inside thigh, just below the crotch . . .' She runs a finger down her inner thigh.

'Cotch!' Travis chirps, laughing.

I nod, even though I am unfamiliar with said muscle and can't recall that Martin actually has them. Travis lurches for my penne, having wolfed his spaghetti, and I deposit a few forkfuls into his bowl. Pre-single parenthood – and assuming that none of my kids was in the vicinity – I'd have relished every pervy detail of Millie's sex life. At least it offered a stark contrast to mine, and reminded me that being naked with someone could be fun. For several years mine and Martin's sex life had felt like something that had to be attended to every so often, like clearing leaves out of the gutter. These days, now that I am no longer a sexual being, I don't wish to be reminded that every other adult on the entire planet – apart from my mother and Sam – is indulging in fabulous rumpy on a regular basis.

'Anyway,' Millie says, stopping herself mid-flow, 'what have you been up to?'

'I did a stupid thing at the weekend,' I admit. 'Remember how Martin couldn't take the kids to Thorpe Park because he was going with – I flick my gaze at Travis '– you-know-who?'

Millie nods and pops a sliver of fish into her mouth.

'I went anyway, with the kids and Sam. We ran into them. It was so awful and I'm such a bloody berk . . .'

She clasps a hand over mine. 'Oh, sweetie, what did you do that for?'

'I don't know.' I prise the pepper-grinder from Travis's grasp.

'You're not a berk, Cait. You feel pissed off and angry, and that's fine – that's *allowed* – but you've got to stop obsessing over—'

'I don't obsess! Why does everyone think I'm obsessed?'

'OK. Listen, I know what you need . . .'

'Don't set me up,' I hiss at her. 'I'm not interested.'

Over the past few months, Millie has attempted to match me up with various males. Sad and desolate scenes with one or both of us desperately trying to dredge up excuses to go home.

'I'm not talking about men,' Millie cuts in. 'I mean work. A new job. That thing you do, writing about arse disorders and stuff – it can't take up all of your time . . .'

'It's not just arse disorders,' I say defensively. 'I do health features and daily tips for the site.'

'That doesn't sound too arduous.'

'I don't want arduous,' I say, laughing. 'I only work part-time, remember?'

Millie flicks a glance at Travis, who is extracting a lightly nibbled penne tube from his mouth.

'Don't want it,' he grumbles.

She winces as I pluck it from his fingers and casually drop it on to my plate. 'Wouldn't you like more work? Something to take your mind off . . . all the Martin stuff?'

'Not really. I don't want to put Travis in nursery more than two days a week.'

Her look says, 'Why ever not?'

She really doesn't get it. Most women need to earn a living, and even those who don't tend to yearn for something more challenging than swilling out lunch boxes and pairing up children's socks – even if it only amounts to writing about foul breath and haemorrhoids. Yet we still want to spend time with our kids, despite their shoddy table manners.

'Here's a suggestion,' Millie announces. 'Harriet's been ill for a couple of months now, and my PA's virtually been doing her job for her, sorting through all the letters and emails and choosing the five she needs for her page every week. To be honest, she's not too happy about it. I mean, it's not in her job description . . .'

'Which page does Harriet do again?'

'Problem page. Agony aunt. You know, Distraught of Durham, Pissed off of Penzance . . .'

Ah, yes. I remember: 'Can't you find it in your heart to forgive your philandering swine of a man? The poor darling couldn't help himself.'

'I'm sure I've told you about Harriet,' Millie rattles on. 'She's the loony who's always chopping bits off herself and sending them away for analysis.'

'Ugh, which bits?' I hope this won't prove too gruesome for Travis's tender ears.

'Her hair, I think.'

'That doesn't sound too bad. It looks pretty shiny and healthy in her photo, doesn't it? Surely she's not about to drop dead . . .'

'God only knows,' Millie says with a shrug. 'Anyway, it's a pain in the butt. I think Harriet needs a proper break, so I need to sort out a temporary replacement. Trouble is, agony aunts aren't exactly easy to find. They're hardly crawling out of the wood-work.'

I snigger, picturing women with there-there smiles slithering out between gaps in the restaurant's panelled walls. 'Do you need one? Couldn't you just drop the problem page until she's better?'

Millie looks aghast, as if I have suggested she invites Travis for a sleepover at her flat. On his sole visit there, Travis jettisoned a box of Lil-lets into her toilet. 'It's the most popular part of the magazine,' she insists. 'It's providing a valuable service to our readers.'

I splutter and Travis cackles with delight. 'No it's not. It's a chance to gloat over other people's misfortunes.'

Millie grins, and her eyes glint mischievously. 'Well, there is that. Anyway, we can't do without problems. The readers would have a fit.' She pushes back a swathe of hair that's escaped from its tortoiseshell clip and is swinging jauntily over one eye. Millie is an absolute beauty: all honeyed hair which gleams as if illuminated from inside, coupled with disarmingly wrinkle-free skin. That's the child-free for you. They look about fifteen years old. They have their cuticles oiled and their bums scoured with Dead Sea minerals. They don't know the names of the Tweenies.

'Well,' I say firmly, 'I'm sure you'll find someone. D'you honestly think I'd have the first idea of how to help people?' I omit to mention that *Bambino*'s poncey attitude sends me incandescent with rage. All those pristine children scampering through buttercup fields in Mini Dior dresses. I could hurl all over its glossy pages.

'That's why you're ideal,' Millie insists.

'I don't see why . . .'

'Because you've had . . .' she struggles for a diplomatic way to put it . . . 'plenty of *life experiences*.'

'Jesus, Millie. You mean I've been dumped.'

'It'd be really high-profile,' she charges on, 'and it's regular work. Regular *cash*. I bet you're skint, aren't you? When did you last have your hair cut?'

'The summer of 1942.'

'Honestly, it's money for old rope. You're a mother and a writer, aren't you?'

'That's debatable,' I say.

'And your kids are healthy and well balanced, so you must be doing something right. You must *know* stuff . . .'

'That doesn't mean I'm qualified to advise other people.' I decide not to mention Jake's decidedly unbalanced cleaning fetish.

'Neither is Harriet! You don't need qualifications to be an agony aunt. Anyone with half a brain can do it. You just need common sense, a good turn of phrase and sound like you know the answers to everything.'

'Is that all?' I edge a wine glass away from Travis's grappling hands. 'I'd feel like a fake,' I add flatly.

'Don't you feel like a fake when you're writing those health tips? I mean, what d'you really know about fungal feet and premature baldness?'

'Um, nothing . . .'

'And look at me, editing a parenting magazine when I've never changed a nappy in my puff and wouldn't want to, thanks. We're all fakes, Cait, when you think about it. We're all bluffing.'

Unless you've spent years training as a surgeon and you're doing a *real* job like fixing people's insides.'

I laugh and she flashes a blinding smile while taking the bill from our waiter. 'My treat. I'll stick it on expenses.'

'Thanks, Millie. I'll get it next time.'

'Will you think about it? The agony thing?'

'OK,' I fib.

While I attempt to de-sauce Travis with a paper napkin, Millie stuffs her purse back into her bag. It looks exclusive, the kind of bag that can only be purchased via a waiting list and certainly doesn't boast a dusting of cookie crumbs inside. She checks her watch, kisses my cheek fleetingly and announces, 'Got to run. Let me know, will you? I'm serious about this.'

'OK,' I murmur.

She pauses. 'I'm . . . I'm really proud of you, you know. I could never do it. After all you've gone through, dealing with the kids on your own . . .'

'Thanks.' My smile wavers.

'All I have to worry about is deadlines and crap like that. I think you're amazing.'

The snort bursts out of my nose as she turns to go.

Travis waves and cries, 'Bye, Billie!' but all that's left is a gust of her Gucci perfume.

4

While Millie zips off to instruct the British public on the Correct Way to Raise Children, Travis and I take the bus to Mimosa House. This is the optimistically named care home where Jeannie, my seventy-seven-year-old mother, is currently bickering with a fellow inmate (sorry, resident).

'I only asked how old you are,' protests the woman in the neighbouring chair.

'None of your business,' my mother snaps, failing to register that her beloved daughter and youngest grandchild are traversing the day room to bestow her with kisses and news from the outside world.

We pause a discreet distance away, waiting for the spat to subside. The TV is blaring – *The Flintstones*, the colour cranked up to the max – and two carers are dispensing tea and biscuits from a squeaking trolley. Behind us, in the corridor, nurses are cackling over something in the newspaper. Despite its purpose – and the fact that my mother lives here – the atmosphere at Mimosa House is reasonably jolly. There is no mimosa, though, as far as I've been able to detect. Just a few dusty dandelion leaves piercing the gravel at the front.

'Whose child is this?' Mum's neighbour asks eagerly, craning forward to inspect Travis. She tips her head to one side and smiles benevolently. 'Pretty girl,' she adds. 'Doesn't look like you, Jeannie, with your heavy jaw.'

'Shut your face,' Mum thunders, drawing in her lips to form a thin line.

'I'm not a girl!' Travis protests. 'I'm a boy.'

'Needs his hair cut,' Mum adds.

'Hello, Mum.' I bend to kiss her papery cheek.

'Where's my breakfast?' she demands.

'It's me, Mum, Cait, your daughter. There isn't any breakfast. It's the afternoon – tea and biscuit time. Look – I've brought Travis to see you. Your *grandson*.'

From her vinyl-covered chair, she scans his face with flinty eyes. Then she slides a bony hand into her brown cardigan pocket and extracts a fistful of Fox's Glacier Mints. For a moment, I assume she'll hand one to Travis. She unwraps one, pops it in her mouth and stuffs the rest back into her pocket.

'Granny, can I have—' Travis starts, but I shush him.

'These people,' Mum mutters, 'they come in the night and take my purse and my eiderdown.' She slides a hand beneath her seat cushion as if the thief might have stashed said items there.

'Mum,' I say gently, crouching down to her level as there are no seats free for visitors, 'I'm sure no one's taken your things. You said that last time, remember? And we found your purse in your handbag. I'll ask Helena if she's seen it.'

Helena, Mum's key worker, is warm and comforting, like a milky pudding. Sometimes I wish she was *my* key worker.

'That witch,' Mum hisses, spraying minty spittle. 'She thinks I don't know.'

'Uh-huh,' I murmur.

Travis totters away and stands in front of the TV.

'Thinks she's better than us with her dad a chemist and not having to join the army,' Mum rattles on. 'Bone bloody idle! The things they get on the black market – the lamb and the chocolate – and of course she makes her own lemonade out of chemicals from the hospital . . .'

Here we go.

'Some of us,' she growls, with an angry crunch of her mint, 'know the meaning of hard work. Building ships with our bare hands. Riveting steel plates. Manning the furnace.'

La-di-da.

'We worked hard in them days, you know.'

'Yes, I'm sure you did.'

I scan the day room as Mum chunters on. She truly believes that she ran a Clyde shipyard single-handedly, operating enormous cranes and ripping steel plates with her teeth. When these shipyard rants started, I knew that things weren't right. My heart would plummet as she tailed off, scrabbling for words. As far as I'm aware, the only jobs Mum had were working in her father's tobacconist shop in Glasgow's East End and terrorising my brother and me. She had me at forty-two years old, when my brother, Adam, was thirteen, which was considered beyond ancient back then. I was a mistake, obviously. 'An accident,' she'd delight in telling me, when her words still made sense. 'You half killed me. I got pleurisy after giving birth to you and I was never the same, 'cause they sewed me up wrong.' She made herself sound like a defective handbag.

'And her,' she rages now, causing her downy-haired neighbour to drop her digestive, 'she's got a damn cheek!'

'Mum, no one's doing anything to you.'

My head is starting to ache. Travis has yanked off his shoes and left them on the carpet where anyone could fall over them and smash a hip. As I force them back on to his feet, I wonder what Millie is doing right now. Having her eyebrows threaded, or her breasts exfoliated? I doubt if she has tended her own brows for a decade.

'Granny,' Travis announces, swinging round from the TV, 'we went to Forpe Park. Daisy got wet. We saw boobies.'

Mum frowns. 'Whose boobies?'

'Daisy's,' Travis explains. 'Daddy *ger*-friend.'

Mum glowers at me. 'Haven't you found yourself a nice man yet?'

'No, Mum, but I'm working on it, and I'll report my findings as soon as there's anything to tell.'

'I'm not surprised, you being that stout.'

Stout? She always does this – implies that I'm morbidly obese. I'm a size 12, for crying out loud. Hardly gym-honed, a tad spongy round the middle from three pregnancies – three pregnancies, Mother! – but not quite two-seats-on-an-aeroplane-

sized either. Who does she think she is? Eva Herzigova? In line
for the next Calvin Klein underwear campaign?

Mum grins savagely at me. A fragment of mint gleams on her
lip. How did Dad manage to stay married to her without moving
permanently to the attic? Perhaps her vitriolic streak is why he
decided to depart from this earth almost twenty years ago. He'd
willed that fatal heart attack to happen, brought it on by piling
thick slabs of butter on to his toast. It was his only escape from
Jeannie's ill humour.

Mum and I slump into silence, as usually happens during my
visits. Some of the inmates are chatting idly, but their conversations take so many unexpected twists and turns that most look
utterly lost. I keep trying to coax Travis away from the TV, but it
draws him in by some powerful magnetic force. The woman
beside Mum is gazing so fondly at him I can't bring myself to tell
him off. Mum takes another mint from her pocket and flicks its
wrapper on to the floor.

To test me – or maybe to amuse himself in a perverse way –
Martin once suggested that Jeannie move in with us. 'Jake and
Travis could share a bedroom,' he said. Never mind their seven-
year age gap; didn't families of fifteen used to cram together in a
room the size of a cutlery drawer?

Was he out of his *mind*? As it was, our marriage was hardly in
sparkling form. Perhaps that was the plan, that Jeannie's arrival
would sound the death knell for us and provide the escape clause
he craved. Like Dad and his butter. I wouldn't have put it past
him. I agreed, however, that something had to be done. Although
carers were dropping in to prepare Mum's meals, she'd been
found wandering the streets of Hackney at unearthly hours –
forgetting that she'd lived in London for fifty-three years – and
trying to blunder her way to Glasgow Central Station.

I suggested she move into Mimosa House.

'It's your decision,' Martin said, his voice tinged with dis-
approval.

'Do you really feel OK about putting Mum in a home?' My
brother's words echoed around his Manchester loft.

'Of course I don't. Tell you what, Adam, maybe she could move into your spare room? I've always thought you must be terribly lonely rattling around in that massive apartment all by yourself.' Despite the 200 miles between us, I could sense terror flashing in his eyes.

'Um, well,' he blustered, 'maybe a home's your only option.'

My option? Oh, of course. I was Big Chief Baddie. Cocky, capable Adam had always been Mum's darling son, and now has a flourishing website design business. What had I ever done? Facilitated my own conception with the sole aim of destroying her health. I was never going to make anything of myself with my sturdy thighs. When he left home, Adam's room was preserved and shown to visitors, like John Lennon's. Mine was filled with clothes horses and the deceased twin tub.

'Hi, Caitlin, Jeannie's in great form today, isn't she?' Helena emerges from the manager's office as Travis and I break for freedom. She seems to *like* my mother. It would be churlish to say, 'Actually, no, I found her to be particularly evil today.'

'Yes,' I say, 'she seemed really chirpy.' Which makes her sound like a budgerigar.

Cool air hits my face as we step outside. Our visit lasted approximately fourteen minutes, of which I am extraordinarily proud. Sometimes we have it wrapped up in ten. Yet, as usual, I'm tinged with guilt as I take Travis's hand. Helena seems to have unearthed a different Jeannie – a Jeannie who's frequently 'in great form' and often has the other inmates 'in stitches'. Of course it's different for Helena. Caring for Mum is her job. Being her daughter is more complicated.

Visiting Mum tends to plunge me into low-level gloom, a situation best remedied with a steamy bath in which I've poured all manner of sweet-scented gloop. I sink deep, enjoying the calm that descends on the house once the children are in bed. Millie jammed this week's *Bambino* into my bag and I flip through it idly. There's a feature on playing in the snow with your children, as if you might need a 2,000-word article to tell you how to do that. 'Relish the moment as your child experiences snow's downy softness and catches a snowflake on his tongue.' Yeah, yeah. And has a fistful rammed down the back of his jacket by his foul elder brother. Naturally, the apple-cheeked children in *Bambino* never pick up what looks like a stone for their snowman's nose but which turns out to be frozen dog doo.

I skim through the fashion pages – zingy hand-knits fashioned from Peruvian alpaca – and settle on Harriet Pike's problem page.

Dear Harriet,
How can I stop my daughter nagging to be bought things every time we go shopping? It has escalated to the point where we can't even go into ordinary shops, like a chemist's, without her pleading to be bought an Alice band, nail polish, lipstick, novelty bubble bath and numerous items which she does not need and I cannot afford.

It's exhausting, stressful and I worry that I have inadvertently brought up a spoilt little madam. Sometimes I do buy her a small treat to keep her quiet, but that just seems to trigger an avalanche of nagging.

Please help.
Desperate, Plymouth

Dear Desperate,
Nagging in shops is a stage that virtually every child goes through. However, you are probably part of the problem. In buying her treats, you are sending the message that nagging is effective and reaps rewards. Never mind the nine times you've said no; the occasion when you crumbled is the one she'll remember. So, no more spontaneous purchases. That's my absolute rule. By giving in to nagging, you're fuelling a child's greed. Try instead to switch the focus from buying to actually *doing* things with your daughter, like reading together, making collages or baking cookies. Such activities should distract her from rampant materialism.

> Perhaps you and your partner are setting a poor
> example in always craving the latest laptop or plasma-
> screen TV? Remember that children often pick up on and
> mimic our most unappealing traits . . .

Poor Desperate! She spills out her fears and what does she get in
return? A verbal slapping. Rampant materialism, for God's sake.
What are we talking – a hairband and a bottle of Matey? Never a
trip to Boots goes by without Lola bleating for a fish-shaped soap
or a box of 'boutique' tissues in a flower-sprigged box. One time
she nagged for a bottle of Listerine, thinking it was some newfangled drink that turned your tongue blue. Anything with a
barcode on it, basically. Does this mean that she, at seven years
old, is a rampant materialist too?

'Don't take your daughter shopping,' Harriet concludes, 'until
she stops expecting you to succumb to her every whim.'

And what should Desperate do when she *needs* to go shopping? Lock up her daughter in the airing cupboard? There's no
mention of a husband or boyfriend. She writes 'I', not 'we'.
Perhaps she, too, has been binned by her husband in favour of
some young slapper with pert breasts. I slam *Bambino* on to the
side of the bath. Clearly, Harriet Pike has never produced
children of her own. It's generally the child-free who glower
at you as your kid drops his pants by the sensory garden for the
sight-impaired and starts peeing.

I loom over *Bambino* and scowl at Pike's picture. You can tell
from her face that she believes you'll cause irreparable damage
by allowing your children to watch more than four minutes of
TV a week, and that their pleas for a hair bobble are – of course!
– all your fault for not locating vast expanses of pristine snow for
them to frolic in. No doubt Pike would reckon that I shouldn't be
lying in this bath, but filling it with non-GM grapes and jumping
on them to make juice for my deprived babies. Adam and I were
raised on boxed Vesta curries. By rights, we should be dead.

I clamber out of the bath, skewering my heel on Travis's
plastic pterodactyl. As I dry myself, I realise that blood from my

foot is blotting the towel and dripping on to the chequered vinyl floor. There are wine-coloured daubs, like evidence at a crime scene. Cursing under my breath, I try to clean the floor with a spongy wipe, but the blood keeps oozing out so I concentrate on binding my foot in loo roll. Thus bandaged, I hobble upstairs and peep in on the kids, who are all zonked out in their beds, then slip gratefully into my own.

Things could be worse. I could be Desperate of Plymouth with her wilting hair and murky shadows under her eyes. All she did was go to the chemist's, probably for something innocuous – a box of plasters or a packet of Rennies. Normal stuff that you don't stop needing just because you're a mother. Like me, she'll be lying in bed right now trying to calm her racing heart and reassure herself that the terrible scene in the shop wasn't really her fault. What do agony aunts know about real people's lives?

My heel throbs urgently. I want to phone that Pike woman this minute and tell her to take a damn hike.

5

'Sorry to land this on you, Caitlin. I know things are difficult at the moment.' Ross attempts to beam sympathy across his cheap-looking desk. What he's actually landed on me is the fact that vitalworld.com has gone bust, thus rendering my latest batch of copy surplus to requirements and sending my outstanding invoices into some weird, shadowy zone involving creditors' forms and court. Then, after some unspecified period, I 'might' get paid 'eventually'.

The Vitalworld offices are in Camden. As I was summoned here at short notice, I've had no option but to bring Travis with me.

'When did you know this was happening?' I ask, trying to keep the agitation out of my voice.

'Only found out yesterday. You know how it is with these things . . .'

'Uh-huh.'

Of course I don't know. I feel helpless. It's hardly feasible to launch into a rant while keeping one eye on Travis, who's having tremendous fun filling one plastic cup after another from the water-cooler. It's a Purity Springs model – Daisy's company – which seems particularly cruel. Its turquoise droplet-shaped logo glows in the periphery of my vision. It looks like a teardrop. I wonder if Daisy has been here, and if any of the Vitalworld staff have enjoyed her deluxe after-sales service too.

'So I'm redundant,' Ross adds lamely, 'as of the end of the week.'

'That must be, um, worrying.' I try, unsuccessfully, to look as if I care.

'I'm sure you'll get plenty of other work, Cait. You've been great. Fast, reliable, never let us down. I'm so sorry it's ended like this.'

'Yes, me too.' Now I'm a second-hand car: good runner, full service history.

As Travis and I leave the office, I realise what an utter twit I've been not to see this coming and to have relied on Vital-world as my main source of income for so long. For months now, they have repeatedly 'lost' my invoices and palmed me off with crap about system problems. I didn't used to be such a wimp. Along with the telly, Martin took my courage and guts and jumped all over them with his bloody great size-eleven feet.

We wait for the lift, with Travis jabbing its buttons randomly. Harriet Pike would suggest that if I object to my infant's button-pressing tendencies, I shouldn't take him to places that have buttons. I should leave him at home to poke crayons into sockets.

'Where we going, Mummy?' he asks as we step out into the fug of Camden Road.

'We've just got time to go home, get the car and take the TV in for repair.'

'Telly fixed!' Delighted, he charges headlong into my legs.

No matter how hard you toil with your collages and cookies – thank you, Pike – all children really want is a functioning screen.

Now all I have to do is find a way to pay for the damn thing.

The TV hospital is in Bethnal Green Road, about half a mile from home.

'I don't see many of these,' the repair boy says, sniggering at our deceased appliance. 'Where the heck d'you get it?' He has a broad smile and is in his late twenties at a guess – a mere boy from an addled mother's perspective.

'From a friend's attic, actually.' I'm still panting from hauling the dratted thing in from the car.

TV Doc's eyes glint with amusement. 'Is it steam-powered?'

I find myself smiling back as Travis barges past him in order to access the alluring buttons of the display TVs. 'Probably. It's Fanta-powered now, anyway. My daughter sloshed a drink down the back and it just, um . . . went off.'

He nods sagely. He is still young enough to be termed cute; once a man passes thirty, his cuteness has begun to morph into something else.

'Fanta,' he repeats.

'Yes. I don't normally let her have it,' I add quickly, as if he might be an undercover accomplice of Harriet Pike's.

He arches an eyebrow in an undeniably flirtatious manner.

'She'd normally have water or fresh juice,' I charge on, 'but I needed to finish some work and she'd spotted it in the fridge and . . .'

Confusion has clouded his eyes.

'Teeth,' I add. 'Acid erosion and all that.'

TV Doc smiles. 'Don't have them myself. Kids, I mean. Listen, the best thing you could do with this heap of junk is dump it. Don't let your husband take it apart and start fiddling with it. He'll be wasting his time.'

I want to tell him, 'I don't have a husband, a job or, as you're aware, a working telly.'

'Do you sell second-hand TVs?' I ask.

'Sure. Hang on and I'll see what I've got reconditioned in the back.'

For Travis, the day is panning out marvellously. First the water-cooler to play with in Ross's office; now a shop filled with flickering screens and no siblings to dictate what he watches. He has settled happily on the tatty carpet, a beatific smile on his face. I speed-read a gaudy red-and-yellow sign:

> Quality repairs on all major brands of TV's, VCR's, Compu-
> ter's, Laptop's, Security System's, Camcorder's and Vacuum-
> Cleaner's. Competitive Rate's. No hidden Cost's. Ask Darren
> for Quote's.

So many things can go wrong these days, not least the use of apostrophes.

Before he'd commenced his shiny new life, 'broken things' had been Martin's domain. It had hit me that I was man-less on a practical level when I'd dragged our wheelie bin on to the pavement for refuse collection. There's an awkward corner you have to turn, and the bin toppled over like an enormous drunk person, spewing festering rubbish everywhere. I stood there in my dented slippers staring at sweetcorn tins and bread wrappers, and conscious of Mrs Catchpole next door gawping in horror from her path. 'Dearie me,' she muttered, hurrying in through her front door and slamming it behind her.

The bin had cracked. There was no Martin to fix this, no strapping husband to make everything all right. Fuelled by anger and determination, I charged into the house, flew back out with a roll of bin liners and stuffed in every last putrefying chicken drumstick. I mended the bin's crack with thick black tape and bunged the bin bags into it. Then I went back inside and enjoyed the longest shower of my life, with no adult male grumbling, 'What are you *doing* in there?' See, Martin? Who needs a farting, bollock-scratching man to fix things?

'What's that man doing?' Travis demands from the floor.

'He's trying to find a new TV for us.'

'This is all I've got at the moment, if you want reconditioned.' TV Doc has emerged from the back room, brandishing a portable TV.

'How much?' I ask.

He quotes a price which seems ridiculously low.

'Are you sure?'

'Yeah, no problem. Leave me your name and number and I'll call you if anything else comes in. This'll tide you over for now. Are you after a combo or an LCD or a plasma screen?'

He gives a cheeky look, which I shoot back. 'Just one with, you know, pictures.'

He grins and hands me a pad on which to write my name and number. As we leave, he winks in a way that could be plain creepy, but somehow manages to be cute. Yes, he's definitely the right side of cute. The blush whooshes up from my chest.

'See you around, Caitlin,' he says.

'See you, um . . .'

'Darren.'

'Thanks, Darren.'

I'm still beaming stupidly as I drive our new fourteen-inch baby home.

Buggeration. Martin has showed up half an hour early to collect the children for a weekend of joy and splendour. He's stepping out of his car looking spruce in dark jeans and an expensive-looking soft grey sweater. Handsome bastard.

I watch his approaching form through the living-room window. No one is ready. I have yet to pack the kids' clothes. (Although their possessions are accumulating at Slapper Towers, and Martin is perfectly capable of operating a washing machine, I cannot stomach the idea of her laundering their stuff. I can picture her wincing as she examines grubby collars and greying whites.)

'You're early,' I remark as I let him in.

'Better than late, isn't it?' He saunters into the living room as if he owns the place, which he still does (well, half of it) and frowns at our new TV. 'What happened to the telly?'

'It shrunk.'

'Seriously, where's that crappy ancient thing Millie gave you?'

'Lola poured a can of Fanta down the back.'

'Fanta?' he repeats, slanting his eyes.

'Yes, you know – the fizzy orangey drink.'

'Since when did Lola have Fanta?'

Fury fizzles inside me. 'Are you criticising me for giving her a treat for completing her school star chart?'

This is a fib. The Fanta was a bribe, not a reward.

'Of course not,' Martin blusters. 'I just thought we agreed they wouldn't have fizzy drinks.'

Oh, we agreed lots of things – for instance, that we wouldn't screw other people.

'I can't believe you're lecturing me,' I snarl, wondering when this will become easier and we'll be able to 'manage' each other, like tolerant work colleagues, without spite.

'Sorry,' Martin murmurs, perching on the sofa's threadbare arm. 'Guess I'm just upset about last weekend.'

'What, because we went to Thorpe Park too?' My voice is clipped, like a doctor's receptionist's. It's not a voice I like.

Martin sighs and glances upwards, as if trying to penetrate the ceiling with his gaze. Jake and Lola are supposed to be choosing their clothes. Lola will probably interpret this as embroidered jeans, rainbow tights and the old-lady furry hat that she insisted on buying at the school car-boot sale, but no sweaters or pants.

'Hello, Daddy.' She wanders into the room, dragging her zebra-striped wheelie suitcase, closely followed by Travis and Jake.

'Hi, guys,' Martin says, beaming. 'We're going to have such fun this weekend, aren't we?' He touches Jake's shoulder as if testing if paint has dried.

'What are we doing?' Lola asks warily.

'I thought we could go to the zoo, and there's a space exhibition at the Science Museum – they're showing a 3-D film. It sounds brilliant.'

'Great,' Jake enthuses.

'I wish Mummy was coming,' Lola whispers.

'You don't want me there,' I respond quickly. 'You'll have a great time with Daddy.'

She blinks at him. 'Can we see the penguins?'

'They're not at the Science Museum,' Jake scoffs.

'No, I mean at the zoo . . .' Hurt flickers in her eyes.

'Of course we can, darling,' Martin says hurriedly. 'Right, is everyone packed and ready?'

'I'll just fetch Travis's bag,' I murmur, grateful for an excuse to vacate the room.

Martin follows me upstairs. I feel so self-conscious with him clomping behind me, and canter up the final few steps to shake him off. He goes into the bathroom and bolts the door behind him. *My* bathroom, to dribble all over with his wee.

I snatch Travis's bag – a matted *Magic Roundabout* Dougal – from his ravaged bed and hunt for his beloved Captain Hook's hook.

'Why is there blood on the bathroom floor?' I hear Martin asking the kids as I head back downstairs. 'Did someone cut themselves?'

'I think it was Mummy,' comes Lola's reply.

'Oh,' Martin chuckles. *That's all right, then.*

'No one's cleaned it up,' Jake adds pointedly.

I stand in the doorway and hand the Dougal bag to Martin, then follow them out to the pavement. There's a kiss each – excluding Martin – and mumbled goodbyes. Lola lingers on the pavement as Martin chides her to get in the car. It's as if she's reluctant to leave me.

'Come on, Lols,' Martin says. 'Hop in.'

'OK, Daddy.' She climbs in, mustering a smile through the window. My heart aches as I smile back. Jake's too busy chatting to his father to wave back, but I'm treated to a sharp rap on the glass from Travis.

'Bye,' I say, pulling a fake grin before turning and hurrying inside. The house always feels so empty when they've gone.

So here I am, stuck for forty-eight hours with no work to keep me occupied. I never thought I'd actually *miss* mild bladder weakness.

Actually, I'm not quite alone. Perched on my desk is Jake's sea-monkey tank. Sea monkeys sound exotic, maybe a blend of baboon and squid. They're actually tiny white dots – dandruff-like dots – that drift aimlessly in water. And that's it. There's no stroking, no cuddling, no cute tricks. If you expect them to chase a ball or fetch a stick, you're on a highway to nothing. With a magnifying glass, you might be able to identify miniscule wriggling legs. They're that interesting. No one shows any interest in the dandruff until they suspect that one has died, at which point Lola declares that each flake had a name and was loved dearly. Not by Jake, obviously; he asked for the tank to be removed from his room, presumably on hygiene grounds. It now lends an air of professionalism to the nerve centre of cutting-edge journalism.

Although seemingly still alive, our latest hatchlings are unlikely to offer much in the way of engaging company on a Friday night. I run through my list of alternatives. Sam? Not an option. He and Harvey are visiting friends in the Lake District. My assorted mummy-friends? All happily un-dumped. On a Friday night, un-dumped parents book a babysitter and go out to dinner, or snuggle up with a DVD at home. And Millie? Not sure I can face another instalment of her scintillating sex life.

I eye the sea monkeys and swear that they're gloating. *Get you, Nora-No-Mates, all alone on a Friday night. Go watch your sad-person's portable telly.* How did this happen? I have lived in London all my life, yet have found myself with no one to play with. I've lost touch with most of my old colleagues with whom I'd while away evenings on cheap wine. That's what happens when you're the first in your group to have babies. Either I wasn't able to come out or they'd assume I couldn't and wouldn't ask. Anyway, back then, being with Martin and our close circle seemed enough for me. Most of my school friends have relocated to suburban semis or honeysuckle-strewn cottages in the country. Maybe we should have done that – moved on, done something different. I bet none of their husbands have been tempted by after-sales services.

I fish out a soggy Cheerio that Travis must have flung into the tank. God, I hate Friday nights when the kids are at Martin's. 'It can't be all bad,' Marcia once announced outside school. 'I guess one good thing about being a single mum is all the time you get to yourself. It's almost enough to make me want to leave Casper!' I grinned ferociously, wanting to punch her. I never used to be like this: constantly suppressing violent urges and growling at sea monkeys.

Perhaps I'm turning into my mother.

A copy of *Bambino* is lying on my desk. I pick it up, open it at Harriet Pike's page and read:

Dear Harriet,
How can I get my life back on track when it feels so
empty? I love my kids and I love being their mother, but
it's not all I want to be. I used to have a fun, stimulating
job, but gave all that up after having my first baby eight
years ago. Since then I have had two more children. The
working world where people have real conversations, not
poopy-nappy conversations, seems so distant and for
'other' people – people with smart shoes and full diaries. I
have what my husband calls a 'little part-time job', but it
doesn't fulfil me at all.

What can I do? I want something for me, to make me
feel young and alive again. This sounds so selfish – it's not
how mothers are meant to feel, is it?

So how are mothers meant to feel? After all, we're not *just*
mothers. Beneath the nit-zapping and homework supervising,
we're still the person we once were. Still the young woman who
flirted with strangers and got tiddly on wine.

'I feel so guilty,' the woman adds.

Well, don't, I tell her silently. Stop that right now. You've
invested nearly a decade in your children's care and it's time to
do something for you. Yes, I know it's hard. You say you loved
your old job – isn't there some way back into that world? The
door may look closed, but I doubt if it's secured with an
enormous rusting padlock. Give it a nudge. Sign up for a course,
or blow the dust from your address book and call up every one of
your old colleagues. Let them know that you're not merely alive
and functioning beneath mounds of putrefying laundry but are
ready to greet the working world with open arms, to grasp it by—

Heck, what am I thinking, assuming I know the first thing
about this stranger's life? I check the name: Searching for
Something, Milton Whippet. I have never heard of Milton
Whippet, yet I feel as if I *do* know her, because she could be
me. And I suspect that she's having a pretty crappy Friday night
too.

She might even be stuck in the kitchen watching dandruff float by.

Would it really be so difficult to respond to letters like hers? Maybe I'd even enjoy it. Perhaps – my heart quickens at this – it's the 'something' I've been looking for. To be Harriet Pike. No, not Harriet. Me. Caitlin Brown, as I was before I married Martin and became Mrs Collins and kind of *withered up*.

My gaze rests on her name. Searching for Something.

I think I might have just found it.

6

'I knew you'd change your mind,' Millie declares in the glass cubicle that separates her from her lowly staff. 'Don't worry about Harriet and how popular she was,' she adds, 'doing all the radio interviews and talk shows and stuff.'

'Talk shows?' I repeat.

Millie flips back her hair. 'She's quite a celeb, you know. A childcare guru with her books and DVDs and that slot she had on breakfast TV.'

Fuck. Bollocks. I haven't watched breakfast TV for years. 'Are you sure you want me to do this?' I ask.

She grins reassuringly. 'All I want is for you to cover for her until she's better, OK? You'll be great.'

I gulp down a kernel of self-doubt. 'So how d'you want it?'

'Short. Snappy. Don't blather on too much.'

Words aren't really Millie's thing. She prefers to swoon over fashion shoots and check that her 'team', as she calls them, are including enough luxury baby socks fashioned from eyelash of yak.

'I mean,' I try again, 'd'you want me to be sympathetic and caring or, um . . .' I want to say 'shoots-from-the-hip-ish', like Pike, but can't bear to.

'Just be yourself. Draw on your life experiences. Make sure there's a nice mix of problems – an affair maybe, some emotional trauma, some practical stuff, potential suicide perhaps . . .' She guffaws. 'Honestly, Cait, it'll be a walk in the park. I only need five letters a week.'

I try to exude confidence, but my gaze drops to Millie's desk. It's not how you'd expect a glossy magazine editor's desk to be –

i.e. bearing only a vase of cream lilies and a front-row ticket for a Dolce and Gabbana show. Millie's is a jumble of rival magazines, the nicotine pellets she sucks manically to help her quit cigs and a half-eaten bagel with a curl of salmon lolling out like a tongue.

'So what do I do?' I ask.

'It's really easy. Just choose problems from the letters and emails that come in. Harriet gets about a hundred a week so there's no shortage of angst out there.'

'Really? I can't answer all of those, Millie. I'd be up all night . . .'

'You don't have to answer them all, dimwit! There's a line on the page that says, "We're sorry, but Harriet cannot reply to letters personally." Were you thinking you'd have to visit them personally? Let them cry on your shoulder? Take them all on holiday with you?'

'No, but—'

'No one expects you to be their *friend*.'

A girl with tumbling auburn curls pokes her head into Millie's office. 'D'you have a minute, Millie? Just wondered if you could settle something with the cover.'

Millie swoops up from her chair. 'Won't be a minute, Cait . . .'

Though the glass walls I have an excellent view of the comings and goings of Britain's weekly parenting bible. When I'd inhabited the real, working world, rather than the fish-finger-grilling world, I'd had short stints on parenting magazines. Their offices had been chaotic and overcrowded, as magazine offices tend to be, with raggedy posters stuck up haphazardly on every available wall. There'd been teetering piles of baby equipment – walkers, cots, buggies, car seats, high chairs, activity arches, changing mats, sterilisers – which had been called in for consumer testing. So much *stuff*. It's a wonder it didn't put me off having kids of my own. Sometimes a few spruced-up mothers would be clutching their babies for a casting. They'd try to affect a casual air, but you could tell they were desperate for their child to be chosen for a fashion shoot or, better still, the cover.

It's not like that here. Radio Four burbles in a distant corner, and there's an alluring coffee aroma, which I'd kill for right now. There are no half-assembled cots, no cries from bored babies.

Millie once explained that *Bambino* offers an alternative, infinitely more fragrant universe to the poo-smeared reality of child-rearing. 'We only put in parenting features to stop mums feeling guilty about buying it,' Millie admitted, which sounded a bit screwy to me (like a man pretending he reads *Playboy* for the motoring articles). So, once you've read some waffle about sandcastle construction, you can get on with drooling over handbags.

'So,' I say when she returns, 'what shall I do with all the leftover letters?'

Millie picks up her bagel, studies it for a moment and jettisons it into the waste-paper bin. 'I've no idea what Harriet does. Throws them away, I suppose.'

All those heartfelt letters? These people are desperate. Surely you don't spill your fears to a stranger in an unyielding white shirt unless you're skidding towards the end of your rope? 'You mean . . . put them in the bin with the rubbish?' I ask.

'Of course.' Millie laughs. 'If they're emails, just delete them. What else would you do?'

I can see her point, but it seems totally wrong. 'OK,' I say. 'Five letters a week. How long d'you think you'll need me?'

'Three or four months tops, I'd imagine, until the old trout's better. Honestly, Cait, I'm so grateful for this. You're really helping me out.'

I know she doesn't mean it, and that there are numerous writers who'd be far more suited to this than I am. Millie is being a friend to me, tossing me regular work as a distraction from Martin and Slapper.

It might be just what I need. But can I really advise strangers when I've forgotten who I am?

With an hour to myself before I pick up the kids from school and nursery, I rip open the bulging manila envelope that Millie pressed into my hands. There are dozens of letters to Pike, ranging from immaculately word-processed documents to barely legible scrawls. Some are blotted with food – chocolate frosting, perhaps, or runny egg. There's an abundance of blotchy, leaking biros. I wouldn't have thought that *Bambino* readers, with their pomegranate smoothies for babies, would stoop to using *biro*.

I tip the letters on to the kitchen table and stare at the pile. Heck, at least I'm not the only parent who fears that they're cocking things up. But where to begin? Closing my eyes, I let my hand hover above them, like that of a medium trying to communicate with the dead.

My fingers find a corner of paper. I open my eyes.

Dear Harriet,
Ever since we've had our little boy, who's now a year old, I have felt as though my husband has become a stranger. He often comes home late after work (via the pub) then settles on the sofa, where he invariably falls asleep. It's breaking my heart. We were so close and in love before Matthew was born, and had wanted a baby so much. Now my husband won't lift a finger to help, and I am worn out from alternately nagging and shouting and pretending I am capable of doing everything myself. And then, of course, I seethe with anger. I have turned into an embittered martyr, Harriet, and I hate it. Is it any wonder he never wants sex (mind you, neither do I) when I'm so foul-tempered?

Sometimes I think we're just clinging together for the sake of our son. I am on the brink of asking my husband to leave, but fear that I'd be making the biggest mistake of my life.

What should I do?
Ginny, Lincs.

Dear Ginny,
How the fuck should I know?
Love, Caitlin

No, that won't do. I am agony aunt on Britain's weekly parenting bible, so I'd better dredge up something.

Should she leave him or not? I study Ginny's elegantly looped handwriting, awaiting inspiration. Nothing. The sea monkeys drift lazily.

Damn, this isn't going to be easy. Get it wrong and I could be partly responsible for the break-up of a marriage, which, although not rosy-glow perfect, is probably just suffering from a new-parenthood slump. Could Ginny sue me? *The defendant, an unqualified jobbing journalist, advised our client to begin divorce proceedings. As a result, she has suffered considerable emotional distress.*

I fling down Ginny's letter and rake through the others for a more trivial problem, but can't find any. Nadia from Upminster fears that she has obsessive compulsive disorder, often hurrying home from playgroup to check that she hasn't left a gas ring on. Gutted from North Wales found condoms in her boyfriend's jeans pocket. Guilt-ridden from Derbyshire is planning to move to Tuscany with her married boss and doesn't know how to break it to her children. It seems that no one has minor concerns. If they do, they don't bother writing to Pike about them. These women are on the brink of walking out on their men, of leaving their children, of setting their hair on fire. One woman is sleeping with her sister's husband: 'I know it's wrong, and I hate myself every time I'm with him, but I can't bear to let go of the one good thing in my life.'

She expects *me* to tell her what to do?

Fury and misery emanate from the pile. I can virtually smell it. It's probably impregnating our kitchen table, seeping into the cracks. With half an hour before school pick-up, I gather up the letters and dump them beside my PC. My new file entitled 'Prob Lady' will, I hope, lend me an air of efficiency and purpose. I start to type:

Dear Ginny,
I'm sorry to hear that things are difficult for you. Have you tried telling your husband about how abandoned and desperate you feel?

Oh, please. Spare the droopy counsellor-speak. I delete and try again:

> Dear Ginny,
> It's quite clear that your husband is an utter pig.

No, no. It may be true, but it's hardly going to help her.

> Dear Ginny,
> The first year with a new baby is never easy. You are exhibiting definite signs of post-natal depression.

So I'm a doctor now, am I? Despite having spent not one minute studying medicine, I have somehow become a world-renowned expert on post-partum illness.

What *do* I know exactly? How to be a secretary in a magazine office and a half-arsed freelance writer? How to paint Lola's nails, make Travis squeal with delight with raspberry-blows on his belly and apply Jake's verruca lotion?

I type:

> Dear Ginny,
> I suggest that you make an effort to meet other women who will understand what you're going through.

Right, like the hatchet-faced women at Three Bears parent and toddler group, to which I'd hauled Lola for 'creative play'? I'd decided it wasn't for me when Chief Bear, a formidable woman in a vast poo-coloured gathered skirt, had emerged from the kitchen bellowing, 'Caitlin, did you do teas and coffees today?'

'Um, yes . . .' I'd muttered.

'You used the sugar bowl from the pensioners' lunch-club cupboard, not the Three Bears cupboard!'

I hadn't known whether to apologise profusely or start weeping, so I'd just shrugged and tried not to look scared.

'You used the WRONG SUGAR BOWL!' Chief Bear had thundered.

At which point, to avoid being bound to a rack and having boiling oil flung at me, I'd grabbed a startled Lola and stuffed her into her buggy. As we'd barged home, I'd decided that being trapped in a dingy kitchen with a grumbling fridge had to be preferable to Three Bears.

Anything was preferable to Three Bears.

I re-read Ginny's letter, trying to glean inspiration by breathing deeply, like bellows. I feel quite light-headed as I type a reply.

My mind is racing when I set out to pick up the kids from school and nursery. I am hopelessly out of my depth with these problems, but isn't it better to feel scared – to feel *something* – instead of muddling through each day with a head full of to-do lists and the various ways in which I could inflict pain on Martin and Slapper?

I realise, with a small stab of joy, that I haven't thought about them all afternoon. *And* I've managed to cobble a reply to Ginny's letter.

In the street, I spot Sam and hurry to catch up with him.

'You look pleased with yourself,' he ventures. 'Something nice happen today?'

'I'm not sure,' I say, proceeding to fill him in on my dazzling new career as we stride towards school.

'Sounds exciting,' he says, grinning.

'I think it could be.'

Yes, I'm a fake, and desperately unqualified to meddle with strangers' lives. I am also free from writing about tongue fur and the gunk that collects between toes.

Which is a step in the right direction. Isn't it?

7

'You're going to be a *what?*' Rachel snorts.

Whoops, I must have inadvertently said that I'm plotting a new career as a pole-dancer or an escort. Rachel is the only woman who talked to me at Three Bears toddler group, consoling me over Sugar-bowl-gate. So grateful was I to see her each Thursday afternoon, we fell into a friendship and soon decided to hang out in the park instead, where no one would tell us off. When Martin left, she invited the kids and me round for numerous suppers and picnics on her lawn. Pummelling some kind of dough on her kitchen table, she is a gleaming example of what might be achieved when I, too, become a Proper Mother.

'An agony aunt,' I repeat. 'You know, replying to problem letters that people send into magazines . . .'

'My God, Cait. That's hysterical. No offence or anything, but who bothers to write to magazines?'

'Desperate people who have no one else to turn to.' The thought of all those Desperates out there is quite terrifying.

Rachel shakes her head, causing her curls to dance around her shiny cheeks.

I don't expect her to understand. Over the years we've knocked around together, she has made it clear that she believes motherhood is something that comes 'naturally', and that it'd be a whole lot easier for everyone if mothers would simply stop whingeing and get on with the job. She has Eve, an eerily well-behaved six-year-old only child, plus a doting husband. I live in hope that a smidge of her sortedness will rub off on me.

'What are you making?' I ask, to swerve her off the agony-aunt track.

'Oh, just pasta dough.'

'*Just* pasta dough? You make your own pasta?'

'Yes, it's really easy. Flour, eggs, water . . . But never mind that. You, being an agony aunt . . .' Her shoulders start quivering again.

I gawp as she rolls out the creamy dough and proceeds to feed it through a steel contraption. Fresh pasta, I ask you. What's wrong with the dried stuff in packets?

'Don't you think we make such a big deal of bringing up children these days?' she muses.

'It *is* a big deal,' I protest. 'It's the biggest deal there is.'

Rachel frowns. 'We've never had *any* problems with Eve.'

'What, none at all? Ever?'

'Um, well, I do get a bit annoyed when she loses her gym shoes.'

Bloody marvellous. In this family, that's as bad as it gets. A mislaid elastic-fronted plimsoll. Sometimes I wonder if being friends with Rachel is actually good for my psyche.

I tune into the chatter drifting down from Eve's bedroom. Even Jake seems happy here, pottering about in the garden by himself. There's a wooden sandpit out there that Guy, Rachel's husband, knocked together in under an hour. In this family, everything seems to work as it should. Guy might not be the most exciting man on the planet – unlike Martin, he doesn't cause women's underwear to ping off as he saunters by – but at least he's *here*.

'You are lucky,' I say quietly.

Rachel stops turning the pasta-maker handle and tips her head. 'Oh, Cait. I'm sorry if I sound smug. I think you're doing a fantastic job, I really do.' Kindness emanates from her brown eyes. By rights, Rachel should be filling in for Harriet Pike.

'Thanks,' I say, unconvinced.

She re-feeds the dough through the machine. This time it comes out tagliatelle-shaped, just like the tagliatelle you can buy at Tesco for 98p. She tosses the anaemic ribbons into a pot of bubbling water. Herby aromas rise from a simmering tomato and basil sauce.

'How's Jake been lately?' she asks.

'The usual. All mutters and scowls. It's as if he's fast-forwarded to adolescence.'

She smiles sympathetically, looking particularly auntie-ish today with her plump face flushed pink from all the winding and simmering. 'He's probably still adjusting to you and Martin living apart. It's nearly nine months since he left, isn't it? That's not so long for a child . . .'

'Yes, that's what Sam reckons too.'

Rachel grins mischievously. 'Been spending a lot of time with Sam, haven't you?'

'Don't you start . . .'

'I know you're just friends, blah, blah, but—'

'It's not like that with Sam and me,' I cut in. 'There's no . . . sexual chemistry. He's not interested, and I'm not interested, and—'

'What's wrong with him?' She frowns, as if attending to an injured child.

'Nothing, but . . .'

'Shouldn't you be open to opportunities?'

'Rachel,' I explain, as patiently as I can to someone who's been with her man for 900 years, 'there *aren't* any opportunities.'

She sighs and dishes up the pasta into jaunty striped bowls. 'Rally the troops, would you? I think we're ready.'

I call the kids and they clatter downstairs and in from the garden, clamouring around the table with a frantic scraping of chairs. Everyone tucks in without fuss, even though fresh herbs are distinctly visible. (In our house, attempting to sneak greenery into a dish is a crime punishable by death.)

'So much better than dried pasta, isn't it?' Rachel enthuses.

'Yummy,' Lola agrees.

'Lovely,' I say, thinking: sorry, but it feels like *worms*.

'Who are my aunties?' Lola asks as we walk home.

'You only have one real one,' I explain. 'There's Auntie

Claire, Daddy's sister. You've got your uncle Adam, but he's not married any more so—'

'Who's my agony aunt?' she cuts in.

I laugh. 'You don't have one, sweetheart, and I hope you'll never need one. It's not a real aunt. Not someone who's related to you. It's a lady who works for a magazine, and if you've got problems you can write to her and she'll try and help.'

'Oh.'

While Lola clutches my hand, Jake mooches several yards behind as if wishing to minimise the chance of being seen in public with me. Travis stops to examine every chunk of loose plaster in the wall, every crushed chip carton and grubby bottletop on the ground.

'No, hon, that's dirty,' I insist, tugging him away from teeming bacteria.

'Why do people write to that lady?' Lola won't let this one go.

'Well, an agony aunt's supposed to be clever and wise and know the answers to lots of things.' I cringe inwardly.

'Why?'

'Sweetie, you're just saying "why" all the time to keep me talking. You're not asking real questions.' It's Lola's favourite game: Why? Why? Why?

'I'm not,' she huffs. 'I just don't understand why they write to that lady . . .'

'Maybe they don't have anyone else to talk to.'

She grins, pulls her hand free and bounds towards our house. 'I don't need an agony aunt,' she yells back, ''cause I've got you, Mummy.'

I glow all over. Maybe I am doing something right after all.

Later, when everyone's been shuffled off to bed and I have a few moments to myself in the sitting room, I stumble upon a feature in *Bambino* that makes me snort with laughter. It's called 'Single and Loving it!' which strikes me as protesting too much. You never see 'Happily Married and Loving It!' or 'In a Fabulous

Relationship and Over the Fucking Moon!' I am compelled to read on.

It's actually a list of the amazing things a single woman can do when there's no pesky significant other to wreck her fun. These include:

- Lying diagonally across your bed with no one telling you off for taking up too much space.

Why would I want to do that? It seems extravagant and wasteful. Tragically, I still keep to my side, leaving space for an invisible man.

- Wallowing in a luxurious scented bath at 7.30 p.m.

What, with three children to get suppered, bathed, pyjamaed and storied? *Bambino* is a parenting magazine. Aren't they supposed to understand?

- Flirting with a stranger in the park, just for the hell of it.

How does one flirt again? Please remind me. I vaguely recall something about eyelash fluttering. If I tried that, I'd look unhinged. Plus, I'd probably pick on the man who'd club me over the head and drag me into a bush.

- When you're feeling wobbly, remind yourself of all the things you don't miss about your partner.

That's more like it. There's plenty I don't miss about Martin. Road rage, for instance. The nerve of it, that anyone had the audacity to drive on the same road as us! In a perfectly normal and responsible manner!

Him: 'Jesus, look at that – what the hell's he doing? God, this drives me mad. What's he PLAYING at? Bloody idiot.'

Me: 'He's indicating right, and, look, he's performing a perfectly safe right turn.'

Him: 'Fine, OK, so *I'm* in the wrong, am I?'

Nor do I miss his polite enquiries as to whether we have any milk/loo roll/bacon, being seemingly incapable of checking for himself. I don't miss his throaty snoring. Or his habit of calling me 'the wife', as in, 'I'd love to come, Damon, but the wife says we need to show our faces at the school car-boot sale. You know how it is . . .' As if I'd invented school and its fundraising activities just to spite him.

I curl up on the sofa, wondering why I loved him so over-whelmingly. What had possessed me to send flowers to his office, and buy a hideously expensive gold ring for his little finger? Having children had changed everything. Apparently I'd had no time for Martin any more, the poor neglected cupcake. Imagine: attending to our baby's dirty nappy rather than massaging his aching back. We'd fluttered like moths in separate parts of the house, coming together – though not literally – for exhausted fortnightly sex.

Ugh, the sex. The faked orgasms, the way he'd roll off with a satisfied grunt and turn his back to me. The lack of any post-coital conversation whatsoever. I hadn't expected detailed discussions about how it had been for him, but a few words would have been nice. Like, 'That was lovely,' or, 'Goodnight, darling,' or even, 'If you're thinking of going downstairs, honey, would you fetch me a glass of water?' That's just common manners, isn't it? Rachel's Guy isn't much in the looks department (mid-brown hair plus ginger gene which has burst out, startlingly, in the form of a carroty beard), but I'll bet he says sweet things after they've done it. Heck, even Millie's one-night stands lie around chatting afterwards, if her stories are to be believed.

I slam the magazine shut and head down to the kitchen to locate wine. There's one message on the answerphone; I must have missed a call while I was upstairs reading *Titchy-Witch*.

'Hi, Caitlin,' comes a voice I don't recognise. 'It's, um, Darren. From the TV shop. Hope you don't mind me calling you . . .' Awkward pause. Weird, maybe he works evenings. 'I, um, wondered if you'd like to go for a drink or something? No problem if not, just thought, yeah, um, thought I'd ask . . .'

It comes out in a rush. I'm so gobsmacked I don't even write down his number.

Darren, the TV Doc. A boy, virtually a *baby*, asking me for a drink. I replay it and he definitely says Caitlin. Caitlin with the laughable antique TV, a three-year-old child and two more that he doesn't know about. Didn't he assume I'm married? 'Best thing you can do with this heap of junk is dump it. Don't let your husband take it apart and start fiddling with it.' Cheeky boy. Was he fishing, or do I simply have an air of the dumpee about me?

Embarrassingly, I play his message for a third time, snatching one of Travis's Chunky Wax Crayons for Little Hands to scribble down his number. What did Rachel say about being open to opportunities? A drink with a cute younger man . . . why the heck not? What harm could it possibly do?

I'm grinning, and my heart's thumping in a slightly hysterical manner, as I tap out Darren's number on our banana-shaped phone.

8

'What I can't understand,' Sam says, poring over the heap of *Bambino* mail on my kitchen table, 'is why they're so different. The awful, tragic letters people send in and the trivial stuff they print in the magazine. The ones about the kid nagging in the chemist's, or little Popsicle wanting to invite too many kids to her birthday party . . .'

'I've only ever read one serious letter on Pike's page,' I tell him. 'When Daddy Strays' pings into my mind.

'But this lot –' Sam swoops his hands over the pile – 'these are people whose lives are falling apart.'

I hand him a mug of coffee and plonk myself on the chair beside him. 'You know what? I reckon Harriet never bothered answering real letters. She just made up her own. Ones that would be easy to answer. It's easy to be rude and confrontational when there's no risk of offending a real person.'

Sam chuckles and peers at Pike's page. I left the magazine lying open in the hope that inspiration might emanate from her photo. It hadn't worked. It felt as if she was *spying* on me, appalled by the pile of muddy wellies by the back door and the murky sea-monkey tank.

'I'm sure you're right,' Sam declares. 'There's something shifty about her.'

'It's not a bad idea, is it? I could make up some trivial problems of my own. It'd be easier than grappling with this lot.'

'What would Millie say?' he asks.

'I don't think she'd mind. Hey, why don't you help me make some up?' I dive for the computer, dragging over an extra chair for Sam, poised for fun.

'Um, I wouldn't be any good at that.' Sam stays put at the table.

'Oh, come on! You've got an overactive imagination. What about all those stories you make up for Harvey?' I pat the chair encouragingly.

He colours slightly. 'Stories aren't personal. Men don't talk about personal stuff.'

'I don't mean *real* problems . . . Unless you have some? That'd be even better! Tell me something – anything – that's bothering you and I'll try to figure out some answers. It'll be good practice, like mock GCSEs before the real exams.'

Sam's jaw tightens. 'Sorry, Cait. I can't help you with this.'

I frown at him. 'Really? You don't have any problems at all?'

'No,' he says firmly.

'Not . . . not even a tiddly one?'

'Not a tiddler, no.'

'Lucky you.' I laugh uncomfortably.

He shrugs and looks away.

'Please, Sam, I just need . . .' I tail off, realising that he's willing me to shut up. What the hell have I said? His eyes are guarded. This isn't like him at all. Something must be worrying him, something I've dredged up with my big gob and stupid game. I feel a stab of hurt that he won't share it with me.

'*You* make them up,' he says, brightening as he ambles towards my desk. 'I'll help with the details.'

'Right,' I say, less enthusiastically now.

Still, we manage and the mood lightens. With Sam's help, I concoct five problems that sound feasible and become so immersed in formulating replies that I start to feel sorry for Sally of Lincs., whose daughter's overuse of the F-word is getting her into trouble at school. As for Sickened of Inverness, whose husband insists on two full rounds of golf every weekend, leaving her to ferry their children to a myriad of activities, I could almost bomb up to Scotland and punch him. I try to invent a problem about whether an elderly mother should move into a home, but tail off and look at Sam.

'Are you sure you feel OK doing this?' he asks tentatively.

I shift on my chair. 'No, not really . . .'

'Can you imagine making them up week after week? And all those people emailing and writing letters, desperate for help.'

'Oh, shut up,' I say, laughing.

Grinning, he checks his watch and gets up from the chair. Harvey is sleeping over in Jake's fragrant room. Jake begged, and I'm trying to make things better between us.

As Sam leaves, he says, 'You know what? I think you should forget about that Pike woman and just be yourself. You don't need to make up the letters, Cait. You can tackle the serious stuff.'

I shiver in the doorway. 'It's not that easy . . .'

'Don't people tell you things? What about that cab driver whose wife had cancer?'

'Yes, but . . .'

'And the old lady we met in the park who was gutted because her granddaughter had dropped out of uni – remember her?'

'That's different,' I insist.

He pulls his jacket around himself, shivering. I wish he'd stay longer. Just being around him makes me sense as if my life's, well, almost normal. Rachel makes me feel so inadequate sometimes. With Sam I feel less alone.

'People tell you stuff, Cait,' he adds, 'because they know you're interested and will listen.'

The smile warms my face. 'OK. I'll give it a go.'

As we say goodbye I realise I haven't even mentioned my forthcoming casual, doesn't-mean-anything drink with Darren.

Having reconvened with the sad and the desperate, I settle on five genuine dilemmas. The strange thing is, answering them isn't as difficult as I'd imagined. I try to picture myself sitting beside each woman in a bar and figure how I'd react if we fell into conversation and she poured out her worries, the way people do sometimes after a few drinks. Lola totters into the kitchen in a half-sleep, and I gently steer her back upstairs to bed. Jake and Harvey have crashed out top to toe beneath a muddle of astronaut duvet. Travis shouts for me on the pretence of wanting a drink, but really, I suspect, because he needs to know that there's one parent who hasn't left him.

Back at my desk, ideas start to form. It all falls into place, as if these women and I are really talking, without noticing the hours slipping by. When I've finally finished, I check the time. It's 2.37 a.m. I'm not even tired. It's been challenging and – dare I say it – fun.

Maybe I can pull this off after all.

Thursday evening, 6.25 p.m. How to de-mother yourself in ten simple steps:

1. Bribe children with trashy dinner scoffed in front of *Wallace and Gromit* while you bolt yourself in the bathroom to shower and defuzz.

Not because I am anticipating that Darren will glimpse defuzzed areas. After all, I shall be returning home to three innocent, sleeping children plus Holly, our peachy-skinned nineteen-year-old babysitter. However, it's beneficial to the old, battered ego to feel less gorilla-like on such occasions. It seems terribly unfair that while certain areas – e.g. breasts – droop and wither with age, pubic hair exhibits newly abundant growth, as if liberally dosed with hormone-rooting powder.

2. Ensure that showering/defuzzing happens as swiftly as possible, as someone is bound to need the toilet – i.e. this toilet, even though there's another perfectly serviceable one downstairs.

Right now, Lola is urgently hammering the locked door. 'Mummy, what are you doing?' she yells. Then, 'Is the toilet an appliance?'

3. Once dried and lotioned up, select jeans, wedgy shoes and floaty top for understated foxiness.
4. Examine reflection by staggering about on bed, as if drunk, in order to view various sections of one's appearance in the dressing-table mirror.

Hmmm. Not sure I've got it right. Top is terribly transparent, breasts pitifully un-pert. An image of Slapper at Thorpe Park pings into my mind and I switch to a black knee-length dress, fancy patterned tights and high boots.

5. Take style pointers from a seven-year-old.

'Why are you standing on your bed?' Lola enquires, striding into my bedroom.

'It's the only way I can see all of myself in the mirror.'

'Where are you going?'

'Just out with a friend, love.'

Despairing shake of the head. 'Don't wear that dress. It makes you look like a witch.'

6. Think: what do thirty-five-year-olds actually wear when they venture out after dark?

I no longer know. Can I get away with a shortish skirt as long as it's 'teamed' (I do love a bit of fashion-speak) with opaque tights, or would genuinely young people start laughing or retching? Once, as a joke, I asked Jake if low-rise jeans were acceptable for a woman of my advancing years. 'Only with a really long jumper,' he declared, shuddering visibly. 'I once saw an old woman in a hoodie,' he added.

'Really old?' I said. 'What sort of age exactly?'

'Even older than you,' he gloated.

Favoured terms when it comes to fashion for thirty-five plus: well cut, classic and investment dressing, all of which make me want to keel over with ennui.

7. Ensure that you look like you haven't tried too hard, that your yumminess is entirely natural.

This seems the sensible option. Unless Darren asked me out as some kind of prank, he must have found me attractive. It's a startling concept, and suggests that I should just go as myself. I settle on the floaty top and trousers plus strappy sandals for a smidge of foxery.

8. Moisturise addled face.

At the back of the bathroom cabinet I find a pot of cream which promises a 'youthful, dewy glow with visible results in one month'. Can't it act faster? I need results in one *hour*.

9. Apply make-up, erring on less-is-more approach, and 'tame' hair.

Miraculously, my paltry selection of budget cosmetics seem to have a prettifying effect. My eyes look less dead, my mouth more shapely and wanton (steady!). I pull up my hair into a messy attempt at a bun, yanking out some kinky bits to 'frame' my face (see, I do skim *Bambino*'s beauty pages) for a less matronly look. At last, my appearance doesn't scream, 'Mother.'

Downstairs, our babysitter, Holly, is chatting to the kids. They love her visits. Unlike me, it is acceptable for her to use words like 'cool' and 'wicked'. (Jake once informed me that I should never say 'cool', not even in a temperature context – e.g. 'I could murder a cool drink.)'

10. When officially de-mothered, to the point at which strangers would cry, 'No! It's just not possible!' on learning that you have actually produced children, trip lightly downstairs, avoiding partially constructed knights' castle in the hall.

'Wow, you look lovely,' Holly announces.

'Thanks.' I feel chuffed even though she, in contrast, is *naturally* lovely and doesn't require a ten-step anything.

All that remains is to plant fleeting kisses on the heads of my sweet-smelling offspring and swish off into the night.

N.B. The aforementioned steps should ensure that even the shabbiest mother greets the outside world feeling pleasingly smooth-skinned and luscious. At least, that's what the magazines tell you.

Unfortunately, they never say what to do when you're shitting a brick.

9

By the time I reach Circa, the new bar in Shoreditch, I have managed to bring myself down to a calmer state. Breathing exercises during the short cab journey helped. Millie showed me how to inhale slowly and deeply, hold my breath for a count of three . . . and *release*. It's a tactic she uses prior to stressful meetings. (How stressful can things become in a soothing office populated by immaculately coiffed adults?)

As I push open the etched-glass door, I feel nothing scarier than mild giddiness. After all, this is nothing to flip out about. It's not as if I am remotely interested in getting involved with Darren, or have him lined up as a potential boyfriend. I have already written him off as sweet, undeniably easy on the eye and useful for sourcing a reconditioned TV, but, at a guess, around a decade too young for me. It's a bit of fun, that's all.

The dimly lit bar is around half full, and there's a hum of low-level chatter. The barman is mixing drinks in a showy way, spinning round for spirits and lemon. I perch on a barstool, order a white wine (large) and scan the room, prickling with anticipation.

The first few sips slide down easily and I start to feel more positive about the evening's possible outcomes. Maybe Darren and I will become friends. He might start coming round for coffee and fix various defunct appliances for me. When it's warmer, he might lounge in our back garden with his T-shirt off. That'd make Mrs Catchpole next door choke on her false teeth.

I imagine him introducing me to his equally fresh-faced friends. They won't blather on about the rigours of potty-training or the MMR jab. They'll discuss music and film and clubs. (That part's scary: I haven't been clubbing since my twenties.) Their fridges will house only a bottle of vodka and a hunk of cheese for late-night snacking. None will own a pasta machine. I'll have to guard against making any embarrassing gaffes, like starting sentences with, 'When I was your age' or talking about school, nursery, the Three Bears toddler group, Martin, Daisy, Poppy . . . (God, there's a lot I won't be able to mention. What the heck *will* I talk about?)

Somehow, I have managed to arrive early. I glimpse my reflection in an artfully tarnished mirror, relieved that the purplish lighting masks my under-eye shadows. The bar is filling up now, and I catch the eye of a man who's standing with a cluster of similarly dressed males (casual work trousers, shirts, loosened ties) by the window. The man smiles and waves. I smile half-heartedly back and it takes me a moment to realise it's Guy, Rachel's husband, devoid of ginger beard.

His face looks scarily naked.

Still clutching his beer, he bounds towards me, grinning broadly. 'Caitlin, I thought it was you! Out and about in a drinking establishment. Gosh, don't you scrub up well?' His eyes slide over my body.

I smile tightly and edge back on my stool. 'Just waiting for someone actually.' It's odd, running into him here – out of context, in a young people's bar – when I've only glimpsed him building sandpits and tending his herbaceous borders. He is also, I surmise, a bit pissed and is sweating profusely around the temples. It's not a flattering look.

'Night out with the girls?' he enquires.

'Um, no, I'm just meeting a friend.'

'*Boy*friend?' He makes a frog-like gurgle.

'Not exactly, no . . .' I glance around desperately.

'Lucky fella. If you don't mind me saying, Caitlin, you're looking lovely tonight. Never understood why Martin went off with that, that . . . other woman. Met her at work, didn't he? Secretary or something?'

'No, he—'

'Why go out for a hamburger when there's steak at home, eh? Hurhur!'

I almost choke.

'What time is he due, this fella of yours?'

'Now, actually. Eight o'clock.' I check my watch and try to transmit desperate go-back-to-your-colleagues vibes. One of Guy's cluster keeps gawping at us, as if something outrageous might happen and he doesn't want to miss it.

Guy frowns at his watch. 'I make it a quarter past and my watch is *never* wrong. Looks like you've been stood up.'

'I don't think so.' Actually, now he's pointed this out, I do think so. My underarms are sweating and my glass is tragically empty.

'That's men for you. Heartless bastards. Come on, let's get you another drink. Come over, join the party. Can't have a lovely woman like you sitting all on her own. God knows who might pounce, hurhur . . .'

Unable to concoct a single reason why I cannot possibly do this, I sit, mute, while Guy orders another glass of wine for me and traipse after him across the room.

And what a desperate bunch they are. All around Guy's age – late-thirties – laughing too loudly and clearly thrilled to be among young people at night-time. (Actually, I was thrilled too, until approximately three minutes ago.) There are brief hellos and the group resumes its conversation.

'So where were we? Oh, yeah,' says the one with greying Brillo-pad hair, 'so I creosoted the fence, thought I could get away with one coat—'

'Hope it wasn't actually creosote, mate,' Guy chips in excitedly. 'It's a banned substance.'

'Yeah, no – it's that other stuff, the green-and-white can with the owl on the front . . .'

'Did you brush it on or use a spray?' Guy enquires.

My eyes flick between them. Their faces are flushed, their eyes gleaming like polished jet.

'I sprayed. Much faster,' says Mr Creosote, his cheeks trembling like half-set jelly.

Darren has stood me up. It was a prank after all.

'You get better coverage with a brush,' Guy warns, and the others murmur in agreement.

I could weep. Here I am, having followed the ten-step programme *and* booked a babysitter, and for what? To be trapped in a debate about wood preservative. Jesus. All around us, people are laughing and chatting animatedly and greeting each other with hugs. I'm seized by a desire to be one of them. Not Caitlin Brown, dumpee, trapped with middle-aged men discussing their fucking fences. Will I ever care about such matters? I guess I should, if I am ever to become a Proper Mother like Rachel. Mrs Catchpole often enquires when I'm intending to cut back the cherry tree that overhangs her garden, as if it's threatening the very fabric of her home.

A stunning girl with a curtain of golden hair drifts past and Mr Creosote stares pointedly at her legs. I wait for a gap in the conversation to announce that I am feeling unwell and need to rush home immediately for medication and rest.

'So,' Guy asks, as if suddenly remembering my presence, 'what does he do, this fella of yours?'

'He's not my fella,' I reply tersely.

'I mean your date. Your *hot* date.' He pronounces it '*hat*'.

'He fixes TVs.'

'Oooh!' Guy's eyes bulge a little. 'Not a high-flying journo like yourself, then. Bit of rough.'

Creosote guffaws. 'Useful profession, though, if you need your aerial adjusting.'

'Or someone to *twiddle your knobs*,' cuts in a man with a neat row of rabbity teeth.

I try to laugh, or at least smirk, to show that I can handle a joke, but my mouth appears to be paralysed. Guy and his buddies are in full swing now. They should be on the fucking stage.

'Watch he doesn't give you any interference,' roars Creosote.

'Or try to turn you on,' cackles the rabbity one.

I have deteriorated from revelling in my new-found youthfulness to feeling about 300 years old and on a fast track to Mimosa House. My wine is lukewarm, but I still swig it desperately.

'So,' Guy cuts in, 'who's looking after the kiddies tonight?'

'No one,' I reply. 'I stuffed them into the cupboard and chucked in a couple of biscuits. They'll be fine.'

He drops his gaze to my breasts. 'Oh, really, haha . . .'

'Um, Caitlin?'

I swing round. It's Darren, an extremely cute and appealing prospect compared with Guy's entourage. Cute and appealing, period. Perky smile, fudgy-brown eyes, hint of stubble around the jaw.

'Hi, Darren.' I smile, and he kisses my cheek.

'Sorry I'm late – a few problems at work . . .'

'That's OK. Nice to meet you all,' I say, managing the fakest of grins as I steer Darren away from the comedians.

'We can have a drink with your friends if you like,' he says.

'They're not my friends. And no, I don't like.'

We both laugh, and I glance over my shoulder. Creosote makes a poking motion with his index finger, like someone turning on a TV.

The night can only get better.

And it does, with Darren's banter offering a delightful contrast to Guy's entourage.

'So this woman came in to pick up her video,' he tells me, 'blaming me for the fact that it was stuffed with money. As if I'd put it there – two or three hundred quid's worth of coins, which was why, of course, it was broken—'

'Travis does that,' I cut in. 'He has the posting fetish, this desire to push things into little slots.' I clamp my mouth shut. Children are supposed to be off the agenda tonight.

'She says, "I don't know how that got in there,"' Darren continues, 'and I say, "I assume you have kids . . ." And she goes, "Yes, but little Sweetiebums would never do that . . ."'

I laugh, trying to blot out the spectre of Guy and Creosote from the periphery of my vision.

'So,' Darren says, 'how come a nice girl like you ended up single?'

'How did you know I'm single?' I ask, twirling the stem of my glass. 'I mean, what made you phone me?'

He smiles. 'I kind of took a gamble.'

'Don't believe you.' I smirk.

'OK . . . I realised I'd seen you before, in that posh deli by the museum . . .'

He'd noticed me? I always assume I'm invisible when out and about. 'You were buying lemons,' Darren continues, 'and talking about pancakes, and your little girl was saying, "Do I have to go to Daddy's this weekend?"'

'Right,' I say, a little startled.

'That sounds a bit stalkerish. Sorry.' He grins ruefully, and his eyes hold mine.

'No, it's OK.'

'And after you'd been in the shop with your old telly, I kept looking at your number and thought, Well, she can only say no.'

I don't know how to respond. I'm not used to this. It's not like riding a bike or swimming: you really do forget how to behave in this kind of situation.

'Well,' I tell him, 'I'm glad you did.'

Dear Pike, I muse, as we stroll past Guy's gang, who are guffawing drunkenly by the cigarette machine, what would you recommend as proper etiquette at the end of a first date?

We're on our way to dinner now – a cheap Italian. I was too harassed and nervy to eat with the kids before I came out and now I'm ravenous.

Darren's hand folds around mine as he chats about his East London family and the business his dad passed on to him. He mentions stuff he gets up to at weekends: like clubbing (yikes). Bit of DJing (double yikes). It feels slightly odd, holding hands with someone over the age of seven, but I try to relax and do the breathing thing again, although more subtly this time. Don't want Darren thinking I'm having a seizure, being old and everything.

Who cares that I was probably in secondary school when he was in nappies? I haven't asked his age. Haven't dared to. Maybe it doesn't matter. It feels like both of us are keen for the evening to go on and on. But what happens at the end? I feel too long in the tooth for snogging down some dark alley, much as I'd like to, as Darren has the most delicious-looking mouth. In fact, I'd be up for kissing him, absolutely. I wouldn't even worry about Holly detecting a just-snogged look about my lips. Heck, I think my libido's woken up.

My mobile starts ringing. I snatch it from my bag, panicking that it's an emergency at home. Christ, it's Mimosa House.

'Hello?' I say shakily.

'Oh, Caitlin.' I recognise Helena's voice immediately. 'I don't want to worry you, but—'

'Is Mum OK?'

'I'm sure she is. I'm sorry, and it shouldn't have happened, but she's somehow managed to wander outside. You know how she lurks by the door with her coat on? A visitor must have assumed she was on her way out and held the door open for her . . . At least, we think that's what happened.'

'Oh, God. How long has she been gone?'

'An hour or so. We've searched the streets around here, been into all the shops and restaurants, asked anyone who might have seen her. The police have someone out driving around looking for her. I don't want to worry you, Cait, but you know how vulnerable Jeannie is . . .'

My stomach lurches, and my instinct is to call Adam – to share this with him – but what can he do in Manchester?

'I'll come over right now,' I say quickly.

'I think that's best. Maybe you could think of places that might mean something to her, anywhere she might go.'

I glance at Darren. Concern flickers in his eyes. 'I'll try, Helena. I'll be with you as soon as possible, OK?'

'What—' Darren starts.

'My mum. She's gone missing. She lives in a care home and . . .' My eyes blur, and my mouth is trembling.

'Can I do anything?' He touches my arm.

I shake my head. 'I've got to go, help them look for her . . .'

'Let's get you a cab.'

I look around wildly, but there's no cab in sight. Then I spot it – a bus, pulling into the stop ahead. I plant the briefest kiss on Darren's startled lips and run.

10

Where the hell has she gone?

I try, as I hurry through faint drizzle in my unsuitable sandals, to thrust myself into Mum's muddled world. Before Mimosa House, she'd lived in Hackney, which could be Jupiter for all she knows now. No point in trying to be logical. Mum doesn't know one day from the next, and the seasons are indistinguishable; she once raged that no one had given her any Christmas presents in August. There are no friends I can think of, or people she might be trying to find. Petty arguments killed any friendships years before she moved into the home. Last Christmas, she received only three cards: one from me and the kids, one from Helena and a whopping padded satin thing from Adam that came in a flat white box. You could smell the guilt emanating from it. As far as I know, there's no one else in her life, unless you count the ever-patient GPs, hairdressers and chiropodists who frequent the home and tend to various parts of her. I must tell the kids that should I show any signs of becoming like Granny, they must set me up in a tiny cottage by the sea with limitless alcohol and strong fags, as I fully intend to take up smoking again. Martin is fervently anti-smoking – the reason I gave up, in fact. I shall save all my fag ends and dispatch them to him in a Jiffy bag.

Mimosa House is in sight. My head swims with a terrible image of crushed Fox's Glacier Mints glinting in the road, or her old brown cardigan flattened by a tyre, with a pigeon pecking at it. Helena is hovering anxiously in the foyer and buzzes me in. She is trying to emanate calmness, but I can see fear in her eyes. 'I've been racking my brains,' she says, 'and there's only one place your mum ever talks about.'

'Glasgow? She wouldn't have gone to King's Cross, would she, and caught a train?'

Helena smiles kindly. 'I think that's unlikely.'

'And the police have been out looking for her?'

'Yes. We've still got staff out looking too. She can't have gone far, Caitlin.'

I nod, feeling helpless and sick. Mum could have been mugged – although she has nothing to be mugged for, apart from her mints – or knocked down by a car. Her road sense is worse than Travis's. I picture her in some alley or shadowy corner of the park, alone and scared. No longer vexed Jeannie ticking me off for letting myself go.

'Caitlin,' Helena says gently, 'please don't cry. We'll find your mum. Let's go.'

As we set out, I'm thinking, Glasgow. It's where she belongs, even now; she has only ever *tolerated* London. Dad, a Londoner himself, had promised that they'd have a better life here. As if in defiance, she'd talked about home constantly, which had tipped into the shipyard fantasies. Jeannie the shipbuilder, slamming in rivets with her bare fists.

'Helena,' I say suddenly, 'I have an idea.' Ships, rivers, water.

'What is it?'

'The canal. I just have a feeling . . .'

'It's worth a try,' she says, and we hurry along dank side streets, calling her name.

'I'm Jeannie!' cries a drunk man, tumbling out of a ratty-looking pub. He sings after us, 'I dream of Jeannie with the light-brown hair.'

We reach the bridge that spans the canal. There's a flight of steps on each side leading down to the towpath. While Helena hurries down one, I take the other. There are moored narrow-boats, some with yellowy glows at their windows. Now my hunch seems ridiculous, that Mum might have mistaken a murky East London canal for the Clyde.

Folk music drifts lazily from one of the boats. There's a sweet, woody smell of dope. I clack along the towpath in my spindly sandals. One of the heels feels unstable and I pray that it won't snap off. Boots would have been better after all.

Although I'm almost too scared to look, my eyes skim the water. Silvery reflections shiver on its surface. There are a few floating cans and a plastic milk carton. What if Mum hasn't floated, but is lying at the bottom with the rusting shopping trolleys and God knows what else?

How the hell will I tell Adam about this?

He was right. Mimosa House isn't the right place for her. Not safe enough. It's the twenty-first century, for God's sake; aren't they able to instal a security system that's capable of foiling an old lady with dementia? It's not as if she hasn't tried this before. She has crept into the kitchen and towards the open back door while the chef was having a ciggy. She's lurked by the front door, hoping to attach herself to someone else's family as they leave. Helena has found her rattling the bar on the fire-escape door in a bid for freedom. Imprisoned – that's how Mum feels. Incarcerated with lots of old people talking nonsense and a blaring TV that seems permanently tuned to *The Flintstones*. Tears drip down my cheeks, and a sob escapes. If I'd done what Martin had suggested and moved her in with us, she'd be alive now.

'Scuse me? Are you all right?'

The voice gives me a start. A head has popped up from the folk-music boat. A stocky, bearded man emerges.

'I'm just looking for someone,' I say quickly.

He grins and a gold tooth glints. 'Feisty lady, Scottish, worked in shipyards all her life?'

Relief swells over me like a wave and I hurry towards him. 'Yes, have you seen her? Is she OK?'

The man beckons me closer. 'Jeannie's in here. She's good company, your mum. A lovely old bird.' He takes my hand and helps me over the railings.

I step on to the deck, which wobbles uncertainly, and follow him down a short flight of creaking steps. There's a thick smell of woodsmoke. Low benches run along each side, on which several young men and women sit, tightly packed as if on a train, plus Jeannie with her tweed coat buttoned up to her neck.

'Mum!' I exclaim, peering into the gloom. 'What are you doing here?'

She jabs a finger at the table. They are playing cards. A couple of cigarettes and a joint emit smoke from a scallop-shell ashtray. 'Playing poker,' she retorts. 'What does it look like?'

'Everyone's been worried sick! I've been charging about all over the place looking for you—'

'She's a ferocious player,' the bearded man cuts in. 'You've been having a nice time with us, Jeannie, haven't you?' He winks at me.

'Nice to find young people with manners,' Mum mutters. 'You're looking awfully done up, aren't you? Are you going somewhere?'

'No, Mum.' I don't have it in me to be angry.

'Those trousers do nothing for your hips.'

A girl with a pale, luminous face giggles into her hand. She's probably the age of my babysitter.

'Come on, Mum,' I say gently. 'Let's go.'

'You're a spoilsport, you are. Always ruining my fun.' Her eyes gleam in the tea lights' glow.

I squeeze past the tight row of knees to take Mum by the hand. 'Thanks for looking after her,' I say. 'Come on, Jeannie, I'm taking you home.'

'Back to those bloody old people,' she growls as we leave.

It's 3.20 a.m. With creeping horror, it dawns on me that I am having my *Bambino* photo taken in seven hours' time. Millie insisted that I have a professional photo taken for the page. Imagine fretting over such a trivial matter when your own mother could have fallen into the canal or been taken hostage by boat-dwellers.

Naturally, all of this is completely my fault. This is what happens when you go out with a strange man, drink alcohol and start thinking that perhaps sex isn't such an appalling concept after all.

II

'Heavy night last night?' Carmen scans my face as if it's a substandard garment on a sale rail.

'Just a few drinks with friends,' I reply.

'Hmmm, I'll need to cover up here, here and here.' Her French-manicured nail flicks my chin, the sides of my nose and under-eye zones. 'And here and here,' she adds, indicating my hairline and jaw.

I glimpse my reflection in the studio's dressing-room mirror. To Carmen, who's accustomed to making up professional models, I must look like a corpse.

'What sort of make-up d'you usually wear?' she asks.

'Um, Rimmel, bit of Maybelline . . .'

She winces. 'I mean colours. Which spectrum d'you feel comfortable with?'

What does she mean? I don't *have* a spectrum. 'I don't wear much make-up,' I say, 'unless I'm going out, then it's just a bit of eyeshadow and lip gloss.'

She emits a gravelly laugh. 'Trust me, I'm a doctor.'

Despite my horror at having my photo taken by a proper photographer – in a proper studio with blazing lights – I have begun to feel less anxious about the whole deal. Carmen appears to be wearing no make-up apart from a slick of brownish gloss on her full lips. A natural beauty, smelling fresh and lemony. I feel reasonably safe in her dainty hands.

'All I'll do,' she continues, 'is bring out your eyes and lips, sticking to the pinky-brown palette. Flattering shades to bring out your natural glow.'

Natural glow! I like the sound of that. Haven't had one for at least a decade.

'You'll still be you,' Carmen adds, 'but more so.' She smiles reassuringly and I smile back. I'm not sure what the pinky-brown palette is exactly, but it sounds unthreatening.

Travis, I am relieved to note, is chatting happily to Adrian, the photographer, in the main studio. 'I like Captain Hook,' he announces. 'Captain Hook cool.'

'I like him too,' Adrian enthuses. 'D'you have one of those plastic hooks that you wear instead of a hand?'

'Yeah! Daddy bought it. An' I got jacket and trousers.'

I'd tried to persuade Millie that I would be available only on Travis's nursery days, but now it seems I needn't have worried.

'We're lucky to be able to book Adrian,' she'd told me. 'We have to work around *his* availability.'

Carmen selects products from three enormous make-up boxes and sets them out on the dressing table. For a natural look, she seems to have chosen a heck of a lot. There are eye shadows in dozens of shades ranging from shimmery beige to black. *Black* eye shadow? I hope she's not intending to use it. I feel far too ragged to pull off the smoky-eyed temptress look, and I'm not sure I'd be convincing as a goth. She opens a palette of lip colours and removes the lids from four bottles of foundation.

'You're a tricky colour,' she murmurs, 'so I'll have to blend.'

'Right.' No one has said this before. I wonder if it indicates an underlying medical problem.

Clearly, Carmen is leaving nothing to chance. Armed with brushes, applicators, eyelash-curlers and flat circular sponges that look like breast pads, she sets to work. As in the hair-dresser's, I avoid my reflection, focusing on an oily smear on the wall just beneath the mirror.

'Your little boy's a real sweetie,' Carmen remarks, soothing my nerves with strokes of her blusher brush.

'Thanks. He has his moments, but he's a pretty good boy.'

'He's so cute! Nothing like you, is he? Does he look like his dad?'

My molars clamp together. 'Yes, he's his image, actually.'

Carmen chuckles. 'He must be a honey. Your man, I mean. Lucky you.'

'Uh-huh.' I hate it when this happens. My kids are, admittedly, head-turningly cute, and that's not just me being boastful. Strangers ooh and ahh in the park, even with Jake, who you'd assume would be too old to be cooed over. Rather fortuitously, my offspring have inherited Martin's dark-eyed intensity, rather than my insipid blue-grey eyes and light-brown hair. In fact, they bear no resemblance to me whatsoever, which is galling when you're the one who lugged them around for nine months and lay screaming and sucking on gas-and-air, feeling as if your entire lower half was about to burst open. Martin's handsomeness has been distilled into our children, the smug arse.

'Nanananananananana, *Batmaaan!*' blasts Travis.

'All done,' Carmen says with a grin. 'What do you think?'

I look up. Slowly, the image comes into focus.

And it's truly terrible.

I mumble something unintelligible. In fact, I am incapable of speech. No words could convey the true horror of what I see before me. Carmen lied. I am not myself only more so. She has transformed me from being reasonably presentable with a faint air of knackeredness into what I can only describe as . . . a man.

A man in drag. The kind of unconvincing trannie you feel desperately sorry for, with his over-done face and bouffant hair and massive farmer's hands. The sort you want to take aside and say, 'Look, love, cut the flouncy blouse and false eyelashes and all that slathery lipstick. It's too much. Women don't do their make-up that way – at least, they haven't since 1975. Come home with me and we'll have a cup of tea and try something more feminine.'

Seemingly unconcerned with my reaction, Carmen is packing away her things. I keep staring. It's beyond awful. I will appear in a national magazine looking like a Bert or a Norman. My man-face face gawps at me as Carmen cleans her lip palette with baby wipes. In some other universe, Travis continues to trill the *Batman* tune.

'I . . . um . . .' I stutter, fearing that if I stare long enough, I will detect an Adam's apple and a hint of beard growth.

Carmen is humming now, seemingly having forgotten that I exist. She certainly doesn't care what I think of her handiwork. How dare she lull me into a false sense of security? Natural glow indeed! I'd be no less pissed off if I'd asked a painter to redecorate my living room – not that I can afford to employ tradespeople – and instead of the creamy white I'd asked for, he'd painted the goddamn room purple.

'Mummy!' Travis cries. 'Where's Mummy?'

'Just coming, darling,' I manage, as Carmen gives my hair a cursory backcomb and liberal dose of foul-smelling spray. Fantastic. Now I am sporting an unyielding dome. Who back-combs their hair in this day and age?

By now, I am beyond caring. I'll just have to go with it. At least I'll give Millie a laugh when she sees the pictures. Then I can throw myself off London Bridge and be done with it.

'She's ready,' Carmen sing-songs.

I am no longer Caitlin, but 'she'. And I smell weird, as if my entire body has been dunked in melted-down old-lady make-up. I smell like Mimosa House, minus the faint whiff of wee and meaty dinners.

I stride purposefully from the dressing room to the main studio, where Adrian has positioned a soft leather seat for me to park myself on. Travis is sprawled belly-down on the floor, where he's playing with a pile of multicoloured cables. I hope they're not live electrical cables. Surely Adrian or his whey-faced assistant would have stopped him if they were . . .

'Right. Lovely.' Adrian appraises my appearance, his mouth twitching with unease. 'On the chair, please, Karen.'

'It's Cait—' I start, just as Travis looks up, his face crumpling in horror as he sees not his loving, pancake-making mother, but some bloke called Bert who's stolen my clothes.

'Mummy!' he screams, sending the cables flying.

'It's OK, darling, it's *me*,' I protest as he spins away, colliding with a light stand and sending it crashing to the floor. There's a metallic clang and a tinkle of breaking glass.

'Christ, my light!' Adrian barks.

I spring out of the seat and try to gather up Travis from his huddled position in the corner. He writhes out of my grasp, still wailing as if I'm some dastardly child-thief. 'Want Mummy!'

'Travis, darling, I *am* Mummy.'

'Don't like Mummy face!' he shrieks.

Carmen regards the scene with amusement, one hand plonked on her skinny hip.

'It's just make-up,' I soothe. 'I'll take it all off.'

'Horrid Mummy! Bad Mummy!'

'Shhh, sweetheart . . .'

'WANT DADDY!'

'I try to grasp his hand, but he flails wildly, punching my thigh and kicking furiously. Finally, as his fury morphs into sobs, I manage to coax him towards the leather seat.

'Sorry about your light,' I murmur.

'These things happen.' Adrian rolls his eyes towards his assistant – a sharply angled boy who has so far failed to acknowledge me and is already setting up a replacement light. 'They could have warned me,' he adds, 'that there'd be a child here today. It's not really *appropriate*.'

Oh, isn't it? Maybe I should have employed the stuffing-him-in-a-cupboard trick. Bet Harriet Pike didn't cause any bother when she was having her photo done.

Travis is so distraught we end up doing the pictures with him plonked on my lap, whimpering like an injured pup. No matter how I try to radiate empathy, I am conscious of my jaw being unnaturally clenched.

'Smile, Travis,' I murmur.

'Oh, don't worry about him,' Adrian mutters. 'I'm cropping out the kid.'

Now Travis, like me, is nameless.

Carmen swoops over my face with her powder brush. 'You have a terribly oily T-zone,' she reprimands. 'You're breaking through.'

No bloody wonder. Travis is still gulping silently. As we leave the studio, I glimpse the three of them – Adrian, his assistant and Carmen the Witch – swiping beers from a battered fridge and flipping them open with a desperate air.

'Nasty Mummy face,' Travis whimpers in the stairwell.

Hell, I've forgotten to scrape off the damn make-up. 'It's just like dressing up,' I assure him. 'You know, like when you play Captain Hook.'

He remains unconvinced. How long before we're home and I can hose down my face? Half an hour at least. Half an hour in public with my Bert face on.

In the studio's cobbled courtyard, I scrabble in my bag for my purse. Thirteen quid and a few coppers. Not nearly enough for a cab. I grasp Travis's hand, intending to find a café with an abundant supply of loo roll with which to wipe my face. We march through a series of junk-cluttered alleys, eventually finding ourselves at a bustling roundabout. Nothing looks as it did when we came here. There are gloomy warehouses and factories with crudely painted signs, but no café with limitless loo paper, and therefore no chance of making myself look normal.

We march on, bracing ourselves against the cold March winds, both too gloomy to speak, until the Underground sign comes into view. Thankfully, the Tube carriage isn't crowded. Perhaps we'll manage to get home without my having to make eye contact with anyone. Each time I blink I'm conscious of something like eighteen layers of lash-lengthening mascara. I feel like my eyelashes have been dunked in tar.

Darren flashes into my mind. Young, carefree Darren, who was under the illusion that he and I might have fun together. That seems laughable now.

In the carriage, an elderly man is filling in a crossword, and a bunch of backpackers are checking guidebooks and maps. On the opposite seat, to the left, a woman sits with her head bent, her glossy black hair hanging around her face, engrossed in the contents of the file on her lap. She's wearing a grey pinstriped trouser suit and is plugged into her iPod.

'Want biscuit,' Travis murmurs.

'We'll be home soon. You can have a snack before we pick up Lola and Jake.'

'Want biscuit with 'ole in the middle.'

'I think there's some in the tin.' I'm so done in after the shoot that I'll let him hog as many as he wants. He can have the whole bloody packet. *And* Fanta, if there's any left in the fridge.

'WANT. BISCUIT.' His voice blasts down the carriage. The man with the crossword rustles his newspaper irritably. The woman coughs. One day, in a parallel universe, maybe I'll enjoy Tube journeys with an iPod.

'Biscuit!' Travis screams.

'Yes, when we get home, but not if you have a tantrum.' Breathe deeply, hold it in and release. Breathe. Breathe. 'Avoid eye contact,' Pike advised on last week's problem page. 'Never, EVER pay attention to a tantrum in a public place. As long as your child is safe, simply ignore him until the tantrum subsides. I might add that parents who over-indulge their children are merely encouraging these outrageous displays.' Crossword man regards Travis disapprovingly. Bet his children never behaved like this.

'Don't like Mummy,' Travis declares. 'Mummy not my friend.'

'Good.' I stare fixedly at the file on the woman's lap. She closes it and my gaze rests upon the teardrop-shaped logo on the front.

Purity Springs. Personal Service Always.

She glances up and our eyes meet. Something spins between us in the carriage, a ball of horror. I inhale sharply.

'Hello, Daisy,' I croak.

She yanks out her headphones. 'Oh, hi! Sorry, Caitlin, I didn't see you.' Her voice is high-pitched, and she giggles uneasily. At least she has the decency to look mortified. Her face is immaculately made up, although she looks bleary around the eyes. She's probably been up half the night shagging the pants off my husband.

'Finished work for the day?' I ask curtly, although at 2 p.m. it's unlikely.

'I – I'm on my way to see clients at Liverpool Street.'

'That's nice.' *Are you planning to shag them?* I want to ask.

She straightens the file on her lap. Crossword man folds up his newspaper noisily.

'Settled into your new flat?' I venture.

'Um, yes, it's lovely. Er, I mean . . . you know. It's quite ordinary really, but it's, um . . . fine.'

'I hear it's a penthouse,' I add.

'No, it's nothing like that.' Her laughter tinkles out like shards of glass. 'There's no room to swing a cat. We call it the penthouse as a joke.'

'Oh.' Bloody hilarious.

'What's a planthouse?' Travis asks, mercifully distracted from his biscuit craving.

'A very expensive flat,' I explain loudly, 'on top of a big building. Only very rich people can afford them.' I regard her coolly, hoping that if I stare hard enough, my gaze will penetrate her frontal lobe and cause irreparable damage.

'Really,' she insists, 'it's quite tiny.'

'Size isn't everything,' I reply.

Daisy nods mutely and glances around the carriage, settling her gaze on the emergency handle. What a cow, she'll be thinking. Is it any wonder that Martin left her for me? Look at her poor, starving child, desperate for a biscuit, and her face all caked in—

Shit. I'd forgotten my face. What am I thinking, trying to freak her out? Daisy's the one with the penthouse and architect boyfriend and nicely done make-up. I am the ladyboy with bouffant hair and lips dripping with grease.

'Well, see you around.' She leaps up and stuffs her folder into her bag.

'Bye,' I manage, as the train pulls into Liverpool Street.

'Nice seeing you both.' She grins broadly, any hint of nervousness gone.

'Bye-bye!' Travis says with a cheery wave.

Daisy waves briefly and swoops off the train, her heels clacking on the platform. I swipe my oily lips against the back of my hand. They leave a scarlet smear, like a wound.

12

Carmen's warpaint is an absolute swine to get off. I haven't worn mascara since Jake was born – due to the fact that it's the only item of make-up that doesn't magically melt away while you sleep – so I don't possess any remover or even cotton wool to wipe the wretched stuff off. (Daisy, I'd imagine, has pastel-coloured cotton-wool balls in a pretty glass jar from Liberty. And probably has her eyelashes *dyed*.)

In the sanctuary of our bathroom I moisten a wad of loo roll and rub my eyelids. Although the mascara is smearing nicely on to the under-eye zones, there's still a ton of it stuck to my lashes. What's this stuff made from – creosote? Maybe Guy and his mates would be able to offer assistance with its removal or suggest a non-gunky substitute. I fear that I'll never blink normally again My eyeballs will wither up through lack of lubrication.

I make another loo-paper wad and scrub at the charcoal patches under my eyes. Now my skin looks raw and is stinging like buggery. Great. Now I look like I've been sobbing for weeks. With no time for further face-scouring, I set off with Travis to collect Lola and Jake from school, conscious of everyone checking out my stressed, puffy face.

There's nothing like the school-gate cluster to heighten your unease if you're not feeling 100 per cent.

'Hi, Cait!' chirps Bev Hartnett, bastion of the PTA, in disastrous drapey blue trousers that might possibly hail from the New Romantic era.

I grin tightly and turn away, but there's no escape.

'What's happened to your face?' she asks, feigning concern.

'I, er, had my photo taken.'

'What, for your passport or something? Are you going away?'

'No, it was for, um, a work thing. A magazine thing.'

She gives me a curious look. I will the school bell to ring and the children to rescue me from Bev's unfaltering gaze.

'Went to a horrible place,' Travis announces. 'Lady put fing on Mummy.' He jabs a grubby finger at my lips.

'Caitlin,' cries Rachel, beetling over to join us, 'you look terrible! Have you been crying?'

'I was assaulted,' I explain, 'with a mascara wand.'

'Really? Oh, come on. You've had one of those department-store make-overs, haven't you?'

'God,' Bev chips in, 'I never let them anywhere near *my* face, even when they're giving out free samples.'

Yet more mothers drift towards us, all focusing intently on my ravaged face. I feel naked and glance around desperately for Sam.

Millie texts me: HOPE SHOOT WENT WELL BET U LOOKED GORGEOUS LOVE MX.

'You owe me one,' I growl at my phone.

Sam waves from across the street and arrives by my side as the children surge from the building. While he raises an eyebrow, and is clearly studying my swollen eyes, he refrains from quizzing me in public. For that I could hug him, if Bev wouldn't interpret it as evidence of our rampant affair. Can't wait for the Easter holidays for a break from all this.

Over the next few weeks I crack on with my page, grateful for regular work to temper my rage when Martin announces that he, Daisy and Poppy are going to Sardinia for the Easter holidays. 'It was only a cheap deal,' Martin mutters. 'One of those last-minute things.' What's 'only' about whizzing off to Sardinia? There's no *only* about it.

I've heard nothing from Darren since our date. Even he didn't want to meet up again, he could have called to see if I'd managed to find Mum. Clearly, he's too young to comprehend what it's like to have an aged parent. His own mother is probably around forty-five. I feel hurt, and vaguely cross; after all, he'd called me and made all the moves. When I'm out shopping locally, I try to avoid passing the TV shop. If I can't avoid it, I walk on the opposite pavement with my head twisted unnaturally to one side.

Newsagents, too, are challenging. Every time I glimpse a copy of *Bambino* I'm reminded that time is ticking away to the dreadful day when my first problem page appears. Then I'll be outed as a man, and life as I know it will be over. It makes Darren, and even Sardinia, pale into insignificance. Perhaps I could buy up every copy and have a gigantic bonfire in the garden. Or at least relocate to another country.

In early April, the Easter break arrives finally and I wait at the school playground railings as Marcia and Bev discuss their forthcoming jaunt to southern France. A two-family holiday. How very jolly. I once suggested to Martin that we might consider going away with Rachel and Guy, and he'd given me a look to suggest that he'd rather saw off his own penis than holiday with another couple and their child.

In that instance, perhaps he was right. A fortnight of creosote conversations, and no means of escape, is quite horrifying.

The school bell rings shrilly and Jake appears at my side, dumping his schoolbag at my feet as if it's my duty to carry it home. 'What we doing for the holidays?' He meets my gaze defiantly.

'I haven't planned anything, Jake. I thought we'd just play it by ear.'

He looks disgusted. 'You mean we're not going away?'

'Not everyone goes away at Easter,' I explain hotly as Lola pelts to my side. 'I'll take you somewhere in the summer, and Daddy will too, so you'll have *two* holidays.' What a lucky, lucky boy from a broken home he is.

Sam and Harvey weave their way through the throng towards us. 'Heading straight home?' Sam asks.

'Sure,' I say, eager to escape the Easter-holiday chatter.

'*Everyone* goes away at Easter,' Jake mutters, falling into step beside me.

'Oh, right,' I say. 'Like everyone's got an Xbox, and everyone takes Starbursts for playtime snack.' I'd fallen for that one when Jake had started school, stocking up on so many multi-packs that it was a miracle his teeth hadn't crumbled to dust by the end of the first week. I soon learned that most parents around here send their children to school with apples, raisins or bite-sized rice cakes.

'Eve isn't going away,' I remind him.

'Yes she is,' Lola announces. 'She's going to Center Parcs.'

'Are you sure?' Damn, I remember now that Rachel booked it at the last minute. I start to explain that Center Parcs costs a fortune, and that most families go there for their main holiday – not a tiddly extra at Easter – but tail off as it's clear that no one believes me. 'What about you, Harvey?' I ask. 'You're staying at home, aren't you?'

'We're going to Cornwall,' he says brightly.

'Are you?'

Sorry, Sam mouths.

'We're staying at my auntie Julie's hotel,' Harvey enthuses. 'Dad says if it's warm enough I can learn to surf. It's gonna be brilliant.'

'That's great,' I say, dripping with disappointment. I'd en- visaged lots of Sam-time over Easter. 'Is Bryony Ellis going away?' I ask hopefully.

'Canary Islands,' Lola chirps.

'Jamie Torrance?'

'Corfu,' Jake mutters darkly. 'Where's that? Can *we* go?'

'No,' I snap. When did this start, this taking several holidays a year? This jetting off to the Canaries or Greece every time there's a bloody bank holiday or in-service day? The only holidays we had during my entire childhood were to boarding houses in Lyme Regis or Littlehampton. No doubt Jamie Tor- rance's parents will be taking the Romanian au pair, in order to minimise contact with their son. I've heard his mother bragging that on their last holiday, they'd only had to deal with him at lunch and bedtime. My kids should realise how damned lucky they are to have a mother who enjoys their company, at least some of the time, and wants to *be* with them.

'Well,' I muster, 'we'll have just as good a time at home. We can go to the cinema and swimming pool and the park and—'

'The park!' Jake repeats bitterly. 'I hate the park. It's cold and boring.'

'You didn't used to say that. You used to love it.'

He sighs dramatically. 'Yeah, when I was about four. I'm ten years old, Mum.' As if my suggestion is as inappropriate as taking him to a *Thomas the Tank Engine* fun day.

'There's loads on over Easter,' Sam cuts in, but Jake isn't having any of it.

'Sadie Bloom's going to Disneyland Paris,' he mutters.

'You think I can afford to take you to Disneyland Paris?' I say, aghast. 'You don't even like Disney! All those films you used to love – *Peter Pan* and *The Jungle Book* and *The Lion King* – didn't you ask me to take them to the charity shop? Aren't they babyish too, like . . . like the park?'

'No!' protests Lola. 'They're *mine*.'

'*I* like *Peter Pan*,' Travis murmurs.

'I don't want *Peter Pan* to go to the charity shop!' Lola wails, and a tear slides down her cheek.

'Well, Mum says it's going,' Jake gloats. 'You're too old for it. Poor children can have it.'

'I hate you,' Lola sobs. 'It's not fair.'

'Honey,' I say, squeezing her hand, 'I'd never give your things away without asking you first.'

'But Jake said—'

'Never mind what Jake said.' I glower at him. How did my adorable little boy turn into a mean brat? 'Well done,' I growl, 'for starting the Easter holidays on such a positive note.'

'What did I do?' He throws out his arms.

Under my breath I mutter, 'Happy fucking Easter.'

'I heard that!' Jake crows. 'Mum swore. She said eff.'

'So what?' *So fucking what?* is what I really want to say.

'Jake,' Sam starts, 'I think what your mum means is—'

'What I mean,' I snap, 'is that I can't help it if every other person in your class gets whisked off abroad every time there's a—'

'Cornwall's not abroad,' says Jake. 'It's in England.'

I know where Cornwall is, smartarse.

'Can *we* go to Cornwall?' Lola asks through her tears. 'Can we go to Sardine-a like Daddy?'

'Want my hook,' demands Travis.

I feign deafness. I want to be home now, with the duvet pulled over my head, hidden from clusters of mothers across the street who are pretending not to tune in. Silly Caitlin, with no plans for Easter. Wouldn't you think she'd have arranged something? At least a trip to California? Poor little mites.

'Where's my Captain Hook hook?' Travis whines.

'No idea,' I mutter as we round the corner into our street.

'Did you take it to the charity shop?' asks Lola.

'My *hook*! No parity shop!'

Jesus H- Christ.

'Why can't we go to Cornwall?' Lola wants to know.

'Can Harvey come for tea?' Jake asks.

'No!' I roar, causing Sam and Harvey to murmur hasty goodbyes and flee for the sanctuary of their own home, when in fact I'd planned to ask them to come in and hang out with us for a bit. Maybe even stay for supper.

I stab my key into the lock.

'How many Easter eggs are we getting this year?' Jake asks as we tumble into the house.

Over the next few days, spurred on by images of the kids' schoolfriends zipping across the Med on inflatable bananas, I work my backside off to pack every second with excitement and fun. We visit the Natural History Museum, where Travis skids delightedly on the polished wooden floors, Jake mooches with a face as flat as a slab of concrete, and we calculate that it would take 1,697 Lolas to fill a blue whale. We have dim sum in Chinatown, see a movie, go to TGI Friday and Hampstead Heath, where Travis skids on dog poo . . . Who needs sodding Sardinia?

Despite our packed schedule, I realise with alarm that I miss Sam. Perhaps it's not Sam per se, but adult company. London – at least my corner of it – has virtually emptied. By the end of week one, I'm so shattered after our myriad of activities that I fall asleep while reading Travis's bedtime story, lurching back into consciousness as he pokes my face.

A postcard arrives from Martin depicting a turquoise sea shot through a crumbling stone arch.

> Hi, folks!
> Having a great time in Sardinia. Beaches are amazing.
> We've been snorkelling and to the amphitheatre and eaten some incredible food. (You'd love the seafood, Jake!) Hope you're having a great Easter hol!
> Lots of love,
> Daddy xxx

I glare at his stunted handwriting, his infuriating fondness for exclamation marks and kisses. Then I rip up the card into tiny pieces, fling it into the pedal bin and dump the kids' leftover pasta on top of it.

> Dear Daddy,
> Are you trying to rub it in, you stupid arse? You could have taken our kids, or would that have unbalanced your precious one-to-one?
> Without love,
> Your ex-wife
> P.S. Are there man-eating sharks in Sardinia? I do hope so.

I also pray that his skin, prone to sunburn, has lifted off in one angry, lobster-hued sheet. Bitter and twisted? *Moi*?

★   ★   ★

By the start of week two, my missing Sam has developed into a full-blown ache. Passing his house makes me feel scratchy and glum. I'd have thought he might have texted or phoned, but he's probably too busy charming Cornish surf babes to think about us.

And I wonder why this makes me feel a little bit strange.

I want him here, sharing stuff like the blue whale and dim sum – even the poo on the heath. The only adults I have spoken to are Mum and assorted inmates and staff at Mimosa House, plus the girl in the café on the heath who charged me something like £200 for a coffee and three fizzy oranges. (Fizzy oranges, Martin! Stick that in your snorkle and smoke it!)

My world has shrunk. In a desperate moment I catch myself muttering to a yellow Sticklebrick. I pore over holidayhomefinder.co.uk and manky-arse-smelling-hovels.com in search of a last-minute bargain – someplace we, too, could enjoy amazing beaches and incredible food. ('You'd love the seafood, Jake!' Choke on a langoustine, shithead!) The only vacant cottage I can find is on the outskirts of Hull. There's an interior photo. Its living-room carpet looks like it's suffering from some kind of fungal growth.

Then something wonderful happens.

A text from Sam: HEADING BACK TOMORO WHY NOT MEET US AT CAMPSITE NR OXFORD FOR I NIGHT ITS FANTASTIC HAVE STAYED THERE BEFORE WILL CALL WITH DETAILS SX.

Completely fantastic idea. Yes, I hate camping. I can't grasp the logic of uprooting one's family from a reasonably comfortable home with proper beds to a rocky field with a stinking toilet block. However, with three more interminable days to fill, and a tent in the attic that Martin bought in a fit of robust outdoorsiness, we're already there.

Stuff Sardinia, Martin Collins. With a grin plastered all over my face, I text back: LOVE 2 CX.

13

As we drive towards Oxford, it strikes me how little time Jake and I spend together, just the two of us. There isn't the opportunity. Maybe that's why he's so hacked off these days. With Jake beside me, and Lola and Travis snoozing on the back seat, I decide to broach it again. The cleaning thing. The spending £1.25 of his own money on Mr Sheen thing. We have left London far behind, and the vast expanses of green have lifted my spirits.

'Jake,' I venture, 'would you tell me if something was worrying you?'

'Mmm.' Eyes fixed ahead.

'I mean . . . you don't seem like yourself. Like your *old* self, I mean. Before Dad, um, moved out. I'm just a bit worried.'

Shrug.

'You never used to tidy and polish and stuff.'

Squirm in seat.

'Why d'you think you do that?' I try to maintain a calm, gentle tone. 'You don't have to, you know. You can be really messy like you were before. It's totally fine. I wouldn't mind at all.'

'Mmblm,' is all he says.

'In fact I'd *like* it,' I charge on. 'It's how kids are supposed to be, isn't it? You can worry about being boring and tidy when you're grown-up.'

Pause. 'Dad wouldn't like that.'

I flick a glance at him. 'You mean, Dad wouldn't like it if you were messy?'

'Yeah.'

Tension fills the car. I can virtually hear it buzzing in my ears like flies. The sun has ducked behind a cloud. 'Jake,' I say gently, 'is Dad's place really tidy?'

'Yeah.'

'And d'you think . . . that's why Dad lives there instead of with us? Because –' I cough to clear a rattle in my throat '– because they're not messy like us?'

Jake nods. His eyes have moistened, and he turns away quickly.

A lump rises in my throat, and I place a hand on his knee. 'Honey, that's not the reason. I tried to explain that when Dad moved out.' Jake stares pointedly at undulating fields. 'He just didn't want to live with me any more,' I add. 'It was about us – me and him. Not you or Lola or Travis.'

'Yeah,' he says, sounding as convinced as if I'd tried to resurrect the tooth-fairy myth.

'So you thought if you made your room really nice, Dad would come back?'

Jake nods.

'That's what you want, for us all to be together again?' My chest feels tight, and tears prickle the backs of my eyes.

'Yes,' he whispers.

'Jake, hon, I'm really sorry.' It's all I can say.

What I want to do is pull over and hug him, but that would wake the others and trigger a barrage of questions about why we've stopped here when there's nothing to see, and why are we cuddling and crying? So I hammer on, through light April drizzle now, with a listless grey sky hanging over us.

All this time Jake's been Mr Sheening to try to lure his dad back, and I hadn't realised.

A bumpy gravel track leads to Sunny Acres Campsite. I park up at the entrance and put my arms round Jake, expecting him to shrug me off, but he doesn't. He feels small and thin and vulnerable. I try to blink back hot tears, but some smear in Jake's hair and I quickly rub my face with my sleeve.

A man wanders past with his jacket hood jutting over his face like a funnel. As Lola stirs in the back, I rest my hands on Jake's shoulders. 'Darling,' I murmur, 'I'm sorry, but me and Daddy aren't going to get back together. Sometimes it's worse when people do that – stay together when they're not getting on – because they're screaming and arguing all the time. You wouldn't like that, would you?'

He stares down. ''Spose not.'

I squeeze his hand. 'C'mon. Let's go to reception and find our pitch. Sam said it's lovely here.'

Jake opens the passenger door and peers around. 'No it's not, Mum. It's horrible.'

'It's *fine*,' I insist, climbing out. 'The weather's rubbish, but I'm sure it'll brighten up and—'

'No, I mean *that*. Look. We're all gonna be poisoned.' He points at a notice shrouded in clear plastic on the side of Toilet Block A: 'IMPORTANT WARNING DO NOT USE WATER DUE TO CONTAMINATION.'

'Well,' I bluster, 'we won't drink it. We'll buy bottled water from the shop.' Clearly, standards have slipped since Sam's last visit.

'What about showers?' Jake asks, narrowing his eyes.

'I'm sure it's fine to shower in.'

'But what if it's not? It might give us skin diseases.'

'Jake, for goodness' sake—' I'm stopped in my tracks by Lola and Travis lurching out of the car, firing questions.

'Is this where we're going to sleep? In that little house?'

'No, Lola, that's the toilet block.'

'Where's Sam?'

'He's coming later.'

'Are we're gonna be poisoned? I heard Jake saying—'

'No, of course we're not. D'you think I'd let that happen to you?' I march round the car, slamming the doors that everyone's left wide open. 'Come on, let's find out where we're supposed to pitch our tent.'

'In the rain?' Lola wails.

'It's not rain. It's drizzle. Let's try and cheer up, shall we? This is our *holiday*. It's going to be great.'

I smile manically, but no one smiles back.

★   ★   ★

My plan had been to pitch our tent and have dinner ready for Sam and Harvey's arrival. In a burst of enthusiasm I'd packed lamb cutlets, shallots and a bunch of rosemary into our coolbox. As seasoned campers, we wouldn't be huddling over tepid baked beans and slug-like sausages, *oh* no.

Under Travis and Lola's authoritative gaze, Jake and I lug the tent from the boot and dump it on our allotted expanse of sodden ground. Our pitch – I believe that's the correct camping term – is situated next to a super-tent, with several annexes, and Toilet Block B, which has the same warning about the water.

We haul the tent from its nylon casing. There seems to be a heck of a lot of it, with numerous bits of string attached. 'Where are the instructions?' I ask, delving into the bag.

'I bet there aren't any,' Jake announces, and I'm sure I detect a hint of smugness.

You'd assume that by now, in the twenty-first century, someone could have invented a self-erecting tent. One with a button you would press and the thing would ping up.

'We'll manage fine,' I bluster. 'I think you feed the poles through these channels.'

I now recall that I have never actually put the thing up. On our sole family camping trip, to the New Forest, Martin had taken charge of such matters. Jake and Lola had been deemed too little to help, and Travis had been nestling in the warm, tent-free environment of my womb. We'd returned from the children's play area to find proud father hammering in the last of the pegs.

Then Martin had contracted food poisoning. I'd cooked, so it was probably my fault. As we'd failed to bring loo roll – also my fault – he'd spent the night lurching to the toilet block with fistfuls of socks on which to wipe his rear.

'That pole doesn't go there,' Jake scolds me, snatching it from my grasp and sliding it swiftly into its correct channel.

Within minutes the basic structure has taken shape. Miraculously, Jake appears to have inherited his father's tent-erecting gene. All seems to be progressing nicely when a tremendous wind – strong enough to knock Travis off his feet, at which he screams in delight – sends the tent billowing skywards like gigantic out-of-control knickers.

'Shit!' I yell.

'Shit!' Travis cries excitedly, causing a tubby man erecting a silver tent to glower in our direction.

'Grab it and peg down that corner!' I cry desperately.

'You've got the hammer,' Jake protests.

'I gave it to you!'

'No you didn't—'

'Need some help?' An elderly man has emerged from the nylon stately home next door to watch our performance.

'No thanks,' I pant, gripping a flailing guy rope.

The man shakes his head and chuckles softly.

'It's hopeless, Mum,' Jake rages as I haul our temporary home to heel.

'I'm hungry,' Lola announces.

'So am I,' Jake mutters.

I glare at them. 'We can't start cooking until the tent's up. We have to *prioritise*.'

'What's "prioritise"?' Lola asks, seemingly unconcerned about our lack of accommodation.

I ignore her.

'What time is it?' she insists.

'Dinnertime,' Travis announces with a grin.

Perhaps the wind will die down. Then we'll knock up the tent in a jiffy and have as lovely a time as anyone who can afford to go to sodding Sardinia. I scan the site for a similar tent to ours, intending to prowl around and take notes on its construction. There aren't any. Perhaps ours was discontinued. It looks rather mottled and mildewed; maybe it contracted a disease in the loft.

The drizzle has subsided, and a hippyish young couple have emerged to play cards at a folding table. It doesn't seem windy around their tent. As far as I can make out, it isn't windy anywhere apart from at our pitch. It seems to have its own micro-climate. No wonder it was vacant.

A man in biker's leathers sips a beer outside a tiny igloo tent. A

smattering of middle-aged couples prepare dinner at their
stoves. The air fills with delicious aromas. God, everything
smells incredible. The children have begun to look pale and
hollow-cheeked, and I swear that Travis has lost weight. It's 6
p.m. Even if we manage to pitch the tent, I still have to connect
the camping stove to its rusting gas bottle and get creative with
lamb and rosemary. It should be marinating by now. Sam and
Harvey are due any minute. Our neighbour from the stately tent
is observing us from a fold-out chair. His wife, who looks about
eighty, is dragging an airbed from the back of their Volvo and
attaching it to some whizzy device, which inflates it instantly.
We, too, have airbeds, but no blow-upper gizmo like theirs. Just
a tiddly foot pump which I now recall drove Martin into an
apoplectic rage.

The woman drags the inflated bed across the battered grass.
'Beautiful evening,' she says.

'Yes, isn't it?' I muster a smile.

She proceeds to unload sleeping bags, a wicker hamper, a
camping stove, an extensive assortment of pots and pans, and a
small white dog – the rat-faced variety that are forever poking
their quivering noses around your groin – and, incredibly, a TV.
Travis's eyes light up when he sees it. It's so humiliating, sitting
here on the tent bag surrounded by bored, fidgety children, while
someone older than my mother creates a luxurious home-from-
home.

Slowly, with Jake's assistance, I make a half-arsed job of
pitching our tent. If not fully erect, it's at least in a state of
semi-arousal. While the kids pile into it, I lay out the airbeds and
pump with the foot thing until my knee starts making peculiar
clicking noises. I will *not* ask to borrow our neighbours' inflator
machine. I am Caitlin Brown, single mother of three, and am
perfectly capable of managing everything all by myself.

Despite twenty minutes' pumping, the first airbed lies flaccid
and useless. It brings to mind Martin's appendage when I'd gone
all-out in the foxy-lingerie department – black balconette bra,
coordinating knickers, stockings and suspenders, the whole

caboodle – in an attempt to perk up our sex life (not yet realising that he'd been directing his attentions elsewhere and that there wasn't enough arousal to go round).

I pump faster, my leg pistoning manically. The point at which we'll tuck into lamb infused with rosemary seems a long way off. I'm missing Bethnal Green, our scabby house, even the sea monkeys.

'When is dinner ready?' Lola asks, popping her head out of the tent.

'Soon,' I mutter. Marvellous, isn't it, how the youth of today expect meals to appear instantly when it's apparent that no food preparation has taken place?

'Hey, love!' our neighbour shouts from his chair. 'Can I give you a hand with that?'

'Think I'm nearly done,' I call with fake gaiety.

He gurgles with amusement and sips from his glass. He's drinking *wine*. Talk about rubbing salt into the wound. There's a popping noise and the pump's tube pings out of the foot bit. It won't fit back in. Perhaps it's been over-pumped and is suffering from nervous exhaustion, as I am. When I examine it closely, I discover a small rip in the rubber. What am I supposed to do now – blow the beds up with my mouth? Christ, I'll end up being stretchered off to hospital with collapsed lungs.

The elderly woman throws me a sympathetic look. She's putting up the cooking tent now. Their camping stove has its own tent. As does the yappy dog; they've brought a kind of nylon kennel.

I'm beginning to feel distinctly under-equipped. Tears well up and I blink them back angrily. I will *not* break down and start girlie-blubbing in front of all these seasoned campers. Then, just as I'm considering tearing down the tent, flinging our lamb to the yappy dog and driving back to London, my world brightens. Sam's car pulls into the site. He and Harvey tumble out and instantly the whole living-under-canvas experience seems bearable.

'Hey,' Sam says, 'your tent's up already! I'm impressed.'

'Easy,' I boast.

He studies the flaccid airbed. 'Hang on. I've got a pumper-upper thing in my car.'

'Oh, Sam,' I say, laughing. 'You say all the right things.'

'Here you are, dear,' the old lady says. 'We had plenty left over so we thought you and the children would like some.'

Normally, I'd take offence at a stranger trying to force her food on to us, but her stew smells wonderful and our camping stove hasn't yet made it out of its box.

'Thanks so much,' I say, taking the bowls gratefully.

We fill our faces, and the kids tear around the site, finally crawling into our tents, exhausted.

Which leaves us – Sam and me – and a bottle of chilled sauvignon that he'd had the forethought to pick up on the way.

'So,' I say, 'what did you get up to in Cornwall?'

Sam stretches out on his side on our tartan blanket. 'Oh, just the usual stuff,' he says quickly.

I sip my wine and try to read his expression. It's not like him to be evasive. 'Martin sent a postcard,' I venture, 'to tell us what a fabulous time he's having.'

Sam winces. 'That was kind of him.'

'To be honest, I'd rather be here than in Sardinia.' I mean it. The air is still now, the sky smattered with pinprick stars. I can't remember the last time I noticed stars. Maybe this is what those *Bambino* writers mean when they bang on about getting back to nature with your kids.

'I'm glad you came,' Sam murmurs. 'Thought it might not be your kind of thing . . .'

I snigger. 'Neither did I.'

He looks at me and there's a flicker of something. Like he's *really* looking at me, as if I'm different somehow and not just Cait who's handy to hang out with.

He sits up and rests an arm round my shoulders. My entire body tenses, and I shiver involuntarily.

'You're cold,' he murmurs. 'Better get tucked up in your tent.'

'Yes, you're probably right.' I gather myself up, even though I'm not remotely tired, even after all that tent-grappling.

As quietly as possible, I unzip our tent and wriggle in. I don't want to be packed off to bed by Sam. I want to sit up with him, talking, feeling the warmth of his arm round me after months of being starved of touch.

The realisation astounds me. I want Sam to touch me. I want *him*. Slithering into my clammy sleeping bag, I zip it up to my neck, as if that might shut out the feelings. I wriggle to get comfortable and my foot strikes something hard at the bottom of my sleeping bag. Travis's hook. I fish it out irritably and toss it aside.

Jake stirs, murmuring softly.

'Did I wake you?' I whisper.

Unintelligible response.

'Are you cold?'

'No, I'm fine.' From Jake, this counts as crazed enthusiasm.

He turns over and eventually the tent fills with his soft snores. Lola murmurs in her sleep, and Travis, sensing my presence, snuggles closer, gusting stew-breath into my face. There are bursts of distant laughter, and a faint breeze ripples the tent.

I wonder what Sam's doing now – if he's still sitting out there, and why he was so keen for me to go to bed. I lie patiently waiting for these wanting-Sam feelings to go away.

They don't.

I screw up my eyes tightly and try to think of other things, like Martin suffering multiple jellyfish stings in Sardinia, but it doesn't work.

Then I hear a tent being unzipped and soft footsteps on the grass. 'Cait?' comes the whisper.

Sam. Maybe he's been lying there too, his head filled with similar thoughts. Perhaps he's decided that being trapped between a dog-tent and Toilet Block B could be pretty romantic with the right person. My hands are clammy, and not just from being trapped in cheap nylon.

'What is it?' I whisper back.

'Come out here. I want to show you something.'

I peer at the kids – three blissed-out faces amidst a jumble of sleeping bags and blankets – and creep gingerly over them. There's a rasping noise as I unzip the tent. Lola flinches but doesn't wake. I crawl out, and Sam is standing there, waiting for me. He is ruffle-haired in a saggy sweater and ancient jeans, and looks utterly lovely.

'Is . . . something wrong?' I ask.

'Quite the opposite.' He smiles, indicating his own blanket that he's laid out on the damp ground.

Oh, my God.

'Come here, let's lie down. There's something I want you to see.'

I feel dizzy. But I do it anyway – lie a few inches from him so there's no touching, wondering what the hell to do next.

'Look up at the sky,' he says.

And I do. Now I get it. There are shooting stars. Tiny explosions streaking the inky sky.

It's incredible, as if they've been put there for us. We don't touch or even talk. We just stare up at the flashes of light.

I lie there on Sam's blanket, watching stars fizz and pop, mirroring the fizzing and popping in my heart.

14

Back in London, the feeling hovers above me like a cloud.

Shooting-stars night. Lying beside Sam on the damp blanket. The two of us watching the sky explode. I tell no one, aware that Millie would blow it up into a Big Thing and bully me mercilessly to 'make something happen'. Rachel, too, would badger me to 'take it further' – not that there's anything *to* take. Nothing happened. No hand-holding, no touching – certainly no kiss. We watched the stars. We glimpsed the old couple canoodling by their dog-tent. Then Sam and I said goodnight and went to bed in our separate tents. Which suggests that I'm deluding myself horribly, and that he does not – and never will – regard me as more than a friend.

It's affecting the way I behave around him and I panic that he's noticed. I fret about behaving unnaturally, which has the effect of making me behave *really* unnaturally – a simmering ball of self-consciousness, incapable of normal conversation. I feel as awkward as Jake must have done when he was forced to be one of the Three Wise Men in the school nativity and muttered, 'I bring you Frankenstein.'

I want to tell Sam how I feel and to hell with it – that something changed for me that night, that I felt alive again – but know he'd laugh in my face. Or be horrified and run off and vomit in the toilet. Or, by far the most humiliating option, give me a gentle talking-to along the lines of, 'Cait, you're a wonderful friend, and I'm really sorry to say this, but I don't feel that way about you. I'm sorry.' After which I would be forced to commit hara-kiri with our bread knife.

As a distraction technique, I work into the night on my page, answering letters personally, even though Millie warned me not to. I tried throwing them away, getting as far as dumping a few in the bin, but ended up retrieving them and giving them a quick rinse under the tap.

I pore over moist, partially smudged writing:

Dear Harriet,
Please help. My boyfriend and I split up last year. We have two small children and they have taken the break-up quite badly. Now my ex is hinting that we should get back together. At the time, he said we had grown apart and that although he loved me, he wasn't 'in love' with me any more. Now he says he made a mistake. He wants to come back. Should I give him a second chance?

I enjoy your page very much and was sorry to read that this week will be your last for some time. I hope your replacement offers equally sage advice. You're certainly a hard act to follow.
Confused, Kidderminster

I type:

Dear Confused,
You talk about your children and ex-partner and hardly mention yourself. How you feel about him. Whether *you* believe that you have a future with him.

I tail off. So what should she do? I gawp at the screen, scratchy-eyed and incapable of coming up with a suitable course of action. Of course she shouldn't let him come back. But what if she still loves him? Who am I to dictate what she does? I thought I'd settled into this, and have been rattling off answers – dozens of personal replies – without too much trouble. Now I'm stuck, my confidence shredded, my head full of ridiculous Sam-thoughts.

Tossing the letter aside, I choose a problem about interfering grandparents instead.

★   ★   ★

It arrives next day, Monday morning. The bulky A4 envelope looks so innocent, lying among a soul-sapping array of junk mail, bills and a pamphlet emblazoned with the disconcerting message: 'EEZEE-CLEAN CARPET-CLEANER. "I CAN'T BELIEVE HOW MUCH DIRT CAME OUT OF MY CARPET. THE WATER WAS BLACK!" – *Brenda, Welwyn Garden City.*'

I pick up the brown envelope and clutch it to my chest. I should be cajoling the kids to get ready for school, but I need to see this, to have the horror over and done with. Ripping it open, I yank out the magazine and flick to my page.

As predicted, the photo is terrible. It's also bloody *huge*. For reasons known only to themselves, either Millie or some smart-arse on the art desk has seen fit to give it maximum space. Pike, in her crisp white shirt, had occupied something like three square centimetres. My picture is four times the size, with a pink border round it which screams, 'Look! Check out this twerp! Who does she think she is?' Even worse, it looks like I'm pouting, as if I reckon I'm a proper model in an advert for Lancôme or Max Factor. I could sob. There's not a pouting gene in my body. I'd been trying to make comforting noises and reassure Travis that this wasn't some unconvincing trannie but *me* – the very woman who'd nurtured him in her womb and sported a 36H Bonne Maman nursing bra with pre-moulded zip cups.

Hurrying down to the kitchen, I frantically consider my options. Damage limitation would involve resigning from the problem page. I am also tempted to undergo drastic face-changing surgery so no one recognises me. Aren't face trans-plants available these days? One of those would do.

'Are we late?' Lola skips into the kitchen still wearing her Pluto nightie.

'God, yes, we'd better get a move on.' I snap out of my trauma and yell upstairs to Jake and Travis, wondering if it would look terribly weird if I wore a balaclava on a warm late-April morning.

Jake appears fully dressed apart from his shoes. 'You don't care,' he growls.

I glare at him. Has he somehow managed to see the magazine

and has realised he'll be teased mercilessly about his man-mother? No, not possible.

'Where are your shoes?' I ask him.

'You don't *care*,' he repeats.

Ah. So the perked-up Jake, who'd been so helpful on our camping trip, has reverted to the Jake who blames me for all that's wrong in his life. Even though his father is the one having fabulous rumpy while I haven't glimpsed a naked man since the Edwardian era.

'What is it,' I say levelly, 'that I don't I care about?'

Travis appears beside him and peers round his brother's legs.

'My verrucas,' Jake announces.

I almost laugh. 'I thought they'd all gone.'

'Well, they haven't.'

'Why didn't you tell me? I don't have time to go round checking everyone's feet, Jake. There are six feet in this house—'

'There are eight,' Lola states smugly. 'When Daddy was here, there were ten.'

'Yes, thank you, Lola . . .'

'Other mums check feet,' Jake adds. 'Other mums *care*.'

'Oh, really? Whose mum has time to perform daily foot checks?' My voice is shrill and ugly.

'Everybody's!' Jake rages.

'Right, like everybody goes to Disneyland Paris at Easter. If your verrucas have come back, just tell me and we'll put the runny stuff on again.'

'I *am* telling you. I'm telling you *now*.'

'How many do you have?' I try to keep my voice even. Calm, unflappable mother.

'About forty-five,' he retorts.

'Forty-five? Jesus! Are you kidding? Take off your socks!'

'I'll show you later,' he says mildly, meaning, *If you haven't cared about the pain and discomfort I've endured these past weeks, a few more hours aren't going to make any difference.*

I bob down and reach for his sock. 'No!' he roars, jerking his foot from my grasp.

'Don't be silly! It won't take a minute—'

'What's a verruca?' Lola enquires.

'It's a little warty thing with a kind of root.'

'A root?' she exclaims. 'What, like a tree? Ugh!'

'Jake,' I snap, 'keep your foot *still*. I need to see them.'

With the foot trapped under one arm, I tear off the sock, but he kicks out furiously, propelling himself backwards and smacking the back of his head on the doorframe.

'Oh, my God! Are you OK?' I scoop him up and hold in my arms, raking through his hair to check for some terrible gaping chasm. There isn't one – there's no blood at all, although a spectacular lump is already beginning to form. He sobs into my chest. Tears pour down my own cheeks.

'You hurt me,' he gulps. 'You hurt my head.'

'Darling, I'm so sorry.' His face feels sticky and hot.

'Will he have to go to hospital?' Lola asks brightly.

'Ambulance!' Travis announces, banging his milk cup on the table.

'No, I don't think we need hospital. Jake, how do you feel, sweetheart?'

'All right.' He's just like the old Jake – *my* Jake – allowing himself to be cuddled and held. I can feel the urgent thudding of his heart. 'Can you see OK?' I murmur. 'Does everything look blurry?'

He nods. Does this mean he *can* see normally, or that his vision's impaired?

'I was only trying to get your sock off, and the way you kicked . . .' I try to hug him again, but his body has stiffened and he's edged away from me. It's like trying to cuddle a freezer. 'D'you have a headache?' I rant on. 'D'you feel sick or anything?'

'I'm OK!' Pushing me away, he staggers up and lands heavily on a chair.

'Jake has forty-five verrucas with roots,' Lola sing-songs.

'*I* wanna burooka!' storms Travis, flinging down his cup.

I stand there, stranded in my own kitchen, not knowing what to do next. There are three children present, with one adult, and that adult is me. It is the adult's job to make decisions, to know what to do at all times. It's what we're *for*. I am not a bona fide adult. I can't even inflate a fucking airbed.

If I make Jake go to school – which starts in precisely four minutes – he might pass out and choke on his own vomit in the loos. If I keep him at home – and I'll still have to drag him out while I take Lola to school – he'll spend all day radiating hatred.

Jake whispers something that sounds like, 'I want Dad.'

I swallow hard. 'Do *you* think you're OK to go to school?' Nice one. Pass the buck.

'Yeah,' he grumbles.

'Come on, then. Let's get coats brushed and teeth on.'

That always lightens the mood in our house. Today, nobody laughs.

We hurtle towards school with me dragging Travis like a pull-along toy. Hell, I'm no better than a child-beater. The least I can do is get my kids to school on time.

'I'll get a late mark,' Jake gloats, adding silently, *And it'll be all your fault.*

We arrive, panting, at the gates, which I march through with Jake protesting loudly behind me. 'What are you doing? You can't go into school! Parents aren't allowed!'

'Yes I can, Jake. I want to talk to Miss Race so she can give you one of those "I bumped my head today" stickers. Then all the staff will know to keep an eye on you.'

'A sticker?' Jake rounds on me. 'I'm ten! I don't want stickers. Stickers are for little kids!'

Ignoring him, I push open the main door with the kids skirmishing behind me.

'Oh, hello, Jake.' Miss Race has emerged from the office. She favours clothes in the olive-green/mustard spectrum. (Since my encounter with Carmen, I've started thinking in spectrums.) I suspect that she's had a session with a sadistic colour consultant.

'Um, Jake bumped his head this morning,' I explain. 'I wondered if you could make sure he's OK.'

Jake pulls in his shoulders and glares at his feet, as if trying to shrink into himself.

'Oh, poor you,' Miss Race gushes. 'Gosh, yes, I can see a nasty lump. What happened?'

'He, um, fell against the door,' I babble, aware of the guilt creeping all over my face.

'He didn't!' Travis shouts. 'Mummy pushed him.'

Miss Race squints at me. 'Oh, dear.'

'It was an accident,' I say with a stupid wittery laugh.

'Hmmm.' Her lips crinkle. 'Well, you will tell me if you feel strange or ill, won't you, Jake?'

He nods, and his look says, *My own mother tried to maim me.*

Miss Race's look says, *We know about people like you, and notes will be kept on file.*

Faking jollity, I kiss Lola and Jake goodbye – he virtually retches – and lead Travis outside to the deserted playground. 'Come on,' I announce, 'let's do something fun to cheer ourselves up.'

'What?' he enthuses with a little skip.

'Let's go shopping for verruca lotion.'

15

Clutching Travis's hand, I step into the chemist's, grateful for its soothing aromas after our challenging start to the day.

A woman with violently highlighted hair swings round from the homeopathic remedies display. 'Caitlin Brown!' shrieks Bev. 'I've just seen it – that hilarious picture of you in *Bambino*. Aren't you the dark horse?'

My face clenches as she flutters towards me. She is joined by Marcia, who hurries over from the toothbrushes, and Charlene, another PTA mother, who's gripping a prescription in a paper bag.

'It's just, er, a temporary thing,' I bluster, 'to fill in while the real agony aunt's off sick.'

'You look *different* in your photo, don't you?' Marcia crows.

'Very glam,' fibs Charlene, baring her teeth.

'Um, thanks.' I try for a grin, but my face freezes. It feels like rigor mortis is setting in.

Travis is twizzling round all the bubble baths so they're facing the wrong way. Christ, I know *Bambino* is popular – market leader and all that – but I hadn't realised I'd be outed within minutes of it going on sale.

'Did you have to do special training?' Marcia arches an eyebrow.

'No, not really . . .'

'So just anyone off the street can start giving advice? Just like that?' She laughs witheringly.

'Yes, I suppose they can.' My mouth twitches as I tug Travis away from the singing toothbrushes. There's a scrambled chorus as they burst into song:

Sing, sing, sing with me,
Sing a little song.
Brush, brush, brush your teeth today
And then you can't go wrong!

'There I was,' Charlene continues, 'expecting that sensible woman, Harriet-Whatserface with the neat hair. But, no, it was you, our very own Caitlin—'

I have become Our Very Own Caitlin, like some end-of-pier variety act.

'Dishing out advice like a proper expert!' Bev cuts in. She throws back her head and guffaws, startling an elderly customer who's hovering by the massage oils.

'It's no different to any writing job, really,' I say firmly.

'Except you're influencing people's lives,' Bev says dramatically.

Marcia frowns. 'Hope you don't mind me saying, Caitlin, but it's not what I'd have said. You know, that letter from the woman whose husband falls asleep on the sofa—'

'Yeah,' Charlene interrupts, 'I thought you were too hard. On the man, I mean. He's been working all day, hasn't he, and he comes home to a trashed house—'

'Does she expect him to come home from a hard day at the office and be Mr Entertainment?' twitters Marcia.

'I wrote what I felt was right,' I mutter. 'And it's the woman who wrote in, remember. She's the one who's asking for advice.'

'Yes, but shouldn't you give a balanced view?' Marcia's eyes glint mischievously.

To my relief, Rachel saunters into the shop. She might shame me with her impeccable mothering skills, but at least she's on my side.

'Saw your first page!' she announces, grinning. 'It's fantastic, Cait. Isn't she good? Doesn't she sound sympathetic, like someone you'd want to confide in?' She glances round at the assembled group.

'Um, yeah,' Marcia says. 'Actually, Caitlin, I have a problem myself . . .'

So have I. How to extract myself and get the hell out.

'I wanna toothbrush!' Travis sings.

'You don't need one . . .'

'I do,' he insists. 'It's chewed up.'

Marcia's smile has set. 'Could I write to you about Genevieve?' she asks.

'You can write about anything you want,' I say sweetly.

'It's school stuff. She's not being stretched. Would you answer a letter about what to do with a gifted child? How to encourage her to achieve her full potential?'

'Oh, d'you think she is?' Bev trills. 'Have you had her assessed by a psychiatrist?'

'Psychologist,' Marcia corrects her, and the ensuing psychiatrist-psychologist debate allows me to detach myself and barge towards the counter.

In defiance of Harriet Pike, I buy Travis the singing toothbrush he's been clutching. ('By giving into nagging, you're fuelling a child's greed!') It's only when we've stepped outside, leaving the others chuckling merrily by the thrush remedies, that I realise I have forgotten the one thing I went in for.

Travis and I pick up Jake's verruca lotion from another chemist's in Bethnal Green Road.

The laugh activates somewhere deep in Sam's belly, bubbling up until he's swiping tears from his eyes. He had invited us back to his house after I picked up Jake and Lola from school.

'God, Cait,' he manages, 'you're right. Should I start calling you Brian?'

I am mortified, and momentarily speechless.

'Sorry,' he adds, his voice wobbling with mirth, 'but it's just so, so . . . overdone. You're so natural and pretty and don't need all this, this . . . stuff on your face.'

'All right,' I snap.

He edges closer on his beaten-up sofa and touches my arm. 'Haven't upset you, have I?'

Stuff shooting-stars night. I am a laughing stock.

'Of course not,' I say quickly. 'I'm just feeling a bit sensitive about it, that's all.'

He glances at the magazine that lies open on his coffee table. 'Maybe they could've gone a bit easier on the lipstick . . .'

'Uh-huh.'

'And the black stuff around your eyes . . .' Sam's shoulders start quivering again.

It's OK for him, with his thriving graphic-design business that he manages to keep rattling along without it interfering with his being a dad. *He* doesn't have to snatch at crumbs of commissions that happen to flutter his way. Harvey is a cheerful, well-balanced kid who has never, as far as I'm aware, wielded a can of Mr Sheen. Sam and Amelia, his ex, are on friendly terms. (They still send each other birthday presents, for crying out loud.) To think, as we'd watched the stars, I'd dared to hope that he might feel something for me.

'I thought it'd be a step up from the tongue-scraper stuff,' I mutter. 'Remember what happened last parents' evening? When I went into Lola's class to see her work and there, on the wall, was a picture of me at the computer. And underneath it she'd written—'

' "My mummy writes about bum creams," ' Sam splutters.

'So I thought this job,' I say hotly, 'would be better than that.'

Sam eyes my photo. 'Well, you might find yourself attracting a cult following.'

I grab the magazine, roll it up and stuff it into my bag. There's only one thing for it. I'll have to resign. My brief career as an agony aunt is over before it has properly begun. Sam is still honking away like a hysterical child and trying to snatch the magazine from my bag.

'Just forget it,' I bark at him.

'Hey, I was only—'

'Yeah,' I growl. 'Well.' Now I've turned into a petulant seven-year-old. Fantastic. Nothing like showing yourself in your best light.

He gets up, shrugs and wanders away to the kitchen, leaving

me fizzing with fury and humiliation. I hate him. I hate all men. My future life will be one of celibacy. When the children leave home, I'll live in a manky pee-smelling attic with mangy cats.

I don't even *like* cats.

On Wednesday Millie calls to check that I received my copy of *Bambino* with my mush in it.

'Yes, thanks,' I say tersely.

'Not annoyed, are you?'

'No, it's just that the gender-realignment drugs are making me feel a bit weird today.'

She snorts into the phone. 'Oh, hon, your page is fantastic. We've had a great response here, and there's a pile of mail for you already.'

Mail addressed not to Pike, but to me. My responsibility. People expecting answers from *me*. Shit.

'Millie,' I say hesitantly, 'I'm sorry, but I don't know if I can pull this off.'

'What are you talking about? You're loads better than Harriet. Far more sensible and empathetic. Anyway, what else would you do now that arse-cream site's gone bust?'

'I could, er . . . write distinguished articles for esteemed publications.'

'Fuck off.' She cackles.

'Honestly, Millie, I'm not sure it's really . . . me.'

'Of course it's not you,' she insists. 'The photo's awful. That idiot make-up artist totally wrecked you, and Adrian let it happen. I can't believe it. Couldn't you have said something, got her to scrape it off and make it more natural?'

'I . . . I thought that's how it went. That I needed to be caked in make-up because of the lights or something.'

'No, darling,' she says with exaggerated patience. 'I want you to look like *you*. You're supposed to look approachable so people will feel happy confiding in you.'

'Right.'

'Anyway,' she continues, 'we've decided it'd be better to have your kids in the photo. Give you more authority. More kudos – you know.'

'But it says on the page that I have three kids.'

'That's not the same as seeing them,' she insists.

'Millie, I'm not sure they'll cooperate. Travis can't sit still for more than a minute, and Jake . . .' I picture him scowling into the lens – if he even agreed to come to the studio in the first place.

'Come on, they're so cute and they'll love the attention. Can we re-shoot next week? There's not much time on this.'

'Jake and Lola are at school,' I remind her, 'so it'd have to be late afternoon or at the weekend.'

'Couldn't they have a day off?'

'To have their photo taken?' I bluster. 'Of course not.'

Millie sighs. 'It'll be *educational*. They'll learn about, um, the photographic process. Lighting and composition and all that. They'll be the talk of the school!'

Sure, that'd go down a treat with Miss Race. Having first assaulted her elder son, mother then interrupts her offspring's education with the sole purpose of furthering her poxy career. Millie doesn't seem to understand that kids of Jake's age don't *want* to be the talk of the school.

'Sorry, but they're not taking time off,' I insist. 'I'll ask them, and if they'll agree to do it, maybe we could arrange something for a Sunday.'

'No good. Photographers charge double time on Sundays.'

Fantastic. *Bambino* can afford to send the fashion team to Kenya and hire elephants as 'props', yet Millie baulks at slinging her photographer a few extra quid.

'Saturday's a bit cheaper,' she adds.

'This Saturday is Mum's birthday . . .'

'But she's in an old folks' home,' Millie reminds me.

'They do let them out occasionally, you know. I've promised to have her round for a special birthday lunch.'

Millie pauses. 'Will she . . . *know* it's her birthday? I mean, she's got dementia, hasn't she? Doesn't she think the Blitz is still happening?'

'Sometimes, yes, but—'

'So you could pretend that the *following* Saturday's her birthday . . .'

'I can't lie to Mum about that! I'm not rescheduling her birthday, Millie. Not for a photo shoot.'

'Why not?' she asks calmly.

'Because . . . on her proper birthday she'll get cards from the carers and they'll have a sing-song and a cake.'

I can virtually hear Millie's brain whirring, like the tiny motor inside Travis's toy train.

'They could postpone the sing-song and cake,' she suggests.

Great! Let's add 'forces care staff to reschedule confused elderly mother's birthday' to my fast-growing list of misdemeanours. 'No, Millie. We'll have to do it some other day.'

'Please. We've got to sort this as soon as possible. I want to stop using your trannie picture as soon as we can.'

'So do I,' I say witheringly.

'OK, I know what we'll do. Let's say Saturday afternoon at your place. Your mum can sit in the corner and watch. It's just a quick shot – ten minutes max. It'll be more interesting for her than all that singing and crochet they do.'

'All right,' I mutter.

'It'll be *fine*, Cait.' Millie's voice softens. 'A little old lady sitting in the corner will hardly get in the way.'

Martin shows up when we're home from school. It's not an official Daddy Visit, but he's been doing this lately – squeezing in extra get-togethers during the week. Since his trip to Sardinia, in fact, but who am I to suggest that they're guilt-induced?

This time, the devoted angel has even left work early in order to be with them. He has booked tickets for a six o'clock film, which will make Travis horribly late for bed. He has also brought presents. This is a new one, dispensing small gifts each time he sees them, and not something I approve of at all.

'Thanks, Dad!' Grinning, Jake holds up the Tin Tin T-shirt to his chest.

Lola snatches the mirrored brush, sweeping it through her hair theatrically.

'A blowy-up ball!' Travis cries.

'Well,' Martin says, glowing now, 'I heard Mummy burst your other one in the garden.'

'Yeah, on purpose.'

I start to protest, then clamp my trap shut. The children are pleased to see him and I musn't spoil it. *Good parent* bestows presents. *Bad parent* neglects son's verrucas, causes head injury and allows lamb cutlets to go rancid on camping trip. Wasteful Mummy!

It still feels odd watching Martin pottering about in our house with the kids hopping excitedly around him (even Jake – *especially* Jake). It's almost as if Water-Cooler Slapper, and the subsequent disintegration of our family, never happened.

'Dad,' Jake announces, 'I hurt my head on Monday. They made me wear a stupid sticker at school.'

Oh, no. Verruca-gate. I'd hoped that this wouldn't come up.

'Did you?' Martin says. 'What happened?'

'Mum was fighting with me and hit my head on the door—'

'Jake!' I protest. 'It wasn't like that.'

Martin flings me a filthy look, then delves through Jake's hair. 'This is an awful, serious-looking bump,' he murmurs. 'Did it bleed?'

'Yeah,' growls Traitor.

'No it didn't!' I cry.

'Even so,' Martin soothes, 'I can see it must have been terribly painful. I hope you had Monday off school.'

'No. Mum made me go for the whole day.'

Martin glares at me.

'I . . . I was trying to check his verrucas,' I protest, 'and Jake wouldn't let me take his sock off—'

'Verrucas?' Martin repeats. 'Haven't they gone yet?'

Apparently fucking not.

'We're treating them,' I snap.

Lola stops brushing and observes me with wide, fearful eyes.

'Has he been to the doctor?' Martin asks.

Anger sizzles in my stomach. 'Have you taken him to the doctor lately?' I want to yell. 'Or the dentist? Have you been to a school parents' meeting or tried to erect a tent in a fucking force-nine gale?'

'I don't think he needs the doctor,' I reply in a strangled voice.

'Well,' Martin guffaws, 'with the verrucas and lump on your head, you're not exactly in the best of health, eh, Jake!'

Jake smiles ruefully. To stop myself from losing it completely, I grab the tub of sea-monkey food and scatter some into the tank. Too much, probably. Overfeeding is the commonest cause of sea-monkey deaths.

'Are you staying for tea, Daddy?' Lola asks in a timid voice.

'Um, if it's OK with Mummy I'll just have a quick coffee, then we'll get off to see this film.'

'There's some in the pot,' I murmur. Which will be lukewarm by now, and muddy at the bottom. Good.

Martin pours himself a mugful. 'I saw you on that problem page,' he ventures.

I frown at him. 'Wouldn't have thought *Bambino* was your sort of magazine.'

'Daisy buys it sometimes. I think it's quite good actually. Plenty of ideas for interesting stuff to do with the kids.' Immaculate kids frolicking in designer frocks? Yes, I can see it would be right up her street.

'They're re-shooting that photo of me,' I add.

'That's good.' Martin manages a smile and I grimace back.

'They want the kids in it this time.'

'Do they? Why?'

'To prove that I know what I'm talking about.' I laugh hollowly.

Martin frowns. 'And you think that's . . . OK, do you?'

'I don't see why not.'

'Can I be in the photo?' Lola asks, tossing her freshly brushed hair.

'Of course you can, sweetheart. Um . . . d'you have a problem with this, Martin?'

He shrugs. 'I just think it's something we should . . . be careful about. Parading them like that . . .'

'I'm not *parading* them! It'll be just like, like . . . a holiday snap.'

Martin sniggers. 'It's a bit different from holiday snaps, Cait. It's a national magazine. But I suppose it's your decision.'

On your head be it, is what he means, *when they're screwed up and in therapy, you child-beater, you.*

To avoid further conversation, I start cracking eggs for the kids' supper.

Jake peers into the glass bowl. 'What are we having?'

'Omelette.'

'I don't like them. I can't eat eggs.'

'Neither can I,' Lola announces, frowning. 'I'm allergic.'

'Lola, you're not! You *love* eggs. What about pancakes? They have eggs in—'

'But they're not eggy,' Jake cuts in.

'Tell you what,' Martin says, 'why don't I take them to Pizza Express seeing as you don't have much in? There's still time before the film.'

'Yeah!' Lola yelps. 'Can Mummy come too?'

'Um, d'you want to come, Cait?' Martin's face softens and something snags in my throat. I can't go through with this. Can't sit at our usual round table by the window. It had seemed ordinary then, with Jake always choosing the pizza with the egg on top (see, he *does* like eggs) and Lola asking yet again why Venice is in peril. Travis and I would share the salami one; he'd peel off the oily discs, sliding them into his mouth like coins. I can almost smell oregano and Peroni beer.

'No thanks,' I say brightly. 'It'll be good for the kids to have some time with you on their own.' *Without Slapper and Pink Princess* is what I mean.

'Sure?'

'I've got some work to get on with anyway.' I muster a broad smile.

They all head out together, babbling over each other and barely remembering to say goodbye, except Lola who grins bravely. 'I'll bring you some pizza back if they'll let me,' she says.

'Thanks, sweetie, but don't worry about me. It'll have gone cold. You tuck in and finish it all up.'

She nods. Jake is already musing that a cartoon movie that's suitable for Travis will be too babyish for him.

'Hey.' Martin turns and meets my gaze. 'Look, I don't want you to think I'm blaming you for Jake's bump . . .'

'It's OK,' I murmur from the doorway. 'I suppose it was my fault, in a roundabout way.'

They pile into the car, and Martin plugs in everyone's seat belts, even though Jake can do it by himself. He's about to climb into the driver's side when he stops again and looks at me. 'I'm sorry, Cait,' he adds.

Sorry for what? For implying that I'm an unfit mother, or for screwing up our lives? I fake a smile, but only because Lola is staring out at me. 'Nothing to be sorry for,' I say lightly.

He shrugs and gets into the car. As they drive away, I remind myself that they're as much Martin's children as mine, and that they love him desperately. I must try to be mature enough to remember that.

But he's still a self-satisfied bastard with a fondness for snug-fitting pants.

16

In the day room with the other inmates, Mum looks normal-sized. Here in the passenger seat of my car, she has assumed the dimensions of a tiny, startled bird.

'I don't know where you're taking me,' she mutters. 'I was having a nice time with them old people eating cake and in you come and spoil it.'

'You're coming to our house for lunch, Mum,' I say brusquely. 'I thought you'd like to spend some time with the kids on your birthday.'

Her milky eyes bore into me. 'What kids?'

'Your grandchildren: Jake, Lola and Travis. Look how excited they are to see you.' I glance into the rear-view mirror. Three doleful faces gawp from the back seat.

'Will that doctor be there?' Mum asks.

'No, Mum, there's no doctor. There will be a photographer, though – he's called Adrian and he's a really nice man. He's coming after lunch to take our photo for a magazine. I told you about him, remember?'

'Don't want no photo taken.' She fluffs up the back of her perm. 'My hair's never been right since they did it.'

I breathe slowly and deeply. *Breathe. Breathe.* 'It's just me and the children who are having our picture done, Mum. You can sit and watch. It shouldn't take long. It'll be *fun.*'

Mum nods, digesting this, as I park outside our house. Taking her arm, I ease her out of the car. Mum seems to be having a frail day. Not a clambering-over-railings-to-play-poker day.

'Where are we going?' she barks as I guide her downstairs.

'To the kitchen, Mum, for lunch. It's OK. I'm here to look after you.'

She blinks at me as if my being here is quite the opposite of reassuring. Lately, I've become nervous about taking Mum out of the home. There are no capable nurses, no Helenas with their pastel-blue tunics and soothing words. So many things could go wrong, and I'd be fully responsible. She could fall, or fly into an unprovoked rage. (Only this morning she tried to whack another inmate with a teaspoon at breakfast.) And what if she needs help on the toilet? It doesn't bear thinking about. I have never seen Mum naked and now doesn't feel like the right time to come over all free and relaxed with each other.

Lunch is tortuous. I have cooked the plainest, most World War Two-esque food I could think of – stew and dumplings – but it's not going down well.

'What *is* this?' Jake asks.

'It's steak.'

'What kind of animal is steak?'

'Cow.' *Very expensive cow*, I want to add.

'It doesn't look like cow,' Lola chirps. Mum glares down at her plate as if surmising that Lola is right and I'm probably trying to poison them all with braised roadkill.

'That's because it's stew,' I explain. 'It's cooked in a kind of gravy.'

'What makes it thick?' Jake enquires.

'Cornflour. You make a little paste with—Just *eat* it, would you?'

Mum's eyebrows shoot up. Christ, when will we emerge from this stage in which every ingredient and cooking method must be explained in brain-juddering detail? Every time we sit down to eat it's like a bloody cookery exam.

'Why are there cakes in the gravy?' Lola asks.

'They're not cakes. They're dumplings.' My patience is stretched taut and could twang at any moment.

'I don't like them,' she says.

'That's because you haven't tried them. Look, they're lovely!'

Fixing her with a challenging stare, I fork in a whole dumpling, which plugs my entire mouth. It has the texture of teddy-bear stuffing. Mum has pushed hers aside and dumped her cutlery on the table. What was I thinking, bringing her here? She didn't want to come. She has barely eaten a thing; doesn't she like my cooking, or does she need feeding these days? Should I have cut up her meat into smaller pieces? I could never do Helena's job. That woman is a saint.

With difficulty, I manage to gulp down the dumpling. I can feel it shifting lumpenly to my stomach.

'Well,' Mum announces, 'I'd better be getting the bus.' She shoves back her chair with a scrape.

'Mum, there's no bus. I'll drive you home when the photographer's finished. Are you sure you can't manage any stew . . .?'

She flings me a beseeching look. 'I want to go home. Don't want no photos.' She struggles up from her chair and totters across the kitchen with the kids gawping after her.

'Bye!' Travis calls out, waving his spoon.

'What's wrong with Granny?' Lola cries.

I fly after Mum, putting an arm round her shoulders, but she brushes me off angrily.

'What have you done with my hat?' she asks.

'You didn't have a hat, Mum.'

'Someone's taken my gloves!' Her eyes are startled, and her bony hands are trembling. She's scared of me – her own daughter. If only Golden Boy Adam were here, Adam the computer whiz, whose farts receive rapturous applause. He'd never force dumplings on anyone.

The bang on the front door makes all of us jump. Shit, it must be Adrian. Lunch has been such a trial I've lost track of time. Guiding Mum upstairs to the front door by the hand, I open it and find Adrian laden with tripod and numerous silver cases. So much for a quick shoot.

'Hi, Adrian, this is my mum.'

'Oh!' Mum brightens. 'It's your fella.'

'Nice to meet you, Mrs, um . . .' He tails off distractedly.

'Jeannie. Jeannie Brown.' Mum flashes her teeth at him and straightens the collar of her brown cardigan. The bus has, apparently, been forgotten.

We shuffle through to the living room. The kids have raced up from the kitchen and are at our heels.

'I thought this room would be best,' I explain, 'being bright and airy and spacious.'

'Hmmm.' Adrian scans it. Through his eyes I take in the light-sapping pistachio paint that Martin chose, the fading armchairs, the assortment of stuff the kids have made – birthday cards, collages, clay owls, jam jars painted with wobbly strokes – which teeter on the mantelpiece. I am incapable of throwing anything away that they have produced. At some point our collection will reach critical mass and burst into the street in an explosion of glass fragments and owl beaks.

'It'll do, I suppose,' Adrian says briskly. He rolls his eyes at Mum. 'Last shoot didn't really work out, Mrs, um, Jeannie. Wasn't the look they wanted.' His tone suggests that this was my fault. That I'd insisted on eight layers of lipstick and winged iridescent eyeshadow.

'Oh,' Mum says, clearly baffled.

'Maybe you could get ready, Caitlin,' he adds, 'while I set up the lights.'

'I *am* ready.' I grin at him in readiness. Fuelled by my *irresistible* dumplings, which now lie in my stomach like bricks, I have never felt more ready in my damn life.

He frowns, and his eyes skim my carefully chosen floral-print dress and cardie, a look I'd hoped suggested kindness and empathy. Surely I couldn't possibly look scary in a floral dress. 'Oh,' he says blankly. 'So we're going for a casual look.'

Casual? Even with that dratted stew bubbling away on the hob, I'd managed to blow-dry my hair, polish my shoes and apply light make-up. Maybe he prefers the Carmen school of cosmetics? A little back-combing, perhaps? Violent blusher stripes?

'I can change if you like,' I tell him, but Adrian has lost interest and is hunting around at skirting-board level for sockets.

'Don't want my photo taken.' Jake thrusts his hands into his jeans pockets.

'Oh, come on,' I insist. 'It's no big deal.'

'Yeah, it is. It's for a stupid ladies' magazine.'

'It's not just any old ladies' magazine. It's for parents, all about bringing up your children properly.'

'Ha!' he says bitterly, briefly touching the bump on his head. 'Well, I won't be in it. I'm going upstairs.'

'No, Jake,' I hiss.

'Yes, Mum.'

I stare at him, trying to simultaneously plead and instil fear into his heart. After all the goddamn things I have done for him, the interminable years I've spent helping him to construct Meccano. (I am tragically inept at construction.) All the dirty pants I've washed and trainers I've scrubbed and he won't do this one piddling thing to help me out.

'Please, Jake,' I say weakly.

'No.'

'Horrible meanie!' Lola elbows him in the chest. 'We've got to help Mummy.'

'Ow! Don't touch me, pig!'

His roar shocks all of us and causes Mum to jolt in her chair in the corner. She'll probably have a heart attack and it'll be all my fault. Travis waves his Captain Hook's hook excitedly. Lola's bottom lip trembles, and her eyes wobble with tears.

'Hey, kids,' Adrian announces like some jolly uncle, 'I'm sure if you cooperate, Mummy will treat you to some enormous, wonderful thing when we're done. Won't you, Mummy?'

I'm not your mummy, I want to sneer. 'Yes, um . . . of course I will.' I smile savagely.

'What?' Lola asks. 'What will we get?'

'Can I have a GameBoy Advance?' Jake enquires.

Jesus Christ.

'Or an Xbox? Everybody's got an Xbox. Jamie Torrance has an Xbox *and* a PlayStation 3.' He folds his arms triumphantly.

Adrian is grinning at me. The 'you-poor-fucker' smirk of the child-free.

'You can choose a book,' I mutter.

'A book?' Jake carps. 'That's not an enormous, wonderful thing.'

I could happily stamp on his foot, verrucas or no verrucas.

Mum is gazing adoringly at Adrian with her head tipped to one side. 'Glad to see you're back,' she announces. 'That woman hasn't been the same since you went off with that other girl. Doesn't know if she's coming or going. Look at the state of these poor kids.'

I chuckle inanely, wondering if it's possible to dissolve through mortification.

'They look fine to me, Jeannie.' Adrian positions us on the sofa, as if we're incapable of independent movement. Incredibly, and probably visualising Xboxes, Jake allows his legs to be crossed neatly at the ankles.

'You've got to work at a marriage,' Mum rattles on. 'Young people today expect everything on a plate.'

'I'm sure you're right,' Adrian murmurs, a small tic appearing beneath his left eye.

'Are you married?' she snaps.

He blinks at her. One minute he's being welcomed back into our family fold, the next he's being quizzed on his marital status. I forget that not everyone is accustomed to Mum's tangled thoughts. 'Um, well, I live with—'

'What's her name?' Mum demands.

Adrian smiles stoically. 'Um, Lewis.'

Mum's forehead crinkles.

'That's a man's name,' Lola retorts.

'Yes, it is,' I say, hoping, as Adrian starts shooting, that my grin doesn't make me look unhinged.

'It's the least you could do,' Mum snaps at him.

'What's that, Jeannie?' Adrian asks.

'Make an honest woman out of her.'

Adrian smirks, casting me a look over his camera. Jake sits stiffly by my side. I wonder if the cloud of simmering resentment around him will show up in the pictures, like a Ready Brek glow. While Lola is a model of obedience, Travis – who's plonked on my lap – refuses to take off his hook.

'That hook thing makes him look a bit, um . . . deformed,' Adrian mumbles.

No one has the will to prise it off him. He could sport a fake wooden leg for all I care.

It's over. Adrian is packing up, slamming precious equipment into cases and displaying a distinct eagerness to escape.

'I want to go home,' Mum shouts the instant he's gone. 'Where's my bus?'

To my relief, by bedtime Lola at least seems to have forgotten about the enormous wonderful thing. She snuggles close to me in her bed, smelling sweetly of bubblegum foam from her bath.

I start to read her story. There's a small shuffling noise behind her half-open door. 'Jake?' I call softly. 'Is that you?'

He ambles into view in rumpled checked pyjamas and stands awkwardly in the doorway.

'Are you OK?' I ask gently.

He nods.

'Want to sit with us? We're reading *The Water Babies*. D'you remember that from when you were little?'

I feel silly for asking. Ten-year-olds aren't interested in *The Water Babies*.

'Yeah.' He smiles. 'I remember it.'

I'm surprised, and pathetically grateful, when he ambles over and joins us on the bed.

'Move up,' I urge Lola. 'Make room for your brother.'

Begrudgingly, she shuffles along about a tenth of an inch. Jake squeezes in beside me and I start to read. We've reached the part where Tom falls in the river, but it isn't really Tom – just the shell he's left behind as he enters the Water Babies' world.

'Mum,' Lola cuts in, 'did Tom die?'

'Yes, but he was unhappy and now he'll have a better life.'

'How can he have a better life if he's dead?'

'It's . . . a sort of afterlife,' I tell her.

'You get reincarnated,' Jake explains, which isn't what I mean, but I don't correct him. It takes me back, with him snuggled up at my side, to the old days before everything unravelled.

'Will *you* die?' Lola asks.

'Everyone dies sometime, sweetie, but I hope it's not until I'm very old.'

She bites her lip. 'Will you be like Granny when you're old?'

I laugh and stroke her hair. 'I don't know.'

'Mum,' Jake murmurs, and I brace myself for more questions of a life-and-death nature, 'I don't really want you to buy me a GameBoy Advance.'

The tension that's gripped me all day subsides a little. 'That's good. I'm really proud of you for helping me today, Jake. I know you didn't want to be in the photos, but you did it anyway.'

He nods thoughtfully. 'I really want a GameBoy Advance, but I know we don't have much money and can't afford it.'

'Well, that's true.'

He grins, breathing out spearmint. 'So I'm gonna ask Dad for one.'

The house is blissfully silent as I creep downstairs to check my emails. My new *Bambino* account is up and running and I have mail – real mail from real *Bambino* readers who, despite my terrifying man-face, seem to be under the illusion that I can help them.

The first one reads:

> Dear Caitlin,
> Is it so wrong of me to fantasise about leaving my little boy strapped in his buggy and legging it to the train station to somewhere like, I don't know, Paris, and never coming back? I had my passport photos taken yesterday . . .

And the next:

This morning, while trying to coax my bickering kids out of
the car, I had an overwhelming urge to slam the boot down
on to my head. Am I normal?

Berserk Mother, Wakefield

And another:

Since our little boy was born seven years ago, my husband
has changed from being a reasonably attractive man and
keen squash player to an overweight, hygienically challenged
slob who hasn't cleaned his teeth for several months. Do you
think I should have an affair?

Suzanne, Bucks.

I feel ridiculously chuffed that they have chosen to contact me,
out of all the agony aunts on the dozens of magazines out there. I
pull out a notebook from my desk drawer and start to make
notes.

Another email pings in.

Dear Caitlin,

I was delighted to see that that dreadful Pike woman has
been replaced and was hoping that you, as the new agony
aunt, might offer more balanced and sympathetic advice to
parents. (I am a single father.) But no, you come across as
so terribly earnest, going all out to convince us that you
understand what normal parents are going through.

With all the make-up you're wearing, and your hair done
up into some kind of bouffant, I can't help suspecting that
you don't really have children at all. If you do, you are
obviously nannied up to the hilt. How can you possibly
know what it's like in the real world when all you have to do
all day is preen yourself in your posh office?

Yours in anger,

R

I glare at the screen. How dare this creep insult me without
knowing the first thing about why I took this job? Millie begged

me to do it. I only agreed because I can't bring myself to ask Martin for more money.

How bloody *dare* he?

'Never reply to emails personally,' Millie advised me. 'You'll only encourage lunatics with too much time on their hands.' She's right; why bother acknowledging this jerk when I barely have time to communicate with my own kids?

But I can't help myself. With my heart juddering furiously, I fire off a reply:

What the hell do you know about my life?

17

It's a gloriously sunny late-April afternoon when Sam and I bring the kids to the park to run riot with their water guns. His sleekly muscled legs, clad in baggy shorts, are already lightly tanned. His chest bears a faint suggestion of hair and is infinitely touchable. Even his feet are quite fetching, as men's feet go – no gnarled nails, no toe-hair sproutings. (Martin may be head-turningly handsome in your smooth, DFS-sofa-model kind of way, but his weirdly skinny feet let him down tragically. Ha.)

I catch myself appraising Sam's body and quickly rearrange my face. 'You're burning,' I warn him. 'Better put on some sunscreen.'

'Never use it,' he protests.

I laugh and pluck the garish orange bottle from my bag. 'What is it about men and sunscreen? Martin was like that. Look – your shoulders are a tiny bit pink.'

'I've never had sunburn in my life,' he protests.

'God,' I splutter, 'that's such a *man* thing. Being immune to burning. Refusing to ask for directions when they're lost.'

He smirks. 'OK, boss. Slap some on.' And he plonks himself before me with his beautiful bare back in my face.

I hesitate. Heck, for a graphic designer who spends great swathes of his time holed up in front of a computer, he is extremely well honed. Slathering on his sunscreen will involve touching his *bare, naked flesh*. Help. I do this in the most non-sexual manner possible, rubbing briskly as if removing a stain. 'There,' I say in a businesslike voice.

'Thanks,' he purrs. 'That was really . . . sensual.'

'Shut up,' I mutter, silently cursing my hot cheeks.

We sit in silence for a few moments, watching the kids charging through the paddling pool. A vision of loveliness in miniscule cut-off shorts – they're smaller than most of my knickers – rollerblades past us. I check to see if she registered with Sam. He watches her for a moment, then flicks his eyes back to me.

'Cait . . . there's something I want to tell you.'

My breath tightens. Lola is complaining loudly that Jake squirted the back of her head, but I block her out. 'What is it?' I ask.

He runs a hand through the grass. 'I, um . . .'

Oh, God. This is it. Shooting-stars night – he felt it too. Like me, he's tried to push his feelings aside for the very reasons I have. Because our sons are friends, and *we* are friends, and it's all too entwined and embarrassing—

'I, um . . . It's about Amelia,' Sam murmurs.

No, I don't want to hear this. 'Oh, right.'

'We slept together,' he says flatly.

I open my mouth, but nothing comes out. Some brat squirts my neck, but I ignore it. Cold water dribbles down the back of my T-shirt. 'Did you?' I say finally.

'I don't really know why I'm telling you,' he adds.

Neither do I, I think bitterly. Does this mean they're getting back together? I daren't ask. 'When . . . when did it happen?' I manage.

Lola and Jake are squabbling about whose turn it is to be armed with the Super-Soaker, rather than the substandard ordinary water gun.

'In Cornwall during the Easter holidays.'

'Just before we went camping?'

'Uh-huh.'

Why didn't you say? I want to ask. *Why did you lie there with me on your blanket and let me believe something special was happening?* I curse myself for being so ridiculous. Sam hadn't made me believe anything. It was me. My ridiculous malfunctioning brain had dreamed up the whole thing. Caitlin idiot Brown.

'I . . . I thought you'd stayed at your sister's hotel?'

Sam nods. 'Amelia came over for a night. She'd had some row with her boyfriend, called me to sound off about him.'

How terribly cosy. How very grown-up and mature. The park, which a few moments ago had seemed vivid and green and full of life, now seems flat and listless. I want to go home.

'You know how it is,' Sam continues, 'when you've known someone for ages, and even though it's obvious it'll never work there's still this connection, this . . . frisson.'

I don't know that feeling. A mangy dog sniffs around our bag of picnic supplies and I shoo it away. It growls at me and pees on the grass.

'Isn't frisson that curly lettuce you get in bags?' God, I'm a twerp. I deserve to be executed.

Sam smiles. 'I think that's frisée. The purply stuff.'

'No, that's radicchio.'

Go on, fuckwit, babble on some more about salad. Just what the situation requires. 'Or lollo rosso,' I suggest as a drenched Lola thunders towards us.

'Anyway,' Sam says with a small laugh, 'confession over.'

I don't know what to do next. Congratulate him? Ask how he *feels* about it? 'I suppose we all do those things,' I mutter.

He frowns. 'Can you imagine it happening with Martin?'

'No, I don't think Martin would sleep with you.'

Agh. Pathetic joke. 'I mean,' he insists, 'd'you ever wish . . .'

'Sam, I'd rather stick pins in my eyes.'

We snigger as Lola lands on my lap, soaking me. 'What's funny, Mummy?'

'Just a silly joke.'

'Tell me.'

'No, hon . . .'

'Why not?' She turns angrily.

Because it's really not funny at all. 'Here, let me towel your hair before you get cold.'

'I'm already cold,' Lola complains.

I can't look at Sam as I help her to dry off. This will change everything, I just know it. Me and Sam, doing this kind of stuff together. Him never ticking me off for my shoddy parenting skills. Just being there whenever I need him. Never shaming me by not only owning but *using* a pasta machine.

He'll get back with Amelia. They'll be a couple again, a symmetrical family with everything as it should be. If I were a faintly decent person, I'd be happy for him, but inside I'm crushed.

It's not a pathetic attempt at one-upmanship. It's not: *Listen, Pants-a-Flying Sam Blackwell. You're not the only who's seeing some action with the opposite sex. You know what? I am too. Or I shall be. Just you wait.* No, I wouldn't stoop so low.

Well, it's only a *tiny* bit of that.

One undeniably cute young man is waiting for my call. OK, weeks have passed since our date, but *subconsciously*, he's waiting. He could have lost my number, and, anyway, I have nothing to lose – because all was already lost after Sam's confession in the park.

With the kids installed in front of the TV, I find Darren's shop's number on yell.com and creep towards the phone. My bravado ebbs away as I tap out his number, and my tongue acquires a sandpapery texture. An answerphone plays its message and bleeps.

'Hi, Darren?' I say tentatively. 'It's Caitlin. Caitlin Brown with the, um, disappearing mother . . .'

There's a click. 'Hi, Cait?' Darren says, sounding pleased. 'Great to hear from you. Sorry I haven't phoned. With your mum and all that, I thought maybe your life's a bit complicated to have me butting in . . .'

'Oh, no,' I blurt out, too eagerly. 'My life's . . . fine.'

A small silence.

'Was your mum OK? You seemed really worried . . .'

Rather belated concern, I'd say, but I don't want to seem bitter. He sounds so chirpy, so unencumbered by ex-spouses and elderly parents. 'I found her playing poker in one of the canal boats. I think she'd mistaken it for the Clyde.'

'Uh?'

'It's a river . . .'

'Oh, right.' Darren laughs. It's a warm, easy laugh that makes my shoulders un-clench. 'These mistakes are easily made,' he adds.

Lola bounds into the kitchen in her velour Scooby Doo dressing gown, complete with ears, tail and matching paw gloves. 'Mummy—'

'Shhhh!' I hiss at her.

'What's that?' Darren asks.

'Just my daughter. Hang on a minute . . . Lola, what d'you want? Are you thirsty or something? You can see I'm on the phone . . .' Oh no. I am committing the heinous crime of talking to my child while attempting to conduct an adult phone conversation.

'No,' Darren says, 'I mean that weird hissing noise. Sounds like something's wrong with your phone.'

'Can I speak to Daddy?' Lola bellows, trying to snatch the receiver with her paw.

'It's not Daddy!' I mouth at her.

'Who is it?'

'Go *upstairs!*' When will I ever get a smidge of privacy? When?

'Are you doing anything tomorrow night?' Darren asks.

'Woof!' Lola barks. 'Woof, woof, woof!'

'No, um, I think I'm free tomorrow.' I waggle my eyebrows furiously. Lola whirls round the kitchen, barking and thrashing her doggie tail.

'D'you have a dog?' Darren enquires.

'No, I . . . Lola, *shush.*'

'We could go for dinner or something, try that new place where the Spice Garden used to be.'

Lola hangs her head like a scolded hound.

'That would be lovely,' I say, cutting her from my line of vision and praying that Holly will be free to babysit. It should be Martin's turn for the kids, but something's come up, yet again.

They're going to the theatre. Slapper, the silly cookie, only booked three tickets.

'Eight o'clock?' Darren suggests.

'Great. See you tomorrow.'

I bang down the phone.

'What?' Lola asks.

'*What* what?' I can sense my brain cells disintegrating.

'What'll be lovely? Are we going out?'

I can't help smiling. 'I'm meeting a friend tomorrow night, that's all. I'll see if Holly can look after you.'

'Oh.' Her face falls.

'What's wrong, honey? I thought you liked Holly, and I hardly ever go out.'

She nods and her velour ears flop dolefully. 'Are you going out with a man?'

I pause. 'It's no one you know.'

She grips my hand with her paw. 'I don't want a new daddy.'

I crouch down and hug her, breathing in her bubblegum smell. 'Lola, I promise there's no need to worry about that. There'll never be a new daddy.'

Her face softens, and she allows me to lead her upstairs. No, Darren certainly isn't new-daddy material. We're managing perfectly fine without one, at least most of the time. A bit of fun is all I'm looking for – to feel like Caitlin again, instead of Director-in-Chief of Lunch Boxes.

Another point in Darren's favour is that he's taken my mind off Sam shagging Amelia for, ooh, all of thirty seconds.

18

So, tell me about your life.

R x

I kick off the strappy sandals that have been biting my ankles all evening. I bought them especially for tonight, as my other pair were scuffed to buggery from clopping along the muddy tow-path during my hunt for Mum. Well worth forty-five quid, plus the de-mothering process and babysitter's fee. Remind me to never indulge in such fripperies again.

I wince at the 'R x'. A kiss! How very friendly. How damn forward. Millie's voice booms in my head: 'Never reply to emails personally. They're all crazies out there.'

OK, R With a Kiss. How about this:

First you insult me, and now you want to know about my life. Let's start with yesterday, shall we? My friend Sam and I take our kids to the park. It's there that he confesses he slept with his ex. Which is allowed, right? They're both adults and have somehow managed to break up while still liking each other. All very healthy and admirable.

Not me, though. Oh, no. I skid backwards to adolescence, where I'm driven insane with jealousy – because, you see, I wish it was me. That Sam had slept with, I mean. Lately I've been spending inordinate amounts of time fantasising about what it would be like and imagining . . . Oh, let's not go there. Suffice to say, I am tragically deluded.

It's all very sad and pathetic.

Still with me, R? OK. Fuelled by unhealthy emotions, I phone Darren, who's extremely cute and about a tenth of my age. I'm so pissed off about Sam and Amelia that I don't care that Darren clearly isn't interested in me. Not really. Or he would have phoned after our first date, wouldn't he?

Anyway. For some reason – pity probably – he suggests we go out to dinner. It's a Moroccan place where there's fruit in with the meat, which Darren's not so sure about, but the night's going well nonetheless. Wine's flowing. He's quite touchy-feely over the meal. At one point his fingers brush against my leg and I feel a definite stirring below. He is extremely flirtatious and flattering, and these things matter when you haven't had sex since Henry VIII's time. Tonight, I think, it's going to happen.

I'm not talking the full works. After being dumped without ceremony by my husband, I'm not quite ready to go there. But a snog scenario, bit of a cuddle – that would do nicely. Caitlin Brown, mother of three and former sexless android, is on the brink of feeling alive again. I'm so excited I can hardly swallow my lamb.

We're halfway through our main course when this couple walks in. I don't recognise the man, but the woman I do know – Bev Hartnett, treasurer of the PTA, without whom the very fabric of our community would crumble to dust.

I type on, splurging it out, hammering the life out of my keyboard.

'Caitlin!' she gushes, giving Darren a cursory glance. Oh, joy, they're seated at the next table to us. Bev drags her chair virtually next to mine, ignoring her poor bastard husband because she has far more pressing matters to attend to, like: had I heard that the year-six trip to Provence might be cancelled due to lack of funding? What do I think of that supply teacher, the one with the short skirt and cleavage? Would I be interested in manning the guess-the-stuffed-bunny's-birthday stall at the summer fête? Failing that, would I volunteer to go in the stocks to be pelted with pies? It's all for a good cause.

'No thank you,' I tell her, figuring precisely where the stuffed bunny could be stuffed.

'Would *you* be our stocks man?' she asks Darren.

Like a child, he has lined up his apricots on the side of his plate. They look like slugs.

'It's not really my thing,' he mutters, glancing around desperately for an escape route. I can almost hear him formulating a plan to go to the loo and make his bid for freedom through the window. And I wouldn't blame him.

'Come on,' Bev gushes. 'Don't be a spoilsport! All the kids do is throw pies at you, and they're not real pies – just paper plates of shaving foam. It's hysterical!'

'Oh,' he says weakly.

'A handsome, strapping boy like you! You'd bring the crowds in.' She licks her lips in a horribly suggestive manner, as if that might swing it.

She looks middle-aged and desperate. I feel likewise. In contrast, Darren appears even younger. He shoots me a 'help me' look, as if he's in pain.

'You'd look great in the stocks,' Bev adds. 'D'you work out? I bet you do. You don't get a body like that from lying on the sofa with a bucket of KFC, ha, ha, ha.'

He cringes visibly. By now it's apparent that she's pissed. She strikes me as the type who's rat-arsed on one glass of wine and says 'aperitif' without irony.

'It's for school funds,' she adds, leaning over and flashing her perma-tanned breasts. 'Think of your children's education.'

'I don't have any children,' Darren mutters, and I see his life flashing before him.

'Well, one day you might! How long have you two been together anyway?' She has joined our table properly now, and her husband is pretending to study the wine list for the millionth time.

'We're, um, not, er . . .' Darren starts.

'No, we're not,' I say firmly.

'We're just, um, you know . . .' he babbles, wiping sweat from his upper lip.

'Bev,' her husband hisses, frantically beckoning her back to their table, 'I think they want to be left alone.'

She does a cartoon 'whoops!' face and hoicks her chair back to their table. But it's too late. Nothing feels right. We're not talking any more. Darren's eyes look a little less melty. I see him glancing furtively at the glass door as if he's planning to launch himself through it, leaving a Darren-shaped hole.

As we pay the bill, Bev is talking loudly about the perimenopause. 'I'm sure it's happening, Barry,' she booms, 'because my face is getting hairier and I'm plumping out in the middle.'

Darren and I head for the door. We say goodbye on the corner of Bethnal Green Road.

There's no kiss. There's certainly no prospect of getting intimate with him at any point in the future. I suspect that he'd rather share a bed with ferrets.

I come home, with pulsating wounds on my heels from my sandals, to a message from you.

So, R, there's a slice of my life. Is that enough for you?

I stare at my words. Seeing the night laid out before me makes me feel even more wretched. What a screw-up. To think I'd assumed that tonight might be some kind of turning point, one of those crucial steps that the magazines talk about.

I don't plan to send the email and am just about to press 'delete' when Lola bursts into the kitchen and flings herself, hot-faced and sticky with tears, into my arms.

'Sweetie,' I cry, 'what's happened?'

'I had a nightmare!' She scrambles on to my lap. I hold her close and stroke her scorching cheek.

'Shush, darling, you're OK. It was just a bad dream. I'll come up and tuck you in.'

'Thanks, Mummy,' she whispers.

I can't help feeling grateful that she needs me so much; she's a fine antidote to Jake. As her sobs subside, I glance at the screen: 'Your email has been sent to rp68@yahoo.co.uk.'

I must have hit 'send' accidentally.

Holy fuck.

Lola stares up, her eyes still brimming with tears. 'Mummy,' she breathes, 'you said the F-word.'

PART TWO

At *Bambino*, we believe that childhood is to be treasured.
Our children do not belong to us, but are merely on loan.
So we should cherish every moment.

Millie Dawson, Bambino *editor's letter, 7 May*

19

Caitlin,

May I just say I sympathise completely. This is the prat who, at the ex-wife's jolly New Year's Eve gathering (yes, I actually agreed to attend such an event), saw fit to drink himself into a fury, insult her golf-sweater-wearing 'partner' and then attempt to snog her in the kitchen. Despite the fact that she has gone all demure since walking out on me and taken to wearing pie-crust collars. Is that what they're called? They're kind of pleated and poke up at the neck.

So, I am no great player in the relationship stakes either. I'm sorry to hear about Sam and Darren, and for the harsh tone of my first email. I'd had a bad day and took it out on the unbearably pompous *Bambino* magazine, which my wife subscribed to and which won't stop coming in the post every blasted week, even though I cancelled the direct debit and keep phoning them in what I hope is a masterful manner.

I've tried to tell them that my wife doesn't live with me any more. That she's with a halfwit who talks in management-speak – 'It's a win-win situation' – and dyes his hair to cover the grey, for fuck's sake. It's like a bit of her plopping through the letterbox every Thursday to laugh in my face for sending Billy (our six-year-old son) over to her place in age three-to-four pants. They still fit him, so what's the problem?

Oh, and that day I emailed you, we'd gone to the chemist's for nit lotion and Billy had unscrewed the top

from a bottle of bubble bath and made a little pink puddle
on the floor, which he then skidded in.
Regards.
R x

This is eerie.

I, too, have an aversion to the word 'partner' *and* pie-crust
collars, which should be rounded up and burned on some
specified date. I reply:

Dear R,
I would no more try to kiss my ex-husband than a slab of
three-week-old haddock I'd found in a park bin. But I
sympathise with you too.
C

To my surprise, he fires a reply straight back.

Hello, Caitlin,
Do people leave haddock in park bins where you live?
Sounds like a health hazard. You should get on to the
council. Oh, and I hope I don't sound rude, but . . . do you
always wear as much make-up as is shown in your photo?
I'm not criticising . . . it's just I'd imagine your face doesn't
need it.
Thought I'd share that.
R x
P.S. Haddock comes in fillets, not slabs.

It's 1.27 a.m. and I am not remotely tired. There's something
about R's tone that I like. He makes me smile. At any rate, he's
doing a fine job of taking my mind off Bev Hartnett and her
stuffed-bunny stall.

Hi, R,
I'm sure the PTA mob around here will be on to the council
directly. As for your kind comments, I usually favour a more
natural look. On this occasion I was taken hostage by a

maniac with a make-up sponge and shackled to a chair while the photo was taken.

C x

P.S. You're up late.

Hello, Caitlin,

Billy's birthday tomorrow. Trying to get everything ready. Is anything sadder than the aftermath of a kids' party with those slowly deflating balloons sellotaped to the kitchen door and bits of cake mushed into the carpet? This year, I've decided to take Billy and his friends to the park with a load of balloons, games and unsuitable food. No cleaning – genius, wouldn't you say? Am hoping that spillages will be eaten by pigeons and squirrels.

R x

I type:

I am concerned that cake will prove unsuitable for wildlife, esp. if buttercream icing is used. However, top marks for allowing your son to celebrate his birthday surrounded by nature, instead of some horrid soft-play centre. I do hope you're supplying home-made boysenberry flapjacks sweetened with organic apple juice.

Good luck and goodnight.

Caitlin x

He pings back:

Naturally! Thank you, Cait, and goodnight.

R x

Cait, as if he's a friend. Only Martin, Sam and friends I've known for years – like Millie and Rachel – call me that. To the PTA mob, I'm always Caitlin (or, more accurately, *poor* Caitlin).

I log off and head upstairs, noticing for the first time the withered end of a party balloon trapped beneath yellowing sellotape since Lola's birthday in January.

Seeing it there makes me feel a little less alone.

20

'What did I tell you?' Millie barks into the phone.

'Not to reply to anyone personally.'

'I do know what I'm talking about,' she barges on. 'Harriet had email stalkers desperate to be her friend. Did I tell you about the weird stuff she got in the mail?'

'No,' I say warily.

'Oh, all kinds of stuff came in for her. Little cling-filmed packages of pubes, that kind of thing.'

'Pubes?' I repeat, aghast.

'Yeah. You know what people are like about agony aunts.'

'No,' I say, shifting uneasily on the edge of the table. 'You never mentioned any of this when you asked me to do her page. What *are* people like?'

She sighs. 'Some of them see you as a sort of . . . outlet. Someone to talk to, even if they don't have a specific problem. They want to confide in you just because you're *there*. They regard you as, I don't know . . . some kind of all-knowing being.'

'You're joking,' I mutter.

'Well, it's understandable really. When your picture's in a magazine and you're discussing personal stuff, they can become a bit . . .' She clears her throat. 'Obsessed,' she concludes.

'Right. So I'm setting myself up to be stalked, is that what you're saying?'

'No, I didn't mean that,' she says hastily. 'Just that . . . you need to be careful. Have your antennae out. Don't get into a personal thing with anyone, all right?'

'OK,' I mutter.

She laughs. 'Sorry, didn't mean to freak you out. You're doing a brilliant job, Cait. It's exactly what I want. You know we had to re-write Harriet's copy every week? She still sounded barking, even then. Your copy comes in and we hardly have to touch it—'

'When *is* Harriet coming back?' I cut in.

'Um . . .' Millie hesitates. 'She's, er . . . she's not coming back. I've told her I want you to do the page permanently.'

'Did you?' I exclaim. 'Without checking with me first? What did Harriet say?'

'She . . . she was pretty pissed off, to be honest. Said she couldn't believe I'd dragged in any old person to take over her page. I explained that you have years of experience and that you wrote about arse creams and all sorts for that health website.' Millie sighs. 'Anyway, she's only a freelancer, and not on a contract or anything, so there's nothing she can do.'

I am aghast. 'I wish we'd talked it over first.'

'C'mon, Cait, what else d'you have to do?'

'Nothing, but . . .'

'You're getting twice as much mail as she did. It could be the start of a whole new career for you. Listen,' she adds, 'I've got a meeting in a minute, so I've got to dash . . . Will you do it?'

A new career? I'm not sure that I want one, but at least it's a new *something*, which can only be a good thing. 'OK,' I say warily, 'I'll do it.'

'Brilliant. Your new picture's gorgeous, by the way. I was worried that the old one might have scared off readers, brought our circulation down.'

'Thanks.'

'Any time. Promise you won't contact that weirdo emailer again?'

She does the screechy *ee-ee-ee* thing from the stabbing scene in *Psycho*. I wind up the call having vowed not to offer the mysterious R one more word of encouragement.

I keep my promise that evening, prowling around the computer as if it's a sleeping animal that if woken, might savage me with its teeth. The following day, I allow myself to log on to my email account and am relieved to see that R hasn't contacted me again. I'd like to fire off a quickie, just to ask how he got on with the party in the park (neat idea – must remember for when Lola demands to fill the house with eighteen E-number-fuelled classmates), but manage not to. Whenever the urge becomes particularly strong I conjure up an image of cling-filmed parcels of pubes, which does the trick.

My *Bambino* mailbag does an excellent job of keeping me occupied. The problems are fascinating – like overhearing intimate conversations on the bus – and make me feel marginally better about the crappiness of my own life. When you're wrapped up in your own woes, it's easy to forget that so many other people are dealing with ten tons of shit. Perhaps Millie was right and the job does suit me perfectly. Admittedly, I have always harboured an unhealthy interest in other people's private lives. As a prying teen, I could think of nothing more fun than rifling through my parents' wardrobe. When I'd unearthed a sex manual filled with photos of a couple demonstrating various positions, I'd been overcome with delight and spent many a happy evening leafing through it.

In my favourite picture, the woman was doing a shoulder stand on the bed, supporting her hips with her hands, while the man was kind of leaning into her, the right way up. I couldn't fathom that one at all and had tried it out (just the woman part, obviously) on my bedroom floor. Mum had walked in and remarked, 'Glad to see you're doing some exercise. You could do with it. You've really put on the beef lately.' Although my feelings were hurt, I was relieved that she hadn't figured that I'd been copying the woman on page seventy-eight.

Boggle-eyed from poring over the problem letters, I haul Jake's clean laundry up to his room, leaving a trail of socks as I go. He's on hands and knees madly scrubbing at something on the carpet with a bunched-up J-cloth.

'What are you doing, love?' I ask. 'It's nearly nine o'clock. I was just about to ask you to put your light out.'

'I'm trying to get this stuff off the carpet,' he mutters without looking at me.

'What? Get what off?'

'*This.*'

I dump the laundry on to his bed and crouch down to investigate. 'Oh, that's just a coffee stain. I must have sloshed some on the carpet while I was putting stuff away.'

'What were you doing in my room?'

I gawp at him. 'I told you. Putting things away. That's what mums *do*, isn't it? Are you saying I'm not allowed in your room, Jake? Is that what you mean?'

The ridiculousness of a ten-year-old scrubbing his carpet pales into insignificance. Apparently, I am now barred from certain areas of the house. *My* house, on which I pay the mortgage, or at least half of it. Jake utters something like, 'Mrruh.'

'Can you talk to me properly?' I snap. 'I can't understand "mrruh". I'm unfamiliar with that word.'

He peers up at me through lush, dark lashes. Disdain oozes from his narrowed eyes. 'I said no.'

'You mean I'm not allowed in here at any time? Not even to make your bed?'

Jake shrugs. 'I make my own bed. I know how to put a duvet cover on, and a pillowcase.'

Aren't you the clever one. 'Or hoover?' I ask.

'You hardly ever hoover. Can't remember the last time you did. It's so dusty in here I could get asthma or an infection or anything.'

'For God's sake, I do my best! What are you, a health and safety inspector? I thought we'd talked about your cleaning thing, Jake. It's not healthy. It's not *right*.'

He stiffens his lips, a gesture which instantly hardens his face. And I feel it then – my chin quivering, like a little kid's. Like someone whose ice cream has toppled from its cone and landed with a splat on the pavement. My vision is blurring. Jake regards me with a look of faint triumph. What have I done to deserve this? I know it's not ideal, living apart from his dad, but who's the one shagging someone else? I might have been too ordinary for

Martin, or a crap lay, having never suggested the woman-does-shoulder-stand thingy, but I refuse to believe it was completely my fault.

'Why are you being like this?' I ask shakily. 'It's not like you. Not like my Jake. Is something happening at school? You're not being bullied, are you?'

His look could curdle milk. 'No.'

'Is it about me and Dad?'

He edges away from me and resumes scrubbing the stain, mumbling something into his pyjama top.

'Pardon?' I say, too loudly.

'I said . . . that stupid magazine. Everyone's seen it. Lola found it in the kitchen and took it in her bag and now the whole school's laughing at me.'

'Oh, Jake, of course they're not!'

'Yes they are. And when the new one comes out, with me in the picture instead of just you, it's gonna be even worse.' His voice wavers.

'Darling, I'm so sorry. It's just my job. I need to earn money, you know.'

'When are you stopping?' he demands. 'When's that old agony aunt coming back?'

'Jake . . .' I run my hand across the damp patch on the carpet '. . . I'm not giving up. Not for the moment. *Bambino*'s my main source of income. Don't you understand that?'

'Fine,' he says, like an embittered grown-up. 'I don't see why you can't go back to writing about spot cream and all that.'

'Because the company went bust, darling. Listen, no one will care about a photo in a silly magazine. They've had their laugh about it and it'll all be forgotten. I bet no one mentions it again.'

He shoots me a scathing look, as if I'd insisted that his Christmas presents were fashioned by elves in a workshop. Christ, I'd only come up to put his laundry away. My head is thumping and my chest feels horribly tight. Maybe I'll have a seizure and he'll be half orphaned and have to live with Martin and Slapper and Pink Princess in that bloody great penthouse.

With a wave of dread, I realise that Jake would probably enjoy that very much.

'I'm sorry you feel like this,' I murmur.

'Leave me alone.'

'You mean . . . you really don't want me in your room? Ever?'

'No.'

'Not even to clean it?'

Jake shakes his head. 'I clean it myself now. Haven't you noticed?'

Fine. Bloody fantastic. I haul myself up from my crouched position, give his laundry pile a little shove, so it cascades all over his bed, and march out of the room, skidding on a sock. 'Suit yourself, Mr Bloody Perfect,' I mutter while stomping downstairs.

'I heard that,' he snarls after me.

I'm seething as I slam down on to the wobbly chair at my desk. Seventeen emails, including one from R:

Hi, Cait,

Hope you don't mind me barging in on your Friday night.
I'm sure – at least I hope – that yours is proving to be more
enjoyable than mine. Billy and I have just had a bit of a
fracas. He's just informed me that I embarrassed him at his
party by joining in the games and singing 'like a silly man'.
Is it better to be a not-really-there dad who hides behind the
newspaper all day? Who uses the *Telegraph* as a shield?
 Crap isn't it, this parenting business?
 R x

'Yes, it bloody is,' I reply, my breathing ragged and tight.

I pause, about to press 'send', then quickly add a few details: about the son who despises me, and being banned from a room in my own house, when we used to lounge around on his bed for hours retelling the funniest scenes from a film we'd just watched. When Jake had liked me and not regarded me as if I were an embarrassing stain.

I type on and on, my anger fading as I spill out the hurts of the past few weeks. In some magazine I found on the bus, one of those relationship gurus had suggested putting difficult feelings into words – in a journal, perhaps, or a letter you don't plan to send. Perhaps they were right. It *is* helping; my heartbeat feels normalish at least. I have never been so open with anyone – not Sam, because I couldn't bear for him to regard me as Chief Whinger; not Rachel, because she wouldn't understand; and not Millie, because . . . well, she *definitely* wouldn't understand. I don't censor myself, or hold anything back, because R is not a real person who'll ever know or judge me.

He's just words on a screen.

21

'How long has this been going on?' Sam asks over dinner on his terrace. It's a warm May evening, and barbecue smells drift from a neighbouring garden.

'Three weeks or so,' I say.

'He sounds creepy, contacting you out of the blue like that. Why won't he tell you his name?'

'I haven't asked, and I don't really want to know. Knowing his name would make him more real and then—'

'You like it that it's anonymous?'

'Yes,' I say through a full mouth. Why is Sam's bolognese rich and tasty whereas mine turns out anaemic and ill-looking?

'But it's not anonymous, is it?' he insists. 'At least, not from his point of view. He knows your name, your kids' names and what your job is . . . You haven't told him where you live, have you?'

'No, of course not!' I say defensively. 'I know he lives in North London, though he hasn't said where.' Sam looks so concerned, giving me the big-eyed look, that I burst out laughing. 'It's a few emails,' I add, 'with an anonymous person, like a chatroom or something. What's the harm in that?'

'I feel uneasy, that's all. The way he says exactly the right thing to make you feel better. Or something happens to you and – by some spooky coincidence – something similar has happened to him.'

I glance at Sam. A hint of awkwardness flits across his face, almost as if he's *jealous*. 'Are you suggesting he's spying on me?' I ask.

'Maybe. He could be out there now, peering through that hole in the fence . . .'

'Or going through my bin, looking for old knickers . . .'

Sam grins and the awkwardness melts away. 'Bet he buys loads of copies of *Bambino* and cuts out your pictures to paper his downstairs loo . . . What does he call himself again?'

'R. Just R.'

'R for arsehole.' Sam chuckles as we pile up the bowls and carry them inside. Now I feel foolish. I haven't told Sam that I've begun to look forward to R's emails, even getting up early to check my inbox before the kids start clamouring for cereal. And Sam is wrong: I know a lot about my new friend, which is how I regard him. I know he emails in a flurry during Billy's bathtime, then again late at night until 1 or 2 a.m. I know he loves kite-flying with his son, despises soft-play centres and McDonald's, and is trying but failing to teach himself guitar. He's told me how crushed he was when his ex-wife announced that she no longer loved him and that she'd been sleeping with someone from work. How he'd bottled up all the anger and had only been dragged back to semi-normality by throwing himself into bringing up his kid.

Nor do I tell Sam that R makes embarrassing incidents – like Travis tipping forty tampons out of their box in Superdrug – seem funny. I know he'll fire back something to make me smile.

'It's like the people who send in their problems to me,' I explain as we load Sam's dishwasher. 'They don't know me, so there's a distance there, which makes it feel safer to share things.'

'He's your own private agony uncle.' Sam laughs dryly.

'Yes, I suppose so.'

He turns to make coffee. It feels like he's deliberately avoiding my gaze. 'Have you heard from Amelia?' I ask, to break the silence.

'Yes, I've seen her actually.'

'So what happened?' I ask lightly.

'She . . . came up a couple of days ago. She was in London for an interview and stayed the night. Well, when I say she stayed . . . she actually left before Harvey woke up.' He laughs hollowly. 'How dumb is that? Hiding the fact that you slept with your child's mother?'

'I, um, suppose you don't want him thinking you're back together and being disappointed.'

'Mmm.'

A silence descends. 'Is she thinking of moving back to London?' I ask in an overly perky voice. God, the effort of pretending I don't care.

'Well, she lost her job in Cornwall, so it's a possibility, yes.'

I frown at the back of his head. 'Sam, what d'you think will happen? Do you want to get back together?'

He turns round and hands me a mug, but I still can't fathom him out. 'Honestly, Cait, I don't know. She's all torn up about splitting up with her boyfriend.'

'I've never asked you this, but . . . why did you break up? I know she left, but—'

'Look what I've got, Dad!' Harvey tumbles in from the garden with a handful of writhing worms, followed by Jake, who appears to have forgotten that I'm the most despicable person on earth.

'Look at mine,' he yelps, uncoiling his hand to reveal a shiny-backed beetle.

'Lovely, Jake . . . What are you planning to do with it?'

'Can I bring it home?'

'Yes, of course you can.' Am I such a terrible mother when I allow live bugs in the house? Actually, I am relieved. Bugs = dirty = normal, grubby-fingernailed child. Not Obsessive-Compulsive Mr Sheener.

'You'll find jam jars under the sink,' Sam says. 'Remember to punch some holes in the lid and put plenty of soil and leaves in there.'

My mobile beeps and I fish it out of my pocket to read the text: MEETING FRIENDS AT THE CROWN IN COLUMBIA ROAD 8PMISH WD BE GREAT IF U CD COME DARREN X.

The smile sneaks across my face. 'Something nice?' Sam asks as the boys charge outside for further creepy-crawly collection.

'Darren, the TV-fixer, remember?'

'You're seeing him again? After the Bev fiasco in the restaurant?'

'Yes, tonight. He's just asked me for a drink. Martin's picking up the kids, so there's no babysitter worries.'

'Sounds great.' He smiles lamely.

'And it's better than spending Friday night with a tank of sea monkeys.' I head towards the back door to round up the kids from the bottom of Sam's garden. 'Anyway,' I say, glancing back at him, 'what are you up to tonight?'

We have a joke, Sam and I, about our lamentable social lives, answering such questions with a blasé, 'Oh, I thought I'd pop along to a private view at the ICA; then there's an all-night party at Tracey Emin's studio. Apart from that, nothing much.'

'She's, um . . . coming over,' Sam says hesitantly. 'Amelia's due in about an hour's time.'

My entire body seems to deflate. 'That's great!' I say, mustering a wide, fake grin, the effort of which almost causes my face to crack.

Back home, I busy myself by packing the kids' weekend bags. Lola is jammed by my side, helping to pair up socks from her drawer. Jake, who's impatient for King Daddy's arrival, keeps asking why he's not here yet. Travis is in the garden, attempting to find further specimens for our bug collection. I plan to de-mother myself when they've gone. It's less stressful than enduring their bathroom-door hammering and Travis catching me sprinting naked across the landing and going, 'Eugh.'

He's late. Martin is *never* late. When he finally shows up, at seven forty-five, he is creased around the eyes, as if severely sleep-deprived. His usually pristine hair looks as if it's been sat on. 'Sorry I'm late,' he mutters, giving me an unexpected kiss on the cheek, which shocks me, as if a stranger had lurched over and pecked me in the street.

'You look awful,' I tell him, having dispatched the kids to gather up their favourite toys. (No matter how ready we are, there's always a scramble for last-minute 'essentials'.)

'Cheers.' He smiles weakly and perches on the sofa arm.

I peer at him. In spite of how much I despise him, I'm concerned to see him looking so haggard. He will, after all, be in charge of our children for the next forty-eight hours. Right now, he barely looks up to the job.

'Bad day at work?' I persist.

'I, um . . .' He glances down at his shoes, then blinks up at me. 'I haven't been to work today. Me and Daisy have been having a few . . . problems.'

'Oh dear.' My heart bleeds.

'Issues, I suppose you'd call them.' Joyless chuckle. 'About the kids . . .'

'What about the kids?'

Here it comes: Sorry, but while I'm happy to pop round in the week bearing gifts, I'll have to cut down on weekends. You know how it is. Space issues, ya-di-ya. And we're going to be terribly busy building an annexe with en-suite bathroom for Pink Princess . . .

'She . . . Daisy worries about the effect they're having on Poppy. She's been quite withdrawn at school and finds it hard to make friends and—'

'And you're saying this is our children's fault? Christ, Martin, you only have them every other weekend. That's when you're not going to the theatre or *Sardinia*—'

'I know, and I'm *not* saying that. She, Daisy . . .'

'How are they affecting Pink— Poppy exactly?'

'Just . . . by being there. It's pretty awkward. Lola hardly speaks to Poppy.'

'Well,' I snap, 'I'm really fucking sorry. What on earth d'you expect? That she'll embrace her as a step-sister?'

He meets my gaze and his eyes looked desperately sad. My own left eyelid is reverberating, as if an insect has landed on it.

'Mummy!' Travis calls from the stairs. 'Where's my hook?'

I tear my eyes away from Martin and try to normalise my voice. 'Probably in your bedroom, sweetie. I'll help you find it in a minute.'

'Cait,' Martin hisses after me, 'I'm not going to do anything. I won't change how things are, with the kids staying with me. They're my priority. I'll make it work out.'

'Yes,' I growl under my breath, 'you bloody will.'

As I embark on Operation Hook Hunt, with Travis making ineffectual forays into his pant and sock drawers, I try to ignore the feeling of dread that Slapper is planning to screw things up between the kids and their father. Whatever I feel about him, they adore him and need their time with him. Where men are concerned, kids are so unblaming. Mine seem to have forgiven him for seamlessly replacing me with Slapper. Martin only has to tell a feeble joke to have the three of them screeching with laughter, as if he warrants a one-man show on the comedy circuit. I suspect that, even if I were capable of fashioning life-sized prehistoric creatures from salt dough, I'd evoke only a lukewarm response.

Martin's role is that of entertainment manager and dispenser of impromptu gifts. Mine is to delve around the dusty pipe at the back of the toilet hunting for lost toys. The Mum-Dad equation is, I feel, horribly unbalanced.

They leave, with Travis scowling through the back window of Martin's car, as if blaming me personally for the disappearance of his hook.

'This is Caitlin, the famous writer.' Darren kisses my hot cheek and beckons me to join his friends at their table in the corner of the bustling pub. I laugh, and he introduces me to each face in turn: fresh-faced boys (not men but *boys*) and girls who undoubtedly read *Elle* and *Glamour*, and wouldn't touch *Bambino* even if they found it abandoned on the train. I'll bet there's not a stretch mark or a thread vein between them.

This is where I want to be – not trapped with Bev Hartnett and her perimenopause.

Drinks are flowing at an impressive pace. Within minutes any smidgen of self-consciousness has ebbed away, and I've stopped fretting about Slapper objecting to our kids' presence, and Jake finding me so objectionable, and the fact that Sam is probably immersed in a passionate deep-throat snoggy scenario with Amelia right now. None of that matters. I feel like Cait, my pre-motherhood self.

A girl with golden streaks running through her chestnut hair bubbles with excitement about her new job as a PA in the City. Her first job; she's just starting out in life. I feel a twang of envy. Another is moving out from her parents' place and in with her boyfriend. 'We're thinking of going for a vintage look,' she announces, 'with one of those cool sixties lamps that curves over in an arc, and maybe beaded curtains.'

I love the frivolity of it all. Lamps and beaded curtains. Not pedal bins and blocked waste pipes. Darren's friends discuss films, music and clubs, and I don't bother to pretend that I'm familiar with a wide array of recreational drugs or have exotic body piercings. I soak it in, temporarily inhabiting a fish-finger-free world. There's no swapping of recipes, no talk of guess-the-stuffed-bunny's-birthday stalls. With Martin showing up so late, I didn't have time to dress up, and now I'm relieved. Everyone is wearing skinny tops and low-slung jeans. Maybe dressing up is something you have to do only when you're starting to crumble around the edges. When you have 'flaws' (magazine-speak) to 'conceal'. Anyway, I feel fine in my faded jeans and baby-blue lambswool sweater.

The Crown is noisy and pleasingly old-fashioned. It's the kind of cosy, unpretentious place that Martin and I frequented during our early years, when we'd left college and taken to throwing occasional sickies from work to spend extra time together. I feel myself slithering towards mild giddiness, as I did during those ever-stretching afternoons.

'I can't believe you have three children, Caitlin,' the PA girl announces. 'I thought you were around the same age as us.'

'It's the lighting in here,' I reply, laughing, not minding that she's lying through her pearly teeth.

As we leave the pub, someone shouts, 'See you again, Caitlin!' I feel ridiculously happy, as if I have left all my worries behind on the Crown's battered oak table.

'So,' Darren says eagerly, 'where to now?'

I like that. The assumption that I needn't scamper home before I turn into a pumpkin.

'We could have a coffee at mine,' I venture. (The old 'coffee' line! Martin used to tease me that the first night he'd come back to my flat, said promised hot beverage had never materialised).

Darren grins, and his fingers curl around mine. His friends have dispersed; it's just us, on a warm, lazy May night. 'That sounds good,' he says.

We don't talk much as we stroll along my road. I steal glances at him; his mouth is full, curved and sensuous, highly kissable. My heart quickens as I remember that I'm wearing a black-and-white spotty bra, mismatched pink knickers and haven't shaved my legs.

Oh, well. Relationships aren't made or broken over stubbly shins.

I fish out my keys at the front door and realise I'm trembling slightly. Will I have the nerve to go through with this? Surely sex is one of those things that you soon get the hang of again – like riding a bike. You're rather wobbly at first, and might fall off and graze yourself, but as far as the basic mechanics go – which bit goes where – I feel reasonably confident that it'll all come flooding back to me. Like helping Jake with his fractions.

No, no. I'm bloody crap at fractions.

Darren touches my face, nudging back a loose strand of hair as I try to stab my key into the lock. Then he kisses me. It's a languid kiss that makes me shiver all over and drop my keys on the flagstone with a clatter. I imagine Mrs Catchpole peering out and sucking in her lips. A mother of three, the youngest of whom often runs about in the garden stark naked. Look at her now, making an exhibition of herself with a man, in full view of our street! That family's gone to the dogs since that nice Martin left.

A rogue thought flashes into my mind as I retrieve my keys. Darren is twenty-five, which means he was *born in the 1980s*. Good God. We step into the house, and I flick on the hall light.

'Ugh,' he says with a shudder.

Damn, this is where it all comes crashing down. I'd looked OK in the corner of the dimly lit pub. Now, faced with the sight of me close up beneath the dazzling bulb, he is sickened.

'What *are* these?' he asks, peering at the bug jars that the kids lined up on the shelf.

'Oh, those.' I laugh, awash with relief. 'They're our pets.'

It happens quickly then. There isn't much chat, and coffee is certainly absent. In fact, the kettle doesn't feature at all. We are kissing on the sofa like teenagers, kissing and kissing with a keenness that I haven't experienced since the early days of Martin and me.

We're undressing each other and I no longer care that my underwear clashes and my shins are bristly and I haven't had the chance to slather my body in extract of papaya, or whatever you're meant to do prior to such an event. Darren's body is lean, lightly muscled, clad only in snow-white briefs.

'Let's go upstairs,' he murmurs.

'Yes,' says the eighteen-year-old that I've become. Desire whirls in my stomach as I stagger up from the sofa, knocking Travis's Playmobil airport from the coffee table on to the floor. We arrive in the hall, holding hands and giggling and shivering slightly.

'Hey, gorgeous,' Darren says, pulling me towards him. His mouth is on mine, tasting beery and faintly cigaretty in a strangely pleasant way. 'You,' he murmurs, 'are so sexy.'

'Come on,' I murmur, tugging his hand, 'let's go up—'

Driiiing!

Jesus, the bloody doorbell. We spring apart.

'Who's that?' I whisper, staring wildly from the front door to Darren, as if he'd have the faintest idea.

Driiiing! *Driiiiiiiiing!*

Shit. Bollocks. I mime, 'Shhh,' with a finger pressed over my mouth. My eyes are bulging, about to pop.

If we stand there, deadly silent, whoever it is will go away.

'Who . . .?' Darren mouths, rubbing his goosepimpled upper arms.

I mime a flamboyant, 'How the hell should I know?' and conceal as much of my body as I can by folding my arms over myself. Trapped in my own hallway, in clashing bra and knickers. A draught sneaks in under the door. Someone is out there, no longer jabbing the doorbell, but waiting.

Someone staggering home pissed from the pub and winding up at the wrong house. Or a burglar casing the joint, as they say on TV. Or the person who sends pubic-hair trimmings to agony aunts.

Or a madman with an axe.

Darren's mouth has tightened, his eyes clouded with exasperation. The commotion that had been going on in his snow-white pants appears to have dwindled to nothing. I feel chilled, and horribly underdressed. In one of the jars, Jake's shiny-backed beetle crawls over a leaf.

Glancing fearfully at Darren, I creep towards the door, trying to silence my breathing as I peer through the spyhole.

It's a hideous thing that looms there, distorted by a fish-eye lens. It stands with its mouth set in a grim line and its eyebrows swooped down in frustration. The draught teases my bare toes.

It's Martin.

22

Something awful has happened. It must be one of the kids. If it was a minor accident or illness, he'd have phoned or dealt with it himself. Martin wouldn't show up like this unannounced.

'Go upstairs,' I hiss at Darren, flapping him away as if he were a wasp. 'My bedroom's first on the right. Go up and be *quiet*.'

He opens his mouth as if to protest, then shrugs and trips lightly upstairs. I watch his white-pant-clad bottom until it disappears into my room.

Slowly, I open the door a few inches and poke my head round it. 'What's happened?' I demand.

'Don't worry, it's nothing terrible,' Martin says distractedly. He takes a step forward as if to come in, but I stop the door with my bare foot.

'So what are you doing here? It's nearly midnight—'

'Aren't you going to let me in?' He knows, I'm certain, that I'm sporting nothing but my ancient pink pants that are losing their elasticity and a spotty bra that's gone bobbly on the cups. I can feel his eyes boring through the three-inch-thick door, mocking me.

'I'm . . . I'm a bit busy right now,' I bluster. 'If it's nothing urgent . . .'

'It's just . . . Travis is really upset. He can't get to sleep without his hook.'

'His *hook*? You've driven over here for that?'

'Yes.' His voice is flat, and faintly accusing. After all, *I* lost the hook. Bad, bad mother.

'You came for a toy? Jesus, Martin! He'd have gone to sleep eventually. You could have given him something else – doesn't Poppy have toys? – or lain down with him until . . .' I tail off as a

particularly rancid image flashes into my mind: Slapper cradling
Travis and saying, 'There, there, darling, Mummy's been silly,
but don't worry, we'll make everything all right . . . Off you go,
Martin, there's a poppet, see if that idiot ex of yours can find it.'

I could vomit right here on my doorstep.

'He *won't* go to sleep,' Martin insists. 'He's beside himself.
Wet the bed and everything.'

'Wasn't he wearing his night-time pants?'

'He was too distraught for night-time pants!'

'Too distraught for night-time pants!' shrieks a boy on the
opposite pavement, and his girlfriend's laughter ricochets down
the street.

'All right,' I snap. 'I'll see if I can find it.'

'Can I come in, for God's sake? It's raining.'

Fine droplets are speckling the shoulders of his suede jacket.

'Just a minute,' I mutter, groping the overloaded coat hooks
for something with which to cover myself. Lola's stripy poncho
drops to the floor. I snatch Jake's despised orange Pac-a-Mac – a
waterproof garment that Bev insisted on donating to us in a
bulging carrier bag of cast-offs, 'Because I imagine times are
pretty hard for you, Caitlin, and you must be stretched finan-
cially.' I pull it over my head and yank it down with difficulty. It's
age nine to ten. It barely covers the gusset of my knickers.
Transmitting a desperate plea to Darren (Please, please stay up
there until Shagpants has gone), I let Martin in.

His mouth twitches with mirth as he appraises my nylon
covering. 'Interesting attire, Cait. Going somewhere special?'

'It's raining,' I mutter.

'Yes, but not inside. It's quite dry in here. Were you about to
have a shower but didn't want to get wet?' The guffaw explodes
out of his nose as he tails me into the living room. It would be no
trouble at all to turn round and slap him. I'm horribly aware that
my arse is sticking out below the Pac-a-Mac.

Martin settles himself on the sofa, his eyes lighting upon the
tumble of clothes strewn all over the floor. Darren's socks are
bunched up, clearly having been pulled off in haste. They are

large, fluffy-soled, obviously man-socks. There's a T-shirt, his jeans, his jacket flung on to the table. Why should I explain? Why?

'Wait here,' I say sternly, 'and I'll have a rummage through the toybox in the kitchen.'

I leg it downstairs, upend the box – 'Can't your children keep their toys in their bedrooms?' Bev once enquired, when she'd barged in and demanded coffee – and rake through the mountain of tat. No hook. A gorgeous, sexy young man waiting upstairs in my bedroom and no fucking hook.

Think. Think. When did Travis last have it? Please, please let him not have left it at Sam's. No, he'd worn it on the way home. I'd pointed out that it would get scratched and ruined if he kept running it along walls, and then it had fallen off and nearly been run over by a car. He'd poked Lola in the bottom with it as we'd come into the house. Then I'd packed the kids' weekend bags, and they'd been squabbling in the kitchen, except . . . Travis had gone out into the garden. That was it. He'd been using it to rake through the soil to find worms. Shit, that means going outside in the dark and the rain – we have no outside light – and stumbling through the borders.

I scan the kitchen for suitable footwear, but all I can find are Lola's size-11 denim sandals with plastic daisies on the front.

Barefoot, I unlock the back door and creep out, squinting into the gloom. My mild drunkenness has worn off, my libido scooted away to find some other woman to attach itself to – a proper grown-up woman who deserves to be pleasured in bed. I tread on something hard and spiky and let out a squeal. It's the tusk of a small plastic elephant. My hair hangs limply around my face, and the damp Pac-a-Mac feels disgusting against my bare flesh.

'Caitlin? Is that you?' A reedy voice wavers over the fence.

'Oh, hello, Mrs Catchpole. I was just, er . . .'

'Isn't it a bit late to be gardening?'

'Yes, ha, ha. I, er, think I left something out here.'

'What is it?' she asks.

'A . . . a hook.'

'A book? What sort of book?'

I sense her raisiny eyes on me, and an unspoken voice: 'For God's sake, woman, where are your trousers? Are you trying to make a spectacle of yourself? Behaviour like this can bring house prices down. This used to be a respectable area, and now look at it. You never flaunted yourself when your husband lived here – that charming young man who screwed the legs on to my flat-pack table.'

Her face juts over the fence like a puppet's. 'Why don't you look for it in the morning?' she suggests.

Why don't you go back inside? I think desperately.

'I, I really need it now.'

'Must be an important book,' she rattles on. 'Is it yours or one of the children's?'

'Mine.' I flash a tight smile, my head flooding with a terrible image of Darren tiring of lying in wait in bed, venturing downstairs in his snow-white pants and coming face to face with Martin in the living room. It would be awkward at first, then there'd be some blokeish hur-hur-ing, and Martin would nip down to fetch some beers.

Darren: 'So you were married to Caitlin?'

Martin: 'Still am, at least legally, ha, ha . . . So, thought your luck was in tonight, did you?'

Darren: 'Yeah, can you believe it? Have you seen what she looks like in that raincoat thing?'

Much hilarity, further cracking open of beers.

How I despise men. All men, Sam included, drifting back to Amelia like an untethered boat.

Trying to blot Mrs Catchpole from my vision (she's wearing a candlewick dressing gown, is she trying to bring on pneumonia or what?), I rummage desperately through straggly lupins and sections of broken toy garage, cursing myself for letting the garden run wild. When Martin was here, it was tidily pruned. He'd spend hours snipping and tweaking, and had started to make noises about acquiring a shed. I plunder a weed-infested hebe, urging the wretched accessory to reveal itself. Is Toys 'R' Us open at this hour? Maybe Martin might consider making an emergency detour.

Then I spot it. A glimmer of silver behind the dwarf rhododendron that Mum donated several years ago, and which has never produced a single flower although it had been *smothered* in blooms in her garden, so I can't have looked after it properly. I snatch the hook and try to wipe it clean on the front of my Pac-a-Mac – it has become *my* Pac-a-Mac – and wave it gaily at Mrs Catchpole before hurtling back into the house.

Martin is standing stiffly in the middle of the living room with his hands clasped behind his back. 'Here.' I jab the hook at him.

'Thank you.' His gaze drops to my bare, muddy feet.

'So you can go now,' I add.

He twitches with the effort of making no further comment. I march to the hall, beyond caring about my appearance, and open the front door for him.

'Caitlin!' comes an eager male voice. 'Are you coming to bed? Has he gone yet?'

I stare up. So does Martin. We both gawp at Darren, who – realising now that we still have company – has frozen, naked, at the top of the stairs.

'Ah,' Martin says.

'Jesus.' Darren slams his hands over his genitals.

'Just . . . just go, Martin,' I mumble, overcome by nausea.

He steps out into the night, clutching the hook, with an infuriating spring to his step. 'Bit young for you, isn't he?' is his parting shot.

I sink on to the bottom stair. No amount of grinding my knuckles into my eye sockets can erase the terrible scene. I'm sweating profusely under the nylon, and my toes are gunked together with mud.

'I assume that's the ex,' Darren says gently, parking himself beside me. Mercifully, he has snatched a towel from a radiator and swathed himself in it.

'Yes, that's Martin.' My voice is emotionless. I could happily stab myself in the heart with Travis's cutlass if that, too, hadn't been lost.

'Come on, don't worry about him. Let's go upstairs.' Darren gives my shoulder a friendly squeeze and kisses my cheek.

'OK,' I say wearily, although the last thing I feel capable of is lashings of energetic sex. We trail upstairs, and I perch on the edge of my bed, trying to summon up a smidge of that lovely tipsiness that had made me feel so sparkly on the walk home. But no – I am utterly sober. *Beyond* sober in fact. My faded bedspread, my pallid legs – everything looks horribly drab, as if we're inhabiting some bleak reality-TV show. Any glimmer of desire whooshed off to another continent the second Martin pressed the bell. Being confronted by his fish-eye face through the spyhole acted like some newfangled sober-up pill.

'Maybe you should wash your feet,' Darren remarks with a chuckle.

'God, yes. Won't be a minute.' I head to the bathroom to de-mud and try to dredge up some saucy thoughts. Sluicing each foot under the bath tap, I flinch under the cold water. There are no saucy thoughts. Nothing. My head's too full of shame to accommodate anything sexy or fun. I attempt to substitute Darren for Sam, but all I can visualise is him marauding his naked ex, which makes me feel even more desolate. It's as if some joker has slammed down a gigantic lever – the kind you find in cobweb-strewn cellars – rendering me sexless, destined to die alone, surrounded by piles of yellowing newspapers.

It wasn't always like this. In the early years of Martin and me, I'd only had to climb into bed with him for my pyjamas to fly off. 'You'd better buy some stronger pyjamas,' he'd joked, and I'd told him that I'd searched London for the strongest pyjamas known to womankind – made from cast iron, impregnated with willpower – but nothing could stop me from wanting him. 'Good,' he'd said, smothering me in kisses.

By the time I return to the bedroom, Darren is reclining, minus towel, on my bed. 'Come here,' he murmurs, patting the space beside him.

'Let me take this thing off,' I murmur, starting to hock the Pac-a-Mac over my head.

'No. No. Keep it on.' He smirks.

'What?' I almost laugh.

'Leave it on. It's kind of . . . sexy.'

'Are you joking? I'm all sweaty inside and—'

'Good,' he growls, beckoning me closer. I sit awkwardly beside him, and a hand worms up the front of the Pac-a-Mac. We start kissing, and I try to relax, but all I can hear are the amplified sounds of rustling nylon. My head fills with Pac-a-Mac thoughts – of camping, trying to put up the tent and blow up the airbeds and ripping the foot pump. I pull away and turn my back on him.

'Hey,' he says softly.

'I'm sorry, Darren. This doesn't feel right.'

He runs a finger down the back of my neck. 'Relax, Caitlin. You're so pretty, you know. I've always liked –' he clears his throat '– older women.'

Older women? I swing round to face him. He wants to sleep with me because I'm *older*? 'What do you mean?' I ask weakly.

'Older women. I just like older women.' He tries the neck-stroking thing again, but I shrink away.

Jesus. Maybe I should be flattered, but it doesn't seem right – like being found attractive because you're a size 24 or a dwarf or something. It feels *freakish*. When men make lustful noises about 'mature' women, they're usually referring to Joanna Lumley or Susan Sarandon, but I am barely of the same species.

I am Caitlin Brown, clammy from the Pac-a-Mac, with the tops of my thighs sticking together.

'You older women,' Darren continues, his eyes glazing alarmingly, 'really turn me on. You're experienced, you've been around, you know your onions.'

Oh, save me.

'You've seen *life* . . .'

Hot breath gusts into my ear, and an arm slides round my waist.

'Darren,' I announce, scrambling up from the bed, 'I think you should go home.'

23

The instant he's gone, I rip off the Pac-a-Mac, scrunch it into a ball and fling it across the room. My entire upper body is pink and clammy. The zip has left a livid imprint on my décolleté.

I storm through to the bathroom. Usually, I let the shower gush for a few moments, only stepping in when it's steamy and hot. Tonight, to punish myself for supreme idiocy, I barge right in, shuddering as the icy water hits my body. Twithead woman, thinking I can possibly have a normal social life – a sex life, dammit – like just about everyone else on earth. I shower for ages, trying to sluice away my anger and mortification. It doesn't work. Not even my lilac-scented body-wash raises my spirits, because it can't wash out my head.

I picture normal people's fun Friday nights: Sam and Amelia, squished up close on his velvety sofa, reminiscing about their early years, when they were still happy, still a family, and mulling over whether it might be possible to have all of that again; Martin returning with Travis's hook (all hail Superdad!) and making Daisy wet her fancy knickers with laughter over my Pac-a-Mac display; Millie and some man in advertising whom she met in a bar last week, tottering around Soho, enjoying London, enjoying *life*; Darren arranging to meet friends at a club and telling them, amidst much hilarity, how it went arse over tit with that older woman with the Stone Age TV; even Rachel, cosied up with gingery Guy after a hard day's baking; even my *mother*, for crying out loud, oblivious to the world beyond Mimosa House as she wanders the corridors, stopping to chat with the night-shift girls; the whole of London, relishing its Friday night. And me, worn out and faded, like a T-shirt after too many washes.

I pull on my dressing gown, make a mug of strong tea in the kitchen and glare into its depths. It's 1.15 a.m. From outside comes a mass giggle as a crowd of young people head home – or, worse, are just setting out. Too depressed to contemplate sleep, I wonder what to do with myself. This is, after all, my child-free weekend, supposedly offering limitless potential for fun. What would I choose to do more than anything? I picture Sam and me lying on a damp blanket watching shooting stars and quickly bat the image away.

Rachel once confided that whenever she can't sleep, she gets up and batch-cooks an entire week's worth of meals. I could do that. Whip up a pasta sauce or a stack of tuna fishcakes while everyone else in this city is getting drunk and dancing and copping off with each other. I could make a fucking marinade. Perhaps I could saw off my own humiliated head and marinate that.

I could, if I so desired, rifle through the drinks cupboard and have myself a party. Who needs other people to have fun? I yank open the cupboard door and glare in. Disappointingly, there's only weird stuff in there that no one ever drinks, like Kahlua and Noilly Prat, which Martin insisted on buying in duty-free for the drinks parties we never had. Anyway, glugging such concoctions would surely lead to a vomiting/passing-out/stomach-pump situation – a level to which even I, in my wretched state, have no wish to plummet.

Whatever I choose to do, I will not sit hunched over the computer at 1.27 a.m. like some tragic Nora-No-Mates. I will not check my emails with a desperate gleam in my eye. NO emails. NO computer. I am a strong thirty-five-year-old mother of three, in charge of my own destiny.

I log on. Nothing. Not a damn thing. Even R thinks I'm a laughing stock, and he's not even a real person.

No readers' emails either. They've figured that I'm a phoney and have sent their woes to Dorothy Hindman at *Your Baby and Toddler* magazine.

Maybe my connection is down, or there's some blockage in

the wire, like the time Lola used flannels to wipe her bottom and
the Dyno-Rod man had to clear the obstruction in our pipe.

Bing! An email pops in. I click on it hungrily:

> Worried about the loss of erection? EVEN if you have no
> erection problem, buy CIALIS to bring back romantic
> moments that u lost in past. CIALIS! Make your lovemaking
> incradible today. Ladyes will say thank you! Visit now for
> 70% discount oofer!

I scowl at the screen. What the hell is this stuff? Some kind of
plant extract, or one of those pumping devices that can supposedly increase a penis's length and girth? I am an agony aunt. I'm
supposed to know this stuff. Whatever it is, it seems to have an
unfortunate effect on the part of the brain responsible for
spelling things correctly.

I Google Cialis and learn that it is, in fact, an almond-shaped
pill to counteract erectile dysfunction, and that thirty pills can be
whizzed to my home address – 'in discreet packaging' – for
$395.

Why am I reading this tripe? I don't even *own* a penis, let alone
one that malfunctions. At least that's one thing I don't have to
worry about. Another email pings in:

> Tired with flakid penis?
> Want sex all night long?
> Girls don't love u no more?
> No need doctor forget problems now! Viagra shipped to
> you direct!!!!!

More sex! It's everywhere you look. You can't leave the house
without being confronted with some snogging couple who look
as if they've either just done it or are pelting home to disrobe as
soon as humanly possible. It's a wonder anyone gets any work
done. Even Sam is getting some, a factlet that could well propel
me towards the Noilly Prat were it not for another email that
pings my way:

Hi, Cait,
Well, it's nearly two in the morning and here I am, sitting at
my PC after a pretty disastrous date. I hope you don't mind
if I share it with you.

Please do. More sex talk is precisely what I need right now.

It was arranged by a friend who seems to have got it into his
head that I need 'fixing up', as if I'm a leaky roof. So off I
went to meet this girl – let's call her S – and she's drop-dead
gorgeous. Long, fair hair . . .

So R fancies blondes. Zzz.

. . . with an amazing sexy mouth and big blue eyes.

I consider switching off the PC and trying that head-marinat-
ing thing instead. Would it fit into our biggest salad bowl, I
wonder?

Anyway, things start off well enough. Bit of chat, filling in
our backgrounds – you know the kind of thing.

Actually, I don't. What I like to do on a date is prance about in
age nine-to-ten rainwear with my arse hanging out.

So, after a couple of hours, I ask her back for coffee.

Two hours? Fast work, mister.

Which she does. Things are going nicely when she starts
wandering around my living room, which is pretty
dishevelled, as you can imagine, and says, 'Hmm, I wouldn't
have gone for the cold palette in here, not with that north-
facing window. I'd have chosen honey tones to bring in
some warmth.'
    I hadn't realised I'd gone for the cool palette, or even that
I had a north-facing window. By now she's started touching
the curtains, which are too heavy and opaque, apparently – I
should have gone for a lighter texture and tone. And while
doing this, she's saying, 'I can see that you have a storage

problem,' while eyeing Billy's towering stack of videos and DVDs. I start thinking, I just want you to go home. Please. Now. I don't want to talk about cold palettes or have you tweaking my curtains and scrunching your pretty little nose up. I don't even want to go to bed with you.

I start to feel old, Cait. Old and past it. We have a little kiss, but it's going nowhere. It's a bloody disaster. I feel wooden and stiff, and not in a good way. Can you believe what I do next?

Please, please don't tell me what you got up to in bed. I can't bear it.

I feign a migraine. Jacqui, my ex, used to have them so I know the drill: blinding pain, needing quiet and darkness. 'I'm so sorry,' I tell her, 'but I'm going to have to call you a cab.'

'Ice cream's good for migraines!' my lunatic date announces, barging through to the kitchen and rummaging in the freezer. No ice cream. 'Not very organised, is it?' she shouts. 'There are sausages out of their packet and loose peas everywhere . . . Ooh, look, here's an Arctic roll. I suppose it's better than nothing.' She brings it out, peels off the spongy layer and forces me to eat the ice-cream middle.

Despite my blinding headache – which is genuine now – I manage to phone a taxi and deposit her in it. And that's it. Thanks for listening, Cait. It's so good just knowing you're there.

R x

I smile, flooded with warmth. Actually, I feel all right again. Almost *normal*. Sipping my tepid tea, I tap out a condensed version of my own debacle. His reply is almost instant:

God, Cait, I'd never thought of anything you'd buy in those outdoor shops having erotic appeal. I'm not really the outdoorsy sort myself – tried camping once, with Billy, and woke up in what I can only describe as a small lake at our feet. (The only time I went to Glastonbury, I booked into a B&B.) Anyway, better luck next time! You deserve it. I'm sorry, but Darren is obviously a dickhead.

R x

P.S. Would you like to meet for coffee sometime?

I stare at the last line. Coffee? No big deal. At least, not compared with parading myself in tangerine nylon and having Mrs Catchpole scowling at my crotch.

It's just *coffee*, isn't it? Just hot, brown liquid. Nothing to flip out about. It's not 'Let's pretend hot beverages will be involved when we're really just going to bed.'

Then I remember Millie's warnings about cling-filmed pubes and how I mustn't get into any personal stuff. I type:

Sorry, but life is pretty hectic at the moment, and I don't think it's a good idea to meet up. If it's OK with you, I would prefer for us to remain email buddies.

C x

The cursor dithers over the 'send' icon. Taking a deep breath, I zap it to him. There. For once in my life, I have taken the sensible option. It's something to be proud of – like writing everyone's names in indelible pen in their gym shoes, or washing out the salad 'crisper' from the fridge. Mature, grown-up. Something I have always aspired to be. Like Rachel, with her model child and home-made tagliatelle.

I should be proud of myself. So why do I wish I could snatch back my email and scream, 'Yes'?

24

It's a blustery, hair-flappy morning when Jake's teacher bustles towards me across the playground.

'I was hoping to catch you,' Miss Race says breathlessly. 'Could you pop in for a quick chat? It's nothing serious.' Her forehead creases ominously.

'Of course,' I say, aware that 'nothing serious' actually means 'This is very bad.' It's like hearing, 'My trousers are wet,' or, 'I think I have nits,' but worse.

Most of the children are inside school. Stragglers are clumping towards the main door, seemingly unconcerned about late marks. Miss Race clomps ahead across the playground, her dark hair pulled back severely and secured with a glossy black claw. Her name, conjuring images of a sleek thoroughbred horse, is all wrong for her. I shuffle in behind her, clutching Travis by the hand, praying that she's not going to bring up Jake's head injury again and suggest that we're put on some kind of register. His verrucas have gone. We have single-handedly tripled sales of verruca lotion. I could fetch him from his classroom, strip off his socks and prove it.

She beckons us into the office, where one of the teaching assistants – face the colour of cod, looks about nine years old – is operating the rumbling photocopier.

'It's, um, about Jake,' Miss Race begins hesitantly.

'Right!' I say, too eagerly, as if it could possibly be anything else. Great. A brain-juddering discussion about my son's behavioural difficulties with this whey-faced teenager listening in.

'I know things have been . . . tricky at home,' she continues, 'and it's been an unsettling time for him.'

How I hate my marriage break-up being referred to in such

foggy terms: 'situation at home', 'unsettling time'. It's no better than describing a child as having 'anger issues' when he's just an aggressive little squirt.

'Has something . . . happened?' I ask.

She smiles benignly. 'He's normally such a good, cooperative boy.'

Please just spit it out. Travis plunges a hand into a jar of multicoloured paperclips on the desk.

Miss Race clears her throat. 'His behaviour has been rather challenging lately. There was an incident yesterday.'

I nod, trying to drag my gaze away from the blueish vein on her neck. She is what my mother would call 'heavyset', and today is wearing a moss-green blouse and pleated fawn trousers. I didn't think they made trousers like that any more.

'We have a magnetic board in the classroom,' she continues, 'with the letters of the alphabet, and what you do is stick them on to the board to make words.'

Jesus, shouldn't Jake's year have progressed from such basic activities? Miss Race is holding him back, I'm sure of it. Last term's topic seemed to focus on the importance of washing hands before touching food, and he kept bringing home ridiculously simple reading books. In any other class, he'd be fluent in Russian by now.

'Jake took it upon himself to come in at breaktime,' she barges on, 'and arrange the letters to form a . . . an *inappropriate* word.'

The assistant collects her papers together noisily and flits out of the room. Travis upends the paperclip jar and they scatter all over the desk.

'Which word?' I ask, trying to gather them up.

'A . . . er . . . a bad word.'

'*Which* bad word?' I'm losing patience now.

Travis bats away my hands and carefully drops the paperclips back into the jar. Good boy. At least one of my children hasn't skidded off the rails.

'It was –' Miss Race flicks her gaze towards the office door, in case a child might be lurking there and keel over at the horror of it all – 'the worst one,' she hisses. 'The one . . . we never say.'

'What does it begin with?' Now I feel ludicrous.

'Mumble, mumble,' she says, flushing pink.

'Sorry?'

'Um . . . "f".'

'Uh?'

'It was the F-word. F-U-C-K.'

Deep inside me, a ball of laughter begins to form. Please, God, don't let it burst out. Don't have me snorting hysterically as if I think it's big or clever. I try to focus on bad things, like Mum escaping from the home, and children in poor countries with no clean water to drink.

'Was that it?' I ask. 'Just . . . just the F-word?'

She nods tersely.

'I'll talk to him,' I say, tugging Travis away from the photocopier buttons.

'I'd be very grateful. Jake might use that sort of language at home, but it's not appropriate for school.'

'Of course he doesn't talk like that at home,' I snap. 'I wouldn't allow it.'

'Well, he's picking it up from somewhere.' She gives me a sly look.

'Children hear bad language everywhere – in the street, on TV . . .' Shut up, you ruddy great berk, going straight on the defensive.

'Not before the watershed they don't.' Miss Race sets her lips primly. 'In fact, Jake explained that you say it. I asked him where he learned it and he said, "Mummy." '

'He said I taught him to swear? You really believe that?' Travis is gawping at me. Watching his mother losing it in the poky school office is proving far more entertaining than any photocopier.

'Well,' she says with a wry chortle, 'I did think that was rather far-fetched. And, as I said, it's nothing serious. We just like to keep lines of communication open. I thought you'd want to know.'

'Yes, I do. I'm very grateful. Thank you.' I grip Travis's hand and bid Miss Race farewell, gritting my teeth. Travis's parting gesture is to stab at the photocopier, setting it whirring into action. Lights flash and its innards rumble, as if chortling over my family's shame.

My day takes a surprise turn for the better when Sam and Harvey come round after school. 'Hi, Sam,' I say.

'Cait, I'd like you to meet Amelia.' Sam grins, and his ex-wife shimmers into focus behind him. I note with a start that her arm is casually slung round Harvey's shoulders. Heck, why shouldn't it be? She's his *mother*.

'Hi, come in. Lovely to meet you,' I gush in a strained voice.

'I've heard so much about you,' Amelia says warmly. She has a broad, beaming smile and swathes of corn-coloured hair. Pretty doesn't do her justice.

'Yes, you too,' I manage.

She follows me into the house, stepping gingerly over Travis's train track on the living-room floor. I have accepted that she and Sam are on the verge of getting back together. I've imagined myself at their re-marriage ceremony, wearing a sombre dress and a brave smile.

'Your children are just as lovely as Sam described,' she adds.

Jake turns round from the TV and frowns. Lola beams delightedly.

'We were wondering,' Sam says hesitantly, 'if you'd all like to come out for dinner. Just a cheapie Indian.'

'Oh, Mummy, please!' Lola implores, equating Indian with her beloved jewel-coloured rice. They want me to sit in a restaurant with Sam's beautiful, skinny-hipped ex-wife, soon-not-to-be ex.

I'm not sure I can do this and act normal. 'Um, I was planning to do sausage and mash . . .'

'Aw, we *never* have Indian,' adds Swearing Supremo Jake, as if every other child on the planet is treated to sumptuous Asian cuisine on a daily basis.

'We went on your birthday,' I remind him.

'Yeah, like in November.' He rolls his eyes dramatically.

'It was my idea,' Amelia explains. 'With Harvey and Jake being such good friends, I wanted to meet you all properly. Our treat.'

Right. So they *are* a couple again. 'OK,' I say brightly, 'that'd be lovely.' Dinner with just Sam and the kids would be lovelier, but I shoo the thought away. Anyway, I could do without cooking after my Miss Race encounter (a matter that I still need to broach with the accused).

By a stroke of good fortune, we choose a restaurant where the children are warmly welcomed and Travis is given a cushion to boost him to table-height. I sit opposite Sam and Amelia, which feels rather interview panel-ish. There's no denying how sparkly they are with each other, which twists my insides somewhat.

'Remember my mum,' Amelia says, snapping off fragments of poppadum, 'and that row with Dad over the naan bread?'

'When he draped it over the arm of the sofa?' Sam says.

'And she'd made the curry, and Dad kept asking what kind of meat was in it—'

'And she told him, "It's *meat* meat," ' Sam concludes, laughing.

Amelia tears her gaze away from Sam and looks at me. 'Sorry, Caitlin. It's really rude – all this reminiscing.'

'No, that's OK,' I say quickly. My napkin has fallen off the table, but I don't dare to retrieve it, in case I catch Sam and Amelia playing footsie, or her hand snaking up his thigh.

'Mum,' Jake barks, 'you're not listening.'

'Sorry, sweetheart, what did you say?'

Sam flicks a poppadum crumb from Amelia's chin.

'I said, why did Miss Race want to see you this morning?'

I narrow my eyes at him. 'How d'you know?'

'Josh Haines went past the office. He saw you in there with Travis and you were looking really mad.'

Damn and blast. For some reason Amelia seems to have warmed to me. I'd rather she didn't learn about my substandard parenting skills just yet. 'We'll discuss it later,' I murmur.

'Mum, she's my *teacher*. I need to know what's going on.'

'OK,' I say, aware of Amelia's gaze, 'she said you rearranged the plastic letters on the board to make a bad word.'

He snorts and a few grains of rice shoot from his mouth. 'That wasn't me.'

'She seemed certain, Jake. Said you'd snuck in during break—'

'It wasn't me!' he cries. 'She blames me for everything – she's got it in for me.'

'Stop lying,' I hiss.

'It wasn't fucking me!'

'*Jake!*'

'Hey,' Amelia cuts in deftly, 'that's nothing compared to the trouble I got into at school. Want to know what I did?'

'Yeah,' he mumbles, crunching a poppadum angrily.

She grins and her cheeks dimple prettily. 'I started a swearing academy behind the sports hall.'

'What's a swearing candy?' Lola asks eagerly.

'Academy,' Jake corrects her. 'So what did you do?'

Amelia laughs. 'It's not clever, OK, and I don't want any of you copying this, but I was banned from the school trip to York because of it.' She leans forward and the children move closer, drawn in by her mischievous grin. 'It was a school of bad words.'

'Cool,' Jake breathes.

'A group of us used to meet up at break,' Amelia continues. 'I'd hand out lists of bad words and we'd practise saying them in different combinations.'

'Mum!' Harvey guffaws.

'That's when your toilet mouth started,' Sam teases.

'And because of that,' she concludes, 'I never got to make brass rubbings of Roman remains, or whatever it was they got up to.'

Everyone sniggers and the mood lifts. I'm astounded at how she's defused the tension. Despite her girlie flutterings around Sam, I actually like her – not only for her swearing academy, but her astounding appetite. The only person I've been to dinner with recently is Millie. Her habit of discussing the GI indexes of our various foodstuffs, or some amazing regime consisting of nothing but water with a dusting of cinnamon, tends to kill my appetite stone dead. Amelia has wolfed a naan the size of an oven glove and, besides her own lamb jalfrezi, is now attacking the remains of Sam's balti. Snacking from a lover's plate. How very intimate. A lump forms in my throat, and I gulp it down.

I will Amelia to go to the loo, and try to transmit extra-sensory messages to make her need it urgently. She stays put, laughing and picking at poppadum crumbs from Sam's plate. I crave just a few moments alone with him, to establish precisely what's going on – not that it would be possible to talk surrounded by kids' waggling ears. Amelia is astoundingly beautiful; why has Sam never shared that minor detail? I'd seen photos of her – he gave me a whistle-stop tour of his former life in the form of a chunky-paged photo album – but in these pictures she looked wispy and insipid. She is radiant now in her embroidered cotton top with her hair falling loosely around her face. Her only embellishment is a dainty turquoise pendant. Bet she doesn't require ten de-mothering steps, or blunder about in her garden with her gusset out.

'So, Caitlin,' she says, 'Sam tells me you're a writer.'

'Well, only in a piddling, part-time kind of way.'

'Nothing like building yourself up, is there?' she laughs.

I shrug. 'It doesn't feel like a proper job. My only regular work is the problem page in *Bambino*, a parenting magazine – you've probably never heard of it.'

'The one where the babies wear cashmere?'

'That's the one.'

Sam, I notice, is gazing at her, drinking her in.

'That's quite a responsibility,' Amelia says. 'I mean, giving the wrong advice could mess up someone's life . . .'

'It does feel scary sometimes, although I'm sure some people think I just bash out replies in between cooking the kids' tea and running their baths.'

'What happens to the letters you get? I imagine you can't print them all.'

'God, no, there are hundreds. With the leftovers –' I shuffle uncomfortably '– I, um, stuff them into a cupboard in the hall, and I'm trying to . . . well, I'm trying to answer as many as I can.'

Sam bursts out laughing. 'You never told me you do that.'

'What else can I do? Throw them out as if they're junk?'

Amelia shrugs. 'That sounds perfectly sensible to me. You

know what a hoarder I am, Sam. Can't bear to throw anything away.' She darts him a meaningful look.

'Oh, yeah.' He rolls his eyes, laughing her off. 'It just seems a bit excessive, Cait. Beyond the call of duty. I mean, you're not being paid to do that, are you? How d'you find the time?'

'It doesn't take that long,' I protest.

'*Liar*,' Sam's look says. He pushes back tousled hair and meets my gaze.

'Well,' Amelia declares, 'I think it's admirable, Caitlin. You obviously care about these people.'

She's not entirely right. I have other, more selfish reasons. Ploughing through *Bambino* mail stops me dwelling on Martin and Slapper and, more crucially, Sam and Amelia. There's nothing like a sackload of mail to make you feel, well, *needed*. Even if it can't give you a cuddle or massage your feet.

The evening passes with all of us crunching aniseed sweets and not wanting to leave, even though the kids are splattered with rice and sauce and it's way past Travis's bathtime. Harvey looks more contented than I have ever seen him. It's as if he has found the missing piece to complete his jigsaw. What kind of embittered old trout would I be not to want his parents to be together?

We finally part company at the end of my street. My family and Sam's, feeling suddenly separate. 'Well, Caitlin,' Amelia says, 'it was lovely to meet you.'

'You too,' I say.

'I hope I'll see lots more of you and your kids. They're a real credit to you.' She smiles warmly and for the first time this evening I sense a twist of unease. She's almost too friendly, as if she's taken a course in niceness.

'Thanks,' I manage.

Amelia grips Sam's hand territorially. They turn away, and as they head towards Sam's road I'm tempted to sneak a look to see if they are still holding hands, or if Harvey is between them, forming a chain of three.

Summoning every ounce of willpower, I stride home with my gang, and I don't look back.

25

To prevent my mind from wandering towards Sam-and-Amelia territory, I whip through the witching hour – bath, stories, bed – making Jake's room my final stop, despite my recent barring.

'Jake,' I venture from the doorway, 'I'm not going to make a big deal out of this . . .'

He is propped up in bed with a fantasy novel and one pyjama-clad leg straggling out from under the duvet. 'Out of what?' he asks, flicking his gaze up at me.

I inhale deeply. 'The magnetic-letters thing. You know – in your classroom. I'd just like to know what made you . . . why you thought it might be a good idea.'

'It was a joke,' he says slowly.

'Well, it wasn't very funny.'

'God,' he says, exasperated, as if my gentle probing is akin to relentless interrogation involving dazzling lights and thumb-screws. 'It's not a big deal,' he adds witheringly.

'I'm not saying it is, but it was obviously a big enough deal for Miss Race to summon me into her office, wasn't it?'

'That's her problem,' he snaps.

'No it isn't. It's our problem, Jake, and we need to talk about it.'

'Mummy!' Lola's voice spears across the landing. 'Why are you shouting?'

Hell, I hadn't even realised I was. A lovely evening out, with the curry and everything, trashed by my temper. Amelia would never do this.

'Wish I lived with another family,' Jake growls into his book.

'What did you say?'

'I said I wish I had another family. A family that's not always arguing.'

I scowl at him. 'What d'you mean exactly? Do you have a particular family in mind?'

'Yeah. Sam and Amelia and Harvey.'

I can't believe he's saying this. Clearly, he has forgotten that Amelia doesn't live with her son. At least, not at the moment. Perhaps, when you're cool enough to have established a swearing academy, certain minor details don't matter.

'You do know that Sam and Amelia are divorced, don't you?' I snap. 'They split up years ago, before Harvey started school, so they can't get on *that* well—'

'Yeah, but—' he cuts in.

'They're not perfect, Jake,' I charge on. 'No one is. You might look at them and think, isn't their life great, and aren't they all smiley and happy with a mum who ran a swearing academy, but you don't *know*.' Oh, shit. These are his best friend's parents. Book me in for a brain transplant.

'They *do* get on,' he growls. 'They must do 'cause they're getting remarried.'

I peer at Jake through the gloom. His air of smugness suggests that he knows how this makes me feel, that he can decipher my untoward Sam-thoughts. 'How . . . how d'you know?' I ask, trying to steady my voice.

'Harvey said.'

'Are you sure?'

'Yeah.' He grins savagely. 'They're gonna have a big party like that actor and actress in the olden days that married each other eight times.'

I smile, despite wishing to plunge myself through Jake's bedroom window and land in a mangled heap on the pavement. 'I think you mean Richard Burton and Elizabeth Taylor. And they were only married twice.'

He shrugs. 'Whatever.'

Deep breath. Don't lose it. Don't exhibit any emotion whatsoever. 'Well,' I chirp, 'that's good news, isn't it? Harvey must be delighted. When are they having the wedding?'

'Really soon.' He's gloating, I swear.

'Great! I do love weddings. Remember Uncle Adam's with that party in the big marquee? Wasn't that fun?'

'Yeah, except Daddy was late and you had an argument in front of everybody and you cried.'

'Um, yes . . .'

'And then Uncle Adam and Auntie what's-her-name . . .'

'Cathy.'

'They got divorced. Why does everyone get divorced?'

'They don't,' I say briskly. 'There are lots of happy marriages. There's, um . . .' My brain empties itself of all logical thought. 'There's . . . Rachel and Guy. Bev and thingy. *Lots* of people. Want me to switch off your light now, or are you reading for a bit longer?'

'Reading,' Jake mutters. The look he throws me causes me to back away and hurry downstairs. This isn't right. I am the adult here: *I* should be in charge. Yet sometimes he reminds me of those small, yappy dogs that nip at your ankles and shins.

Dear Caitlin,

My first letter of the night shift reads:

> Is it normal for young children to use bad language? My six-year-old son seems to have fallen into a habit of it – not constantly, but enough to worry me and his father and for his friends' parents to comment on it. (At a recent birthday party, he announced that the jelly was 'shit'.)

I smile, reassured that I'm not the only mother with a potty-mouthed child. Aren't *I* supposed to make the *readers* feel better? Isn't this happening the wrong way round?

The writer continues:

> I'm worried that we must be doing something dreadfully wrong. We don't pepper our everyday conversations with

expletives, but occasionally the odd bad word shoots out. I'd be grateful for any advice you can offer.

Ashamed Mum, Bristol

Dear Ashamed,
Your son's ears are as receptive as satellite dishes, his brain a remarkable filing cabinet for the storage of bad words. Please don't beat yourself up for spouting the odd rude word yourself. Your little boy would still be exposed to expletives in the playground and while out and about.

Granted, some people take great exception to this. I did hear of one family who banned Raymond Briggs's *Father Christmas* in their house, due to the overuse of the word 'bloomin' – as in 'another bloomin' Christmas'. An overreaction perhaps. However, I do appreciate your concern. No one wants their child asking why there are no effing Horrid Henry books at the library. Plus, bad words take on greater weight and significance when they fall from the mouths of babes.

Miss Race, in her moss-coloured blouse, shimmers before me like a spectre.

Explain to your son that grown-ups often find these words upsetting, and that using them may result in fewer playdate and party invitations. But don't blow it up into some international incident. We all know the allure of forbidden fruit.

That'll do for tonight. Maybe Sam's right: wading through leftover angst is beyond the call of duty. A dumpee's way of filling the empty small hours. I'll just read one more email, and only because it's headed 'PLEASE, PLEASE READ THIS'.

Dear Caitlin,
I am emailing you as I have no one else to turn to. Things haven't been good lately. I know a lot of it is my fault, in that I have not always been supportive about the children

coming here for weekends. Having an only child who
stretches me to the limit sometimes, I fear that my parenting
skills are sorely lacking and at times find it hard to cope.

I thought that things would improve when we moved into
the new flat with the extra bedroom, but if anything, they
have become worse. I know Martin feels—

Martin. Will I ever be able to encounter that name without
shuddering? I read on.

I know Martin feels tremendous guilt at what he has put you
and the children through. It's something he seems unable to
reconcile. He wants them to feel happy in our home and feels
that I don't support him, when I am trying my very best.

I blink at the screen, rigid in my chair. The fridge growls
ominously.

You're probably shocked that I'm emailing you out of the
blue when we have barely spoken. The truth is, I don't know
what else to do. I don't have many friends that I can turn
to. Many of them disapproved when I got together with
Martin, and I know that our relationship has caused a great
deal of pain. And I admire you, Caitlin. You seem so
together and sorted, and have remained dignified
throughout.

I could slam my fist through the PC. That would be dignified. I
could fling the sea-monkey tank at the wall, if it wouldn't cause
mass death.

Daisy ploughs on:

I know what you must think of me. Poppy's father has never
been part of her life. He, too, was a married man, so I know
how hard it is to bring up a child alone and the pressures we
single mums have to deal with.

Another married man! Ah, a theme emerges. A vein throbs in my
neck. So she knows, does she, what it's like to be barred from

your own son's bedroom? How it feels to be caught by your self-satisfied ex in a child-sized Pac-a-Mac? Perhaps I should pity her. It must be terribly hard trying to go about your business, advising customers at bottle-changeover time, when your clothes have a habit of flying off and you accidentally find yourself having sex.

> Anyway, I thought you might be able to have a chat to
> Martin and let him know, in your understanding away, that
> I am perfectly happy about your children's visits, and that if
> I seem tense, it's due to my own inadequacies. Sometimes
> it's so helpful to have a mediator in these circumstances,
> isn't it? And you do a remarkable job in *Bambino*.
> Many thanks for reading this, Caitlin. I'd like to smooth
> things out and see Martin much happier before Jake comes
> to live with us permanently.
> Regards,
> Daisy

Permanently? Is this some kind of sick joke? She really believes that Jake wants to live at the love nest? My heart thuds furiously. How dare she concoct this crap about my son? If Miss Race could hear the bad words whirling inside me, her head would spin off like a frisbee. Jake, residing with Slapper. My darling son, forbidden from sitting on Poppy's chair, and sharing roof-space with 8,000 My Little Ponies. I would rather gouge out my eyes than allow it.

I formulate a considered reply.

> Dear Daisy,
> Thank you so much for your email. Please accept my
> heartfelt sympathy that things have gone rather cock-eyed
> between you and Martin. Have his piles put in a
> reappearance? They do tend to make him rather irritable, as
> I remember only too well during a holiday in Scotland. Shall
> I dig out some info on creams and suppositories from my
> vitalworld.com file and forward it to you? In the meantime,

ask him to tell you about the time the doctor shone a torch
up his arse and said, 'You have a beautiful specimen up
there, Mr Collins.'

As for Jake moving in with you . . .

My fingers grind to a halt. I glower at her email. Creepy phrases
like 'a great deal of pain' judder before my eyes. *I* could show her
what pain's like.

'Mummy!' comes Travis's cry from his room, but I can't get
up from my chair, can't go to him.

Slapper. How I hate her.

'Mummy!' There's a scrambling on the stairs as Travis pelts
down to the kitchen. 'I fell out of bed!' he roars.

I open my arms and pull him close. His cheeks are hot and
damp from crying. 'Oh, sweetheart. Are you OK now? Did you
bump yourself?'

'Yeah. No. I rolled under the bed and couldn't get out. It was
dark.'

I lift him on to my knee and stroke his moist hair, this child
who would no more try to hitchhike to Greece than be parted
from me. This is how it should be. The way children should
regard their mothers, instead of acquiring crazy urges for the
superior facilities at their father's flat.

'Want to sleep in the big bed with me tonight?' I ask gently.

'Yeah,' he murmurs. His fine hair smells sweet, like vanilla
cookies.

'Hang on. I'll finish this and we'll go up.' I delete my juvenile
rant and shut down the computer.

Travis rides upstairs on my hip, even though he's too heavy
these days for this mode of transport. I tuck him into Martin's side
of the bed before changing into PJs and slipping in beside him.

Travis makes my anger fade away, just by being here, breathing into my face. The third child, whose conception we hadn't
planned, and which Martin had been distinctly put out by, but
who greeted the world with an exuberance that had gripped my
heart.

Occasionally, I wonder if Martin would have succumbed to Slapper's charms if we'd stopped at two children. Weighing them up – Travis and a huge, farting adult male – there's really no contest. I lie awake for a while watching him sleep, figuring that life can't be so bad when someone needs you this much. And I start to feel almost lucky. Kids aside, I have a decent-ish home and a job that's grown on me unexpectedly, like an inherited pot plant. I'm not a deranged water-cooler-maintenance girl. My breasts may be lacking in perkiness, but at least I do have a brain, of sorts.

As for Slapper's suggestion that Jake might move out, I've decided on a more concise response, which I shall fire off first thing.

Over my dead body.

Martin looks dashingly handsome as he strides into the steamy café the following morning. Handsome, that is, if you're attracted to chunky six-footers with deep brown eyes and a caramel tan. The girl at the counter, who's dropping marshmallows into tall mugs of hot chocolate, beams an eager smile. I nod curtly as he eases his way between the cramped tables towards mine.

'Cait, what's happened? What's so urgent?' He drops on to the opposite chair.

'Want a coffee or something?' I ask.

'I'll go up and order in a minute.' No need. The girl has whooshed to his side, despite the sign that reads, 'PLEASE ORDER AT COUNTER. THANK YOU.'

'Anything I can get you?' she asks.

'Um, just a latte, please.'

'Can I bring you a cookie or a muffin with that?'

Can I climb on to your lap and attach my lips to your face with that?

'No, just a coffee, thanks.' He smiles wearily and turns back to me. 'Is this going to take long? I really should be at work. There's a client presentation in half an hour . . .'

'You'd better read this.' I hand him the printed-off email.

His eyes cloud as he scans it. 'For fuck's sake. I can't believe she sent this. I'm really sorry, Cait. You shouldn't be involved.'

He barely acknowledges the waitress as she places the coffee before him. I sip mine, which is tepid now. In the sugary warmth of the café, with the kids deposited at school and nursery, I am a model of calm. I deserve a Most Controlled Being Award. A Well Done for Not Losing It certificate, like the architectural awards on the pale-grey walls of Martin's office.

Still reading, he shakes his head despairingly. 'I suppose she thinks you're a *real* agony aunt.'

'Read the last bit. Where she says Jake wants to . . .' My voice splinters.

Martin glances up at me, then scans Daisy's final lines. 'Oh, God, Cait . . .'

'Is it true? Is this what he wants?' My nose starts running and I blow it distractedly on a paper napkin.

Martin places the printout on the speckled table and reaches for my hand. I let him hold it. I don't flinch or pull away. He looks at me the way the old Martin used to, before exasperation and smugness poisoned everything. 'It's . . . it's what he's been saying. At first I thought it was a whim, and that he was just trying to stir things up . . . but he won't let it drop. I didn't know how to tell you.'

'How could it work when Slap— when Daisy finds it so difficult having our kids around? He can't live where he's not wanted.'

'He would be wanted. I'd make sure of that.'

Marcia and Charlene, two of the scarier PTA mums, march in and deliberate over the cakes in the chiller cabinet. I quickly free my hand from Martin's grasp.

'He can't mean it,' I insist. 'He's just saying it for . . . a reaction. Because he blames me for us breaking up.' A tear wobbles like mercury on my lower eyelid. Martin reaches for my hand again, but I clasp mine on my lap, out of reach.

'You know that's not true,' he says softly. 'It was *my* fault. All of it.'

'You mean—' I clamp my mouth shut.

'Hi, Caitlin!'

'Hello, Marcia,' I mutter.

She shoots Charlene a look-who's-here glance while man-oeuvring their laden tray. That's the trouble with living in a family-friendly neighbourhood: numerous school-gate spies noting your every move. Before having kids, I could have got up to anything and no one would have noticed or cared. Luckily, for once they don't stop to talk.

'Do you . . . regret it?' I murmur when they're out of earshot.

'Yes, Cait, I do.'

Out of the corner of my eye I see Marcia biting her eclair obscenely.

'Since when?' My voice has turned brittle.

Martin fixes me with solemn eyes. 'Since . . . since I left you. But especially . . .' He lowers his gaze and I'm overcome by an urge to hold him. The Most Controlled Being Award slips from my grasp.

'Especially . . . when?'

There's a hint of a smile. 'That night with the hook. You remember. When you had some bloke round and were standing there in Jake's raincoat thingy and . . .' He grins sheepishly.

'Right. When I looked like a complete idiot.'

Marcia's eclair wavers in mid-air.

'No, Cait, you looked like *you*. Like the girl I first met, who was so sweet and spontaneous. Seeing you like that – all over the place, not knowing where to put yourself – reminded me how funny you are, and how no one's ever—' He stops.

The waitress removes my cup and flashes a smile at Martin, but it goes unheeded.

'Martin,' I murmur, 'it's too late for any of that.'

'Yes, I know.'

I swallow hard. 'I need to go now. There's stuff I have to get on with at home.'

We get up from the table, and Marcia looks away quickly as Martin pulls me close. The hug doesn't make me feel better, or that I want to be his friend or his girl again, but it does suggest that we're in this Jake business together.

'It wouldn't work, you know,' I add. 'Jake would be miles away from Harvey and the rest of his friends. Getting to and from school would be a nightmare, and changing to a new one . . . do we really want to put him through that, after all the upheaval he's been through?'

'No,' Martin agrees, 'but—'

'And what about his football practice?' I charge on.

'Cait . . .'

'It just won't work, Martin. He thinks this is what he wants, but he'll be miserable.'

'Hey,' Martin says, taking both of my hands in his, 'he wouldn't have to change schools. I'd do the school run on my way to and from work, and he can still go to football.'

'But you work late. You're *always* working.'

'There's the after-school club.'

'He hates that,' I say vehemently. 'And you and Daisy aren't even getting on.' I'm grasping at straws now.

'Whatever happens,' Martin says firmly, 'I'm still his dad and I'd look after him. We have to respect what he wants.'

I pull away, trying to cut Marcia and Charlene from my line of vision. However I stand, I can still feel their eyes boring into my head. 'Of course you're his dad,' I murmur. 'You've never stopped being that.'

Martin smiles and all the years and tension seem to drain from his face. He's no longer the two-timing architect with 500 letters after his name, but my boyfriend again. The man I loved. I could take him in my arms and kiss him right here. That would make Marcia choke on her eclair.

'I think we should let Jake decide,' he says gently. 'Don't you?'

'OK. Let's do that.' I muster a smile, confident that I know what our son's decision will be.

I am his mother, after all.

26

Saturday morning. Sam and I have brought the kids to the cinema. He's left messages the past few days reminding me that the latest child-pleasing blockbuster is due to finish, and that seeing it is essential to Harvey and Jake's survival.

'Have you been avoiding me?' Sam whispers in the flickering darkness. The trailers are on; I'm praying that the film proves as enticing for Travis and Lola as it does for the older boys. I have yet to broach the moving-in-with-Dad issue with Jake. Not that I'm avoiding the subject or anything. I've had a cold, been snowed under with *Bambino* mail, and the right moment just hasn't come up.

'Of course I haven't,' I whisper back.

'It's just . . . you've been pretty elusive lately.' He pauses, and his eyes gleam. 'I've missed you,' he adds.

'I've had a bit of a week, Sam.' I fix my gaze on the screen. Opening credits; a dragon surging across an indigo sky; fiery breath; a deafening lightning crack. Travis snuggles closer for safety. Lola, who hates to show fear, ogles the screen brazenly. I sense Sam glancing at me, trying to read my thoughts. He knows that I am never too busy to see him.

All I can think of now is Sam in a sharp suit, his usually tousled hair freshly cut. Polished shoes in place of his usual battered trainers or baseball boots. A gleaming ring on his finger. I wonder if he still has the one from first time around.

Amelia will wear . . . What? Not a veil, surely? There'll be speeches, toasts, lilac sugared almonds in net bags. Jesus. I can feel a feigned illness coming on. Diphtheria, maybe, or a severe nuptial allergy. 'I'm so sorry, Sam and Amelia, but being in the same room as a tiered cake brings me out in unsightly boils, and I wouldn't wish to ruin your photos.'

After the film, we go to a diner with red Formica tables and music blaring from a chrome jukebox. My burger bun feels like a sponge in my throat. Everyone chats about the film, and Lola draws dragons all over her oily paper napkin. Travis blows noisy bubbles into his lemonade, despite my asking him not to. The restaurant bustles with children and teenagers. Free crayons, colouring books and infinitely tolerant waiting staff make it a favourite family pit-stop.

I gnaw gamely on my burger. I'm desperate to whisper to Sam that Jake wants to live with his dad, and what the hell should I do about this? But with the kids crammed round our table, it's impossible. If it weren't for the impending wedding, I'd have called him in an instant. And now I can't. He has other, more important stuff on his mind, like seating plans and choosing a suit. The thought of Sam in a suit is as ridiculous as imagining Travis wearing one.

The air is rich with the aroma of hot chips. I can't even raise the enthusiasm to sip my Coke. He'll no longer be my friend, my Sam, my anything at all. I have lost him already.

'Hey,' he says as we leave, 'you're awfully quiet today. Don't say those problem letters are getting you down.'

'No,' I say, mustering a smile. 'Nothing cheers you up like other people's angst.'

'Were you scared of the film, Mummy?' Lola asks, grasping my hand.

'Um, yes, sweetheart,' I tell her.

'Silly Mummy.' She giggles. 'Grown-ups shouldn't be scared of anything.'

It's 9.25 p.m., and I'm on the threshold of Jake's room. 'Hon, don't read for much longer. I know you've got your torch on under the covers.'

He extracts it and shines its blueish beam in my face.

'Did you enjoy the movie?'

'Yeah,' he replies, 'it was cool.'

I step gingerly towards the torchlight. 'Jake,' I venture, 'can I come in? I need to talk to you.'

'What about?' he asks airily.

'You seem so . . . so angry with me these days.'

He flicks off his torch, but an image of its beam still glows on the back of my eyeballs. 'You don't keep promises,' he growls.

'What are you talking about?'

'That photographer. Those embarrassing pictures for that magazine. You said you'd buy us an enormous wonderful thing.'

'Actually,' I correct him, 'the photographer said that. But, yes, I suppose I agreed. We'll choose something . . . Could you put on your bedside light for a minute? I can't talk properly in the dark.'

'Why not?'

'I need to see your face.'

He sighs, flicking on the switch. We stare at each other like strangers. 'Jake,' I murmur, 'I know you've said to Dad that you want to live with him.'

He swallows and nods. I detect a smidgen of shame.

'You know it wouldn't be like your Daddy weekends. Going to exciting places like the Science Museum and the zoo all the time. It would just be . . . ordinary. It would be homework and light off when Dad says.'

'Yeah, I know.' He fiddles with the edge of his duvet. The spaceman pattern seems silly – too young for him now. I should have bought him a new one ages ago.

'Have you thought about Poppy?' I ask. 'Having a little girl pestering you who's not even your sister? Wanting your toys and books?'

'Uh-huh.'

I delve for something, anything, to make him change his mind. Pancakes every damn day of the week. Unlimited refined sugar. 'Do you . . . like Daisy?' I ask hesitantly.

'Uh?'

'D'you really want to live with her instead of us?' The 'us' comes out as a squeak.

'She's all right. It's not really to do with her.'

'So what *is* it to do with? Why d'you want to do this?' A tear plops down my cheek and I bat it away furiously. Damn my uncontrollable tear ducts. If only vitalworld.com had marketed some kind of anti-blubbing device.

Jake's mouth crumples, and he shocks me by reaching out with his arms. I hurry to him, and he hugs me so tightly I want to stay that way for ever.

'What is it, darling?' I whisper.

'It's just,' he croaks into my neck, 'I miss Dad.'

12.07 a.m.

Oh, Cait. I'm sorry to hear what you've been going through with Jake. It must be awful for you. Billy and I had a similar situation. He spent a short time last summer with his mother, having assumed that life with her would be filled with sunshine and chocolate instead of being trapped with his grumpy father and nagged to eat his greens. Unfortunately, Jacqui's new boyfriend had just moved in. He's a kind of male Harriet Pike, from what I can gather – a strict, no-nonsense, show-kids-who's-boss type (having no children of his own, naturally!).

For us, as I hope it is for you, it turned out to be a trial separation. I think Billy had wanted to flex his muscles and kick against me. Three weeks in the love nest proved more than enough. Believe me, Jake wanting to live with his dad doesn't mean he loves you any less. You are brave for letting him go and I'm sure in time that he will respect that. It might even bring you closer in the long run. And he'll probably find that he misses you more than he expected.

Heck, what do I know? You're the agony aunt!

Your friend,

R x

I'm poised to type that I've changed my mind, that I would like us to meet after all. Just for coffee. It won't mean anything. I'm just curious, that's all. I need to figure out how he manages to say the right things.

No one makes me feel better the way he does. Millie doesn't get it, Sam's out of bounds now, and it doesn't feel right to share Jake's imminent departure with Rachel. 'We've never had any problems with Eve,' she admitted. How could she possibly understand?

R knows what it's like, and I want to make him real.

I remember Millie's words: 'Harriet had email stalkers desperate to be her friend.'

Obscene missives. Cling-filmed packages of pubic hair. R isn't like that. He can't be. Surely I'd know by now?

My index fingers twitch as one of the kids – Lola, I think – calls out softly in her sleep. All I type is:

Thanks, R. I knew you'd understand.
  C x

27

So many times I've imagined the scene as one by one my children flee our family nest. Jake would be first. We'd have packed his belongings in boxes, and I'd have assembled all manner of essentials: bed linen, pans, crockery, one of those studenty cookbooks that details the importance of vitamins and minerals and includes 'Twenty-Five Ways With a Jacket Potato', as if this would insure him against rickets and scurvy. I would drive him to his student accommodation and meet his room-mates: boys who'd look as if they'd be up for plenty of larking about, but not so far as distracting Jake from his studies or forcing class-A drugs on to him. We'd have had a little chat about dope being OK-ish, but that anything else was seriously scary. He'd roll his eyes in a 'Yeah, Mum' kind of way.

I would drive away feeling sad – probably weeping gently, picturesquely – yet find comfort in the fact that my first-born had blossomed into a bright, independent young man.

That's how it's meant to be. Not like this. For one thing, it's happening around eight years too soon.

'Cait, are you there?' Sam's voice is dulled by the answerphone. 'Haven't seen you all week. Hope you're OK . . . Bit worried . . . Look, Amelia's coming up for the weekend. She wondered – *we* wondered – if you're not doing anything, maybe we could all get together, have a picnic in the park or something if the weather holds out, maybe drive over to the heath . . . Anyway, call me.'

I fold Jake's freshly washed football kit and place it in one of the boxes I cadged from the corner shop. Although he's insisted that he'll need it, he clearly despises the sport. Every time I have watched him play, he has mooched around the edge of the pitch, gazing at clouds or biting the raggedy skin around his fingernails. Yet when I've suggested that he doesn't have to go – that he can give it up whenever he likes – he brushes me off.

The phone trills again.

'Cait, hon, it's me. Are you there?'

This time I pick up. 'Millie, hi.'

'You sound harassed, sweetie. Everything OK?'

I'm surrounded by boxes containing Jake's precious things. There's still tons of stuff in his room. He said that he'll sort through it some other time, which offers a fragment of hope.

'You know Jake's decided to live with Martin?' I tell her. 'Well, I'm just packing up his stuff. It feels so weird, Millie.'

'Oh, Cait.' She sighs, allowing a respectful silence, as if I have announced the death of a pet. 'Still, at least he won't be too far away.'

'That's not really the point . . .'

'And you'll still see him at weekends, won't you, like Martin does now? It'll just be the other way round.'

Such empathy. And what will those weekends be like? R has advised me to play them down, not to cram every second with fun. 'I hated the idea of being one of those Saturday dads,' he told me, 'who bustles his kid from football match to theme park but doesn't make time for normal stuff, like sharing a baguette in the park. So we fell into a pattern of doing simple things – just being ordinary father and son – and I think that brought us closer again.'

'Millie,' I say, 'I really need to get finished here . . .'

'I'll be quick,' she announces. 'Just wanted to say I'm so pleased with your pages and I was thinking you could maybe do more stuff for us.'

'Yes, fine, can we talk about it another—'

'What I want to do is *exploit* you.'

'Huh?'

She laughs, having the decency to sound embarrassed. 'Not horribly. Not in a bad way. I mean, make the most of your talents

. . . To be honest, you're just what we've needed: a writer who actually has children and understands what it's like.'

Well, hello!

'What d'you want me to do?' I ask, as Lola saunters into the kitchen, drops her ancient teddy into one of Jake's boxes and plonks herself on a chair, swinging her legs idly.

'Just a few little soundbites,' Millie explains. 'Words of wisdom that we can scatter through the magazine with a dotted line and little scissor thingies.'

Dotted lines and scissor thingies. Millie is paid vast wodges of cash to come up with such ground-breaking concepts. 'You mean for readers to cut out and keep?'

'Yeah! That's it exactly. And stick on their fridge or whatever. We could call them something like, like . . . "Caitlin's Nuggets". And whenever they're having a stressy moment with the kids, like a tantrum or something, they can glance at your soundbite and it'll make them feel instantly better. Does that sound OK?'

' "Caitlin's nuggets," ' I repeat flatly.

'Just a working title. "Nuggets" isn't right. Ideally, it'd be another C-word so it rolls off the tongue – "Caitlin's Corkers" or something . . . Can you think of a C-word?'

Not one that I can utter in the presence of my daughter. ' "Chunks"?' I suggest to get her off the phone.

' "Caitlin's Chunks" . . . Nope, that's not right. How about "lumps"?'

' "Caitlin's *Lumps*"? Jesus, Millie, it sounds like a disease.'

'Hmm. I really like "nuggets". Shame your name doesn't start with an "n".'

'I'll just change it, shall I?'

'I was joking, sweetie,' Millie says, sounding hurt.

'Sorry. I'm just not feeling very inspired right now. Can I think it over when I've helped Jake to pack up and leave home and everything?'

'Oh. Yeah. I've called at a really bad time. I was going to tell you about that advertising man I went out with, but maybe we could meet up in the week.'

'Yes, let's do that.'

Lola eyes me as I finish the call. 'Have you got a disease?' she enquires.

After dinner, we drive to Jake's sumptuous new abode.

'I can do cartwheels,' Lola announces from the back seat. 'Shall I show you, Jake?'

'What, in the car?' he sneers.

'I mean when we get to Dad's,' she says sheepishly.

No response.

'Jake?' she tries again. 'D'you want to see my gymnastics?'

'Could you answer her, Jake?' I mutter. He sighs dramatically. He is sitting beside me in the passenger seat, staring pointedly out of the side window.

'Jake!' Her voice peaks in desperation.

Poor Lola. It's as if she, like me, can't bear to let him go. No one ignored Jake when he was Lola's age. Martin and I would pore over every page in his homework jotter and laugh uproariously at his jokes. If he'd been able to do a cartwheel, we'd probably have videoed it and invited our friends round for a special screening.

'You can show me,' I murmur, 'when you're back from Dad's on Sunday night.'

Lola digests this. 'Why are *you* taking us to Dad's? It's usually Daddy that gets us.'

'I just . . .' I begin, realising I can't tell her that I have to see Martin's flat – Jake's new home – for myself. I need to place him in it and picture him there when I've gone. 'We just thought it'd be easier,' I say lightly.

And it's not sumptuous. Martin and *famille* reside on the third floor of a flimsy-looking development built in sickly-yellow brick. (You say 'development' these days, never 'estate'.) It looks cheap and bleak, and is called Garfield Court, which makes me think of an over-stuffed tangerine cat. Surely Slapper must have insisted on moving here. It doesn't look like somewhere Martin, architect supremo, would choose to live.

I buzz the intercom and he lopes downstairs to greet us. 'Hi, guys,' he says with a skewed grin, as if this were any ordinary Friday evening. He leads the way upstairs, laden with the heaviest of Jake's boxes, explaining, 'Sorry, lift's broken.' Surely it's too new to be broken? The stairwell smells of fresh plaster and is stark white, the kind that dazzles your eyes.

'Hi, everyone! Come in.' Daisy flicks a tense smile at me, which I return. She hovers in the hall for a moment, clutching a plate of toast, as if she's forgotten what she'd planned to do with it. Although she's fully made up, with rather too much coral-coloured blusher, her lips are pale and her eyes faintly bloodshot, as if we've arrived during the aftermath of a row.

'Hi,' I say curtly, busying myself by ensuring that everyone takes off their shoes.

'Oh, don't worry about that,' she insists, but I sense that this is a shoes-off kind of flat. The last thing I want is for her to complain to Martin that we lack manners. We follow her into the living room, where the only decorative item is an outsized mirror on the cream wall, which must come in handy for Slapper's constant preening. Sofa, curtains, fluffy rug – all are palest cream. Poppy's toys are presumably banned from seeping out of her bedroom and polluting the rest of the flat.

'Shall we take your things into your room, Jake?' Daisy asks eagerly.

'Yeah, OK.' He seems at ease here and has already tossed his (non-cream) jacket on to the back of the sofa, thus marring the muted colour scheme. Good.

Poppy steps tentatively out of a bedroom and quickly scuttles back in.

'It's very, um, compact, isn't it?' I remark as Daisy shows us into Jake's new sleeping quarters.

'Well, we've made it as nice as we could. New bed and chest of drawers, though we couldn't fit in any shelves, Jake, and I know you're a bookworm.' She giggles unnecessarily. 'Perhaps we can find some boxes to fit under the bed.'

'All right,' he murmurs. The duvet cover is striped purple and grey, typically boyish, and is slightly stiff to the touch, indicating newness. And the room smells new, faintly chemical. It's so insipid, and clearly furnished in a hurry, that I can't dredge up one positive thing to say about it. This is where Jake wants to be. Away from the mess, the clutter and the sea monkeys and, presumably, me. My stomach feels like a hollow pit.

'Is this what you're reading these days?' Martin asks needlessly, marching in behind us and swiping one of the novels that Jake has tipped on to the bed.

'Yes, Dad,' he says quietly. He flicks me an anxious glance and I try for a reassuring smile. Then *The Simpsons* theme tune kicks in and he seems to forget the enormity of what's going on and flees to the living room, away from all these self-conscious adults.

Martin creeps away and Daisy and I look at each other. She's wearing skinny jeans and a grey felted top that skims her youthful figure. Mercifully, her breasts aren't on obvious display.

'Caitlin . . .' she begins, and her cheeks flush prettily.

Don't say you're sorry, or that you'll take good care of my son, or my tear ducts will spurt into action right here in this crappy cardboard flat.

'That email I sent . . .' she adds, lowering her gaze to the biscuit-coloured carpet.

'I was surprised,' I say coolly. 'I mean, we've never really spoken, have we? Not properly.' Please don't start on about your relationship troubles. Not with me, not now – not ever.

Daisy smiles weakly. 'I wanted you to know how things are with us. I thought it was important, if Jake was going to come and live here.'

Shut up, shut up, shut up. If I could get away with it, I'd stick my fingers in my ears and start singing loudly, the way Lola does sometimes when I ask her to pick up her pants from the floor.

'The Siiiimpsons . . .' Poppy is laughing heartily in the living room. It's an unfamiliar, gurgly laugh.

'D'you . . . like *The Simpsons*?' Lola asks tentatively.

'Yeah!' Poppy enthuses.

Now they're all in hysterics together, with even Jake laughing his socks off. Maybe, as far as kids are concerned, it doesn't matter which family you're from.

'Daisy,' I venture, 'I know I write a problem page, but yours and Martin's personal stuff . . . it's a bit too close for comfort for me to deal with.'

She laughs uneasily. 'Yes, of course it is. I'm sorry. You just seem so . . . *sensible* in the magazine.'

I gawp at her. 'Well, I'm not really. That's not what I'm like at all. It's just a job, OK? It's what I *do*. Like you and the water-cooler thing.' The sternness of my voice surprises me, and Daisy shrinks away.

'Martin was really angry that I'd emailed you,' she adds.

I shrug.

'He's very loyal to you, Caitlin. He has a lot of respect for you as, as . . . a mother.'

Please, spare me.

'Anyway,' she adds, 'it was silly of me to tell you my personal problems. I bet your friends do that all the time.'

'Not really,' I mutter.

'It's just . . .' she grins lopsidedly '. . . if you weren't, um, connected to my family, I'd write to you for advice about Poppy. How she nags for new toys all the time – any advert she's seen on TV, basically, and we really can't afford them after taking this place on.'

My jaw is clenched and starting to ache. The woman is a fruitcake. 'Daisy,' I say, 'I think you should talk to Martin about that.'

'That's . . . what you'd suggest?'

She actually seems disappointed that I am unwilling to offer a one-to-one counselling session.

'Yes,' I say firmly, and stride out of the room.

While Martin pulls out the sofabed for Lola and Travis to sleep on, the kids settle themselves on cushions on the floor. All four are entranced by the TV. I feel superfluous and utterly lost.

'Well,' I announce stiffly, 'I'd better be going. See you on Sunday, OK?'

'Guys,' Daisy prompts them, 'your mum's going now. Aren't you going to say goodbye?'

'Bye, Mummy,' Lola sing-songs. I notice with alarm that she and Poppy are sharing a cushion.

Jake doesn't even look at me.

'Shush!' Travis growls. 'Am watching TV.'

What should a ditched parent do when she returns to Bleak House? Seek adult company. Despite my fear of interrupting some guest-list-planning session, I call Sam. There's no Amelia. 'Change of plan,' he says lightly. 'Why don't you come over?'

'Are you sure? It's pretty late . . .'

He laughs hollowly. 'To be honest, I could do with some company.'

I set out with a bottle of wine, plus a headful of gripes about my departed son and his new cardboard home, but by the time I've reached Sam's place, the bad stuff's evaporated.

'He'll come back,' Sam assures me, crouching by his CD shelves as he searches for cheer-up-Cait tunes.

'No he won't. This is it, Sam.'

'Has he taken all his stuff? Like everything from his room?'

'Well . . . no. His skateboard's in the garden, but he's probably just forgotten it. There are still loads of books in his room – even some of his favourites – and his Top Trumps collection.'

'There you go,' Sam says softly. 'He's just trying to make a point. I bet he's back by the end of next week.'

Within minutes Martin texts me: JAKE ASKED IF U CD BRING HIS SKATEBOARD, CDS, ART STUFF, TOP TRUMPS & REST OF BOOKS WHEN U COME ON SUN, CHEERS M.

Trial separation? Permanent dumpage more like.

'Hey, Sam.' I show him the text and he meets my gaze. He's looking especially lovely tonight, honey-skinned after a day spent working in the garden.

'It's just a phase,' he says firmly.

I shake my head. 'If anything, this is worse than Martin leaving. When that happened, I could direct all my anger on to him and Slapper, but with this . . .' My eyes prickle. 'There's no one I can be angry with, Sam. I don't know what the hell to do.'

He smiles and puts his arms round me. My heart flits like a trapped bird. 'Which stage is anger meant to be again?' he asks softly.

'Um, three, I think. I've forgotten. Think I screwed up the order a long time ago.'

Sam laughs and pulls me close on the sofa. We sit like that, with my head resting against his chest, even though Harvey could wake up and wander downstairs and be *really* confused, with the impending nuptials and everything. Sam lightly kisses the top of my head, then gets up to pour wine and play a CD.

I don't ask about Amelia. Instead, I play a game with myself in which the wedding isn't happening at all. He's changed his mind. *She's* changed her mind – got back with that boyfriend in Cornwall. She and Sam were being silly trying to turn back the clock.

So I pretend, and it feels like we're our old selves again. In fact, if it weren't for the fact I'll be picking up only Lola and Travis on Sunday, life would be pretty damn perfect.

28

All week I will myself not to miss Jake. This is tricky because I pass his bedroom about eight billion times a day, find his damp PJs festering in the washing machine and his favourite peach yoghurts in the fridge. I swear the yoghurts smirk at me. Neither Lola nor Travis will eat them, and I can't face them, so they end up being tipped in the bin. The PJs, I re-wash and iron with a level of care and attention never before seen in our home.

Plus, I still see him at school every morning. Martin drops him off on his way to the office. This results in him being late to work, but, hey, Superdad is prepared to make small sacrifices for the sake of our first-born.

Every morning so far I've had my teeth jammed together during the walk to school and have been incapable of listening properly to Lola and Travis's perpetual chat about how clever it is that oranges are in fact orange, and how dogs talk to each other in dog language, which we can't understand. The school-bound world crackles around me, as if someone has tampered with my inner tuning dial.

'Mummy, you're not listening!' Lola chastises me on Friday morning.

'Sorry, sweetheart. We'd better hurry up or we'll be late . . .'

'I *said*, Bethany Holden fell in the playground and her eyes went funny with stars in.'

'That only happens in cartoons, Lols. Real eyes can't have stars in.'

'They did! I saw.' She allows her schoolbag to fall from her shoulder and drags it along the ground, narrowly missing a small mound of dog poo.

'Pick up your bag, Lola. It'll get filthy.'

'Where's Jake?' Travis rumbles. 'I want my brother Jake!'

Every morning I've had this and I fear that my head will explode, splattering the school-gate crowd with juddering brain cells. I want it to stop, for everything to be normal again and not have to endure our two disparate groups (mine, Martin's) stumbling together for a brief exchange at the railings.

'You'll see Jake at the school gate,' I tell Travis, but now his brother's forgotten and he's more interested in snapping a branch off a tree.

Today I spot Martin before he sees me. He still looks self-consciously new to this school-gate lark, in his charcoal work suit and polished black shoes. Jake lurks beside him, with his hair combed in a spooky way. There's an attempt at a parting and perhaps the introduction of some kind of product. *She* must have done it. Martin would never acquaint himself with, with . . . What the fuck is it? Gel, or that serum stuff that looks like snot? Slapper had better not have come into contact with one follicle on my darling son's head.

We have a brief chat about something nonsensical – the weather, thank God for British weather to talk about – while Bev and Marcia gawp openly from the gate. I want to grab Jake – to have him all to myself, if only for a few seconds – and ask, 'So what did you watch on TV last night? Did you sleep OK under that horrible stiff duvet? Did you do your homework, and has anyone checked it? What did you have for breakfast? Have they bought Cheerios, or d'you have to make do with those nasty little square things that Poppy has?'

Oh, and, 'Do you miss me?'

There's no opportunity to do this. 'Hi, Mum,' Jake says flatly, briefly tweaking his weird hair.

'Hello, darling, how's things?'

'All right.' And that's it. He's gone, and Lola has scampered away with her schoolbag all grubby at the bottom, and Travis is crying hot tears because Daddy has hurried to his car, barely saying goodbye. That's the extent of our 9 a.m. exchange. It's not exactly what the magazines call 'quality time'.

I suppose I should be grateful, as at hometime I don't get to see Jake at all. My only opportunity would be to drag one of the huge wheelie bins to the furthest window, clamber on to it and peer into the classroom that serves as the afterschool club. Which might not go down too well with the caretaker.

When he lived at home – at his *real* home – Jake refused point-blank to attend the club. Anyone would have surmised that it's run by members of a sinister sect who sacrifice kittens and force the children to eat stones. Now, it seems, it's non-stop party time, as Jake goes there every day, seemingly without complaint. Some days Slapper picks him up. Mostly, though, it's Martin. I stalked them a couple of days ago, an act which made me feel lowly and pathetic, but I couldn't stop myself. No Most Controlled Being Award that day either.

Travis was playing at his mate Eddie's house, and I'd just dropped Lola at her gym class. I'd intended to spend the hour picking up some shopping and realised, as I was passing school, that afterschool club would be ending. I loitered behind a florist's delivery van, pretending to admire the cornflowers in the shop window. I kept poking my head round the van and spotted parents and children emerging from school. Marcia and her daughter, Genevieve, came out, giggling together and swinging hands like the mother-daughter duos you see on perky TV shows. The kind that try on kooky hats together in department stores. Finally, Martin and Jake emerged, looking relaxed and happy – looking *normal*. Jake certainly didn't look distressed or malnourished.

Rather than heading along the street where I presumed Martin would have parked, they took a swift turn down the narrow alley that leads to the playing field. The way they did that, with no obvious discussion, made me realise that they'd done this lots of times before. The late-afternoon sun cast an amber glow, and Jake was doing a jolly kind of skip-walk. Martin had a football tucked under his arm.

How very pleasing. How thoughtful-daddyish. A quick kick-around in the park on a summer afternoon before heading home to that Lego flat that looks like it would crumble to dust if you so much as farted in it. I wanted to stalk them to the playing field, and wished I had some kind of disguise – like a balaclava, or Lola's Scooby Doo outfit. Their voices faded, and I skulked around the shops and picked up Lola from gym. I tried to chat happily as we walked home, but I couldn't get Jake out of my head. If I learned to play football, would that bring him back? We'd go to the playing field every day. Football, pancakes – anything.

So I stop buying peach yoghurts and I try not to miss Jake. Instead of phoning constantly, which I know he'd resent, I offload to R, who listens no matter what.

Sometimes, though not always, that helps.

'Guess what!' Millie announces, like a child. 'Our survey results are back and your page has come out as most popular. Way more than Harriet's ever was. We need you to stand up and do a little talk.'

'What do you mean?' I ask. 'Stand up *where*?'

'At a reader event we're planning. Nothing too daunting. You'll answer readers' problems, just like you do in the magazine, so it'll be no different really.'

My heart lurches. It's Monday morning. Having rejected his breakfast before we took Lola to school, Travis is now mashing his Shredded Wheat with such gusto that milk slops over the side of his dish.

'Millie, of course it's different,' I protest. 'I can't *see* anyone when I'm working. It's just me and the computer in our kitchen. I'm not being . . . looked at.'

'Yeah, well . . .'

'And I can't answer questions on the hop. I need time to mull them over. It takes me ages, you know, to do your page.'

Millie's snigger rattles out of the phone. I grip the handset with my shoulder while wrestling Travis's spoon from his grasp. In a small act of mutiny he dunks a fist into the gunk. Toddler behaviour that he should have outgrown a year ago. 'Hello, readers, I am Caitlin Brown, *Bambino*'s new agony aunt. You might think I can assist with your problems, but it's quite clear that I know not a damn thing. My three-year-old son still tries to eat Shredded Wheat with his hands, squeezing it gently so the milk drips through his fingers, and my daughter remains firmly attached to the Scooby costume she's had since she was four. As for my other son . . . well, he can't even bear to live with me. So you can see that we are juggling a few "issues".'

'Surely you can predict the kind of stuff they'll ask?' Millie insists. 'Don't the problems follow certain themes?'

'Well, yes,' I admit.

'And what are they?'

'Relationship problems, mostly. Things not being the same since they had a child. Being knackered, snappy, irritable. Blaming each other for not helping enough. No sex. Having nothing to talk about apart from the kids. Being paranoid about a partner having affairs, then actually *having* affairs. Oh, and kids' behavioural problems. I get lots of those: tantrums, sleep problems, faddy eaters, terrible manners.' Travis sticks out his tongue. A tiny Shredded Wheat nest is perched on it.

'See,' Millie gloats, 'you do know your stuff. Come on, we're only talking a couple of hundred readers.'

A couple of hundred? However you look at it, that's a heck of a lot. It's not a PTA fundraising meeting. Those 200 readers will know, at a glance, that it takes me hours to formulate my replies, that I mull them over on the walk home from school, in the bath, in bed – anytime I have a spare moment. It doesn't come easily. I'm too anxious of getting it wrong, of fouling up someone's life. Sometimes I even ask R for suggestions, which probably isn't ethical – confidentiality and all that – but, hey, any port in a storm.

'It'll be great for your profile,' Millie adds in a gentler tone.

'I don't want a profile!'

She sighs dramatically. 'I've already told the big cheeses that you'll be there, OK? Please, Cait. It'll be painless.'

I watch bleakly as Travis picks up his bowl and slurps mush

from its rim. 'It won't be a huge all-singing, all-dancing thing, will it?'

She laughs throatily. 'It's just a tiny, miniscule, blink-and-you'll-miss-it thing.'

We finish the call, her almighty fib shimmering in the air.

Hi, Cait,
Been thinking about you and wondering how your second week's going since Jake moved in with his dad. Did you see him at the weekend? Hope all went well.
   Love, R x

Dear R,
Thanks for asking. It wasn't so bad, actually, though I'd been dreading it in case he'd reverted to his old, loving self (in which case I am clearly the problem) or, worse, I got the cold-shoulder treatment. In fact he was pretty . . . in-betweeny. Normal, I suppose.

I took the three of them swimming to the new place with flumes. To be honest, I wasn't even sure that Jake would want to come. But he did and I was ridiculously grateful – how tragic is that? He showed me the touch-turns that Martin's taught him to do. Martin's always been better with stuff like that than I am. I consider it a major achievement just to get them all changed and in the water without losing anything.

I realised, when Jake was queuing up for the flume that he's changing – physically I mean. He's no longer kid-shaped. He looked taller and has long, strong legs like his dad's. I wondered if there's been other stuff that I haven't noticed. Surely a parent should be aware of everything that's happening to their kids? I felt ashamed, R. As if he's slipped from my grasp without me seeing it happening.

Anyway, we had fun. Jake and I had a swimming race and he beat me hands down. We also went to the park and threw stale bread for the ducks, which I worried that Jake would find boring, but it seemed to be fine. He even reminded Travis to tear up the bread into tiny pieces for the smaller birds. It brought a lump to my throat, seeing them bread-ripping together, Jake being the kind big brother.

I wanted to ask him so many questions, to interrogate him about how things are going and ask what the hell that gunk is that he puts in his hair now, but I remembered what you said and managed not to.

As it turned out, I only had him for the day. Jake had made it clear that he didn't want to stay overnight at our house, even though I'd cleaned his blasted room until it reeked of Mr Sheen Lemon Shine and developed RSI of the entire body from all the scrubbing. Anyway, your advice was really helpful and I think it made things more relaxed and natural between us. So a huge thank you.

Love, Cait x

And it's true: I *am* grateful. R's regular dispatches are forming a kind of operator's manual for a ten-year-old boy. It doesn't matter that Millie thinks I'm a crackpot for involving myself with him, or that I am the one who's supposed to be *au fait* with this parenting lark.

R is always there for me, at any time of day or night, and it feels as if he cares. Anyway, for the moment he is all I have.

29

'I'm coming to your *Bambino* thing,' Rachel announces. 'So are Bev, Marcia, Charlene . . . everyone, really. All the PTA lot and the gymnastics crowd. Paula tried to get a ticket, but it was sold out.'

'*My*' *Bambino* thing? 'That's great,' I manage as we march around Leoni's Larder, a judderingly expensive deli-cum-mini-supermarket where a goat's cheese salad costs something like five thousand quid.

'I know they can be bitchy,' Rachel ventures, 'but everyone's on your side, Cait. They're being supportive.'

'Of course they are,' I mutter darkly.

'It's exciting for them,' she continues, 'and for me. We've never met anyone famous.' She giggles, and I muster a smile as she examines a carton of chicken and couscous. Naturally, it's no ordinary chicken. It's probably been marinated in goji-berry juice and chargrilled over the smouldering embers of rare Peruvian bark.

'I hope everyone's not disappointed,' I tell her. 'I mean, I'm not used to . . . you know . . . *performing*. I'm just going to stand there shaking with a purple face, probably peeing myself.'

'Oh, hon, you'll be fine,' she insists, giving my arm a reassuring squeeze. Travis and Lola are, as usual, scampering around the aisles. Like a well-trained hound, Eve is strolling mutely at her mother's side. I must ask Rachel how she programmed her to behave in such a pleasing manner. It's my fault we're in this preposterous shop at all. The plan had been to have a picnic on the playing field by the sports centre before Eve and Lola's gymnastic display, but my afternoon was gobbled up by numerous calls from Nadia, Millie's secretary, to run through endless details about the reader event.

'What are you planning to wear?' she'd wanted to know. Did she really assume that I plan my outfits a week in advance? I blustered that I was 'considering a few possibilities'.

'Could you perhaps email me your script?' she asked, which nearly made me vomit in panic.

So I'm here, in Leoni's, trying to locate foodstuffs that will be deemed acceptable by my children. Eve, meanwhile, will doubtless be propelled to gold-medal stardom by Rachel's home-made sourdough, which takes three days to 'ferment'.

'Can I have this?' Lola asks, snatching a bottle of elderflower infusion. (Judging by the cost, said elderflowers were fertilised with rare yak dung and trampled by Tibetan monks.)

'OK, but you'll need something to eat or you won't have any energy for gym.'

'I don't like anything.' Lola glares into the chill cabinet as if it contains dead rats.

A pointy-nosed woman swishes past us in a dress of crinkled indigo silk. Leoni's is frequented by the gorgeous of face and willowy of frame – women who have so many food intolerances they'd be safer sticking to water.

'Don't want samwich,' Travis chirps.

With a sigh, I flick my gaze over the delicacies on offer. You used to be able to buy ordinary things around here, like plain sandwiches without juniper berries nestling inside. Being in Leoni's makes me feel like an impoverished oik. I don't know who Leoni is, but assume that her hobbies include chartering helicopters and purchasing Caribbean islands.

'Want cookie,' breathes Travis, lurching towards a display of rough-hewn biscuits.

'OK, you can have one if you choose a sandwich.'

'We *always* have sandwiches,' Lola bleats, and I catch Rachel's sympathetic glance.

'No you don't—'

'We have them in our lunch boxes,' she says triumphantly, 'every day of our lives.'

'Yes,' I snap, 'because you won't have school lunches, even though they've done that improvement programme and now it's all baked artichokes and fillet of venison or whatever it is.'

'School lunches are stinky.' She shudders.

'We'll have to hurry,' Rachel cuts in, 'if we're going to have time for a picnic . . . Won't that be lovely, kids, a picnic in the park while the sun's still shining?'

My duo gazes bleakly at the shelves.

'And we can all have a play,' Rachel chatters on, 'then it'll be gym time and . . .'

I have stopped listening. Someone is watching us. He was perusing the olives and has now half turned to observe us. Six-footish, slim verging on rangy, nicely put together in a slightly rumpled white T-shirt and faded jeans. A little boy of around six or seven wanders towards him and tugs at his hand. 'Daddy,' he says, 'come on, I'm hungry.'

The man glances down at the child, murmurs something and looks back at me. There's a flicker of recognition. The fine hairs on the back of my neck spring up. A small smile crosses the man's lips, and he turns back to the jars, selecting one and studying the label.

I am aware of the hubbub of the shop and Travis making *bleugh* noises by the Greek salads, but everything seems hazy. The way the man looked at me – it was as if he knew me.

R. I breathe in sharply. It could be him. My skin tingles.

'Can I have crisps?' his son asks.

Say Billy, I will the stranger. Say Billy, then I'll know it's you.

'You can have a small packet,' he says, 'but you're not eating them before dinner.'

He's bargaining, like all parents do. He throws me a look, and his eyes gleam flirtatiously. I smile back, but my mouth feels wrong, as if it's too big and unwieldy for my face. My flirting muscles have seized up through lack of use.

'What's for dinner?' the boy asks.

The man glances at his son, then at me: a 'kids, eh?' look. 'Cats' brains,' he says, 'then toads on toast.'

The boy giggles. 'What else, Daddy?'

'Eye of newt, wing of bat.' He pings another grin at me.

So unaccustomed am I to flirtatious behaviour in shops, my cheeks are now blazing red. (I am not counting Darren in the TV shop. Look what happened there. I have even had to bin Jake's Pac-a-Mac, such sordid memories did it evoke.) Travis is prodding a humous wrap. Lola and Eve have wandered to the fruit display, where they're shunning non-glamorous species such as apples and pears in favour of pots of blueberries and pomegranate seeds. 'Look, Mummy,' Lola exclaims. 'They're so pretty! Like little beads.'

'Yes, sweetie,' I say vaguely. The man and his kid are heading away from us now, and I want to call out, 'Billy!' just to see if the child turns round. But what if it's not him and his dad gives me a look that says, 'What the hell are you doing, yelling at my kid?' Shouting, 'R!' would be just plain weird.

The man takes the boy's hand, and they turn the corner out of sight. My heart thumps against my ribs. I want to charge after them and cry, 'It's you, isn't it?' but Rachel already looks concerned for my well-being. 'Cait?' she says, 'are you OK?'

'Yes . . . yes, I'm fine.' I force a grin.

'Worried about this *Bambino* thing?'

'I suppose so.'

She narrows her eyes as I snatch Brie and grape sandwiches – the most child-friendly variety in my line of vision. 'Did you see that man?' she adds. 'The one in the white T-shirt? He was looking at you . . . really staring. Bit creepy, wasn't he? D'you know him or something?'

I scan the aisle for flapping ears. 'There's this man,' I hiss, 'who emails me, got in touch through the magazine. We've become . . . sort of friends, although we've never met, and I know this sounds stupid, but I've got this strange feeling . . .'

'What kind of friend?' Rachel hisses back.

'Well, I confide in him. Tell him stuff about Martin, the kids, pretty personal stuff.'

Her eyes widen. 'Why on earth d'you do that?'

'I . . . I just fell into it. It felt . . . safe.'

'And you think that was him? That staring guy?'

I shake my head. 'Like I said, I'm probably being stupid.'

She frowns, glancing around wildly and catching the eye of a scrawny teenage boy, who freezes under her glare. He scuttles off, as if fearing that she might wrongly accuse him of filling his pockets with lemon-stuffed olives.

'Cait –' Rachel turns to me '– what do you know about this man?'

'That he has a son, and is single, and lives a couple of miles away.'

'And that's it?'

'Yes.'

'What's his name?'

'Um, R.'

She casts me a despairing look, as if I've just plunged a grubby hand into the help-yourself salad display. 'He could be anyone, Cait.'

'Yes, I know.'

My heart plummets. I don't have it in me to object as Lola drops a pot of pomegranate beads into my basket. Or the gigantic cookie flung in by Travis. All the sympathy, the advice, the gentle ego-boosts: what do I know about him really? He might not even be a dad. Billy could be a complete work of fiction concocted to draw me in. R could be eighty-seven years old with a criminal record. Or a pervo flasher, a stalker or a Hannibal Lecter who's planning to make a handbag out of my skin. I've started to believe that he's there for me, and scamper down to the kitchen as soon as the kids are in bed to see if he's mailed me – which he invariably has. It's so pathetic I could slap myself.

Caitlin Brown, get a life.

I feel leaden as we queue up at the checkout. The other women – apart from Rachel, who favours a sagging cardie and worn-out jeans ensemble – are dressed smartly in the Hobbs/

Jigsaw mode and are all, without exception, wearing heels. Their appearance would lead one to believe that their last hairdresser appointment was more recent than nine months ago. Their perfumes mingle pleasantly.

I glimpse my reflection in the mirrored tiles. The whole wall is a mirror; what possessed Leoni to think that this was a good idea? My hair is suffering a frizz attack, and there are bruise-coloured shadows under my eyes. And there I was, feeling superior to Rachel in her baggy old cardie, when at least she can get it together to knock together a picnic. *And* stay married, even if it's to an oily twerp.

I pay for our contribution, and the male sales assistant – wooden beaded necklace, hint of the surfer haircut about him – doesn't even make eye contact.

There's no sign of the man from the olive section, or his little boy.

'Yuck,' Travis cries, prodding a sandwich on the conveyor belt.

'It's just cheese,' I murmur. 'Cheese with grapes in.'

'That's not cheese.'

'It's Brie.'

'Don't want bee! Want sausage.'

I shut off my ears.

'Don't like it,' he rages, punching the cellophane-wrapped packet.

I glower at him, trying to scare him with my fierce-mummy face. 'Shush, Travis. Stop whingeing this minute.'

'Children in Africa would love that sandwich,' Rachel murmurs.

'Want SAUSAGE!' His cry ricochets around the shop, causing customers to grip their bunches of tarragon fearfully.

'Stop this,' I bark at him. His eyes bulge as he crumples, wailing, to the floor. 'Travis!' I hiss. 'There aren't any sausages here.'

'There are!' His mouth is a cave of misery.

'This. Is. Not. A. Sausage. Shop.'

'Oh dear,' Rachel murmurs. Of course she never has any problems with Eve. Why did I think this would be a good idea – to come to Leoni's and force poncey food on to my kids, which will probably have Lola spewing all over the sports-centre floor?

Something outside catches my eye. It's that man again, straightening up after fastening his kid's shoe. I freeze as his gaze meets mine through the glass.

'Hello,' he mouths. His eyebrows raise, and there's a tweak of a smile.

Travis hauls himself up and scans the window to see what's caught my attention. 'Who's that man?'

'I don't know.' I turn away from the window.

'It's not Daddy,' he growls, and his bottom lip shoots out, pink and gleaming.

'No, darling, it's not.'

He blinks at me, moist-eyed. 'There *are* sausages. Look.'

I follow his jabbing finger to the cooked-meat counter. Above it hangs a colossal salami, bound in mesh, speckled with creamy fat, long enough to span a small river.

'I think,' I murmur, 'that's a bit big for our picnic.'

As we leave, causing a visible ripple of relief from the other shoppers, Rachel turns to me. 'Was that him? The one who was staring through the window?'

'I didn't notice,' I murmur.

Rachel shakes her head, and I glimpse pity in her eyes. 'Oh, Cait,' she says, 'we're going to have to find you a man.'

30

Although the gymnastics display doesn't start for twenty minutes, the sports hall is already teeming with revved-up parents brandishing cameras and babbling on the low wooden benches. Bev and Marcia try to draw me into conversation, but I'm still agitated by the possible R sighting in Leoni's, and not in the mood for chit-chat.

Like an obedient hound, I trail after Rachel as we search for somewhere to sit. As there's no space on the benches, we bag a corner of floor, kicking aside a curled-up waterproof plaster and a discarded crust before plonking ourselves down. We have already helped Lola and Eve to wriggle into their leotards, while Travis checked every locker in the changing area for forgotten coins. I do wish he wouldn't resort to such blatant scavenging.

'You hear of all kinds of things going on,' Rachel muses, 'with the weirdo types you meet in chatrooms.'

Oh no. She's still on about my pervo emailer with the serrated knife and black bin liner to stuff me into. She forgets that I am rather long in the tooth for paedo-type grooming.

'It's not a chatroom,' I correct her, but there's no point. She won't allow a computer in her house, so fearful is she that it might infect Eve's brain, even though I have pointed out that you can download Nigella's canapé recipes and all kinds of wholesome stuff. I mean, it's not *all* horse porn.

I scan the rows of parents who are seated uncomfortably on the benches. There are several lone dads. A few have sons of around Billy's age. This is beyond pathetic. It's Lola's big moment, her annual performance on the bar and horse and other instruments of torture which, through some genetic quirk, she seems genuinely fond of. Months she's spent practising her forward rolls on the living-room floor, and I'm scanning the hall for another glimpse of the Leoni's Larder man. Get your priorities right, woman.

'Hope you're not nervous about this reader thing', R had emailed this morning. 'What makes you any less equipped to do this than that awful Harriet woman? I know you'll be brilliant, and I'll be rooting for you.'

The thought of R rooting for me evokes a warm, treacly feeling, which is quickly cancelled out by the terrible fact that the event begins – speedy calculation – in twenty-six hours' time. Thursday evening, 7 p.m., Jacob's Court Hotel, Bloomsbury. Introduction and open question and answer session with our very own agony aunt, Caitlin Brown.

Caitlin Brown, whose younger son is extracting the grapes from his sandwich and grinding them into the floor with his foot. 'Stop it,' I hiss, rifling through my bag for tissues to wipe up the mess. All I can find is a mangled serviette from the diner, covered in Lola's dragon drawings.

Across the hall, she hops around nervously, flailing her skinny limbs. Her group's coach, an Amazonian girl with hair scraped back into a severe ponytail, seems to be giving an inaudible pep talk. Lola scans the hall for me and I wave encouragingly.

Twenty-six hours. Anything could happen in twenty-six hours. I might fall prey to a terrible virus and be carted off to an isolation ward. The kids would be scooped up by Martin, who'd do fun, spontaneous things with them; then they'd all jolly on home, where Daisy would dish up a sumptuous roast. (Actually, she wouldn't. Lola has let slip that Daisy's cooking 'doesn't taste of anything', which gave me a brief, if pathetic, stab of pleasure.)

Or an accident. I might be run over and maimed by a drunk driver. Then I won't have to stand up in front of 200 readers. No, that would be a bugger regarding getting around and doing stuff.

I could die. In the next twenty-six hours I might drop down dead and be spared ritual humiliation. Lola and Travis would move in with their dad – no, not enough space in the Lego flat. They'd all come to live at *our* house. The thought of Slapper using my toiletries causes bile to surge up my throat, but hopefully they'd bring her out in an unsightly rash and she'd stop. After a few weeks of missing me, and occasionally wondering where I'd gone, my family would live happily ever after, with no one forcing them to eat Brie. Would anyone remember to feed the sea monkeys?

'Look, Cait, aren't they sweet?' Rachel murmurs.

Lola and Eve's group are lining up to begin their routine. They *are* sweet, brimming with keenness and none of the cynicism that seeps in as they grow older. Their routine starts simply – they walk gingerly along the bar – and Lola's concentrating so hard I can almost taste it. There are fluid forward rolls and leaps over the horse. She throws me a walloping smile. I grin and wave, overcome by a surge of love for her. She's an easy kid really. She's never flung herself on to a shop floor screaming for sausage. While she goes to Martin's without a fuss, I know she's always delighted to come home to me. Lola never regards me with a blaming eye.

As for Travis, he has now plucked the Brie from his sandwich and is daubing it on to the floor for me to wipe up with my soggy napkin. Sausage tantrum aside, he is generally sunny-natured and still needs me, for which I am pathetically grateful. And Jake? He and I are bound by a fierce, aggressive love that makes me so angry and sweaty I want to stomp away from him, then stomp right back and nuzzle his hair and glean approval. It's so mixed up with him. No one warned me that parenthood would be so complicated.

The group finish and the girls line up. Straight backs, chins high, bodies encased in pink-and-blue Lycra. Lola looks so delighted I want to run over and hug her. The next age group run through their routine, and the next, and it feels like we've been trapped in this dusty corner for several weeks. Yet it's not the done thing to leave, even if your backside is throbbing and you're scared it'll never function normally again.

Finally, it's prize-giving. The kids are sitting in rows on the floor with faces tilted in expectation. An elderly lady with a swirl of silvery hair is brandishing a trophy. Across the hall, someone catches my eye. Expensive-looking grey suit, white shirt open at the neck, dark hair cropped just so. Martin. I'm so shocked to see him my heart flips, the way it used to, when just hearing his voice on the phone sparked a ripple of desire.

Quick check: he's alone. No Slapper, no Pink Princess, no Jake. He catches my eye, does a raised-eyebrow hiya thing. I hiya back. He grins sheepishly, looking ungainly on the bench, with his knees jutting towards his chin. Gymnastics displays, school plays – all the dutiful-parent events, with the exception of parents' evenings – have always been my territory, Martin's professional life being unable to accommodate the odd afternoon off.

'Isn't that Martin?' Rachel whispers.

'Yes.'

'What's he doing here? Did you know he was coming?'

I shrug. 'I'd no idea.'

Seeing him here, looking a little lost among couples and camcorders, makes me soften inside. Travis, who has yet to spot Daddy, yawns loudly and yanks off his trainers. Rachel shrugs off her cardie and folds it to make a plump cushion.

I tear my gaze away from Martin and focus on the silver-haired lady, who's announcing (I can't quite believe it), 'First prize in the junior section goes to our very talented . . . Lola Collins!'

Lola rushes up to collect her prize. I'm on my feet clapping and cheering, and Martin is too, and our eyes meet across the hall, and he's grinning. Lola disappears towards the changing rooms – Martin's heading towards me now, and it seems so normal, like the way we used to be before water-coolers ruined everything and caused all this mess we're still trying to unravel.

'Isn't that fantastic?' he says, arriving beside me.

'Brilliant,' I say, and the hug he gives me feels almost *real*. 'She's been practising really hard. She'll be so chuffed.'

The smile warms his face, and there's no hint of the cold, flinty look that I've become so accustomed to.

'Daddy!' Travis cries, leaping up in his stockinged feet and hurling himself at Martin's legs.

'Hey, little man,' Martin says, ruffling his hair before turning to me. 'Where's Lols? Do we need to collect her?'

'She's just getting changed. She'll be ready in a minute.' A pause settles between us. Rachel's gaze bores into the back of my neck. 'She'll be so pleased you came,' I add.

Martin touches my arm. 'Let's take the kids out,' he says, 'to celebrate.'

I pause. 'Won't Jake feel left out? Where is he, anyway?'

'He's at a friend's. He's made a couple of new mates in our block—' Martin catches himself, as if he's aware of how this makes me feel. The fact that Jake has new friends. That Martin's flat is where he belongs.

Registering Rachel, Martin smiles awkwardly. 'Um, would you and Eve like to come, Rachel? We're just going for a pizza or something.'

'No thanks,' she says briskly, 'I need to get back.' She tries to throw me a look, but it's too tricky to return it. 'See you at the *Bambino* thing tomorrow,' she adds.

'Yes, OK.'

'What *Bambino* thing?' Martin asks.

'Oh, just some readers' event. You know the problem page I'm doing for Millie?'

He smiles. 'It's pretty good. The kids look sweet in the photo, don't they? And it's a step up from those boil-squeezers or whatever it was you used to write about.'

I snigger. His eyes are teasing; he doesn't mean it snidely. 'Millie seems pleased with it. Anyway, she's got me doing a talk. I'm petrified, to be honest. Woke up last night in a panic that I was stranded on stage in my bra and knickers . . .'

He laughs, and I know he's remembering Pac-a-Mac night. 'Worse things could happen. You could be naked. Anyway, I'm sure you'll be great.'

*   *   *

We go to Pizza Express, and those familiar smells hit my face as we walk in. Warm, doughy, the smell of Sunday afternoons when we couldn't be bothered to cook. Lola and Travis, having rejected Leoni's fare, are ravenous.

'Why is Venice in peril, Daddy?' Lola asks, and we all laugh.

Martin looks different, and it's hard to know why. He's still wearing his stiff work clothes, but his face looks softer. 'Martin,' I venture, 'what made you come to the gym hall today?'

'I was just at a loose end.'

'Fibber,' I say, laughing. 'You don't have loose ends.'

He studies the menu, but I can tell he's not reading. 'I wanted to see your performance, didn't I, Lols?'

'Yes, Daddy.' Her eyes are shining. Then her face falls. 'Why didn't Jake come?'

'He, um, couldn't make it.' Martin shoots me a glance. 'It's not your fault, you know, Jake living with me. I don't want you worrying that it's something you've done.'

I glance at Lola, reluctant to discuss this in front of the kids in case I lose it. 'How does he get on with Daisy?' Damn, I've blurted it out in front of small children. Harriet Pike wouldn't approve.

'They're polite with each other,' he murmurs. 'Polite and a bit stiff. You know.'

'No, I don't know,' I say.

'Lola and Poppy seem to be getting on better. Poppy even shares her My Little Ponies – at least the knackered ones with grubby manes. Isn't that right, Lols? You're pretty friendly, aren't you?'

'Yeah,' she says, ever eager to please. I try for a smile, but fail.

Martin toys with his glass, oiling its surface with fingerprints. 'Things are . . . kind of difficult at the moment,' he murmurs.

'Are they?' I ask. 'Why?'

He gives me a not-in-front-of-the-kids glance, which Lola seizes upon. 'What's difficult, Daddy?'

'Oh, choosing pizza. There are so many these days. They keep adding extra ones and it's all very confusing. What are you having, darling?'

'The egg one that Jake likes.' She grins.

'Salami,' Travis declares.

'Me too,' I say, thinking, This is nice, us being together. If Jake were here, we'd feel like a whole family again.

There's a group at the circular table by the window: Mum and Dad, who look as if they're relieved not to be cooking, and two small children who are drawing on their paper napkins. That used to be us, and we thought it was so ordinary.

Our pizzas arrive. As always, Travis protests when I cut his up, even though he's unable to do it for himself. I catch Martin watching me, and I swear there's some warmth there. I don't want to spoil it.

I eat slowly, trying to spin out the meal, already deciding to have dessert. My missing-Martin pang is so unexpectedly strong I have to jam my lips together to stop myself from blurting out something embarrassing. He drives us home, with Lola babbling about her triumphant display, and parks at the end of our road. I'm desperate to ask, 'What do you mean, things are difficult? What's going on?' but I manage not to.

'Well,' I say to him, as the kids clamber out, 'I'm glad you came today.'

He smiles. 'I'm glad I did too. And good luck tomorrow.'

'Thanks.'

I turn to leave and Martin grabs my arm, planting the briefest kiss on my cheek. Its suddenness almost makes me laugh. As the kids tumble into the house, I can still feel it there, quickening my heart like a kiss from a decade ago.

31

I don't wish to de-mother myself to such an extent that *Bambino* readers will assume I'm not really a mum at all, that the kids in my problem-page photo were, in fact, borrowed from a child modelling agency to lend me an air of authenticity. Nor do I wish them to assume that I'm nannied up to the hilt and that any child-rearing insight has been gleaned during my brief scamper through the house between my Pilates class and arse-exfoliation appointment.

On the other hand – and I'm scrutinising myself now in our bathroom mirror, which is frosted with gobbed-out toothpaste – I certainly don't wish to go as me. Brief rundown:

- *Hair*: no longer crying out for a cut, but sobbing helplessly like a child being subjected to the controlled-crying technique (i.e. leave your baby to wail until he falls asleep. Sounds so simple. First night with Jake, I actually bit a hole through my pillowcase while Martin slumbered blissfully. Swine.)
- *Neck*: showing definite signs of wear and tear. Premature withering directly attributable to child-rearing. Millie's neck-skin resembles that of a young nectarine, like the rest of her infant-free colleagues. Her enthusiastic dating regime appears to not mar her appearance one jot.
- *Face*: Jesus wept.
- *Breasts*: flumping slowly floorwards, mercifully concealed by Martin's pale-grey French Connection sweater, which he forgot to remove from our property and of which I am particularly fond. Not because it still smells of him or anything. Absolutely not.
- *Stomach, hips, arse*: while not gargantuan, certainly requiring some kind of industrial support.

After much sweaty deliberation, I choose my knee-length black dress, which fits fine round the middle (if I suck in my stomach at all times) and shows just about the right amount of cleavage and legs. As I walk the children round to Sam's, I am conscious of being looked at differently by strangers – of being noticed.

'Whoa, very nice,' Sam exclaims, letting us in.

'Are you sure?' I gawp down at what now looks terribly funereal.

'Yeah, honestly. I'd have hardly recognised you.'

I take this as a compliment. 'Not too drab?'

'You,' he says, laughing, 'are absolutely not drab. God, they're sexy shoes. Why don't you wear them more often?'

'What, like in the park, or the gym hall?' I ask, laughing.

'Like anywhere,' he says, and my stomach flips in nervy anticipation.

Lola and Travis have already hared up to Harvey's room. For a ten-year-old, he's unusually tolerant of younger children, and bursts of laughter fizzle around the house. I spot it then: a fringed purple silk scarf – a girl's scarf most definitely – strewn over the back of a chair. I inhale deeply and Sam mistakes it for pre-event nerves. 'You'll be great, babe,' he says gently.

Babe? Flustered, I grab my jacket and bag, and reach up to kiss his cheek. 'Thanks for letting the kids stay over. Thanks for everything, Sam.'

He sniggers. 'Save your acceptance speech for the event. Off you go now. You did order your cab to pick you up from here, didn't you? Is that him waiting outside?'

'Looks like it.' I glance through the window. I couldn't face driving, having to find a parking space on top of everything else. I pause, aware of Sam studying my face. I don't know where I'd be without him supporting me through everything. Sometimes it feels as if I give nothing in return. I open my mouth, wanting to thank him not just for babysitting tonight, but for so much more. The cab driver toots his horn impatiently.

'Can't be late for your own show,' Sam says teasingly.

Turning my back on the scarf, I muster some semblance of a

confident smile. Then I stride out, with even my motherish hair feeling less lacklustre now, as 'if that, too, has been Sam-ified.

Although my 'script' has been approved by Millie, I still play it over and over in the back of the cab.

'Hello, my name is Caitlin Brown and I'm *Bambino*'s agony aunt. Every week I receive—'

The driver snorts. I grimace behind his oil-slicked head. Hell, was I talking out loud?

I continue, under my breath, 'Hello, thank you for coming. My name is—'

I glimpse the driver's teasing eyes in the rear-view mirror.

'Hello! Welcome to our *Bambino* reader event! Every week I—'

'Let out for the evening?' he asks, as if I'm a prison inmate.

'Um, yes. Just meeting some friends.'

My name is Caitlin Brown and I'm a halfwit.

An email that came in yesterday pops into my head:

Dear Caitlin,
I really enjoy your page, and your words of wisdom always make me feel so much better about being a mother. I am not writing with a problem as such but for some general advice on how to get back to being the old, confident me who had a sense of humour, a smidge of intelligence and who could read the *Guardian* without fazing off and finding herself gawping at the same paragraph over and over and over.
How can I be a fun person again? I so want to claw back the woman I once was – assertive and confident, like you.
With thanks,
Mashed-Potato Brain, Croydon

Yet again ignoring Millie's never-reply-personally rule, I typed:

Dear Mashed,
You have hit upon something that virtually every mother experiences. The feeling that a vital part of you has been lost. It's only natural, having devoted vast portions of your

time to the care of your child; but there comes a time when the focus should fall back on you. What excites you and makes you happy? I suggest that you set yourself some challenges. These needn't be monumental but should scare you, just a little.

The cab pulls up outside Jacob's Court Hotel. Take your own advice, Caitlin Brown. I am scared, and not just a little.

'I'll be rooting for you.' Where are you, R, when I need you? I pay the driver, climb out of the cab and stride – chin up, back straight, like Lola at her gym display – towards the hotel.

I glimpse my reflection in the glass door. I see a woman who's putting on a passable act of knowing where she's going, and what the heck she'll say when she gets there.

32

Jacob's Court Hotel is in the throes of refurbishment, which lends a chaotic air. There are hessian screens in the foyer blocking off the area where workmen are sanding and plastering, but they might as well not be there for all the screening they do. The air feels dusty, and there's a palpable air of discontent. A woman with the proportions of a barbecue skewer clacks around the hall in spike heels, muttering urgent instructions to workmen.

'Excuse me,' I say, 'I'm looking for the *Bambino* reader event.'

She pulls an icy smile. 'Davenport Suite.'

Like I know where that is. 'Along the corridor to your left,' she adds. 'Follow it round the corner, last door on your right.' She flicks back sleek toffee-coloured hair and narrows her eyes at the workmen.

I set off down the corridor. It's carpeted with a ruby-red runner and has strips of parquet gleaming at either side. There's something unnerving about walking along a long, narrow space. It's too catwalk-like. 'Sexy shoes,' Sam had remarked, and at his place they'd felt right with their skinny ankle straps and just-manageable heels. For a moment I'd felt like the foxtrel mothers who shop at Leoni's.

Now, in the hundred-mile corridor, they just feel bloody high and are pinching like buggery. Either they have shrunk a size since I left Sam's or my feet have puffed up to gargantuan proportions. Where the hell is this last door on the right? Does it actually exist? A chambermaid emerges from a room with a trolley and throws me a sympathetic glance. The corridor turns a corner, and another. I suspect it's leading me right round the building as some kind of sick joke and I'll end up back at reception.

Then I hear it, behind an ornately carved door: a warm, confident voice – Millie's voice. Someone who never has puffer-fish feet.

I step in. Millie waves across the room and makes to head in my direction, but is stopped for an urgent head-to-head by a stressed-looking girl clutching a sheaf of papers. Still an hour to go before the readers arrive (or rather, in Millie-speak, the 'normal people' – i.e. not media people, as if those who work on magazines inhabit some rarefied parallel universe). I loiter by the door, my heels throbbing rhythmically, wondering how to occupy myself. It's at times like this that I wish I still smoked. What is there to fiddle with, now that smoking indoors is illegal? I'd be able to busy myself with lighting up and smoking, and wouldn't feel like a stranded carp.

Stands have been set up round the edge of the conference suite. They're for products I know only from the adverts in *Bambino*: Au Naturelle Baby Purées, Little Padders Footwear, Botty-Bot Pure Terry Nappy System. My poor, beleaguered infants, dragged up on cheap commercial baby mush with the texture of sick, their feet encased in Mum's lumpen knitted bootees (in the days when she still remembered she was a grandmother and clacked her needles with a vengeance). I did try making baby food, lovingly puréeing carrots and sweet potatoes, which Jake spat out in disgust. I gave up after that.

'Hi, sweetie,' Millie gushes, slightly breathless but looking stunning in a swirly-patterned wrap dress that clings fetchingly to her child-free form.

'Hello, Millie.' I am stilted by shyness. This is ridiculous. I have known her for fifteen years. I try to un-clench my back teeth.

'Hey.' She throws a slender arm round my shoulders. 'You look lovely, hon. God, what fabulous shoes. Haven't seen you in heels since . . . I can't remember. Want a coffee or anything? Or a proper drink?'

'No thanks.' My insides are juddering along merrily enough without a caffeine injection.

'Are you OK with everything? You know what you're doing?'

'No.' I snigger idiotically.

'Hey, don't stress. It's just a little thing, OK? No big deal.'

'Blink and you'll miss it. Yes, I remember.' I manage a watery smile.

Millie laughs and swishes away to attend to the more pressing matter of where the waitresses should stand to dispense welcome drinks.

For something to do – as an alternative to sweating and shaking in the toilets, or having lustful thoughts about cigarettes – I peruse the stands and am cornered by an eager girl at the Botty-Bot display. People are starting to wander into the suite, taking their glasses of wine or freshly squeezed juice from the waitresses' trays, and are looking around expectantly. Most don't really fit the *Bambino* image. There are all types – all sizes and shapes – from the downright unkempt to the just holding it together to, occasionally, the scarily groomed. Most, thankfully, look *normal*.

'You're Caitlin Brown, aren't you?' chirps the Botty-Bot girl.

'That's right, yes.' Being recognised is so weird. Already a few women have cast me knowing glances. 'It's her, isn't it?' looks, accompanied by raised eyebrows and whispers. I am hardly on a par with Madonna, or even a Z-list reality-TV contestant, yet it's still unnerving – as if the back of my dress might be tucked into my pants, exposing my ten-denier-clad arse.

'So, what's your feeling?' the girl asks.

'Sorry?'

'On nappies,' she prompts me. 'Terries versus disposables.'

Christ on a bike. Not that one. Disposables it's been for the lot of them – with Travis's rear still firmly encased at night-time, thus qualifying our family for the Planet Wrecker Award. So shoot me dead. The only parent I know who gamely adhered to a terries regime is Rachel. 'Well, I did try using terriers . . .' I begin.

Terriers? What am I saying?

We both laugh. 'I shouldn't say this,' the girl hisses over the stand, 'but I'm only filling in for a friend today. I've got twins.

Two years old. Between them they're responsible for clogging up half the landfill sites in the south-east.'

I am ridiculously grateful to this girl and take one of her sample nappy liners anyway, just to be friendly. I can always use it as a shoe-shining cloth.

'Cait? This is Henry, our MD.'

I swing round to be greeted by Millie, who's glowing prettily, and a middle-aged man with veiny cheeks. 'Henry', she adds, 'meet our famous Caitlin Brown.'

'Pleased to meet you.' My hand shoots out like a robot's, and I try for a confident smile. God, I could murder a proper drink, but am sticking to water (still, not fizzy: less likely to cause an embarrassing belching incident on stage).

'You've made a huge difference to the magazine,' Henry enthuses. 'Stuffy old bag we used to have . . . What was her name again, Millie?'

Her eyebrows perform a manic wiggle. 'Harriet,' she hisses. 'She's here, actually.'

'Is she?' I am horrified, having effectively done her out of a job while she was in the throes of illness.

'I can't understand why she's come,' Millie whispers as Henry glides towards a cluster of suits. 'I didn't invite her or anything. She just turned up, with a ticket, like everyone else.'

'Shall I speak to her or what?'

Millie shakes her head. 'Don't worry about her. Just concentrate on your performance, OK?'

'Performance?' I repeat hollowly.

'Hey, Caitlin! How are you feeling?' Bev gushes, tottering towards me in ill-advised skinny jeans and a marshmallow-pink top. Marcia looms close behind, her black shirt dress clinging elegantly to her curvaceous form. It makes my dress resemble a tube of liquorice.

'I'm fine,' I say brightly.

'You don't look it,' Bev announces. 'You look bloody petrified. I've got a packet of ten Silk Cut in my bag, thought I'd treat myself seeing as it's a special occasion. Fancy sneaking out for a quick puff, soothe your nerves?'

'No thanks,' I say, although I want to, very much. Right now I could smoke the entire packet.

Marcia squints at my dress. 'George at Asda?' she says with a guffaw.

'I think so,' I say, although in truth it's so ancient I can't remember where it came from.

'Yes, I'm sure it is. My cleaning lady has the same one.'

I smile curtly, amazed that Marcia has even heard of Asda, or that she speaks to her cleaning staff.

Rachel scuttles over, looking oddly disconnected without Eve jammed at her side, and gives me a warm hug. Everyone has a gleeful air, as if delighted to be presented with food that they haven't prepared themselves. They snatch at canapés, studying them like Martians who have never encountered Earthlings' food. 'Ooh, look at these!' Bev exclaims, grabbing a pawful of what looks like caramelised fruit wrapped in prosciutto. I'm surprised she doesn't snatch the tray, open her gob and tip in the entire lot.

I nibble a blini smeared with caviar. It's so densely fishy it causes the interior of my mouth to shrivel instantly. I never feel comfortable with canapés. They're like buses, coming thick and fast when you don't need them. Then, when your belly feels hollow and your blood sugar's plummeted, all you can find is an oil-smeared empty tray.

Two hours, I remind myself as Bev slurps her wine. Two hours and I'm out of here, in my safe, silent house. Then I can be normal again.

'Um, hi, Caitlin.'

Amelia. Sam's ex, soon-to-be-no-longer ex, a vision of beauty with rose-petal skin and amber-flecked eyes. 'Amelia, hi!' I gush. 'What are you doing here?' I try not to blast fish-breath into her face.

'I do read *Bambino* sometimes.' She smiles. 'I am still a mum, remember.'

'Oh, I'm sorry, I didn't mean . . .' I shift my weight, trying to ease the biting pressure of the ankle straps.

'It's OK.' She laughs kindly. 'Sam says you're brilliant – that you've practised your whole speech thing with him.'

I shrug, conscious of my blazing cheeks. Yes, we rehearsed a few times over the past week, with Sam posing as Heckling Reader, Indignant Reader, Reader Up for a Fight – every reader type we could think of – but did he have to *tell* her? What other little nuggets does he pass on?

'He's been a huge help,' I murmur. 'In fact, Lola and Travis are staying at his place tonight.'

'Yes, I know.'

Of course she does. Amelia is no longer the shadowy figure who makes occasional forays to London from Cornwall, but part of his life again. Each time I'm at Sam's I scan the bathroom for evidence of girlie occupation – creams, 'feminine' razors, a box of Lil-lets. Nothing yet, apart from the purple scarf on the chair, but it's only a matter of time. I snatch some kind of crustacean in a fibrous wrapping from a passing tray and ram it into my mouth.

Millie assumes her position behind the podium on the stage. The chatter subsides, as if a blanket has descended on the room. 'Hello, everyone. I'm Millie Dawson, editor of *Bambino* magazine. Welcome to our very first reader event.'

I steal a sideways glance at Amelia. Her corn-coloured waves fall prettily around her face. I have to ask. I *have* to.

'How are things with you two?' I whisper.

There, I've done it. I'm such a fizz of sweaty-palmed nerves that it feels like I've nothing to lose. I crunch hard on an unchewable bit of crustacean. It spikes the inside of my cheek.

'What, me and Sam?' Amelia whispers back.

I nod. 'I mean . . . d'you think you'll get back together? Harvey's been saying . . .' God, my audacity astounds me.

'To be honest, that's partly why I came. To grab a few minutes with you. Stupid, I know, because you'll be busy doing your speech and everything.'

'A fabulous selection of guest speakers . . .' Millie continues. Her hair gleams, and her décolleté looks lightly oiled. She's the right kind of shiny. I am a sweaty liquorice stick.

'What did you want to talk about?' I hiss. Oh God, it's all going to come out. Amelia knows how I feel about Sam. She's seen into my head and glimpsed the salacious thoughts I've been having about her beloved.

I am on the verge of dying with shame. I need booze, cigarettes, anything.

She sips her purplish drink. 'I know how he feels about you,' she murmurs, flicking me a sly glance.

Jesus. As if I'm not a scramble of nerves already. 'Do you?' I manage. So he does feel something, more than I've ever dared hope.

'What a good friend you are to him,' Amelia continues, 'how you've been so supportive, hanging out with him and having Harvey to stay over.'

Friend. Supportive. Bollocks, bollocks, bollocks.

'And I thought maybe you'd be the person to tell me if I was being a complete idiot.' She giggles, and big-cheese Henry throws her a stern look.

'I don't get it,' I whisper.

'I mean . . . wanting me and Sam to be together. Do you think he wants that, or would I be ruining everything all over again?'

'I . . . I'm not sure.'

'It's just . . . I thought you, better than anyone, might be able to tell me. It's so scary, Caitlin. I'm terrified of misreading him and getting it wrong.'

The adrenaline that has been coursing through my veins seems to seep away and I'm overwhelmed by a feeling of flatness. I could disintegrate right here, shrouded in George at Asda.

'Yes,' I murmur. 'I think he does. I thought you were getting remarried anyway. Harvey's been telling Jake . . .'

She smiles and her eyes sparkle. 'Of course Harvey says that. It's what he wants, like most kids whose parents live apart. It's not the same, is it, doing the weekend parent thing? I think boys especially need to be with their mums, don't you?'

'Um, yes,' I manage, thinking of Jake playing with his new friend in Lego Towers.

'So you don't think I'm crazy, arranging a kind of meeting with Sam to see if we can work something out?'

'No, I don't think you're crazy.' The caviar repeats on me, even fishier this time.

There's applause as Millie holds up this week's issue.

'I'm so glad,' Amelia murmurs, 'because I have this stupid idea about taking him to dinner to a little French place in Camden. La Rose, it's called. It's old-fashioned, not trendy or glamorous. It has checked tablecloths and candles in dribbly wine bottles – you know the kind of place – but it's special to us.'

'Why?' I really don't want to hear this.

She smiles coyly. 'It's where we went the day I found out I was pregnant. I took the pregnancy test with me and I showed it to him and he was so shocked and excited.'

I forget all this – that they had a life together, with their baby, before Cornwall swept her away. And now she's about to stomp right back in.

'I'm sure he'll love it,' I say. It comes out as a growl.

'Well, let's see if I can pluck up the nerve.'

'And our first guest,' Millie says, 'has been a huge hit since she joined the magazine just a few months ago.'

Amelia claps a hand over her mouth. 'God, listen to me wittering on. You'd better get up there.'

'Yes, I'd better. Good luck with Sam.'

She throws her arms round me in an unexpected hug. 'Thanks. You're a lovely person, Caitlin. I can see why Sam's so fond of you. I couldn't think of anyone else I could talk to about this.'

I turn away, but Amelia catches my arm. 'Imagine them naked,' she adds with a grin. 'Picture everyone in this room stark bollock naked, even the fat guys in suits.'

A snigger bursts out. 'I'll do that,' I say.

'I'm rooting for you,' R told me, and something surges through me. A feeling that I'll get through this alive.

33

And I do. Imagine them naked, I mean – even the big cheeses. So many faces are tilted my way, expecting me to say something funny or clever or both. It feels like my heels have doubled in height and I wobble uncertainly, as if drunk. Every word of my script evaporates from my brain.

'When Millie asked me to be *Bambino*'s agony aunt,' I begin, my voice wavering, 'I wasn't sure if I was up to the job.'

Fuck it. Just be yourself. It's OK to feel scared, isn't that what I told Mashed-Potato Brain?

'I felt such a phoney,' I continue, feeling braver now, 'as a parent certainly, and probably as a human being.'

Small ripple of laughter. Jesus, I've forgotten to do the hello-readers-how-lovely-it-is-to-meet-you thing. Too late now.

'And I'm sure lots of you can identify with that,' I finish in a rush. I scan the room. Bev is stoking her face with canapés. Amelia flashes an encouraging smile.

'So I thought,' I continue – this isn't remotely what I'd intended to say – 'if we all feel like fakes, let's acknowledge that and support each other. I don't know about you, but it's been a huge relief to me to discover that the childcare police aren't about to storm into my house and wallop me with a truncheon for not feeding my children organic aubergine with a blueberry jus.'

What the heck am I blathering on about? It's the stress of having Amelia here, staring at me. My brain's running away with itself. Yet when I skim the audience, I realise that people are laughing. There's a palpable air of relief. Even my shoes seem to have slackened off. My feet must have de-puffed.

'So instead of me preaching to you about the right way to do things,' I lurch on, feeling mildly out of control but beginning to enjoy myself, as if on a roller-coaster ride, 'I thought we could all throw in the most dim-witted advice we've ever heard.'

There's a lull; then someone pipes up, 'You should *wear* your children. You should strap them to your body with scraps of ethnic-looking fabric.'

A flurry of approval and clapping.

'No more than three hours of TV a week!'

'No TV until they're ten!'

'No nursery – ever.'

'All your bread should be home-made, even if you have to get up at four in the morning to make it.'

'Grind the wheat for your bread with your teeth!'

'With your children strapped to your body.'

Laughter fills the room as more hands shoot up.

'Parents who give their children fruit juice should be jailed.'

Millie catches my eye and gives me a flamboyant thumbs-up.

'Children should sleep in the adult bed,' calls out a woman from the back, 'even if it means you're forced on to the floor.'

'Potty-train them at six weeks old.'

'Six *days* old!'

'They should only play with wooden toys.'

And so they keep coming, until I've forgotten that this was supposed to be an ordeal.

'When you hear all this,' comes my newly confident voice, 'you have to agree that one sure route to madness is trying to do the right thing. Feeling fake is natural. It's part of the job. The one thing we can all do for our children is have time for them and listen.'

'Absolutely,' someone murmurs.

'But, please, let's stop beating ourselves around the heads, because the perfect parent doesn't exist. I mean, sometimes I let my kids have Fanta.'

More clapping. My heart is thudding madly, but in a good way – as it might if Sam were to walk in right now, and Amelia were spirited away to another continent.

'Question and answer time,' Millie mouths from the side of the stage.

It's the part I've been dreading. My jaw clenches instantly, and I spot Rachel, willing me to keep it together over the top of her glass.

'So,' I manage, the wobbliness sneaking back in, 'would anyone like to ask a question? Any particular problems you'd like to, um . . . to throw open to everyone here?'

Rachel grins and winks. Amelia is smiling broadly, and her smile is starting to look a little scary. Something doesn't feel right. She's trying too hard to be my friend. Instantly, it all makes sense. Amelia is trying to warn me off him. In sharing her Sam-plans with me, she's saying, *Don't think you can come between us.*

There's an awkward pause. Then a hand springs up and a chalk-faced woman blurts out, 'What can I do about my kids' fights? It starts as soon as they wake up – sometimes they've had at least three before we set off for school.' She looks exhausted and desperate.

'Does anyone else have a problem with inter-sibling fighting?' I ask.

Much nodding and waving of hands.

'Has anyone found strategies that actually work?'

'Star charts!' pipes up Marcia.

'Praising them when they don't fight and ignoring it when they do,' calls out a glossy-haired woman in a tweedy suit. 'Unless someone's being seriously injured of course.'

Much laughter.

They answer the questions, this eager audience, while I stand there in my liquorice dress, somehow managing to wing it.

Millie strides towards me – her wrap dress has unwrapped a tad, revealing a glimpse of lacy bra – and grabs the mic. 'Thank you,' she says grandly, 'to our fabulous agony aunt, Caitlin Brown.'

And it's over.

'Brilliant,' she hisses into my ear as I clatter past her.

'I need a drink,' I hiss back, almost running into – such good fortune – the wine waitress. I snatch a glass and gulp its contents greedily. 'Thanks,' I murmur.

'I never drink at this kind of event,' comes a voice in my ear. I turn, and it's Harriet Pike; her sneer would make small children weep.

'Oh, Harriet, I'm—'

'Yes, I've gathered. You're Caitlin. My replacement.'

My mouth shrivels, and I'm scrabbling for words when Rachel hurries through the crowd towards me, holding out my bag. 'You didn't turn off your mobile, idiot. It's rung at least five times. You'd better see who it is.'

'Thanks, Rachel.' I smile tightly at Pike.

'I'd decided to move on anyway,' she says tersely.

'Right . . .'

'You can't do these things for too long. Seen one problem, seen them all.' She laughs bitterly.

'Yes, I suppose there are certain themes that come up.'

'Anyway,' she adds, 'I couldn't resist popping along today. To see what kind of a hash you'd make of this.'

My mouth drops open. The milling crowd – even Rachel, who's still clutching my bag – seems to melt away.

Harriet's eyes narrow. 'Do you know how long I worked for this magazine?' she hisses. 'Ten years! Since the first issue. I was on the launch team. Bet you didn't know that, did you?'

'No, I . . .' I can feel my face blazing. Her burgundy lipstick has bled into the creases around her mouth.

'Even the name, *Bambino*, was my idea,' she fires on. 'You should have heard some of the dreadful names they were kicking around.'

'Excuse me,' I mutter, 'but I really have to go.' Rachel flings me a let's-get-out-of-here look.

'Mind you,' Harriet retorts, 'we had a proper editor then who knew what she was talking about. Not Millie Dawson, who brings in her friend to take over my page and hasn't a clue about raising children.'

'Do *you* have children, Harriet?' I bark, startled by my assertiveness.

Her lips wither. 'It's not necessarily the mother who knows what's best for a child.'

'For goodness' sake,' Rachel snaps, 'do you honestly think you know better than a parent does? I used to enjoy your page, Harriet, and read it every week, but I didn't realise you had such an attitude—'

'Why are you being like this?' I cut in. '*I* didn't sack you. I had no intention of taking on the page permanently.'

Harriet laughs scathingly. 'With a job like this, one needs a break. I'd been doing it week in, week out, for ten years. Can you imagine what that's like? Millie – your *friend* – encouraged me to take time off, said I needed a rest – planning, of course, to substitute me with you.'

'I'm sorry you feel that way,' I say firmly, 'and I'm sure it didn't happen like that. Now, if you'll excuse me . . .'

Right on cue, my mobile trills. Grabbing my bag from Rachel, I fish it out and hurry to the corridor. It's stopped ringing by the time I take the call. Not five but *nine* missed calls. All from Martin. What's going on? Trembling, I call him, willing him to pick up.

It can only be one thing. Something has happened to Jake.

34

'It's OK, Cait, it's OK. He's going to be all right.'

'What happened?'

'It was just . . . an accident. I can't believe I let it happen.'

'Just tell me what happened!'

'It's his arm. He's done something – fallen on his arm when the car hit him.'

'He got hit by a *car*?'

'Please don't panic,' Martin insists. 'He's been seen in A&E and they're keeping him in, but they just want to check everything's all right.'

'Where? Which hospital?'

Someone touches my arm and I turn to see Amelia. Martin gives me the details and I try to store them in my head. My hands are shaking so much I stab the wrong button to finish the call.

'Caitlin,' Amelia says gently, 'what's going on?'

'Jake's in hospital. He's been knocked over or something, I don't know . . .'

'I'll drive you. My car's over the road on a meter.'

'I can get a cab,' I protest, but she's already marching me towards her beaten-up yellow Beetle with a gigantic sunflower emblazoned on its bonnet.

The car rattles and jerks, and it quickly becomes apparent that London driving and Amelia don't mix. She curses constantly, gripping the steering wheel as if fearful that it might spring from her hands.

This shouldn't be Jake. Not cautious Jake, who has never had an accident in his life. Travis is different; he's been to A&E so many times that he greets the waiting-area toys like long-lost buddies. He broke his willy once, three weeks after Martin left. I'd bought him a toddler seat that fitted over the loo and he'd somehow tumbled forwards, trapping his penis at an unfortunate angle and bellowing for me. I'd run into the bathroom thinking, What now? What's he broken or spilled? I was still smarting from finding him squirting the last glug of my L'Occitane shower gel (a gift from Millie) down the loo. All those bad thoughts I'd had; then I'd found him screaming, with blood dripping on to the floor.

Where was Martin when I needed him? I'd never hated him more than at that moment. Naturally, as soon as he learned of Travis's accident, he was tearing through East London at something like 800 miles an hour to meet us at hospital, where we were told that the damaged appendage would miraculously self-heal.

Amelia is chatting – I wish she'd keep her mind on the road – but I'm not in a small-talk mood. 'So I've definitely finished with my boyfriend,' she says, 'because whatever happens with me and Sam, I realised I wasn't being honest, stringing him along and sneaking up to London whenever I could to spend the night with Sam.'

'That's probably the best thing,' I murmur. Please don't expect me to advise you. Not now.

She lurches to a halt at a red light. 'I probably shouldn't ask this, and it's really none of my business—'

'Amelia, I think you're in the wrong lane.'

'God, am I?' She noses right, triggering a torrent of angry tooting behind us. 'I was just wondering,' she continues, now straddling two lanes, 'if there's ever been anything between you and Sam.'

I swallow hard. 'Of course not,' I say tersely. 'What made you think there was?'

She shoots me a glance. Her sunniness has faded, and her eyes are flinty. I realise now that being chummy towards me has required a monumental effort on her part. She's the one who deserves the Most Controlled Being Award.

'It's just . . . I hear from Harvey that you're around a lot,' she continues lightly, seemingly having forgotten my injured son in hospital, 'and your name's always cropping up.' She barges in front of a rusting Transit van, her knuckles taut as she grips the steering wheel. 'I just wanted to know,' she adds with a dry snigger, 'what kind of competition I'm up against.'

I stare pointedly out of the side window so she can't see my blazing cheeks.

'There's no competition, Amelia,' I say coolly.

'Right. I'm sorry.'

'I haven't been involved with anyone since Martin left,' I add, conveniently erasing Pac-a-Mac night from my mind.

'Well, I can't understand why not,' she says, her voice brightening. 'You're a lovely-looking woman, Caitlin. Ever think of joining one of those dating websites?'

'No,' I growl. Oh, please. She's warned me off Sam; now she's turned into my mother. Isn't it time you found yourself a nice man?

Mercifully, the hospital's in view. Amelia pulls up in front of a huddle of smokers, their faces misted in a pale-grey haze. 'Shall I come in with you? I can let Sam know I'll be late.'

'No, I'll be fine. Thanks for the lift.'

'He'll be fine, Caitlin. Kids break bones all the time.' She squeezes my hand, but any trace of warmth is long gone.

Jake doesn't break bones all the time, I think, tumbling out of the car and striding towards the entrance.

But she's right. The receptionist directs me along a corridor and up two floors to the fracture ward, and he *is* fine. His face is pale and drawn, and his right arm is encased in plaster, but my son still breaks into a grin when he sees me.

'Hi, Mum.'

'Oh, honey.' I put my arms round him and kiss his forehead. He still smells of Jake: sweet as honey. I barely register Martin saying hi from the chair beside the bed and asking where Lola and Travis are, as if I might have left them bundled in the cupboard under the stairs while I snatched my five minutes of fame. He stands up and tugs the faded burgundy curtain around the bed.

'They're at Sam's,' I say quickly, 'sleeping over. Oh, Jake, how did it happen?'

Jake shifts in bed, wincing. 'Me and Dad were playing football—'

'On the grassy area by the flats,' Martin cuts in. 'I passed to him and the ball went into the road. Jake chased it and the car came round the corner . . . It just clipped him, sent him flying, and he landed on his arm. It was my fault really, wasn't it, son?'

Jake shakes his head fiercely. 'No, Dad. It wasn't anyone's fault.'

He looks like a little boy, propped up against white pillows with his brave face on.

'He's fractured his elbow,' Martin adds. 'It was some mess, wasn't it, Jake? All twisted-looking.'

'It was freaky.' Jake grins.

'How long will he be in here?' I ask as Martin drags over a chair for me.

'A couple of days. We're waiting for X-ray results. They want to check that it's setting properly and make sure there's no nerve damage to the hand.'

'D'you think—'

'He'll be *fine*,' Martin insists. I glance at him. Being here together reminds me of the countless school parents' evenings we've attended together. These days I go alone, dispatching potted reports to Martin.

'One of us should stay here tonight,' I add.

'I will. You should get home for Travis and Lola.'

'I told you, they're sleeping over at Sam's.'

Martin frowns and there's a glimmer of the old shark-eye look. 'That's OK, is it? What about school in the morning?'

'I'd planned to go round first thing to pick them up. I'll be there in plenty of time. You don't have a problem with that, do you?' I keep my voice light, for Jake's sake. His dark eyes bore into me.

'It's just . . .' Martin tails off, raking his hair distractedly. Clearly he does have a problem; he's just not willing to share it.

'Sam's been a big support to me,' I murmur.

Martin darts me an I-bet-he-has look.

'Let's not get into this now.'

'I'm sorry,' Martin mutters. 'I just feel so . . . responsible for this.'

'Dad,' Jake says, 'would you mind if . . .' He reddens.

'What is it, son?'

'It's . . . football. I, um, don't really like it. I try, but I'm rubbish, everyone knows I am.'

Martin looks aghast. 'Why didn't you say?'

'I thought you might be cross,' comes the small voice.

'You really thought that?' Martin's eyes moisten instantly.

'Or disappointed or mad,' Jake adds.

'What kind of dad d'you think I am? I don't care about football, Jake. I thought it was what you liked to do.'

Jake shrugs.

'Hey.' I touch his good arm. 'I'll go and see if the shop's open, find you some comics and stuff, get a couple of coffees . . . Is there anything else you'd like?'

'No thanks, Mummy.'

I can't remember the last time he called me 'Mummy', or looked at me that way – as if he's actually fond of me, and I'm not just some random, fun-wrecking adult.

I feel Martin's eyes on me as I delve for my purse. My bag is crammed with wodges of paper – my survival notes for the *Bambino* event, none of which I referred to. There's an oily napkin that the waitress gave me with the fishy blini.

'I haven't asked,' Martin says, 'how did the *Bambino* thing go?'

'It was fine. Actually, I enjoyed it.'

He smiles. 'Thought you would.' A hint of sadness crosses his face. It's still a handsome face, with top-quality cheekbones; he looks like a man who takes care of himself, even with the ward's blue-white striplights draining him of colour. 'Cait.' He clears his throat and looks down. 'I'm so sorry.'

I know then that he's sorry for more than Jake's arm and for trying to crowbar him into some First Division-footballer mould. He's sorry about water-coolers, and shagging in the toilets of Bink & Smithson, and messing up everything we had.

It's too late, of course, but something loosens in me, as if I'm slowly uncoiling. I turn away before he sees my eyes filling.

'Cait?' Martin calls after me. 'Black no sugar, remember?'

My lips twitch into a smile. 'Of course I remember,' I say.

35

Travis and I spend Friday in hospital with Jake, having relieved Martin of bedside duties and seen him stagger off to work with hair askew. (*Work*, I ask you, after spending the night on a fold-out bed. Still, the design of a swanky gym complex in Canary Wharf waits for no man.) The ward and its various fittings thrill Travis. Who needs Thorpe Park when there's a round-the-bed curtain to swing on and drape around oneself like a cape?

Jake, who is still being unnervingly – almost spookily – warm towards me, spends most of the day pretending he isn't *really* watching little ones' programmes (*Tweenies*, *Teletubbies*) that are showing on a loop in the TV room. His lunch arrives on a squeaking trolley. Fish, boiled potatoes, cauliflower florets – all a bleary off-white, apart from a small mound of sweetcorn. A brusque nurse hands him a bulbous red plastic knife and fork, as if he were three years old and incapable of manipulating proper cutlery, and he tucks in with one-handed gusto.

'How are the sea monkeys?' he asks through a full mouth.

'They're fine,' I lie. (Frankly, they haven't entered my radar for weeks.)

'I miss them,' he adds wistfully, and I wonder if this is my Jake talking, or if he'll rip off a mask like a Scooby Doo baddie to reveal someone else's child.

'Do you?' I ask. 'I didn't think you liked them. Remember when you unwrapped the box last Christmas and complained that they weren't proper pets?'

He smirks. 'I said they were rubbish, didn't I? I was disappointed 'cause I couldn't teach them tricks.'

I reach for his hand and squeeze it. As visitors aren't catered for by meals-on-wheels, Travis is wolfing a canteen ham sandwich that looks as if it's been compressed by straightening irons. 'I suppose they were a bit babyish for you,' I venture. 'Sometimes I forget how grown-up you are.'

He shrugs. 'That's all right. I'd rather have a dog, though.'

'Are you joking?'

'No. Yeah.' He pulls a mock scowl that morphs into an ear-to-ear grin as Harvey whips back the curtain.

'Jake, you've got a cast!'

'Yeah.' He displays it proudly.

'*And* you missed school today. You're so lucky. Wish I could break my elbow.'

'How's the patient?' Sam asks, appearing behind him as Lola dives towards Jake. Lifesaver Sam, offering to collect her from school and bring her to me.

'They did X-rays,' Jake enthuses. 'We saw my bones.'

'Cool,' breathes Harvey, forcing his way to the bed's head end and perching on its spongy edge.

Martin returns – he's cut his working day short – laden with provisions. He spots Sam and his smile cements. 'Hi,' he manages, cradling a large brown paper bag awkwardly.

'Here, have this seat.' Sam leaps up. He, too, looks flustered. 'We're going anyway,' he adds quickly. 'Come on, Harv. You'll see Jake as soon as he's out of hospital.'

No he won't, I think miserably. He'll be back with Martin and Slapper, giving me the cold treatment again and having a marvellous time with his new friends in their block and at the afterschool club.

'Oh, I nearly forgot,' Sam murmurs, delving into a crumpled carrier bag that he'd dumped in the corner. 'We brought you a few bits and pieces, Jake, to keep you occupied.'

He hands over the bag and Jake pulls out several well-thumbed books including *The Far Side* and *Calvin and Hobbes*.

'Wow, thanks!' he exclaims.

'That's far too much,' I protest as Lola hops on to the bed, craning to glimpse the pages.

'Charity shop.' Sam flicks a look at Martin, as if he might disapprove of his son being given second-hand goods. My ex-husband is not a charity-shop man. And I see it then – Martin's quick glance that says, 'So, you know Jake's favourite comic strips, do you? And you've had my kids to stay over? Oh, and I hear you've been a huge support to Caitlin.' As if he has the right to prickle over anything.

'Let's get going,' Sam says, grabbing Harvey's hand. He looks as if he might kiss me or Jake, or both of us, then thinks better of it.

And he's gone.

It seems so much quieter now, even though the ward is filling with early-evening visitors. Travis is whingeing to go to the vending machine – so many buttons to press – which he spotted in the entrance area. Jake sets down a comic book on the chipped bedside cabinet and closes his eyes.

'Lola, Travis, why don't you go and watch TV?' Martin suggests, and they scamper away.

Now it's just us and Jake, who's dozing off. We're not talking much, but it doesn't feel awkward. The old closeness has crept back in. An in-this-together feeling that I remember from when Jake was a baby and Martin and I were chronically sleep-deprived. Sometimes, after a small-hours feed, Jake wouldn't settle and Martin would hold him in his arms, pointing out trees and street lamps through our bedroom window. Finally, we'd curl up in bed together, our body clocks so skewed that we couldn't sleep. We'd talk then, barely noticing the creeping dawn.

'Cait,' Martin murmurs. 'There's . . . stuff I need to talk about.'

'What?'

'It's about us. You and me.'

'There you are!' the voice chimes through the ward. Millie strides towards us. 'God, Cait, I've only just found out what happened. Is he all right?'

I leap up to greet her. 'He's fine. Everything's going to be OK.'

She hurries to Jake's side, planting a noisy kiss on his forehead. He swipes a hand where she's left a lipstick smear, as if a bird had deposited something there. 'I couldn't understand why you'd rushed off,' she babbles, 'when you'd gone down so well. Lots of people were dying to talk to you.'

I can't help laughing. 'Millie, it was an emergency.'

She plonks herself on the edge of Jake's bed. 'I know, and I'm really sorry . . . I've been trying to phone you, been so worried.' She laughs. 'I thought maybe you'd had delayed stage fright.'

'Phone's run out of juice,' I tell her.

She sighs noisily. 'None of those friends of yours were any help either. Especially that one in the hideous tight pink top . . . Bev, is it? Half pissed by the end of it, trying to chat up Henry, who's only the MD. Don't those friends of yours get out much?'

Martin clears his throat irritably.

'Sorry, Martin,' she catches herself, 'listen to me babbling on, with poor Jake in his sick bed. Wasn't it great, though, Cait? We'll have to make these events a regular thing. Twice a year, maybe. Pre-Christmas would be perfect.'

Martin smiles tightly. 'Would you like a coffee or something, Millie?'

'Not for me,' she declares. 'Well, only if there are skinny lattes – you know, something decent. Not that vending-machine crap.'

He marches away, and she grimaces at his retreating form. 'God, Cait, this must be so hard for you.'

'Well, it's OK now we know Jake's arm's going to heal and there's no nerve damage.'

'No, I mean with *him*. Shagpants. Being forced to spend all this time together, crammed up in this horrible stinky hospital.'

Millie's citrus perfume seems alien among the disinfectanty smells.

'We're still Jake's parents,' I insist.

'I know, but—'

'It's fine being with him. Kind of comforting.'

She gives me a confused look. 'Well, I think he's really aged. He never looked that haggard when he was with you. *And* he's put on weight.'

I smile. She's being loyal, but it's not what I need to hear, *and* it's not true. It reminds me of the night, soon after Martin had left, when Millie and I were coming home in a cab from a night out and happened to pass the end of Slapper's street. I'd made the mistake of pointing this out and Millie had nagged me to ask the driver to swing round so we could scrawl furious messages on Martin's windscreen. She'd have sacrificed her favourite Chanel lipstick for the pleasure, not caring if we'd ground it down to a gummy stump. Sensible, reasonable Cait wouldn't let her do it. But I loved her for dreaming up the idea.

Jake's eyes flicker open.

'Hi, sweetie,' Millie says briskly. 'Look, I brought you this.' She hands him a mini bagatelle game that Travis begged for in the hospital shop.

'Um, thanks,' he murmurs, giving it a half-hearted ping.

'You're welcome, darling. Take care, won't you? Get better soon.' She turns to me and hisses, 'Hope you don't mind if I shoot off before Shagpants comes back. I feel so awkward around him.'

'Of course not. Thanks for dropping in.'

As she leaves, Jake frowns at me. 'Who's Shagpants?'

'Oh, no one you know.'

He grins slyly at me and we laugh, both knowing he can read every damn thought in my head.

'It's good that Millie's able to conceal her hatred for me,' Martin quips.

'Oh, that's just Millie. Take no notice.' You're lucky, I think; I know what she planned to do with her lipstick.

With Jake awake now, and Lola and Travis tired of TV, there's no chance to ask Martin what he wanted to talk about. When *is* the right time? Perhaps that was the trouble with us all along: no time for each other any more. We'd lost each other.

Where had my R been – or even a sympathetic agony aunt – when I'd needed a little help?

'Are you going to take these guys home?' Martin asks, sipping his millionth vending-machine coffee.

'Yes, I'd better. Travis should be in bed by now.'

Martin gives me a fleeting look. 'I miss all that, you know.'

'What, bathtime? Bedtime? The witching hour?'

He nods. 'All that. The ordinary stuff. Seeing them all first thing, getting them ready for school, doing that thing with the cereal – remember the milk waterfalls?'

'Yes, I remember that.' Swallowing hard, I busy myself by feeding Lola's tired, floppy arms into her coat sleeves, while Martin buttons up Travis's jacket.

I kiss Jake's cheek. He looks up at me and says, 'The doctor says I can come home tomorrow.'

'I know, love. That's brilliant news.'

He bites his lip. 'Give me a cuddle, Mum.'

His request is so surprising that I feel awkward at first, breathing in the scent of his skin and feeling his heart pulse through his pyjama top. I love him so much it crushes me.

I daren't ask what he means when he says 'home.'

36

Morning Cait,

I've been awaiting your full report on the *Bambino* event. As none has been forthcoming, I have to ask: HOW DID IT GO?? I trust that you didn't clam up/faint/run screaming from the building. In fact, I know you didn't. I am aware how fantastic and natural you were, as if you had done that kind of thing countless times before, and that you also looked sensational in your little black dress and those knockout shoes with the strappy bits . . .

I almost choke on my toast. He was there.

Yes, Cait, I have a confession to make. Billy was spending the night at his mum's, and on the spur of the moment I decided to see a film in the West End. By the time I got there, anything half decent was sold out, and I didn't really fancy nursing a drink in some bar. I happened to notice a copy of *Bambino* on a news-stand and you flashed into my mind. I thought, Why not? I hoped you wouldn't mind my turning up out of the blue and that I might be able to project silent support, so I bought the darned mag to get the address of the do.

Even though I didn't have a ticket, it was so chaotic in the hotel foyer with all the workmen that I just walked in. And as I was a little late, there was no one collecting tickets on the door.

Anyway, I have to tell you that your current *Bambino* photo is a marked improvement on the first, but doesn't remotely do you justice. You are lovely.

He. Was. There.

> I hope you'll forgive me for not introducing myself. You
> seemed so busy, talking to clusters of people, and I was
> reluctant to barge in. It just didn't feel like the right time.
> And after your speech you just seemed to disappear.

Driiiiing. The doorbell. I hurry upstairs, just as Lola and Travis
thunder down from their rooms in a race to answer it. It's Martin
and Jake.

'I'm home, Mum!' Jake says, grinning. He's immediately
swamped by his siblings as if they've spent years apart. I find
myself stepping back, melting into bookshelves and walls.

'Mum,' Jake cries, 'when am I getting that thing? That present
you promised when we had our photo done.'

'I can't believe you're still on about that!'

Martin laughs, sending Jake upstairs to change into clean
clothes, and Lola and Travis to swap their PJs for daywear, as if
he lives here.

Sunlight gasps into the living room as I draw back the
curtains. 'Daisy,' I want to say to Martin, 'what's happening
with Daisy and you?' I used to play with her name in my head:
Daisy, a fragile, skinny-petalled flower. Plucking her petals one
by one, then squishing the yolk-coloured centre, her heart.

I'd nurtured wild fantasies about showing up at Purity Springs
in Acton Lane with Jake, Lola and Travis all dressed in their
crummiest, most pitiful clothes and bursting into Daisy's office,
screaming, 'Look what you've done to us! Is this what you
wanted, to ruin these poor children's lives?' Once I'd been
removed from the premises by burly security guards, I'd
planned to hurl bricks through the windows until the police
came to drag me away. Travis would have enjoyed riding in a
cop car. He'd have made nee-naw noises and maybe been
allowed to try on a policeman's hat.

I am no longer troubled by such embittered thoughts.
Although I have lost track of the post-break-up stages, I seem
to have passed a significant one without noticing.

We have an ordinary morning featuring Junior Monopoly and TV (we're still stuck with the portable) until the syrupy sunshine coaxes us into the garden. It feels almost normal, all of us being together – as if the Purity Springs after-sales service never happened. The warm late-June afternoon stretches on and on, lending even our beleaguered back garden a faintly exotic air. Martin and I sit on the back step, each with a glass of Pinot.

'So,' I venture, 'what did you want to talk about at the hospital?'

Travis thunders towards us with a wriggling bug he found under a flowerpot, and now the others are moving every pot in order to capture unsuspecting creatures.

'Lovely, Travis,' Martin says. 'Don't hurt it, will you? Put it back on the ground.'

Travis pouts and shuffles away. 'Sam lets us keep them in jars.'

'Does he now?' Martin glances at me, and tension clouds his eyes.

'The hospital,' I prompt him. 'You wanted—'

'It's . . . Daisy and me. She's moved out until . . . we can work out what's happening.'

'Oh.' I can't say I'm about to crumple with grief. Whooping for joy, or sending champagne corks popping, doesn't seem the right response either.

'She and Poppy are staying with her parents in Hertfordshire.'

'So . . . what went wrong?' I try to banish any trace of glee from my voice.

He sighs deeply. 'I suppose I'm not the kind of man she thought I was. She's much younger, you know.'

'I know that,' I snap.

'And what she wants . . . I couldn't give it. Didn't want to give it.'

'Which is?'

He turns and looks me full in the face. My stomach twists uncomfortably. 'Another baby,' he murmurs.

'She wanted a baby with you?' I'm so grateful to our creepy-crawly collection for occupying the kids.

Martin drains his glass. 'We had a scare. At least, that's how I viewed it. She was furious when it turned out to be a false alarm, as if my negativity – that's how she put it, "your negative attitude" – had caused it not to be real.'

I am astounded. He hasn't talked like this – talked to me properly – for years. I clear my throat. 'Martin . . . why don't you want a child with her?'

His look says, 'Isn't it obvious?' He reminds me of Jake for an instant. 'I already have my family,' he murmurs.

I look down at the flagstones, where ants are scuttling along a crack. 'What are you going to do?' I ask quietly.

He shrugs. 'I don't know. It depends.' It's so unlike him to sound uncertain; not the Martin I know, who I suspect was a fully fledged grown-up at age nine.

'Do you want to come back?' I want to ask. 'Was it just a mistake, and now you want to put things right?' The words pound in my head. He's sitting so close I can sense the warmth from him. I don't know if that's what I want, if it's a real desire or just a yearning for things to be stable and steady again. If he kissed me now, what would I do?

'Cait,' he says, 'Jake wants to come home. To you, I mean.'

'Of course he does,' I say briskly, 'if Daisy's moved out and you're going to be living God knows where . . . it's hardly going to make him feel secure, is it?' My voice rises sharply. Lola swings round and frowns.

'It's not just that. He made a mistake and I think he knew it as soon as he moved in with me.'

Me, not us. As if she no longer exists.

Lola scampers towards us, a glossy black beetle writhing in her palm. 'Mummy! Daddy! Look!'

'Bugs are their new obsession,' I explain.

'Can I keep it as a pet?' Lola demands.

Martin laughs. 'Ask Mum.'

'Thanks.' I grimace at him. It was always 'Ask Mum' at sweat-making moments, and became a joke with us:

'How was I made? How was I born?'

'Ask Mum.' 'Where did the egg come from? D'you mean an egg like that comes from a hen's bum? Like a boiled egg?'

'Jake needs you,' Martin murmurs now.

I'm suspicious. Is it me he needs, or his decent-sized bedroom and all the stuff we didn't get around to packing? Hell, I don't care if he's only after my pancakes. I want my boy back.

We share witching-hour duties, just as we used to. Martin supervises Lola and Travis's bathtimes, and I read stories. Jake jumps into the shower, jutting out his bad arm to keep the cast dry, and unearths PJs from his chest of drawers.

'Am I allowed in?' I peer into his room, where he's clambered into bed.

'Yeah, of course you are.'

I take mock-fearful steps. 'Jake, Dad says you want to come home.'

He drops his gaze and picks at his cast. Lola and Harvey have already autographed it, and Travis has adorned it with a worm drawn in fat felt tip. 'Yeah,' he says, 'I do.'

'Are you sure, hon?'

'Uh-huh.'

'Did . . . something upset you at Dad's?' I venture.

He looks up at me, then flicks his gaze around the room, which I have cleaned to within an inch of its life, an act which has had the unfortunate effect of making the rest of the house appear instantly squat-like.

'No, Mum,' Jake says. 'It's just home.'

Saturday, 10.17 p.m.

Cait, are you there? You've been very elusive lately. Hope my turning up at the *Bambino* thing didn't unnerve or upset you. Maybe I'm being oversensitive and your PC's on the blink. Anyway, just wanted to say hi. I miss you.

R x

I don't reply. I just delete it and take the remains of the wine from the fridge – plus a second bottle, in case the kitchen's destroyed in an earthquake – and head upstairs to Martin in the living room.

I refill his glass, and he tells me about a contract Bink and Smithson have won. I'm only half listening, soaking in the restfulness that descends on the house when the children have gone to bed. 'They're making me a partner,' he says.

'That's brilliant, Martin. About time, after all the hours you've put in.'

He shrugs, knowing that he deserves it.

'Cait,' he adds quietly, 'I've decided it's over with Daisy.'

'Well, you said she's moved out . . .'

'She thinks it's temporary, that we might still work things out, but . . . I wasn't honest with her.' His eyes meet mine. 'I don't love her, Cait. I don't think I ever have.'

'So why . . .?' My voice fractures.

'My fault. I fucked up. I was a terrible husband; I'm a terrible father . . .'

Tears spring into my eyes. Instinctively, I slide my arms round him. He feels so familiar, so right.

He pulls away, mustering a smile despite the tears streaking his cheeks. 'You're wearing my sweater,' he whispers.

'Yes, I often do.'

'I thought you'd have burned it.' He swipes an arm across his face.

I smile. 'I never hated you that much.'

Then we're kissing, and it's like that first kiss in the sleazy Soho pub that we named the Snog Bar thereafter. It's the kiss of our strong-pyjama days.

And we're hurrying upstairs, dizzy on wine and kissing and tumbling into bed with Martin on his side, smelling warm and as sweet as toffee, as if he'd never left me.

It's never stopped being his side.

37

Sunday 6.47 a.m.

Someone's in my bed.

It's not Travis or Lola or Jake. It's an adult male with his legs bent to fit mine and an arm strewn casually across my belly. A *naked* man's arm. It's attached to a body with all the respective bits and pieces in full working order, one particular bit which I was – just a few horribly short hours ago – bestowing with enthusiastic attention.

Oh, God. Kill me now with a pillow or a gun.

Pale sunlight filters through my curtains. I manoeuvre my eyeballs in the direction of the head on my other pillow. Its hair is mussed up in nutty-brown swirls. There's faint snoring. Martin's low, rumbly snore.

Shit.

Sweat prickles my cleavage as the awful details drip, drip into my brain. Our kiss, which had somehow continued all the way up the stairs. (Walking *and* kissing? Who says men aren't capable of doing more than one thing at once?) The bit where we'd torn off each other's clothes, kissing hungrily and kind of *collapsing* on to the bed.

I could weep.

Without moving my body, I slide my gaze around my bedroom. Jeans and knickers are bunched up on the floor, clearly having been yanked off in haste. Martin's T-shirt has been flung with abandon on to my chest of drawers. My bra lies at the bottom of the bed, seemingly with clasp still fastened. Did I yank it over my head or what? Did *he*? How much did we drink last night? My sweater – *his* sweater – lies in a clump by the door. My pillow's sausaged up, my neck bent at an unnatural angle. Even though I still sleep on 'my' side, I'm no longer used to anyone being in my bed. I'd forgotten how big Martin is – all of him, I mean, not the crucial part – and how he encroaches into my space.

I want him out. This is *my* bed. My mouth's interior has shrivelled – why am I so dehydrated? I can taste myself, and it's disgusting: 'Did you know that the tongue is more responsible for bad breath than the gums or teeth?'

Whoops. We polished off that second bottle. Even so, I must have wanted to do it. I cannot blame my actions on alcohol.

As slowly as humanly possible, I creep out of bed and pluck my dressing gown from its hook on the door.

'Hmmm,' Martin murmurs, a small smile flitting across his lips. Maybe he's replaying last night's scene. My arms goose-pimple. I could vomit right here, all over my bedroom floor.

'Cait?' he whispers.

I don't answer.

His eyes flutter open, and he blinks in the morning light. 'You OK, darling?'

'Shhh.' I slap a finger to my lips.

'What . . .?'

'The children will hear you!' I hiss.

Martin grins sleepily. 'It's OK. It's allowed. We're their parents.'

'Don't you think it'd be weird for them, finding you here?'

'Yes, but . . .'

'We've split up, remember? You left me, or did you forget?' My voice quivers.

Frowning, Martin props up a pillow against the headboard and sits up. The duvet falls away, exposing his torso right down to the bit where his pubes drift up towards his navel. I shudder, averting my gaze. I'd forgotten how hairy and, well, *robust* the male form looks against white sheets. Martin's eyes are fixed on me. Even as I turn my back, retying my dressing-gown cord tighter, I can feel them boring into the back of my head.

'You'd better get dressed,' I say sharply. 'It's gone seven – Travis will be up any minute.'

'Cait, please . . .'

'What?' I turn to glare at him.

'You don't regret it, do you?'

What kind of question is that? 'Yes, of course I do,' I bark. I don't tell him that I enjoyed it – loved it actually – and felt alive for the first time since . . . Actually, I can't remember. I don't recall it was ever like that. It must have been, I suppose, in the early days. That's what it felt like last night: strong-pyjama-days sex.

Martin's face creases with concern. 'Cait, you're crying . . .'

'No I'm not.' I perch on the corner of the bed with my back to him and swipe my face with my sleeve. 'Please get up and go home,' I add desperately.

He sighs. 'You really think it'll upset the children to see me here?'

I nod. My entire face feels like it's liquefying.

'But it needn't be just . . . just a one-off. I could come back. The Daisy thing . . . it was only . . .' He pauses, scrabbling for words. 'It was a mistake,' he blunders on, 'a hideous mistake that triggered something I should never have got involved with, and only did because of that pathetic getting-older thing – when you look at your life and think, Is this it?'

'Thanks,' I say witheringly.

'Didn't you ever feel like that before I left?'

I swallow. 'Yes, I suppose I did. I just thought it was normal.'

Martin sighs. 'I've never forgiven myself. Daisy knew it. She realised I'd gone into it without thinking, that I didn't love her the way I love you.'

He reaches out for me, but I keep my hands bunched on my lap. The creak gives me a start. I swing round and Lola's standing there in the doorway in her Mickey Mouse nightie and Scooby Doo feet.

'Daddy!' she yelps, pelting towards him and flinging herself into his arms. 'Did you and Mummy have a sleepover party?'

★   ★   ★

Tuesday, 11 p.m.

Dear R,

I'm sorry I haven't been in touch for so long. Things have
been rather hectic and confusing. Yes, I was surprised that
you'd come to the *Bambino* event and not spoken to me –
but then, I'd had to rush off as Jake had had an accident
(he's OK now) so I couldn't hang around. Oh, apart from
being accosted by our dear friend Harriet Pike. Some lecture
she gave me! She seems to think that Millie edged her off
the mag, suggesting that she needed a little break, when
she'd planned for me to take over her page all along. I can't
believe Millie would be so devious. Actually, I can . . .

Anyway. Here I am, needing to talk. I can't splurge to
Millie – she'd be horrified, would probably excommunicate
me from her friendship circle – and Sam's too wrapped up
in other stuff. What happened is, I slept with Martin last
night. That's right – Shagpants. In my defence, your
honour, I can only say that he was here and wanted me, and
I am sick to the back teeth of pretending I'm doing OK but
feeling so lonely inside.

Martin hung around all day. All bloody day, like he
owned the place! He insisted on making lunch, resisted
making snide remarks about the shoddy selection of offerings
in my fridge, and washed up too. All perky and cheerful,
bounding around the kitchen as if he was on *Masterchef* and
probably confusing the children horribly. (He was such a
grumpy arse when he lived here.)

We took them to the park. It was Martin's idea – his
attempt at wangling an opportunity to talk to me while the
kids mucked about in the play area. All morning Lola had
been firing questions: 'Are you going to live with us again,
Daddy?'

'I, um, I'm not sure what's going to happen,' he replied,
trying to fix me with a look. 'Mummy and I need to talk.'

So, the park. How normal and happy familyish. My God,

did he put in the donkey work – spinning Travis on the roundabout, plus loads of other kids who didn't even belong to us. He pushed Lola on the swing until she begged to come off. This is the man who's usually unwilling to venture into playgrounds without a copy of the *Guardian* to use as a shield. In the olden days, he'd have browsed the whole of *G2* while I hoofed from swings to see-saw to roundabout, consoling myself that at least I was getting some exercise.

He asked me if I'd consider getting back together. He pointed out that we're not even divorced, that I've never asked him to instigate the legal proceedings, which he seems to interpret as a hint that the door to his homecoming has been left ajar. I thought of you, R. How you've brought up Billy on your own and said that life is better in some ways – that at least it's an honest life. I thought, That's what I want. It's got to be better than being married to the wrong person. All these months I have been bitter and twisted while I mourned the loss of my relationship. Not any more.

I saw Rachel in the park. (Pasta-making friend, remember? Do keep up!) She was with Guy, her creepy husband, who patted my arse in the pub. They didn't see us. They were too engrossed in one of those snappy rows that you try to hold in for the kids' sake. They'd brought a picnic, and it was perfectly set out on the grass – Rachel does give excellent picnic – but I could tell by their bitter faces that they were squabbling. Poor Eve, their daughter, had the saddest look on her face.

I thought, Is that what I want? I don't, R. It's just me now – me and the kids. I've made an appointment to see a family lawyer so hopefully we'll be able to set the divorce in motion and sort out the money stuff properly. As you know, being dumped isn't fun. A single mother isn't something I'd ever planned to be. But there are worse things. Like being trapped with a tosser like Guy, who scrambled up from the picnic rug and stormed across the grass, leaving Rachel and Eve staring bleakly after him.

I don't really think of Martin as Shagpants. Not any more. He's a decent dad – a devoted dad, in fact – who made one major mistake.

It feels so good to put these words down. Thanks for listening. For the first time since he left, I feel like the old Caitlin, who I thought was dead and buried a long time ago. Shagging my ex might not have been the smartest way to get over him – no pun intended – but it's worked. I am cured.

Love, C x

Dear Cait,

I'm so proud of you, dear friend. And things could have been much worse. You could have been wearing a child's orange Pac-a-Mac.

R x

P.S. Shall we go out sometime?

38

There's an unfamiliar toothbrush in Sam's bathroom. It's purple and sparkly, like a child's toothbrush, but adult-sized.

I don't think it's Sam's style of toothbrush. By the time I'm back in his garden I've arranged my face into what I hope is some semblance of normality.

'How's Jake settling back in?' Sam asks. He seems agitated today. Rather than sitting on the deck with me, he's slicing back sprawling geraniums, trying to make them behave.

'It's like he's never been away,' I say. 'Only he's different. Cheerier. And he's stopped cleaning his room. Hasn't lifted a bloody finger. Within a day of him moving back in, there were comics strewn all over the floor, manky pyjamas kicked under the bed . . .'

Sam frowns. 'Aren't you pleased?'

'I'm joking, Sam. It's a joke.'

'Oh, right.' He snips off a geranium head in its prime.

An awkward silence hangs in the air. Don't mention the purple toothbrush. Or, for that matter, the fact that I shagged Martin accidentally. Sam hasn't been calling me so often. I've told myself that it's due to Jake's spell at his dad's. Our sons are what brought us together, after all.

'So what d'you think happened?' he asks, turning to face me. The stubbly jaw is a recent development, and it suits him. Hell and damnation to purple toothbrushes.

'He did mention that Slapper's a tidying maniac,' I explain, 'and freaks out if anyone puts down a drink without a coaster, but . . . I think he was homesick. Dare I say it, he actually seemed to miss me.'

'Well, I'm glad,' Sam murmurs. The children are splashing in an inflatable paddling pool that Sam unearthed from his cellar.

'It's over with them,' I add. 'Martin and Slapper, I mean.'

'Why didn't you say? You must be delighted!'

I muster a smile. 'Not really. He's still the kids' dad, and he'll always be that, but who he sees or what he gets up to is nothing to do with me. Not any more.'

Sam exhales loudly, dumps his secateurs on the table and pulls up the chair beside me. 'My God, Caitlin Brown. I never thought I'd hear you say that.'

'And there's something else,' I add with a chuckle. 'Ask me what I'm doing tonight.'

'Um, exhibition opening at the White Cube? Drinks party at Nigella's?'

I blush and he spots it. 'Sam . . . I'm meeting that man. The one who's been emailing for months now.'

'What? For God's sake, are you out of your mind?'

His reaction floors me. 'I'm just curious. We get on so well in our emails . . . It sounds weird, but I know I can tell him anything. I feel close to him, Sam.'

He frowns, and his eyes cloud over. 'Right. OK. Go meet an axe-wielding maniac.'

'Why are you being like this?' He has never raised his voice to me before. The children have fallen silent in the pool and are staring at us.

'Like what?' he mutters.

'So . . . so negative. I'm not stupid, you know. We're meeting in a pub. I'm not planning to sneak off down a dark alley with him – at least not on a first date.'

He laughs bitterly. 'I hope not.'

This is a Sam I've never seen before. Disapproving. Scathing. His mouth has formed a sneer.

'I thought you were my friend,' I say pathetically.

'Of course I'm your friend. I care about you, that's all.'

Yeah right. God, I've turned into Jake, before his personality spruce-up.

'What's the matter, Mummy?' Lola skips towards us, water droplets flying from her hair.

'Nothing, sweetie, but you'd better get dry because we need to go home now.'

'I don't want to go home yet.' She folds her arms defiantly.

'Rachel's babysitting tonight,' I add, knowing that this will delight her. By rights, Lola should have been born to a pasta-making mother.

'Great!' She grabs a towel and shrouds it around herself.

'Jake, Travis, come and get dry.'

'No!' cries Travis.

'Do we have to?' whines Jake.

'Yes,' I call back with impressive firmness.

Wordlessly, Sam distributes towels. Then, as the children peel off wet bathers, he resumes his pruning project.

I don't think he even says goodbye.

An hour later, everyone's in PJs except me. I'm wearing a swishy black skirt, a somewhat clingy lace-edged top and a raspberry cardie flung over the top, a last-minute addition that I hope will dampen the frantic pounding of my heart.

'Too fancy.' Lola, who's sitting cross-legged on my bed, shakes her head. Her hair, still damp from Sam's pool, has clumped into snakes.

'Don't like it,' declares fashion-guru Travis, who's attempting a backward roll on my bed.

I scrutinise my reflection in the dressing-table mirror. Rather than the artfully mussed effect I'd been aiming for, my hair looks quite deranged due to being put up, pulled down, put up and pulled down again.

'Wear your nice blue jumper,' Lola suggests.

I eye it on the bed. It's the lambswool one I wore to meet Darren on Pac-a-Mac night. It feels tainted, as if some of my mortification might be trapped in its fibres. I doubt I'll ever wear it again.

I tear through my wardrobe, briefly studying the dress that Martin had been especially fond of and that I wore so often that its print faded as if bleached by the sun. I glimpse my wedding dress – an ivory silk shift – and quickly shove other clothes along the rail to cover it up. In desperation, I change into trousers with a summery floral dress over the top, which I know is a 'look' at the moment, but feels as if I have plundered a teenager's wardrobe.

'No, Mum.' Jake winces in the doorway.

'Yuck.' Travis scowls.

I'm about to change again when the bell rings, and it's Rachel, my babysitting rescuer.

'Oh, you look lovely,' she gushes as I hurry downstairs. 'Your hair's great like that, all sexy and messy. Where are you going?'

'Um, just meeting a friend for a drink. No one you know.' My cheeks flame instantly.

'Well, don't hurry back,' she says cheerfully. 'To be honest, I'm relieved to be out of the house. Guy's been such an arsehole lately.' Her use of the A-word shocks me.

'What's happened?' I ask.

She grins stoically and flicks her growing-out fringe from her eyes. 'You know how men are. Complain that you don't make an effort any more, that you've let yourself go . . .'

'Oh, Rachel.' I touch her arm.

'But he's right, isn't he? All these mags like your *Bambino* – week after week they're filled with these ridiculous pictures of new mothers in cashmere tracksuits with their hair just so.'

I splutter with laugher. 'None of that's real. It's all made up.'

She musters a chuckle. 'Not if you shop at Leoni's it's not. Anyway, listen to me, burdening you with my woes when you're off out for the night.'

Lola is already delving into the bulging carrier bag of craft supplies that Rachel's brought with her. *This* is the kind of mother I'd intended to be.

'Well, I'd better get going,' I murmur.

'Have fun.' Rachel grins at me, and there's a glimmer of something – envy, maybe – in her eyes.

'Thanks again.'

I kiss the children goodbye – even Jake allows it – and step out into the street. It's only then that I remember I'd intended to change back into outfit number one.

Strange things happen as I stride towards Batters Corner, the junction where people met before there were mobiles and numerous coffee shops (and still do, according to R, if they're soppy romantics like he is). Martin and I met here a few times, although I quickly push that memory from my mind.

A lorry driver whistles from his cab window. Another man, who's heading towards me, turns to watch me pass by and emits a low whistle. What's going on? I didn't manage to get my hair right or apply make-up, apart from a slick of sheer lipstick. It's as if I have suddenly become visible again.

At Batters Corner, there's no sign of anyone who might be R. It's a still, dry evening, and a faint vinegar smell hangs in the air. Batters Corner takes its name from J. & J. Batters furniture store, a long-gone fixture at the wedge-shaped junction. The creamy building still stands, although it's lain empty for years, with dust-mottled windows and a flaking 'To Let' sign. But R was right: it's still a meeting place. A few people are hanging around, trying to affect casualness. There's an Asian boy in baggy jeans, a yellow top and gleaming silver wristwatch, which he glances at far too often to appear truly comfortable. There's a woman of around my age, sharply dressed and fully made up, as if she's glossed herself up in the ladies' mirrors. She loiters for a couple of minutes before zipping over the road to meet a man in a flowing grey coat.

The third loiterer has a silvery fuzz of hair and is wearing a red V-neck and some kind of drapey trousers. He flicks me a glance, his moist eyes lingering over the breast region for just long enough to be creepy. Please, please don't be R. I turn away quickly. There's a man in a suit whose tongue keeps flitting out – a tiny pink dart – to moisten his anxious mouth.

Twelve minutes past eight. The red-jumpered man gives me a 'stood up?' look, as if grateful that he's not the only one who appears to be stranded on a Friday night. I grimace back. A sweet-looking girl in a floor-sweeping skirt hurries towards him. The other loiterers have gone, and now it's just me. R is now twenty minutes late, which counts as either plain rude or simply not coming.

Stranded at Batters Corner. Brilliant. Angrily, I snatch my phone from my bag and call Rachel's mobile.

'Cait, hi,' she exclaims. 'Everyone's fine – you needn't worry. Just enjoy your evening.'

To my shame, it hadn't occurred to me to enquire after my offspring's well-being. 'Rachel,' I say, 'my, um, friend hasn't shown up. I was wondering if he'd sent me an email or anything.'

'An email? Wouldn't he have called?'

'He doesn't have my number.'

'Well, couldn't you call him?'

This is getting worse. I can't tell her the truth – not after the ticking-off she gave me in Leoni's. 'I . . . don't have his number either. I, um . . . I met him online,' I babble feebly.

A pause. 'You've been dabbling with those Internet dating sites?'

'Yes.'

She chuckles. 'It's nothing to be ashamed of. I suppose it's sensible, really, for someone in your situation, though I'm sure you could meet someone in a more *normal* way—'

'Rachel,' I cut in, 'could you log on to my computer and check my inbox? It wouldn't take a minute.'

'Oh, I'm not very techy, Cait. Hang on . . .' The cordless phone crackles as she crosses the kitchen. I hear a sharp tapping noise. What's she doing, trying to turn it on at the keyboard?

'There's a button,' I say, desperation creeping into my voice, 'on the big black box under my desk.'

'What? Ew, there's a banana skin here. Let's get rid of that . . . Right. Shall I . . . press it?'

This woman is capable of fashioning ravioli pillows stuffed with puréed pumpkin, yet is nervous about pressing a button. Does she think it'll blow up in her face?

'Yes,' I breathe, my eyes darting this way and that in case R should appear, awash with apologies.

'Right,' Rachel says. 'It's on.' A trace of confidence has crept into her voice. 'What now?'

Now you have to climb on to the little hamster wheel at the back and start running to power it up. 'Type in my password,' I tell her. 'It's, um . . .'

'Didn't catch that. Are you next to a busy road or something? Where *are* you?'

'Fuckwit,' I say.

'Sorry?'

'That's my password. Fuckwit. I've used it since Martin left.' I snigger awkwardly. 'I suppose it helped me vent my anger or something. Type it in lower case.'

'Right.' I hear her typing it in.

No wonder Jake has a tendency to misuse magnetic letters when his mother displays such a tragic level of immaturity.

Patiently, and still glancing around for R, I explain how to access my email account. You'd think I was a surgeon talking her through a complex roadside operation after an accident.

'There's one email,' she announces.

'Who's it from?'

'Um, let's see . . . It says, "Big Roger." Shall I open it?'

'Yes, please.' My heart lollops against my ribcage.

'Hang on . . . Here it is . . . "Worried you loss erection? Safe secure Viagra hundred and fifteen dollar special price." God, Cait, who sends this stuff? You're not on some kind of . . . medication, are you?' She dissolves into giggles.

'Um, no,' I manage, gazing bleakly at the flaking Batters Corner sign.

Then I hear it, a voice calling, 'Caitlin!' across the street. The tall, lean figure waits for a gap in the traffic before hurrying towards me.

It's Darren. No, not just Darren. He's with the PA girl, the one with golden streaks in her chestnut hair from the pub. 'Sorry, Rachel, got to go,' I blurt out.

'Is that him? The friend you're meeting?'

'Yes,' I say, finishing the call.

Darren and the girl fling each other an amused glance as they approach – a glance that says, 'Look, it's her, the one who keeps bugs in jars and wore the orange nylon raincoat thingy.'

'Hey, how are you?' he says with a smirk.

'Fine, great.' I grin tersely and check my watch.

'Waiting for someone, Caitlin?' the girl asks.

'No, um, yes. But we've changed plans.' A kind of snort-laugh comes out. 'And I'm running late, I'd really better go . . .'

I leg it down the street, Darren's mocking laughter echoing in my burning ears.

39

I can't go home and face Rachel. I don't know where else to go. The thought of sitting in some pub nursing a drink on my own is beyond tragic, but how else can I fill the evening? See a film? Sitting in a cinema is as appealing right now as spending the dog-end of Friday evening on a park bench being accosted by crazies. I could go home, sneak into our back garden and lurk about for a bit. Give Mrs Catchpole a fright.

Bloody R. Millie, Rachel, Sam – everyone was right. Fabulous recent dating history, Cait! Prance around in a Pac-a-Mac, shag the ex, spend forty minutes at Batters Corner with 'STOOD UP' plastered all over your face.

I march on, seething, not thinking where I'm going, and I wind up in the next street to Mimosa House. I could pop in to see Mommy dearest. She doesn't like me especially, and will probably reprimand me for failing to achieve a Kate Moss-like physique, but at least she knows me.

At least, she once did.

'Cait, before you see your mum, there's something I want to show you.' Helena beckons me into the manager's office, indicating a dog-eared book on the desk. It's called *Forgotten Glasgow* and is one of those black-and-white photographic books in which you know you'll find pictures of shipyards and street kids and old-fashioned dance halls.

I pick it up and flip the pages randomly. 'Is it Mum's?'

Helena smiles. 'We were having a second-hand book sale to raise funds for outings. This came in with a load of other stuff. I showed it to Jeannie . . . and something happened, Caitlin.

Something clicked in her. It was incredible, as if she remembered a little of who she was . . . who she *is*.'

I frown, studying photos of children playing on rubble and kicking a football across barren ground.

'Page seventy-two,' Helena murmurs.

I turn to it, and it's a shot of a shipyard in the 1950s, captioned 'The Melting Room'. There's a furnace, its heat escaping in a gasp of white light, and several workers lined up in dark overalls. The picture's so smudgy and grainy it's impossible to pick out the workers' faces. All I can tell is that they're women.

Helena leans over me, indicating a slight, skinny figure at the end of the line, standing a little apart from the others. 'Your mum says that's her. She says lots of women worked in the shipyard during the war, but by the 1950s it was rare, and a newspaper photographer came to take a picture of them. She remembered the day quite clearly.'

I squint at the photo, trying to bring the face into focus. 'D'you think it's really her?'

She laughs. 'Well, your mum's convinced. And yesterday, when we discovered the book, she had a group of residents gathered round while she gave a little talk about it. It was fascinating, Caitlin. She knew just about every place in the photos, and how the metal was melted in the furnace and then shaped and—' Helena catches herself and grins. 'I'm not answering your question, am I? Do I think it's really her?' She closes the book and hands it to me. 'I don't think it matters,' she says.

Mum is crunching a sweet and has a crocheted blanket spread over her bony knees when I find her in the day room. She's the only one here. The other residents will have been taken to their rooms for the night, but Mum's internal clock has become so cock-eyed that bedtime means nothing to her.

'It's you again,' she grumbles, and a fragment of boiled sweet pings on to her lap.

What a lovely surprise, darling daughter! Yes, I really am the same dear old lady who enthrals all these old folk with tales from my youth.

'Just thought I'd pop in to see you, Mum.' I take the seat beside her.

'That's Florrie's seat. You can't sit there.'

'Florrie's gone to bed.'

'Where are you taking me?' she snaps.

'I'm not taking you anywhere.' Honestly, in the thirty seconds I've been in this room, I have aged a decade.

'What d'you want then?' Jeannie growls.

'Look, Mum. Helena showed me this book.' I hold its front cover before her, and she squints at it suspiciously. 'It's all about Glasgow,' I add. 'The places you knew when you were young. I thought we could look through it together.'

'Oh, that.' She cackles, and her freshly permed curls bob around her face.

I flick to the page showing the melting room. 'Helena says that's you. Is that right, Mum?'

We both peer at it.

'Of course it is,' she says gruffly.

I glance back at the page, and my heart quickens. The girl's face is no longer a smudge, but a real person with deep-set dark eyes and an upturned nose, just like Lola's. She has Lola's hair, too – thick, unruly waves – which Mum had tried, unsuccessfully, to stuff under a cap. 'I never believed you,' I murmur.

She chuckles and snatches the book from my grasp. 'Always think you know best, don't you? Little Miss Know-All. Look . . .' She turns the pages slowly. 'This is the market at the end of our street, and this is sports day, which they had every year in the park over the road.' Dishevelled children are having a sack race across a patch of scrubby ground. None look like Mum, but by now she believes that every female in the photos is her. Only Jeannie would assume that there could be three of her in one shot. 'I used to win every race going,' she exclaims. 'Mind you, I was athletic. Built for speed. Not like you.'

The smile plays on my lips as we study page after page. Mum

has shuffled closer – so close I can smell Fox's Glacier Mints on her breath. Being stranded at Batters Corner seems a lifetime away as she chatters on in her wavery bedtime-story voice, as if I am her little girl again.

All weekend I keep checking my emails, not because I wish to be dragged into further correspondence with R, but for the pleasure of deleting his grovelling apology.

It doesn't materialise. All our chats, our shared confidences and confessions – they've meant nothing to him. R for Arsehole indeed. Sam infiltrates my mind – and I can't forget the sparkly toothbrush left on prominent display in his bathroom. It might as well trill, 'Look at me! I live here now,' like the singing toothbrush that Travis nagged me to buy. In the chemist's on Saturday, on an emergency Calpol run for Lola, I avert my eyes from the oral-hygiene display.

On Sunday afternoon, we pop in to see Mum. It's a confusing visit. We leaf through the Glasgow book, and Mum points at the woman at the end of the line in the melting room. 'That's you,' she declares, jabbing her granddaughter's chest. No amount of protest can persuade her that, in 1957, Lola didn't exist.

By Monday morning, now that R no longer features in my life, I feel freer to get on with other things – like polish off leftover cold noodles from the fridge and crack on with a feature Millie asked me to write. It's about spotting the danger signs that one is 'lacking in self-esteem' and 'letting oneself go', which, in *Bambino*-land, is a crime punishable by a custodial sentence at the very least.

I write:

Do you find yourself re-heating coffee in the microwave because you think you don't deserve a freshly made cup?
Do you gobble wrinkled fruit from the bowl that no one else would dream of eating?
Do you wait for forty minutes at Batters Corner for someone who doesn't show up?

I stop typing, figuring that perhaps I'm not the ideal person to write this feature. Virtually every coffee I consume has been microwaved to a highly carcinogenic state. For breakfast, I wolfed a banana that was so ancient I'd practically had to pour it into my mouth.

I turn my attention instead to the pressing matter of the 'problem cupboard' in the hall.

It's stuffed with readers' letters – the ones I haven't got around to answering, yet can't bear to throw away – and symbolises all that I despise about myself: my tendency to put off the inevitable, my lack of direction and courage. Should a clutter counsellor come to our house – Rachel informed me that such people exist, perhaps hinting that I urgently require their services – they would shine a torch into the cupboard and look extremely worried. 'Hmm,' they'd say, 'I can see there's quite a problem here.' They'd diagnose several personality defects, which have resulted in this sorry state of affairs, not to mention the breakdown of my marriage.

Something must be done. I have already found Lola prying in the cupboard, on the verge of showing Eve a handful of random letters. Affairs, divorces, lamentable sex lives – it's hardly suitable reading material for six- and seven-year-olds. I mean, it's hardly *The BFG*. I fetch a bin liner, stuff all the letters into it and haul it down to the kitchen, where, fuelled by an urge to Be Organised, I tip them out on to the table.

Bing! An incoming email. I tear to my desk like a whippet. It's from R and is headed: 'So Sorry.'

Cait,
What can I say? So much has happened over the past few days, yet nothing makes up for the fact that I stood you up on Friday night. I'm so sorry. In a nutshell, here's what happened.

  I'd dropped Billy at Jacqui's as it was her turn to have him for the weekend. Everything seemed fine. Her lover-boy, Kyle, was his usual oily, charmless self. I came home and

was getting ready to meet you when she called, in a terrible
state: Kyle had smacked Billy, for nothing really – just
trailing mud in from the garden across the kitchen floor.
When I say smacked, Cait, I mean really walloped him
across the back of the legs – I could hear him sobbing while
she was on the phone. Kyle had stormed out, accusing
Jacqui of being incapable of controlling her son, and that it
was typical behaviour from a boy who was being brought up
by his hopeless dad.

Well, never mind what he thinks about me. I was livid
that he'd hit Billy and so drove over right away. All I could
think about was how I'd like to punch his lights out.

I comforted Billy, and once he'd gone to bed, Jacqui and I
sat up talking. It came out that Kyle has hit her too. A slap
in the face during a row, that kind of thing. However bad
things have been between Jacqui and me, I couldn't bear to
hear of her being treated like that. So I stayed the night, in
case he came back. Kipped on the sofa, honest – I still have
the cricked neck to prove it.

By morning, Jacqui had decided that it was over with Kyle
and that she wouldn't let him come back. She even hinted
that maybe she and I might get back together. I don't think
she was thinking straight. By the afternoon, all the
resentment and bitterness had resurfaced and we were soon
bickering again.

Of course, Billy interpreted me being at Jacqui's as a sign
that Mum and Dad were back together again and everything
was going to be rosy. Every time I tried to leave, he became
distraught, so I hung around all weekend. It's been pretty
horrendous and it's a relief to be able to share all of this with
you.

To be honest, Cait, I don't talk to anyone else in this way.
Anyway, the long and short of it is, I'm so sorry about
Friday and hope we can arrange to meet soon, if you're still
speaking to me.

R x

I study the readers' letter mountain, as if it might inspire me. After all, don't these people trust me to say the right thing? It doesn't work. After stuffing them back into the cupboard – I have to press my entire body weight on the door in order to shut it – I sit down at my desk and reply:

> Dear R,
> I'm so sorry to hear what you've been through. Don't worry about Friday night – I had a rollicking time at the old folks' home. Of course I'm still speaking to you.
>   C x

Cast-iron willpower, me.

40

Saturday, 7.45 p.m. This time, I don't even try to de-mother myself. I just pull on a sweater and jeans, and tie back my hair into a ponytail. The kids are at Martin's. If I so desired, I could have all the time in the world in which to pamper and preen. The truth is, I just want to be me.

It feels different this time, as if all my nervousness was used up while I waited at Batters Corner. Tonight, I'm almost serene. It doesn't matter what R thinks of me, because whatever happens I'll be home later tonight, and I'll call Martin to check that the kids have settled OK, as I always do when they're staying with him.

Then I'll have a bath and go to bed. That's my usual child-free Saturday night. It hardly sets the world on fire, but it's fine. I'm feeling pretty buoyant, despite Sam letting slip that Amelia has asked him to dinner tonight, and could he have our babysitter Holly's number?

La Rose. That's where they're going. 'It's a quaint little French place,' Sam told me. 'We went there years ago. It was kind of special to us. I'm not sure why she's so intent on going back.' He sounded blasé – dismissive, almost – but I could tell he was only trying to make me feel better. He must know how I feel, how I *felt*, about him. Anyway, that's all over now.

For a moment, I yearned to tell him about my meeting with the divorce lawyer, so he'd realise that I'm capable of being a proper grown-up; yet it didn't seem right, talking about maintenance payments, not with him and Amelia going out to plan their wedding. I gave him Holly's number and rang off.

Millie calls as I'm trying to find my purse and mobile among the debris from the kids' supper.

'Martin asked me if I wanted to spend this weekend at his flat,' I tell her. 'He said, "We could hang out together if you have nothing else on."'

'My God,' she splutters. 'I hope you told him to fuck off.'

'Well . . . no,' I tease her. 'Not exactly . . .'

'Please, Cait, don't say you're—'

'Don't worry,' I say, laughing. 'I told him I'd had a meeting with a lawyer and we need to meet up to go through the legal stuff.' A few months ago, I'd have derived twisted pleasure from seeing him looking so pained. Now, I felt almost sorry for him. He looked tired and drawn, and his Sardinian tan was long gone.

'And will he go for that?' Millie asks.

'I think so. He said he won't make things difficult, anyway. The kids and I will stay in the house, and he'll carry on renting the place he had with Daisy.'

There's a small pause. 'Well, that's good. So what are you up to tonight? I wondered if I could drag you out for a drink . . .'

'I thought you were seeing Mr Advertising?'

She sighs. 'It's kind of . . . dwindled away. Actually,' she snorts, 'he's dwindled back to his ex, so I could do with a bit of cheering up.'

'Oh, hon, I'm sorry. It's just . . .'

'Don't tell me. You're getting all smoochy with Sam.'

'Actually,' I say, unable to resist, 'I'm finally meeting R.'

'You're joking,' she gasps.

'Well,' I say, 'that's the intention. If he stands me up again, first thing I'll do is call you.'

A small snigger. 'Where are you meeting?'

'Just a local pub. The Inn on the Park. Thought it'd be safer than dinner, so if it's awful and I've made a hideous mistake, I can always—'

'Cut and run,' she laughs.

'Millie?' I say hesitantly. 'I thought you'd give me a lecture . . .'

'Honey,' she says, 'you're a grown-up. Compared to my life, yours is pretty sorted. Christ, I don't understand half the features we put in the magazine. All the child-rearing stuff. What the hell am I doing, Cait?'

'But I thought you loved it,' I insist. 'You were so confident at the reader do, the way you held it all together . . .'

'Just an act, sweetie. Anyway, I've been thinking . . .'

'What kind of thinking?'

She laughs softly. 'Maybe it's time I found myself a proper job.'

I spot R as I approach the pub. I just know it's him. He's sitting at an outside table with a beer and a lovely, handsome face: vivid blue eyes, full mouth, a finely sculpted face I feel as if I know already.

The man with the olives in Leoni's Larder. It *was* him. I grin stupidly as I approach, and he stands up and puts out his arms and hugs me. It seems so natural I don't feel a shred of awkwardness.

'Cait, hi,' he says.

'Hi,' I say, pulling back to study his face. 'So . . . are you going to tell me your name, or shall I carry on calling you "R"?'

'It's Richard,' he says incredulously. 'Doesn't it come up automatically on my email?'

'Um, no,' I say, laughing. 'I kind of liked it, though – the mysterious stranger aspect.'

'Well,' he grins, 'I hope the reality isn't a big disappointment.'

'Of course it's not.' My cheeks colour.

'That's a relief. I was scared you might run screaming. Anyway, in case you're planning to scarper, let me get you a drink. What would you like?'

'Glass of wine, please.'

I am grateful for the few minutes on my own to bask in my good fortune. Richard. I turn the name over in my head. It fits him. A sexy, handsome man, late thirties at a guess. Not a weirdo with pallid, mushroomy skin that would suggest he spends 90 per cent of his time hunched over a PC with the curtains shut. No obvious pubic-hair-snipping tendencies either.

My heart quickens with anticipation. It's Saturday night, and he's lovely – not too dissimilar to the picture I'd painted in my head. Who cares about Sam and Amelia? Or Martin having the audacity to think that after one ill-advised shag, I'd be pelting over to keep him company in his oh-so-empty king-sized bed?

Give me a break.

Richard returns with my drink.

'It was you, wasn't it?' I venture as he sits down. 'In Leoni's Larder. And you recognised me, but you didn't say anything.'

He chuckles, and his laughter lines crinkle fetchingly. 'You seemed to have your hands full with the children asking for this and that. I thought I'd wait outside and introduce myself as you came out – I was dying to – but one of the children was having a tantrum . . .'

'Oh, yes.' I snigger. 'Travis wanted the giant salami they have hanging over the meat counter.'

'Billy's got a thing about that too! I usually avoid that shop because of that damn salami, but he'd begged me to go in that day because he loves those fancy crisps they do there. Billy's such a *ponce* about crisps.'

'What, no Walkers?'

'God, no. It's rosemary and roasted shallot or whatever the hell it is they do in there.'

We laugh, but I sense a snag of unease. There's no shyness between us, no stress of not being allowed to mention the kids. Yet . . . it's almost *too* easy. Like chatting to any of the dozens of mothers whom I've sat next to at toddler groups over the years. It's almost like . . . being at Three Bears, yacking to Rachel.

Something wilts inside me.

'Are your kids fussy eaters?' Richard asks.

'Um, yes, they can be.'

He sips his beer and grins ruefully. 'God, here I am, rambling on about children. I vowed that I wouldn't do that tonight.'

'No, it's OK.' I manage a broad smile, but disappointment pools in my stomach. 'What happened with Jacqui? Has she got rid of the boyfriend?'

'For the moment,' he says. 'She's agreed that he won't be there when Billy's staying. If she goes back on that, it'll all have to be formalised through our solicitors.'

I touch his arm and he smiles. 'Not easy, is it?'

His gaze fixes on mine. 'It's been good having you to talk to. That's made it easier. I have to tell you, though,' he adds, blushing, 'how nervous I was about this – meeting you properly at last—'

'Richard,' I cut in, 'what made you email me in the first place?'

He smiles. 'I was intrigued. You came across as so caring, so sweet, and I couldn't quite believe you were for real.'

I blink at him. 'I mean, what *really* made you email me?'

Another sip. His eyes are hesitant. 'Remember I told you that Jacqui had a subscription to *Bambino*?'

'Uh-huh.'

'That other agony aunt, Harriet somebody—'

'Pike.'

'Jacqui lived by her every word. Nothing I did with Billy was right, wasn't what Harriet had recommended. You know, one of our biggest rows was sparked off by a letter in that magazine.'

'Really?' I flick my gaze over the customers at the other tables. There are a few couples, a single guy in a tracksuit and a woman sitting on her own. She is facing away from us; I can see only her ear and cheek. I find myself wondering who she's waiting for.

'There was this letter on her page,' Richard continues. 'Someone had written in about their child waking up in the night and crawling into his parents' bed. Billy does that if he's had a nightmare, but that agony aunt was having none of it. She flew into a rage about setting firm boundaries and never backing down, and that a child should be shown who's in charge . . .'

I chuckle. 'That sounds like Pike. So what happened?'

'That became our regime. Billy would run in and I'd have to carry him back, crying and screaming. Sometimes he was so distraught he'd wet himself.'

'That sounds awful.'

'Or I'd refuse and Jacqui would try to take him back and we'd have a horrendous row in the middle of the night.'

'And agony aunts are supposed to help people. The thing is, though, I'm not Harriet, and you still sent that aggressive email . . .'

Richard shrugs. 'I thought, Here's another one – some perfect parent who reckons she knows it all.'

'It's just a job, Richard. It's what I do. That's all.'

He frowns. 'You really view it like that?'

I shuffle uncomfortably. It's as if he knows that I've ignored Millie's warnings and reply to as many letters as I can manage. Sitting at my desk, at some ungodly hour, chewing over problems from Frazzled of Doncaster or Crap Mother from Leeds . . . as if I can possibly make a difference. 'No, I don't,' I murmur. 'I suppose I take it far too seriously. I'm thinking of asking my brother to design me a website so I can answer the problems more easily – a kind of message board – and I'll be able to post my replies.'

'Sounds like a great idea. You're really cut out for this job, aren't you? It seems to come so naturally.'

I smile and glimpse that woman at the table again. The curve of her cheek looks so familiar. 'Well, at least the work part of my life's going OK,' I tell him.

'And the love life?'

My splutter says it all.

'How are things going on with Sam?' he asks.

The woman turns slightly towards us and—Oh, God, it's Millie, keeping a watchful eye to ensure that I'm not lured down an alley by an emailing maniac.

'Sam's just a friend,' I say firmly. 'Didn't I tell you that he and Amelia are getting remarried?'

'Are you sure?' Richard arches an eyebrow.

I shift in my chair. 'Actually, I know for certain that they're out having dinner right now and she's going to ask him to marry her again.' It splurges out, and I'm mortified to realise that my eyes have misted. Desperately, I try to blink the moisture back in.

'But Cait,' he persists, 'are you really prepared to sit back and let that happen?'

I laugh mirthlessly. 'It's not as if I can do anything about it.'

He studies my face. This doesn't make sense. An attractive man whom I regard as my friend and can offload to about anything – even Pac-a-Mac night and my tussle with Martin – a man who has always been there for me these past few months, and all I feel is . . .

Millie catches my eye. I jump up from my chair. 'Richard,' I blurt out, 'I've just spotted a friend. Would you mind if she joins us?'

'Not at all,' he says, leaning over and touching my arm, 'but can I just ask, why do you pretend you don't care about Sam?'

'Because he's a dad and it's only right that he should be back with his child's mother.'

His eyes are teasing. 'You really believe that? That's how you'd advise someone in your situation?'

I shake my head, exasperated now. 'Millie!' I call out, waving to her.

'Did you think,' Richard charges on, 'that if they were back together, it would force you to get over him?'

Millie is heading towards us, thank God, looking gorgeous in a slinky spaghetti-strapped dress.

'What makes you think that?' I growl at him.

Richard smirks, and his eyes glint knowingly. 'Just a theory.'

'I don't need theories, thanks.'

'And however you try to pretend you don't care, you've got to face up to it, Caitlin.'

'Millie,' I gush, 'this is Richard.' She beams at him, and I can read her thoughts: Well, *hello*. 'Hi, Richard. Lovely to meet you. I've heard lots about you.'

'Good to meet you, Millie.' He shakes her hand. 'Can I get you anything?'

'I've got a drink, thanks. I'll bring it over, if it's OK to join you . . .'

'Of course it's OK,' he says warmly. I catch him appraising her as she retrieves her glass.

By the time she's back, Richard has positioned a vacant chair so she's right next to him, and the pair of them fall into conversation instantly. I try not to think about La Rose and wine bottles dribbled with wax.

They don't talk about crisp varieties. They don't mention faddy eaters or fixations on giant salamis. They laugh and they chat, and although I try to pitch in occasionally, my heart's not in it, because it's snuck off somewhere else.

'How did you get here so quickly?' I hiss to Millie when Richard goes to the loo.

'Couldn't bear the idea of staying in. What kind of sad fuck stays at home on a Saturday night?'

'I do,' I point out.

'But not tonight. I was halfway over town when I phoned you, and when you said you were meeting your weirdo stranger, I thought I'd come too, just to make sure you were safe.'

'Liar,' I say, laughing. 'You wanted to see what he was like. You couldn't help yourself.'

She shrugs. 'Well, yes. He's gorgeous, isn't he?'

'He's . . . OK.'

'Oh, come on.' Her frown upturns into a beaming smile as Richard returns to our table.

Suddenly, I feel as if I don't belong here, that being stuck at home with the sea monkeys would be preferable to this. 'Millie, Richard,' I announce, 'I'm going to head off, OK?'

No one looks particularly devastated. Millie is on full-on flirt mode and Richard is lapping it up. There's so much I don't know about him, but maybe Millie will fill me in at a later date.

It's almost as if I have ceased to exist. I hug her goodbye, quickly kiss his cheek and head home, where there's no one to analyse me, because sea monkeys aren't capable of that.

So Richard thinks he knows me, and how I feel about Sam? I remember the first email I ever sent to him, which said simply, 'What the hell do you know about my life?'

41

As I march home, I figure, Well done, Caitlin Brown. Top marks. Only a seriously deluded twit-head would have assumed that there'd be some spark – something real – between herself and an emailing stranger. I must get a grip. Be a proper grown-up who inhabits the real world. My expectations have burst, like the giant bubbles from Travis's soap-blower machine.

I'm nearly home when my mobile bleeps. I fish it out of my bag; it's a text from Sam. Funny, I'd assumed he'd be otherwise occupied right now in La Rose. Unless . . . he's texting good news. Like, GUESS WHAT! WE´RE GETTING MARRIED. Rather than read it and subject myself to further torment, I stuff my mobile back in my bag and quicken my pace. Right now, I have no wish to be confronted by the gory details.

I let myself into the house. It feels eerily still, as it always does when the kids are at Martin's. Sometimes I feel as if I'd give anything for a few hours' peace; yet when the kids are away, I crave noise and commotion.

The thing I do that I have never told anyone – not even R – is check all the kids' rooms, even though they're not here. Travis's bed is unmade, his floor an explosion of Sticklebricks, which I'd loved as a child and had thought were extinct, but which Sam managed to find at a car-boot fair. Lola's room is unusually tidy, and I wonder if she's been influenced by her stays at Martin's. I don't know if Daisy has gone for good or if Martin will slink back to her now he knows it's truly over with us. I really don't care either way.

It really *is* over now, which feels OK. It might seem rather tragic, prowling around an empty house on a Saturday night, but it's far preferable to waking up with Martin's face on the pillow beside me.

Last of all, I peek into Jake's room. It's not a war zone, and not anally tidy either – just lived in, with a selection of books about pirates and Greek myths strewn over the bed, and his art stuff scattered on the carpet. It looks like a kid's bedroom should be. His football boots lie in a corner, untouched since he came back to me. He now goes to the chess and book clubs at school. Travis is furious that Jake's boots don't fit him.

I head down to the kitchen and play my messages. 'Hi, Cait, it's me, just wondering how things are, how Mum is . . .' Adam. His bi-monthly call to enquire after our mother's well-being.

Message two: 'Caitlin, Ross here. Sorry to call you on a Saturday, but I've been out of the country setting up a deal, talking to suppliers and such . . . Wondered if you might be interested in getting involved in a new site we're setting up? It's similar to Vitalworld, but we're aiming for the upper end of the market, your *Bambino*-reader type. Love your page, by the way. I gather you've attracted quite a following. Give me a call, would you, when you get a minute? Oh, and your outstanding payment should be with you in a couple of days.' Back to tongue-scraper world? I don't think so.

I pull up a chair at my desk to check my emails. Apart from the usual deluge of Viagra-related spam, there's just one:

Dear Caitlin,
I read your page avidly every week and hope you can help with my problem. I am a single father to a ten-year-old son and have a close female friend who happens to be a single mother to three children. We have hung out together for some months now, and at first it was one of those casual school-gate friendships in which neither of you gives much away. However, our friendship has deepened and we now spend a great deal of time together. We gossip and chat as any friends do, but for me at least there is much more to it than that.

For one thing, she's gorgeous. (There, I've said it.) When
she walks into my house, everything feels brighter. I might
have had a terrible day, having argued with my son about
getting his homework done, or not tidying his bombsite of a
bedroom; then in she walks and I feel amazing.

I stop reading for a moment. My heart pounds frantically.

Sometimes I wonder if she might feel something more than
friendship for me. At other times, especially recently, she can be
rather cold and distant and not return my calls. It's so hurtful
and confusing. I drive myself mad trying to analyse her every
move and gesture – the way she looked at me, or didn't look at
me. (I sound worryingly like a fifteen-year-old here. I have to
point out that I am old and ugly enough to know better.)

Which brings me to the crux of my problem. Do I come
out with how I feel about her, and risk embarrassing her,
and myself, and ruining our friendship, or do I carry on the
way I am, driving myself demented? Can you perform a risk
assessment for me, Caitlin? Or at least tell me to get over
myself and get a life?

I'm sure you receive hundreds of emails a day, flooding
into your PC, which sits on the desk in your kitchen, next to
the sea-monkey tank . . .

My hand flies to my mouth. Tears spring up instantly.

I had intended to go out to dinner tonight with my ex, but
decided that I couldn't go through with it. I had a hunch of
what she was planning and I knew it wasn't right and never
will be. I guess I'm not her favourite person right now. In
fact, I suspect that it's because of this friendship that she
was so determined for me and her to try again. Before I met
this person, my ex showed no interest in any reconciliation,
and she certainly knows how I feel about my friend,
although any fool could spot it a mile off.

That is, except her. And that's why I love her.
Demented, Bethnal Green

42

My hands are shaking as I type:

Dear Demented,
Your problem is an interesting one, as I have been
burdened by similar myself. You see, I have a friend too.
A special friend. He has helped me through some
extremely difficult times, but our friendship means more to
me than that. He is the only person who can make me
laugh when seconds before, I was on the verge of
slamming my head in a door.

My feelings have caused me much confusion and
anguish lately. I can now confess how gutted I was to
spot an unfamiliar purple toothbrush in his bathroom
and a woman's scarf draped across a chair. I tried to
avert my eyes, but I couldn't. I hoped my feelings would
go away, as to me they seemed foolish and were
certainly getting in the way of our friendship. But of
course they didn't.

I have to add that he is also completely gorgeous.

So, Demented, my advice to you is to put some wine to
chill in the fridge and see what happens.

C x

I'm about to log off when another email pops in. It's from R.
Richard. I almost don't read it. I hope he and Millie have
arranged to meet again, but my head is too full of other stuff
to dwell on that now.

I do open it; I can't resist.

Hi Cait,

Well, I'm just back from the pub. It was lovely to meet you after all this time. Sorry to write such a brief email, but your friend Millie has decided to come to my place for a coffee and I feel rude clattering away on my keyboard.

So I just wanted to say thanks. For everything. Especially for making me laugh and for allowing me into your life when I was so rude and obnoxious at the start.

You are lovely, Caitlin, and whatever you choose to do next, I hope that all works out for you.

With love,

R x

I know we won't email again. Once you've met someone, everything changes – and, anyway, someone real is waiting for me. I can barely make my fingers behave as I type:

Goodbye, Richard, and thank you for being my own private agony uncle. I wish you luck.

C x

Then I turn off my PC, head upstairs to the hall and pull on my jacket. I check my lipstick in the mirror and quickly run a brush through my hair. I think of Sam, waiting for me.

My heart soars, and I feel as light as dandelion fluff as I set off into the night.

EPILOGUE

'Mummy,' Lola cries, 'Travis says he's the best writer in his class. Is it true?'

'Yes it is,' I say. 'Mrs Farnham told me at parents' evening.'

She frowns, digesting this, and dips a finger into the mixing bowl on the table. I am attempting to make a Victoria sponge for the guess-the-cake's-weight stand at the PTA summer fête. Bev assigned the task to me. I fear that my creation will sit all alone and stranded, without the security of all the other cakes and cookies on the home-making stall. Actually, I suspect that she asked me as some kind of sick joke.

'Let me have a go,' Jake says, marching in from the garden. He grabs the spoon from my grasp. I'm on the verge of telling him to wash his hands first – they're covered in soil; Bev would have a seizure – but something stops me.

Eighteen months ago, Jake would scrub his hands raw when they came into contact with soil. I watch him beating vigorously, the mixture becoming pale and light as a cloud. I pour the cake into the tin and slip it into the oven.

Sam wanders in clutching a slim glass tank – the wormery he and the kids have been making. I'd been so scared about how the kids would react when Sam and Harvey had moved in. Especially Jake. Even though he and Harvey are still best mates, I wasn't sure he'd be happy about sharing a bedroom after having his own all these years. And, scarier still, how he'd feel about Sam and me being together. A few months ago, I'd asked, 'D'you feel OK about Sam and Harvey living here?'

Jake's eyes had narrowed, and my heart had quickened as I anticipated a growled response. 'Yeah,' he said, guardedly, then broke into a grin. 'We've got Sam's TV now. We don't have to watch that crappy little portable any more.'

Travis, too, is delighted with our new, superior TV – and even more so with the vast tub of magnetic letters that Martin gave him for his fifth birthday last week. He is using them to make words on the fridge. And, yes, he probably is the smartest in reception class, although I won't do a Marcia and suggest that he's gifted.

'He's written "Sam",' Lola reports. 'And "sea monkey". But you've spelt it wrong, Travis. It's S-E-A M-O-N—'

'He's only five, Lols,' I chide her.

'Now he's written "TV"!' Harvey announces.

'That's only two letters,' Jake crows. 'Anyone could do that.'

Sam casts me a look and my mouth curls into a smile. It still works, whenever he looks at me; it warms me all over. Cake smells fill the kitchen. I have actually made a real cake, just like Rachel's – something Proper Mothers do. I only hope that any soily bits merge in.

A little while later, Sam lifts the cake out of the oven, and it looks pretty damn perfect to me. The table is cluttered with my work things, and Sam's work things, and he shoves aside a pile of papers for somewhere to put it.

A letter from Mum's solicitor flutters to the floor and I stuff it into the drawer beneath my desk. Mum passed away last winter – five months ago now – painlessly and in her sleep, having lost her ability to recognise me or even Helena. I'd feared that she was nearing the end when she'd stopped asking when I was going to find a decent man. Although there'd been a glimmer of something – curiosity, perhaps, or more likely relief – when I'd taken Sam to see her.

It's strange, but after losing Mum I felt somehow freer and I wanted Sam and me to start afresh – not to live in the house where I'd been so lonely. I didn't want Mrs Catchpole gawping over the fence, wondering why Sam wasn't that nice man who'd built her flat-pack table. I craved a bedroom where Martin had never slept, and where no one had asked me to do pervy things in a Pac-a-Mac.

Sam's place is far too small for all of us, so we're looking for somewhere new, with a bigger garden with plenty of bug-collecting potential, and proper studies for Sam and me.

Sam and me. It feels so right, and I guess it always has.

'Mum!' Lola yelps. 'Travis has written "Harvey"! And he's spelt it right!'

'Well done, sweetheart,' I say. Oh, yes. I can picture the pained look on Marcia's face when Travis collects his Best Writer Award at prize-giving. It'll take every ounce of my concentration not to explode with pride.

'And now,' Lola says hesitantly, 'now he's writing— Mum! Mum, come and see!'

'What?' I ask distractedly.

'He's . . . he's made a *bad word*.'

Sam studies the fridge door, cocks his head and splutters, 'Well, um, that's very creative, Travis.'

'What's he written?' I ask, lurching over.

And there it is, in plastic letters of red, pink and green.

'Travis,' I say in my most serious voice, 'this is a swear word. You do know that, don't you? Who's been saying it?'

The grin spreads all over his face. 'You,' he says.

FIONA GIBSON

Lucky Girl

Everyone told Stella Moon how lucky she was to have a famous dad. She just wished he was more like everyone else's. Then when her mum died, and he hid away in his study, she didn't feel lucky at all.

Now in her thirties Stella has ensured her calm, orderly existence couldn't be further from her chaotic upbringing. Then two noisy little girls move in next door, shattering her peace and turning her life upside down.

At first, Stella feels besieged. The girls hound and stalk her, firing personal questions about her mum, her dad and her excuse for her love-life. But ultimately it's their friendship that helps her to confront the truth about her own childhood and start living life to the full.

A beautifully written, moving and uplifting story about growing up, family secrets and allowing new people into your life.

HODDER

FIONA GIBSON

The Fish Finger Years

What Your Mother Never Told You About Bringing Up Kids

'Raising kids is rather like looking after small, very drunk people'

If you have an embarrassing child who shouts, 'Why is that man so fat?' in the street, or bursts into friends' houses announcing 'It stinks in here', then this book is for you.

Self-confessed imperfect mum Fiona Gibson blends her own hilarious tales of raising three children with nuggets of advice from fellow parents who admit that they too get things wrong occasionally.

What to do when your child throws a plank-rigid wobbler in M&S? How to handle a foul-mouthed monster who's obsessed with the toilet parts of horses? Can parents rekindle their sex life, or is it simpler all round to not bother? Is it okay to uncork the wine before 7 pm?

Funny and refreshingly honest, *The Fish Finger Years* offers a welcome reminder that yours is not the only family for whom a simple trip to IKEA results in cushion fights, tears, and a messy encounter with the ketchup dispenser in the hot dog zone.

HODDER